LANDLORDS

A NOVEL

MIA KIRSI STAGEBERG

TARSAL PRESS ⊖ SAN FRANCISCO

LANDLORDS
ISBN: 978-0-9763711-9-9
First Edition

Published in the United States by Tarsal Press
A division of Silver Bay Books
San Francisco, California

Cover design by Al Marin
Cover images © Mia Kirsi Stageberg

Dedicated to James Peter Brightwolf

1936 – 2006

CONTENTS

AUTHOR'S NOTE

HOLLYWOOD VERSION
1. Harmless Life   1
2. Roach   7
3. Pigeon-blood Ruby   21
4. Objects Closer Than They Appear   29
5. Point Tenderness   37
6. Shaking, Standing, Not Standing   49
7. Serpentization   63
8. Quake and Bake   77
9. Slash and Burn   93
10. What's Wanted, What's Gotten   125

SPECIAL FEATURES
The Trailer   139
Characters Respond to the Film   139
Director's Comments   141
The Made-For-TV Pitch and More   143

INDIE VERSION
11. Holding the Wall   145
12. Roach   151
13. Pigeon-Blood Ruby   169
14. Objects Closer Than They Appear   181
15. Point Tenderness   193
16. Shaking, Standing, Not Standing   211
17. Serpentization   225
18. Quake and Bake   243
19. Slash and Burn   261
20. Through the Narrow Channel   307

EPILOGUE   329

ACKNOWLEDGMENTS

AUTHOR'S NOTE

For every moment the body sees, we need two images that make one. Our retinas work stereoscopically, so we see best when we see both. That is why *Landlords* has two halves that are similar. Though the characters are about ten years older in the second version, what happens is the same.

This is a work of fiction. Liberties have been taken with geology, timelines, and place names. No actual person has been portrayed. Incidents are invented.

The spirit of San Francisco artists living for their work is real.

LANDLORDS

HOLLYWOOD VERSION

1. HARMLESS LIFE

Night comes down on late-1980s San Francisco, with streams of dense fog. Some of these whip up toward the tops of Buena Vista Park, Diamond Heights, and Russian Hill and race over rushing cars on long corridors that weave under bridges. Ocean Beach lies open to its flat dun-colored sand as restless waves pummel in; surfers in black wetsuits stay in the water. Around the city, dune flowers and yellow poppies keep company with tall eucalyptus and palms. On a crowded bus, a little girl starts to cry as people crush against her; and the mother, worn from twelve hours washing hospital floors, shushes her. At bookstores in North Beach, rows of people in glasses take books from shelves and stand reading in charged silence. South of Market, men in leather boots and chaps slap each other's shoulders in bars that vibrate with music. In Golden Gate Park, groups of the homeless gather to secure sleeping places among groves of foliage. An angular man with a shaved head bends down to pick up a coin and says, "Found it. A lucky one."

Tall and pale, a slender woman with a camera in her bag walks to her bus stop. She has delicate features and long light hair with a couple of streaks of grey. This woman, Gretchen, carries herself with inwardness, as though she has pride and comfort in experience she keeps to herself. Sitting, she stares at the worn brick wall of an old factory building. Its closely paned windows, painted over and rimmed by faded red woodwork, contrast with the white sky above. Below, a massive metal mailbox sits at the corner. Next to it's a dilapidated street light. Gretchen looks at ease, although she's just finished a long day at work. Standing, she pulls her camera out of its case and starts framing. She clicks, reframes, clicks until the bus pulls up. Even after she gets on and finds her seat, she goes on shooting through the moving window's glass.

She finally climbs upstairs to an apartment building. Opening the scarred door she says sharply, "Damn, it's cold in here! Freezing!" Shivering, she pulls on a sweater, then calls, "Oscar? Hey, kitty-kitty." A white cat comes to her, sliding against her leg, as she greets him with a caress. The front room, painted grey with butterscotch trim, has an old couch, lamps from the 1930s, and big black-and-white photos of San Francisco streets on the walls. They're hers.

Gretchen sits down with a glass of apricot juice. Then she hauls out a green file folder, "Bills to Pay." Talking to herself, she alternates between rectangular shapes: check-book, register, discardables. Tip-in ads and water control reports gather before her in a heap. She does this every Thursday night; as coordinator for a nonprofit, she's used to organizing papers and dealing with their demands. Sitting behind the last ray of daylight that crosses the white table, Gretchen moves lightly, writes checks in careful script, stamps envelopes. Rain starts to smack against her windows plaintively as she works.

Across town Satchel, a forty-one-year-old man with hair below his collar, has been walking a long time. Along the street, the lights of early night glimmer at all levels: top-floor hotel bars, the welcoming sheet glass of bookstores, neon-sign night clubs, family restaurants. He ducks out of the wet. *Man, this must be the last actual phone booth in North Beach. Thought I'd never find one.* He lifts the receiver, puts in some coins, rubs his neck nervously.

The phone rings in Gretchen's kitchen. She lets it go to the answering machine. The man's high-spirited voice says, "Hey, Gretch . . . I love your phone message. Great to hear your voice. Okay, well, it's me. Pick up." The lines of her face contract, resisting. She freezes, waiting.

The man cusses and slams the receiver back down. He walks out in the rain, stands in it, and his trench coat turns too wet for comfort. Suddenly he says. "No! I'm gonna try one last time." He turns, his hair thrashing in wet spikes, and brings a complaining squeak from the folding door, closing himself into the booth. Determined, he grabs the receiver and throws money into the slot.

After another onslaught of rings, Gretchen sighs. Lifting the receiver, she says, "Hey, Satchel."

"What's happening, babe?"

"So you're coming to town?" she guesses.

"Yeah, baby, can't wait to see you."

"I suppose you want to stay here?"

"Yeah, I'm actually in San Fran. Got a bed for me?"

"I don't, Satchel."

"You know me, I can sleep on the floor, Gretch."

"Don't call me Gretch. It sounds like nausea."

He creases his face. Drawing himself up, he says, "The floor is fine." This time the pause is longer. He goes on with fake cheer, "You're not like this, you know. I remember how sweet you are, so cut it out."

Vigilant, Gretchen says, "We can't get into our old complications."

"We don't have to do the nasty. I just wanna see you. Just—"

"No!" She shakes her head irritably. "You can't just show up like this. Where are you?"

"My band played this cruise ship. It sucked. They kicked us out of a hotel in L.A. last night. The singer got drunk and trashed the room."

"The singer?" Gretchen asks suspiciously.

"Okay, me. See you tomorrow, though. Meet me at The Black Hart at five." He puts the phone back on the hook and shakes his head. *Shit. Do I spring for a hotel? I'm beat.* He plunges back into the rain. *Sleep in the car again then.*

Next evening they sit side by side at the counter of a deserted dive bar. It's dingy, but an ornately carved gilt mirror above the bar surrounds a huge array of bottles. Satchel's jeans are shiny, tight, as though he recently gained weight, but he carries himself with the wanton authority of a rock band's lead singer. He's puffy under the eyes and has a strongly-defined, flushed mouth. He wipes it with the back of his hand and bursts out, "Know what? You're leading a harmless life!"

Gretchen recoils. "Yes," she says awkwardly, "a great alternative to leading a harmful life."

He stands up, bumping into a pool table. Loudly: "It *is* harmful!"

"Satch."

"You can't do that, Gretchen. Can't give all that intensity and brilliance to a . . . a *harmless life.*"

"I knew I shouldn't have come," Gretchen says unhappily, folding her arms close to her body.

"Fuck it, you're hiding."

Then Gretchen sits quietly and dangerously still as he lights a cigarette. She starts coughing. Finally she says, "You have no idea about my path."

"What path?"

"I have a job. And my pictures. It's enough."

His lip curls. "You look like you haven't gotten laid in two years."

"What a horrible thing to say. If it had to be you, I'd rather be—"

"Celibate?" He laughs. "All women want me. You were never an exception."

Gretchen shakes her head. "Satch, go ahead and splash words."

"Just being the little hermit. Makes me so mad. I bet you don't even show your pictures to anybody. Right?"

"None of your business."

He snaps, "Fine, I'm due somewhere in ten minutes. I have a girl to meet." Gretchen tosses her head—angry, embarrassed. Suddenly he adds, "What the hell, I'll drive you home. I'm responsible that way. Besides, you hate to spend money on cabs."

Gretchen takes a deep breath and, after a moment, says reluctantly, "Okay."

Satchel's hooded eyes glimmer. He slugs back more ale, hunches over the counter and asks the owner, "Hey, buddy, how old is your mirror? I can tell the work of a fellow Irishman."

The owner answers happily, "Hundred years plus, man. I keep it in great shape."

Finally they leave. Gretchen tosses her hair and asks, "You drove up from L.A.?"

"The same," he says. "Not sure yet whether I stay."

Gretchen nods. "You always did play it by ear. First the relentless intimacy. Then taking off."

"Just tell me how long it is since you showed any work in a gallery! That's my bottom line, little hermit. Be grateful I care." He gets into the car—same battered orange Volkswagen bug from the old days, multiple dents. Although he leans over and opens the door for Gretchen, she stays on the sidewalk, wounded and taut.

She says, "Why do you do that? Only one reason I ever put up with you—"

"So, and—"

"—is before you started singing it was all about your drums. Because your drumming blows the sky away. It did! I remember, see? But you take advantage!" She slams the door shut and kicks the car.

Satchel blows her a kiss. "Hey, baby! Watch the fender."

Gretchen stubbornly takes the bus, climbs her three flights of stairs, unlocks the door and shivers at the cold in her apartment. When she calls her cat Oscar, he retreats to a corner. She sits down hard on the couch, putting a hand to her forehead. Instead of crying, she picks herself up, goes to the phone and dials. "Hello, this is Gretchen upstairs. When you get through with the second-floor radiators, will you come up and fix mine? It's really bad."

2. ROACH

Ruby, a small thirtyish woman with short dark hair, reaches hard with rhythmic force—painting a canvas that almost covers one wall. Intricate shawls hang over windows of the room. It has open shelves for paints, books, dishes and pots. Ruby dances as she paints. Her shapes under the brush resemble beasts—behemoths and serpents—and proud faces. Powerful arcs swoop across canvas, swelled by rough black outlines. She loads her palette with brilliant colors harsh and lush, squeezing from tubes, thinning, mixing. Her dark eyes flash with obsession, wild love of work.

She changes brushes, lashing lines and smears of green and blue onto canvas. Stepping back to see the results: her painting's a forest turned to lightning. She lays brushes aside, carelessly wipes hands on her gray smock, and sits on the floor with a smile. The smile disappears as she turns her face sideways looking down. Grabbing a torn-open envelope, she pulls out its contents, addressed to Ruby Arena. Paint on her hands smudges the mail with deep blue fingerprints. She grips the papers in a crush—then holds them out before her. In graphs and medical reports the words that stand out are "your biopsy," "breast tumor," and "positive for cancer."

Still wearing her paint-splotched smock, Ruby stands in line at the crowded counter of Caffé Trieste. She forces back her sleeve to look at a watch.

"You know that paint is still wet?" A tousled person taps her on the shoulder. It's Satchel. He's strongly built, though not particularly young. Again he wears the tight jeans; he has expressive hazel eyes, slightly squinting, and a prominent nose. Ruby opens her mouth to answer derisively, but she's interrupted. A hip-looking young man leaps up to point, yelling, "Hey, hey. You're that guy from Dark Matter!"

Ruby faces Satchel and says, "Really? *I* used to be in a band. Retrovirus."

He gives her a winning smile. "Cool. I heard of that. Broke up for the usual infights?"

"Yeah."

"What instrument?" His eyes staring into hers seem sea-colored, and they look large and interested.

"Bass. And a little sax. You?"

"Just voice, baby. Just me."

"You between gigs?" she asks him.

"Aaaah. You could say. Between rocks, hard places and so forth. Between the rock and the roll." He hums a little jazz riff.

Ruby glances at his well-used biceps. "And the band?"

"We hit money-management issues. . . . Say, you wanta jam sometime? I like to get my hands on a drum, but I front vocals whenever."

"Oh . . ." she flashes toward him, intrigued. But then says, "Uhhh. No, I don't really think so. I don't have time for it, for music these days." She checks the time again. "Actually, I'm late—have to skip coffee."

"But you gotta see me work, right? Maybe I phone the guys and we put together one of those shows we blew off."

She laughs uncertainly, but suddenly holds out her long

hand and says, "I'm Ruby. Ruby Arena." She pronounces it A-*reh*-na.

He grasps her hand with both of his. "Satchel Reilly."

"Satchel. Like the suitcase?"

"The same. —Ruby! Ahh. The name of a jewel."

Eleven blocks away, Gretchen walks through North Beach, lugging a large binder. Ruby's walking too, quickly now. She has to get back her apartment. The person she needs to meet there is Gretchen. They arrive the same time, with the sparkle of friends starting to know each other better.

Ruby says, "Hi! God, I barely made it." They start up the dark stairs.

"I'm glad you have time for me. I figured out I should get my work out there more, so I need an artist to collaborate. Some kind of show."

"Well, I'm your girl, Gretchen. I've got an idea for this little place I know on Grant." Ruby unlocks her heavy old wooden door. Inside, Gretchen stops in front of a huge painting full of color and motion.

"Oh, Ruby. Is this new?"

"Still wet!"

"It's powerful. Like a . . . a macroburst of energy from some planet I didn't know."

"That's a great way of describing what it wants to be. I hope it holds true when I finish!"

"You don't know how it'll turn out?"

"Hardly ever. Not a calculating painter. But I want to finish this canvas soon. For our show, right? So. Let's get to your photographs!" Ruby claps her hands. "Put 'em right on the table."

Gretchen lays out her work, photos taken from plane windows and around San Francisco.

"Wow! I can hardly believe this. Your colors!" Ruby points to one and another, seizing on details she especially likes: mountains, foggy sandscape, store windows, contorted tree. "You *have* to show them. Where were these skies?"

"Over the Rockies. The black and white ones are from here, all recent. North Beach, Mission, Tenderloin, other neighborhoods. I should probably choose a theme. Either the aerial photos or black-and-white San Francisco."

"Why the hell choose? The gallery that's good for this handles off-the-beaten-track artists. They won't try to package us to hustle a mil. Mix it up however you want."

"What about you? Do you have a main theme in mind?"

"Hah. How 'bout 'Eighties Madwoman of North Beach Channels Beat Poets?' Can't say if I've even got a style."

"Can I see more?"

"Sure, if you've got time you can see it *all.*" In a whirlwind Ruby hauls large canvases from a side room into the kitchen with little help. Her paintings are full of big hungry, lunging lines and blurs and an occasional face of tenderness, fierce anger, or determination. Ruby moves her hands and touches her short dark curls as she talks—Gretchen nods, taking it in.

Finally the high energy settles. Ruby says, "We should call the LiveWire Gallery. We'll only get a one- or two-day event . . . have to hang our own work, find some friends to help. But hey. Time for a break. Shot of tequila?"

"Whoa. A little early in the day for me."

"Well, a joint?"

"Seriously?"

"C'mon, Gretchen. I deal a little to make ends meet."

"Uh, not my thing."

"A glass of wine then? I got Chardonnay."

"Water's fine."

"Sheesh. Okay." Ruby swings open an old refrigerator.

Suddenly Gretchen gasps. "Oh, my God!" Infinitesimal cockroaches stream from under the refrigerator onto the floor.

Ruby shrugs dramatically. "Yeah, yeah—the freakin' monsters been here forever. Babies just keep spawning."

"That's awful! Your landlord doesn't spray?"

"They don't do jack shit. The less you have, less you can break, prob'ly—"

"That's not even legal. *Do* something, Ruby—make them take action!" Gretchen shakes her head, worried and disgusted.

"I been here two years, and the critters came with the place. Like in charge of the dark. Open your fridge at midnight and they *leap* out from under. I tried sprays. Traps. Voodoo. Nothing worked. Now I ignore the bastards. Poof, they don't exist." Ruby helps herself to a big shot of tequila and hands Gretchen a bottle of water.

"Well, they *do*, and with all that spraying, the fittest probably survived. Look, that one's albino!"

Ruby says, "Yeah, tell me about it. Mutant roaches. Aliens. . . . Hey, know what? I just found out this lump in my breast has to come out. First they thought it was a cyst, but turns out it's a tumor. My crappy housekeeping skills fell apart. Don't even look in the sink!"

Involuntarily Gretchen looks. It's full of dishes splattered with salad, buttered popcorn, spaghetti. She says softly, "Ruby, I'm sorry. Is it . . ."

"Cancer? Looks as if. Have to get it cut out."

Gretchen puts both hands over her mouth. Then she asks, "Is anyone going with you?"

Ruby shakes her head. "Ehh. I can handle it."

"I'll go."

"Really? You'd do that?"

"Sure, I'll be glad to."

"Wow. You're a sweetheart!" Ruby throws her arms around Gretchen. "Yeah! I accept."

Gretchen arrives at the Grant Avenue storefront gallery and knocks. A woman with a long, sleek black ponytail barely opens the door and peeks out. "Hi, sweetie. Your titles, prices—all there. Gimme me a few minutes? It's almost time."

"Yes, I know. Shouldn't I help?"

"Just come back in fifteen. Okay, doll?" Two of Ruby's paintings lean on the wall, unhung.

"Okay," Gretchen agrees uncomfortably. The ponytail woman blows an air kiss, disappears, and relocks the door.

Gretchen meanders down Grant Avenue in her long skirt, emerald green jacket and ankle boots in the dark. She steps into a small market that's nearly empty, walks through thoughtfully. Back on the street, a hair salon has an amber neon sign in Chinese. Inside, only the far green wall and a faint-gold couch can be seen. Gretchen captures the scene with her camera, standing in the doorway. Her face looks as still as if she's forgotten about the show.

In the LiveWire Gallery, long and skinny as a small alley, talk roars above street noise. In front of the large painting that Gretchen called a macroburst of energy, Ruby's holding court. A guy in a tweed vest, silk tie and florid moustache has his arm around her. Intense-looking groups discuss the work on the wall; many move from one painting to another in a ragged line. There are plenty of young art students, along with old-timers. A few older black men with skull caps appear to be jazz musicians. Mixing among the neighborhood Italians and Asians, some in the room look like highly-paid models or wealthy matrons. Gretchen circles around as if hoping for invisibility, at one point even taking out her camera, then shyly putting it away. She glances toward her photographs spread over a whole wall, show-cased with effective lighting. A very tall man's also looking at her pictures, hand on one hip confidently. He's so lean his shoulder blades stand out. He sidles in close to one image—of sun slamming onto a steep street—crosses his arms, and stays there. Gretchen presses forward, watching him. He has grey hair to his shoulders, a long craggy face, blue eyes squinting through a light of his own. Somebody jostles him and he catches Gretchen's eye.

He turns, holding out his large, sensitive hand. "Are you the photographer?"

She blushes. "Yes, that's me. I'm Gretchen Wilson." She shakes his hand, then folds hers together, as though she can't remember where they go.

"Len Considine. This is beautiful work. It's like a love feast of the city. And you have an especially strong affinity for the sky." His skin's brown-tinged in the way of naturally fair people who crave sun. "You're based in North Beach?" he asks.

"No, nearby in the Tenderloin. This is my first show in a long time."

He nods. "I used to hang out in North Beach, but for a few years I've been in Europe and Australia. Just got back." He has a clear, warm voice.

"What did you do over there?"

"Theater. Art activism."

"*Art* activism? What's that?"

"Well, I enjoy trying to interrupt the stranglehold cor-porate interests have on art. It's all over the place."

"In Australia?"

"Sure. Take opera—in Sydney, all that gorgeous music happens at the Opera House. It was controlled by huge sponsors with big investment in South African apartheid. Mandela had done the work, but corporations started undermining it. We had to challenge that."

"Who's 'we?'" Gretchen's still timid.

"Just some friends. We'd dress up like idiot clowns, put on satirical skits right in the lobby. When they threw us out, we'd move it to the front steps. Shouldn't the opera house belong to regular folks? Finally people with the bucks stayed away, and that got some attention, believe me. We hit the house in their fat pocketbook, so they had to listen. They finally even got rid of their contract with a big corporation that lobbied for the apartheid regime."

"Wow," Gretchen says. "That's impressive. But I feel sorry for the opera house. I don't have your energy for that. I'd be happy just to get warm in my apartment."

"What? I *hate* that for you. In North Beach we can't afford studios, maybe even live here anymore. LiveWire's great, but in a single day or two, how many people get to see your work? Most of us aren't gallery artists."

"*You're* an artist?" Gretchen's forgotten her shyness.

"Yeah, I mess around with painting. Learned from some Maori friends over there."

"Interesting."

He pulls out a simple business card and offers it to her. "I think we should have coffee," he says with a smile.

Suddenly Satchel's there, grabbing Gretchen in a massive hug. She protests, "Satch, stop it!" Satchel buries his face in her neck.

Len, the tall man, says, "Hey, you've got to talk to your public. See you." He flashes Gretchen a warm look as he walks away.

"Why?" she exclaims angrily to Satchel. "Why do you do—"

"C'mon, I came here for *you*. Lemme bring you wine and cheese, baby."

As soon as Satchel walks away, he's detoured by a girl with cleavage. Forgetting his task, he's swirled into a group of bearded guys in berets. In the middle stands Ruby, talking to four of them at once.

Gretchen, after greeting luminaries, hangers-on and interested artists for hours, at last lets herself be swept toward Caffè Trieste with the final crowd. It has started raining and, umbrellaless, she protects her head with her hands. The laughing group runs into the café, and someone hands her a glass of red wine. She sips from it, then holds it close to her midriff. Len, the tall man, sits against a front window with people he's talking to. She looks toward him eagerly, but he's surrounded. Nervously she glances at her watch, puts down the glass, moves outside.

She signals for a cab, standing in wind by the street light. Suddenly Len's there, jacketless, with wet hair. His button-down shirt with rolled-up sleeves is peeled wide at the neck. There's a birthmark about the size and shape of an oval quarter on his chest, slightly darker than his skin. Gretchen, covering her hair against the rain, can't help looking at it.

He says, "I hope you're not put off by all the noise. Come back?"

Gretchen doesn't answer, but she looks torn. A lot has happened for her this night. "I'd better go," she finally says shyly, looking at her ankle boots.

"Well . . . you've got my card." He stands in the doorway gazing at her for a long moment, leaning his arm on the frame.

As he turns back, opens the door to go inside, Gretchen calls, "Bye, Len," but it's too late—he hasn't heard. She looks down again, at the damp pavement, smiles sadly, and walks toward Columbus..

Someone runs after her; it's Ruby, under a big black umbrella. Out of breath, Ruby cries, "Hey, I hardly saw you tonight. Wasn't it fabulous?"

"It was great. Really." Gretchen nods and smiles but doesn't stop. Her hands are restlessly jammed into her coat pockets. Rain falls onto her unprotected face.

"What's going on, honey? Where you going? You look all flushed."

Gretchen stops but looks distracted.

"Come on, give! What is it?"

"Nothing. —It's a man." She shakes her head and absently wipes her palms against her coat.

"Oh, wow. You look like a little girl." Ruby and her ample umbrella move closer.

Gretchen says, "Don't."

"But I want to hear! What's the story?"

Gretchen quickly stores away her feelings. "Nothing. I just need to go home and decompress."

"Aw, too bad. But you'll tell me if anything happens with this, this guy?"

Gretchen gives her a quick kiss on the cheek, smiles enigmatically and says, "If there's anything I want to say, you'll be the first to know."

As Gretchen moves away into the increasing rain, Ruby calls, "It's an incredible night. We'll miss you!"

Daylight tries to come through a lace curtain, but it's still raining. Gretchen sits at her kitchen table, holding a steaming mug and mopping her nose. Nearby, a workman kneels by her radiator, fiddling with valves. Gretchen, sniffling, picks up the card Len gave her. She looks blearily at the radiator, then strokes Oscar at her ankle. Suddenly she puts down the mug, grabs the card again and walks to the phone, dials the number,

"Oh! You're home. I thought I'd . . . leave a message. Uh, this is Gretchen Wilson, from last night."

"Hey. Hi there. That's some rain, isn't it?"

"Yes, it really is. I'm snuffling. It's cold in here."

"Well, I'm glad to hear from you. What's happening?"

"Today? Well, actually, I need to take down my photos from—" Right in the middle of her sentence, the worker bangs on the radiator with a crowbar. She laughs. "I was saying *I need to take down my show.*"

"Oh, I get you. Well, could you use company? Maybe some help?"

Surprised, Gretchen says, "Sure. You know what? That would be great."

Soon they're at LiveWire together; Len lifts one of Gretchen's framed photos off the wall and passes it to her. "Want me to help wrap?" he asks.

"No, it's okay. I have my packing system." Gretchen sees him handling her work and likes his careful manner.

"That's good. You know what works for you," he says. She gives him a big smile. He takes down the framed pictures, and she slips Styrofoam triangles over their corners.

They keep working and talking. Len says, "Say, have you noticed that abandoned market on Vallejo?"

"I don't think so."

"That was a family Italian grocery for years. Petta's. It's boarded-up, graffiti all over. Probably even has rats. You should swing by and take a look."

"Really? Why?"

"Because much better things could happen in there. It's a damn disgrace."

She looks at him and says, "Yeah?" as she envelops her photos in bubble wrap.

"Thing is, I'm getting an idea. . . . I'm thinking we could get the owners to let artists take care of it till it's sold."

"What for?"

"We could put work spaces in there. We're artists—we should be taking back the arts."

Gretchen's setting photos upright in a box. "But why would the owners trust us? What's in it for them?"

"How about some of us cleaning it up? We could probably even do plays there. Some terrific stuff. Every single night tourists swarm all over North Beach—we just might sell out! Seriously. I think the owners could go for it."

"You've done successful productions?"

"Sure. Before I was an art activist I was a theater professor at San Jose State. You didn't go there, did you?"

"No, I did art history at Oregon State."

"Like it?"

"Yeah, but I liked getting behind a camera more." Gretchen has all her photos stacked in boxes. The project has gone quickly.

Len stands facing her. His blue eyes in dusty afternoon light look energized. It also seems he trimmed and neatened his hair since last night. He says to her, "That color's great on you."

Gretchen looks at the arm of her thick Irish sweater as if she hasn't seen it recently. "Oh! This? Well . . . thanks."

Leaning on one hip, he says, "Know what? I'd really like you to look at Petta's Market. You're inspiring me, here!"

"What about my photos?" Gretchen asks.

"Leave the box and lock up. It's not far. After that we could grab something to eat, then pick up your photos. Hungry?"

"I'd like to, but I promised to get these boxes out of here by tonight."

"Okay, sure—I'll put you in a cab whenever you want. Come on, it's just a few blocks."

As they walk out, Len impulsively seizes Gretchen's hand. Jaywalking, they run across the street, laughing past a speeding car. Gretchen, breathless, turns her eyes down to her hand still in his, and as she looks up, his eyes ask if he can keep it there. She smiles. As they walk slower, narrow and sharp-turning North Beach streets reflect the light of fresh sun, after the long night and day of rain.

They stop at a boarded-up market, front door covered with graffiti. Gretchen, leaning into the window, exclaims, "God, it's *enormous!* I can't believe this is going to waste." Len stands with her side by side, faces almost touching the smeared window, as they talk about how it must have looked as a thriving neighborhood market—and almost finish each other's sentences.

Ruby kneels on her kitchen floor, halfway inside a large cupboard. Only her backside can be seen. Her hips in a brown maxi dress sway in work rhythm; apron strings flutter behind her waist. A loud thump on her door makes her pull herself up, stretch, and answer.

Satchel, eyes shining, says gaily, "Hey, you look adorable," and touches her hair. "We heading to the gallery? Do we need a dolly or anything?" He follows her in.

"Long as my paintings fit in your car we're fine."

"You always have an intriguing smear on you," he says, brushing powder off her chin.

"Boric acid for the roaches. It's hard to get the cupboard corners. Shelves are full of roach spit and roach crap." Ruby sighs, hunkers down against the wall, and takes a joint out of her apron pocket. Satchel joins her, elbows on bent knees.

"Damn. Nice spliff. And so I got a match for that, princess." He snaps a packet out of his too-tight jeans.

Ruby takes the first toke. "We'll get to the paintings," she tells Satchel, passing the joint to him.

He inhales vociferously. "*Oh, yeah,*" he says, putting an arm around her. He sniffs. "Do I smell turpentine?"

She nods.

"Huh. You know they get that stuff from balsam firs? In Canada."

Ruby doesn't answer. She's staring at a cockroach crawling on the linoleum, using its feelers to touch the floor.

Satchel goes on, "And the ancients in the Mediterranean got turpentine from a terebinth tree. Y'know?"

"I wouldn't," she says.

Satchel clears his throat. "But yeah, it's toxic. Wanta ruin your lungs?"

Ruby frowns. "I just met you and you call me on my shit?"

He laughs, apparently delighted, and gives her shoulder a squeeze.

"Okay," she says, relaxing, "go ahead." She leans against him. "Tell me more esoteric stuff about turpentine."

In a fake-pompous voice he declares, "And so, terebinth is in the pistachio family." He pulls her closer.

"That's silly. Even if it's true."

He laughs, his face close to hers. "Ruby, I'm gonna be your favorite. You'll see."

3. PIGEON-BLOOD RUBY

The county hospital waiting room is crowded. It has blond-wood tables and closely packed chairs; there's a noticeable smell from Ruby's perfume, "Poison," which she saves for crucial occasions. Gretchen, who sits beside her, asks, "How're you doing?"

Ruby bends her anxious face over a magazine, photos of movie stars, all wearing the same dress, headlined "Who's Skinny and Not?" Gripping pages, Ruby stares at silk jackets, turquoise or magenta pants, feathered hair. She's neither listening nor reading.

"What medical thing will they do first?" Gretchen asks, touching her friend's arm.

Ruby says grimly, "Stick a wire into my breast." She puts the pages down.

"What?"

"Seems they know where the tumor is, but there's this other place in there they have to biopsy. Both."

"And the wire is because—?"

"The surgeon can see where to do the biopsy."

"Ruby A-reeeena!" a nurse yells from the hallway door. She's holding a chart.

"A-*reh*-na," Ruby tells her tensely.

"Can I come along?" Gretchen asks.

"No," the nurse says.

Flustered, Gretchen quickly hugs Ruby, patting her on the back. With a panicked face, Ruby hurries after the nurse.

Before disappearing through double doors, she turns back. Gretchen smiles encouragement, gives a little wave.

In a small cubicle, Ruby removes her clothes and puts on the baby-blue, polka-dot gown. It's too short, and she tugs it self-consciously, then struggles to tie it in front. She's led into a room full of machines, and finally a technician in starched white coat arrives. There's no introduction, and as the test setup starts, Ruby's alone and scared.

Summoning her courage, Ruby says, "Good. You're a woman."

The technician answers brusquely. "Yes. I am. We will take images of your right breast first. Open your gown and move up to the machine. Get as close as you can." She pulls Ruby against a tall metal column with two horizontal plates at chest level. "Raise your right arm. Put it up here." She grasps Ruby's breast like hamburger-in-the-making, puts it between plates and arranges it, meat caught in metal. "Now I'll tighten these." She steps on a device and the metal plates noisily mash against Ruby.

She yells. "That hurts! There's a tumor in there!"

"Exactly the point."

"Shit!"

Another technician walks in, compresses his mouth at her exclamation, and without saying a word starts threading a wire into her breast.

"Christ, can't you give me any anaesthesia? Something to numb it at least?"

The nurse says, "No. It will be over soon. We're coordinating by live camera. It's very precise." Ruby clenches her hands, her teeth. *When will they finish with her?*

"It feels like you're defusing a bomb!"

"Almost done with the wire." Only the nurse actually says anything to her. "You need to stay still. It's better and faster for all of us."

Ruby says sharply, "Better? Faster? I bet a lot better and

faster if somebody can afford another way!"

The nurse gives her a hostile look. "Hold still. We have to get this part right. Listen, we'll make you sleepy before you have surgery."

Ruby scrunches her whole being. As the placement wire twists in, strangled moans come from her throat.

After this procedure, an orderly pushes in a gurney. She gropes for the ties to her gown, unable to fix them. The guy says, "I'm your ride, kiddo. Stop wigging out and lie down here." He wheels her to surgery, accidentally smacking into a doorway. "Sorry 'bout that, he says. "Anything I can do for ya?"

She answers shakily, "I want to see the tumor when they take it out."

The next thing Ruby will remember is a white-rubbered hand holding up some sort of bloody, gristle-threaded lump, a ragged ball of uncooked chicken.

Within a day, back home, she starts wondering how—*if*—she can ever be attractive to anybody with one smaller, scarred breast. She will involuntary touch herself there many times a day, her hand looking for the missing parts.

It's less than a week later. Ruby holds a little glass of Pernod. She sits with Gretchen at a small, round balcony table in the North Beach bar Vesuvio. It looks over an immense wall of varicolored liqueurs. Leaded-glass lamps hang over the bar below—dark woodwork, men and women of all ages, and friendly cacophony.

Gretchen says, "I can't believe you got out of the hospital so fast."

Ruby answers, "What they do now. 'Specially when you have zero insurance. They gave me a deal where the government pays part, but they'd rather have the big bucks, yeah? Only one of my biopsies tested positive for cancer, but the asshole surgeon took *two* huge chunks out of my tits. Both places. Jesus! She said she had to."

"*What?* D'you think they were too quick to cut?"

"Damn right." Ruby winces. "If they want me to do radiation or fucking-*anything,* I won't. Bastards!"

"Ruby, come on, if you need chemo, or—"

"I don't! I won't. So, one of my tits is small now. I'm fine. *All crappy cells are out of there;* it's over."

Gretchen shakes her head impatiently. "We'll go back. We'll make a list of questions."

"Why make a big deal?" Ruby's eyes narrow.

"I want to know what you're facing. And *you've* got to know."

"I don't 'got to' anything. Stop it with the bad vibes!" Grimacing, she takes a drink of Pernod and throws back her head, slugging like it's whisky.

For a minute Gretchen stares, then says quietly, "Will you go to your follow-up appointment? Please?"

"I'll think about it. Today I'm just glad it's over!"

"Okay." Gretchen puts down her lemonade. "Hey, I have something to give you."

"That why your backpack looks like you're moving to China?"

Gretchen smiles. "You told me on the way to the hospital that you want to make movies."

"Yeah. Stuff I can show in a bigger way . . . ugly stuff, like what happened to my body, that I can't get, painting."

Gretchen turns to the chair next to her, piled with their coats and bags. "Well, here." Gretchen unzips one, pulls out an old video camera.

"Oh, God! Yours?"

"I don't need it," Gretchen says. "Take it, Ruby."

Ruby reaches out and, carefully avoiding her own chest, lifts it and peers through the viewfinder. Giggling, she says, "You brought a backpack to a bar! Weirdo. I love weirdos."

Someone bangs confidently on Gretchen's door. "Who is it?" she calls.

"Benedict Di Noti. Our family owns your building." She cracks the door to peek. A poised and solid man with curly white hair stands holding a fedora.

"Hello. Are you Gretchen?"

"I'm Gretchen Wilson, yes."

"May I talk to you a moment? I'm checking in with our tenants." She opens the door partway. Di Noti has a barrel chest, small legs. His tightly wavy white hair poufs in front, and he has a strong scent of aftershave. He gives her an amiable, surprisingly young-man smile.

"Uh . . . okay." Gretchen opens the door nervously. He's wearing an expensive-looking brown suit with a purple Oxford shirt and blue tie, an odd combination that looks elegant on him. Gretchen, in house slippers and worn tights, clutches her sweater close.

He stays respectfully just inside the door with his hat in his hand, but his tone's particularly assured. "You've always been a good tenant. I appreciate it." They look directly into each other's eyes.

"Well, thank you, Mister . . . . Denotee? I'm surprised you say that. I've been calling your office every day to fix the heat, and nobody calls back. As you can tell, it's very cold."

He smiles crookedly. "Sorry to hear it. I'll take care of that. The thing is—can I call you Gretchen?"

"I guess . . . I mean call me Gretchen and tell me what 'the thing' is."

Over his black eyes, dark eyebrows hold their own. "This building has been a bum investment. I thought it was in better shape when I bought it. There's no way I could get my money back."

Gretchen speaks up. "Really? Not if you make some improvements? I could sure suggest a few."

He seems taken aback by her forthrightness. "Hm. We can talk about that."

Gretchen nods, waiting.

He goes on, "The thing is . . . Gretchen, you always pay on time. And I notice you're a take-charge person."

Baffled, Gretchen says, "Well, thanks. I wouldn't *not* pay my rent. I just want to be treated fairly."

"That's what I want to talk about. I'm interested in this place being more under tenant control. You like your apartment, right? I see you look after it." He lifts the fedora in a slight wave, like an emcee making an introduction. "Maybe you'd like to get involved running the building."

Gretchen crosses her arms and takes a step back. "No, I don't want to be a super." She'd better shorten this. "I have a job."

"Sure. But maybe I cut my losses, and you rent to own. Pay a little extra each month, become part owner of the building."

"Oh! What do you mean by rent to own?"

"Own your unit. You'd make a down payment for an option to buy at a future time, not necessarily specified."

He keeps standing patiently, almost like someone asking a woman out. Gretchen, confused, finally responds, "I don't know what to say. I'm not sure I could come up with all that cash. What about the heat, Mr. Denotee?"

"I'll have it fixed. I'd *like* you to be part owner of the building. Think it over." As he leaves, she hears his steps echo through the hallway. He has a brisk, upbeat walk.

Gretchen closes the door and goes to the battered chair in front of her desk. She shakes her head. Part ownership of the building? Like share it with his family? Or would it turn out to be a co-op? *I don't want to rule anything out before I find out more.*

✥

"Baby, you lit me the first time I looked at you," Satchel says. He's playing with Ruby's hands in bed.

Ruby laughs richly and asks, "How? My eyes?"

"Your name."

"What? My name turned you on, *looking* at me?"

"Quiet. There's two kinds of rubies—Indian, which is pink. And pigeon-blood, the Burmese. With pigeon-blood rubies, you hold 'em up in morning light and they gotta be *exactly* the right color, or they're not real."

"How do you know?"

He whispers, "Used to smuggle them. In Burma."

"*What?* Shut up, you did not." She pushes his shoulder.

"I had a restaurant in Rangoon. In that situation, you deal with the Triad." He flips onto his back, arms under his head, looking intently at the ceiling. "And, but . . . you can't ignore them; they own everything, anybody. They ordered me to go in a mine and pretend to be a tourist. I got a ruby for them down in there. Pigeon-blood ruby. A damned expensive stone."

Ruby lies beside him. She leans forward on one elbow, thoughtful. "What are you even talking about, Satch? *Pigeon* blood?"

"It's like this. Rubies grade by color clarity, carat and cut. The sellers bring out a dagger, jab it through a pigeon's heart, and put a drop of its blood on a paper. Next to the ruby. That's if you have a good eye. Which I do." His eyes glimmer as he says this.

Ruby moves closer. She says incredulously, "You seriously were a restaurateur in—"

"Damn right!" He throws himself across her, shutting her mouth with kisses.

4. OBJECTS CLOSER THAN THEY APPEAR

Through Gretchen's kitchen window, behind her, clouds push across the sky above a rusty-sign hotel. She stands in front of this window as Satchel tells her about him and Ruby—"before she hears it some other way."

"What do you mean?" Gretchen asks Satchel, her voice rising.

"We're inseparable."

"I can't—what are you saying?"

"Yeah, it's true. Ruby and I haven't been out of each other's sight for six days."

"Where? How?" Gretchen looks horrified.

Laughing, Satchel says, "Babe, you're not taking it in. I stay at her place." He rips a cigarette out of his pocket and lights up. "Hey, sorry if this is weird."

Gretchen coughs and waves her hand. "Satchel, don't."

"Oh, you hate smoke. Forgot."

Gretchen turns her head away. Then she protests firmly, "You had to pick my friend? Damn it, Satchel. How could you *do* that?"

He takes her arm. "Hey, now, that doesn't sound like you." She pulls away and takes deep breaths. He goes on, "Hon, you said we're toast. I didn't want that, but then I met her, before you guys did the show. I didn't know you were close."

Staring, she stands. Quiet. Behind her, clouds still gallop by. She looks down at a small, square light reflection on the floor and asks, "Are you taking care of her? Because she's recovering from surgery. You know?"

"Of course I know!"

"Okay. Okay . . ." She looks worried. "Satch, I have work to do." He knows to leave. And he does.

Gretchen shuts the door, eyes closed. She sits, and Oscar jumps onto her lap. As she strokes him, the phone rings. Gretchen picks it up and says gratefully, "Oh. Len!"

Gretchen and Len sit outside Caffé Trieste, almost into the street, at a small table with a red umbrella. They're drinking coffee. Apparently this is Len's favorite place.

"So come on, tell me, Gretchen. What do you want out of life?"

Gretchen smiles girlishly. "Just keep making pictures. A way that feels right."

"That's all?"

She laughs. "Well, I'm attached to my way of photography, and I love it. I'm old-school—manual, and I don't pose or arrange anything, because it's about looking. I love framing things different ways through the lens. What about you? What are *you* after?"

Len beams. "Nothing less than another kind of world!"

"Wow, such a modest ambition."

"Yeah. Don't get me wrong, I wasn't always idealistic."

"No? Where'd you grow up?"

"Across the Bay. Richmond."

"You have family there?"

"Both of my folks were welders during the World War. Those heavy-lifters working the Oakland shipyards? That was them. Both dead now. Quite a while."

"What was it like growing up in Richmond?"

"I did fine. Some guys whine about how bad it was, running around stealing and skipping school—you know, crazy stuff—we'd get caught. But besides that, my buddies and I also spent time on the beach. Playing ball, goofing. I had a happy childhood."

Gretchen laughs. The breeze lifts her hair. "So what are you like now?"

He says, "Well for one thing, beautiful art makes me happy. Your pictures . . . I'm impressed. Can I see more?"

Quickly, she glances sideways, then back at him. "You can see one now," she says, pulling a photograph out of her bag and handing it to him. It's a moody still of a room.

"Is this a gallery?"

"No, I don't have space for a darkroom anymore, so there's a photo lab I trust to develop my work. But I hang some in my room."

"Your bedroom?" Len repeats, looking at it again. "In black and white, it looks austere." His tone is respectful.

"Is there a reason you're in the Bay Area? You said you had been in Australia."

"Actually, I was kicked out of Australia. For my plays." He gives her a smile that seems a little more proud than embarrassed.

"So now you'll try them out in wild and free San Francisco?" She tosses her head, amused.

"You bet! I'm crazy about San Fran. Hub of the universe. So many talented people, so much we could do!" He shifts eagerly. "And sometimes a chance to check out somewhere else on the globe. If I'm called to do a show."

"Wow," She says uneasily. "You have a lot in motion!"

"Damn right." He looks excited. "A friend of mine in Prague works with life-size puppets. And one of my former students just started helping villagers in India get in better financial shape. He'd like me to come—include me in his grant—but I'll probably just enjoy his letters about it all. There's always great stuff going on."

Gretchen sits thoughtfully. "You seem so hungry for that. These adventures." She looks disheartened.

Len reaches to touch her hand. "Are you okay?"

After a minute she says, "I'm worried about my friend Ruby." She pauses, looking across the street, deciding whether to say more and, if so, what? About herself, his seeming temporariness, or her friend? "She just had breast surgery for early cancer."

Len raises his eyebrows. "Oh, no. What's going on?"

Gretchen tells him about the operation. A large German Shepherd comes up, wagging its tail and nuzzling her elbow. Gretchen strokes his head. The dog moves toward Len, who ruffles him.

Len answers Gretchen, "You know . . . that's what we pay doctors for, do their job. She should let them decide." The dog settles at Len's feet.

"Well, I'm not exactly saying that. I think she should find out why they handled it so aggressively and what they think the deal is. And her options."

"We have her medical life all figured out for her, here!"

Gretchen laughs again. "I'd feel better if she'd call me back. . . . I guess she'll do what she needs to. It's hard to watch." Gretchen drops her hands into her lap.

"Yeah, I can tell."

She shrugs sadly, and her napkin flutters away. She reaches down, but Len picks it up and hands it to her across the table.

"Sorry, I'm distracted," Gretchen says softly.

"Hey," he says, and puts his hand on hers. "No sorry. Let's change it up. I'd like to have a get-together about that market idea. Want to come? You can bring your friend if you like."

They're back at LiveWire—Gretchen, Ruby, and twelve or so others, in folding chairs or crouching on the floor. Len stands by the gallery wall where Gretchen's pictures recently hung. Beside him an easel holds a big tablet. Len smiles, clears his throat, and says, "Hey! Thanks for turning out! Good to see all of you. I want to talk about Petta's Market—an empty space on a main corner of North Beach. It's been turned into an eyesore, a real disgrace. *We* could be using that space."

Len doesn't raise his voice. It's quiet, but it carries. People are listening. "Petta's was a neighborhood grocery for seventy years, and now it's a place for people to piss on in the middle of the night. On a prime corner at the heart of North Beach. Which is pretty much the artistic capital of the Bay Area. It doesn't just offend tourists. It's offensive to *us*. We work out of this part of the world; some of us live here. A lot of us do both, in crowded situations. If you're an artist sitting here, you're probably without a studio. Can't afford the rent anymore. That space could be a fantastic place to work and show our work."

He glances around. People nod. A couple say, "Yeah. Yeah!" Gretchen stands near Len, but off to one side by the wall. Seeing Len in his element, she's intrigued to see how quickly people respond to his idea. New people have been walking in. One of them is Satchel.

Len goes on, "Think about it. All it needs is cleanup; we can do it. If we get the owners to let us use the place, we'll take care of it. Keep it safe for them until they sell. What do you say?"

The talk moves to what has to be done, and people cluster around the big tablet, signing up to find out who owns the building, research North Beach's history of backing the arts, or ask local merchants for support. Someone adds "printing flyers." Somebody else adds "writing flyers." They decide to call themselves North Beach Artists. Len says anybody's free to join the effort, and Satchel hollers, "Musicians?"

"You bet," Len tells him.

Satchel stands up. "I'm in!"

After the meeting, they go on talking outside in gathering dark, most people walking toward Caffé Trieste.

Inside Trieste, tables are shoved together in groups, except for a few under the celebrity-photo wall. The crowd includes aging poets, young travelers, Italian immigrants, and university intellectuals. It's noisy, with many ideas thrown around and tested, plenty of laughter, wine and steaming espresso. At the front window, a bald guy with a trimmed white beard and sweater vest exclaims, "I tell my students, 'Move back ten or twenty steps from the image. Get a bigger perspective!' "

Next to him, a woman wearing a chartreuse scarf tells a man in a tweed cap, "It was *not* a yellowjacket. It was a European paper wasp. Orange feelers . . ." Outside, somebody walks by with a loud ghetto blaster playing "No More Mister Nice Guy." He reaches into an open window to shake hands with a guy in a crocheted beanie.

A bald woman hands a newspaper clipping to someone across the table. "Look! They're showing fifteenth-century Italian paintings. A Piero di Cosimo, 'Maria Magdalena.' "

Len and Gretchen walk in together. Gretchen looks a little like the painting, with her stillness and self-containment. Len stands straight with an air of being where he needs to be. Satchel, already there, holds forth with Ruby at his side. Ruby, though still a bit pale, beams. Her eyes are dancing, and she looks like a recovering woman.

Satchel throws his arms wide and exclaims, "Two thirds of the universe has Dark Energy." He calls to Len, "Hey, man! Over here with us." Len pulls up a chair for Gretchen and takes one himself. Satchel goes on, "The other third of the universe is dark matter—which you can't even see with a telescope. Dark matter! Mixed with the usual atoms."

Gretchen squirms in her seat, seeing Satchel and Ruby together. She turns to Satchel and asks, "How do you come up with that? Two thirds of everything is 'dark energy'?"

Satchel leans forward on his elbows. A little controversy appeals to him. "Ten-year project checking bent light from quasars. Dark Energy was an outer-space idea Einstein toyed with, but he decided it was nuts—and, but now there's evidence. With your gravitational lens, two images of a quasar appear, but they're so close together you can't even tell them apart. So, but modern lenses make images of a *huge* number of quasars."

Len pitches in cheerfully, "They used radio telescopes?"

"Yeah, dude, yeah."

Gretchen asks, "Remind me what a quasar is?"

"So anyway," Satchel goes on, "Dark Energy makes the universe expand—faster, not slower. Nobody knows Dark Energy! You can't see it, smell it—you only get radio pictures of the dance it's doing out there—like flashing light in a dance club!"

Gretchen raises her eyebrows. "Sounds like science fiction."

Satchel laughs, reaches over and taps his forefinger against her head. "Believe, believe, baby! The old Satchmo knows."

"Hey!" Gretchen pushes his hand away.

Len, unaware of Satchel and Gretchen's history, says earnestly, "The way I understand it, a quasar's a starlike mass with a frightful amount of energy, incredibly bright, probably very ancient, probably a black hole powering it from its center. . . . And if dark matter's out there, however *much* of it there is will have a huge effect on our fate. Our galaxy."

Gretchen finally seems interested. She says, "Still, what if 'dark energy' is just a marker for something we hardly know? Twenty years from now, won't there be a different interpretation?"

Satchel answers, "Sure, maybe, but there's already theories to explain it, three of them very strong right now."

Ruby hasn't spoken, but now she says, "Cool." She's hardly taken her eyes off Satchel.

And he feels it. He goes on exuberantly, "Guess what? The three theories also have sexy names: Hot Dark Matter, Warm Dark Matter and Cold Dark Matter."

Ruby smiles broadly. "Rad!" she says, sipping delicately from a shot glass. "Go, Satchi."

Across the room commotion breaks out. A leather-jacketed man with long hair runs toward the door, yelling after a woman who's walking away, "Stop! Marry me, baby! C'mon, marry me!"

Satchel grins. "And Hot Dark Matter has gravitational effects." He swipes two fingers along the rim of his cappuccino and licks off the foam.

Gretchen awkwardly runs her hands through her hair. At the door, the leather-jacket guy keeps yelling, "C'mon, don't leave!"

Len's attention has shifted. Putting his hand on Gretchen's shoulder, he stands up to talk to someone about Petta's Market, "a great chance for a big art space." Immediately he gets in conversation with a middle-aged man in a navy-patterned tie, comparing their views on budget deficit, presidential candidate George H. Bush, and the arms race.

5. POINT TENDERNESS

INSIDE RUBY

Am I getting any sleep at all tonight? Satch snores like a rhino, so I know he's getting some. Maybe it's better awake; I hate dreams that make me cry. Ha, when I was little and we moved from one army base to another, I'd wake up crying . . .

But not in Kathmandu. I'd dream about giant birds, or wise old people, and they knew me. Actually, they loved the hell out of me! The darkness smelled so different, much better than anyplace else. Thick red spices and huge flowers and sweat and animals.

It's so cool to get up in the night . . . go out, walk the streets until I get to Coit Tower. The way the air moves! When it's lighter, see fog. Feels safe. It's nothing like when I've gotta do what a man wants. Like my uncle made me. Satchel . . . fun in bed . . . but was nicer to me at first. Wish he'd move his arm off my stomach, too. God, my body hurts like hell.

She's face up in darkness. Sounds of the building twirp faintly. Cars pass, and a line of moonlight shows under the window blinds. Ruby's forehead's sweaty. She runs her hand over her cheeks and between her breasts.

Turning onto her side, she pulls the sheet close; as she lies breathing, a dark stain shows in the dim light, filling out against the sheet.

Ruby's hand moves into the wetness. Slowly, her body pulls away from Satchel, disengaging his arm. Her bare feet start toward the bathroom.

The light she flicks on is sudden and harshly white. She leans both hands on the sink. Her breast is leaking blood through her T-shirt. A sound of shock comes out of her.

"Ruby?" Satchel calls. "What the hell?"

"Something's wrong. My stitches."

"Let me see."

"No! Satch, no." She shuts the bathroom door with her foot. "Just call my surgeon. Please. Her number's next to the phone!"

"What do I say?"

Ruby's shaking. "Tell her the cut's coming apart and ask what to do. Okay?" She rakes at a cabinet, grabs band-aids that jump out of her grasp and scatter on the floor. Cursing, she pushes a towel against her breast and starts to cry.

Satchel yells, "She's picking up. You talk. If the cord reaches, I'll hand it in."

Ruby reaches through the door to yank the receiver out of his hand, then shuts the door as far as goes, against the jammed cord. She stage-whispers, "It's me, Ruby Arena. You said to call if I have to. My breast is bleeding!" Pause. "No, it's a mess. . . . Tape it? What do you mean, like . . . *adhesive?* . . . Okay, *sorry* I woke you, right? But I'm scared shitless . . ."

There's a longer pause. "I was doing something . . . active in bed, okay? I know, I know. Yeah. . . . I'll be at your office first thing tomorrow."

She turns off the light and feels her way along the wall, back to her room.

Satchel's upturned face is dimly visible, with one arm thrown over it. His voice sounds mournful. "Rube," he says thickly. "This is horrible. I'm covered in bites. You have bed bugs in here!"

"How can you say that when I'm bleeding?"

"If you don't believe me, turn on the light. This place is serious hell."

Angrily, she switches on the light.

Satchel swings the sheet over. "Okay, can't see them now, but they been all over me. Your fuckin' landlord."

"What you should be telling me is you're sorry that we jumped in the sack so soon," she says harshly. "Satchel, I'm *bleeding!*" He doesn't answer. Then she says with tears in her voice, "I should have known I wasn't ready."

Gretchen gives her useless radiator a disgusted kick. She looks out the window, sees the street's wetness. A few beads of light crawl as rain slaps asphalt. She goes to the kitchen stove when a teapot starts to whistle, coming to a boil. Pours water into a cup, drops a teabag into it. There's another piercing sound; it's her phone. She hesitates, then picks up.

It's Len's voice. "Gretchen, I was thinking about you."

"Were you?"

"I just want to know more, I guess. . . . About you."

"Like what?"

"Start anywhere."

It's sudden, but she likes it. She sits down and gathers herself. "Well . . . I always needed to make things visually. Photography really pulls me. . . . Though sometimes with people, I'd find out later I made mistakes." She sips her tea. There's a pause, and she's glad he doesn't fill it.

He's sitting in a wicker chair with his feet on his window sill, looking down at the street. A shabby young guy swings a grocery bag with one arm, buses pass at different speeds, some bushes by the sidewalk gleam darkly.

Gretchen, leaning on her elbow to support the phone, tries to tell more. "Getting halfway through my thirties," she goes on, "I don't *expect* the same. I'm not crushed with disappointment . . . not often. . . . I'm not trying to get a rush of fulfillment from someone. I do what I need to, even if people won't notice or don't like it."

Len's struck by her need to make art, which he likes. Yet he asks, "You don't always feel that attached to people?"

"I *do* . . . but if you have a friend or lover for quite a while, it comes and goes." She closes her eyes to find words for her feelings. "And if you lose that person, you see it in other people, other things that inspire you." She sighs, sets down the cup, tugs the ends of her hair.

Len says, "A while back I lived in a cabin in Northern California on my own."

"What was that like?"

"Slept on the floor. I liked the spider webs on the ceiling, so I left them there . . . like looping ropes."

"Mm. Just how rustic was this?"

"Not like I couldn't walk to the store. But one night, a couple field mice ran around my room. They were hilarious, somersaulting and chasing each other."

"What were you doing there, Len?"

"Street theater was wearing me down, I guess. Wanted to spend some time painting." He rubs his collarbone with his free hand. "Sometimes get a ride from a friend, come to the city."

"What were you painting?" she asks, straightening her shoulders.

"Mmmm. Things that intertwined. Abstract. Say, a lizard's tongue reaching out toward something. Food, or sun. Maybe another lizard." He smiles, remembering this not-so-long-ago phase.

"Color?"

"Vermilion! Lots of it, and dark blue . . . yellow ochre, sometimes cerulean."

"Favorite colors of mine!" she says. Gretchen sips her tea. "Still painting like that?"

"I keep on writing plays. Sort of guerilla theater. But I paint, too."

"What else did you do at the cabin?"

"Uhh. No electricity, not even running water. I carried it from a stream. Nobody knew I was living there. Or they figured I was some hermit or outlaw. They kept away. It suited me. . . . I could spend a whole evening walking around, looking at cobwebs in the rafters, or sketching . . . while the mice had the time of their lives."

There's a savory silence. Len likes the way they can ask each other things and answer them without forcing it.

At last Gretchen says, "I can't believe how cold my apartment's getting. The owner promised to fix it soon. He came by to ask if I wanted to rent to own. He said it would take a down payment and something extra every month."

Len throws his feet off the sill onto the floor. "Oh, no!" he says. "That's a dodgy scheme."

"Really?"

"If your building's old and he doesn't want to make repairs, won't fix a thing, sounds like he wants to unload it. With his rent-to-buy scam, he not only gets more cash now—if you change your mind, you lose all your money. And if he won't contract a specific time to buy and a definite price you can actually swing, you're at the mercy of the apartment's value. It keeps going down? Then pretty soon you're screwed."

"Ah! Hadn't thought of it that way. I'm finding out a lot of new things from you."

Ruby, humming, walks out of her apartment and down the narrow hall, its crumbling walls slick with ancient cream-colored paint. The old elevator comes up, clinking slowly. She opens its heavy black gate and goes into the poorly lit cubicle, which like some old warehouse has no outer door. Although she presses the button for her ground floor, nothing happens. She tries again, then slams her hand against the rickety gate. With a thud, the whole elevator sinks about a foot. Panicking, Ruby clutches her hands to her chest. She crouches, finally finding the emergency button. *Blaaaaaaap!*

When a stooped janitor shows up, he says, "What'd you do, Miss?"

Zhooooop! the elevator falls several more feet, ending with a huge clank. She shrieks.

"Hold on, hold on!" the janitor commands.

"Get me out! Please, *now!*" Ruby begs him, frantic. He fumbles the gate and reaches his hand to her. She wraps her hands around his forearm like a drowning victim, hauling herself to ground level.

"Okay then," he says like a playground monitor talking to a child. "You're fine now," he tells her, turning to leave. He walks away, wiping his hands on each other with the universal "that's that" gesture.

"What the hell! Freak-ass! You're not gonna fix it? You didn't even . . ."

Satchel, coming from the stairway door, runs into her. When she tells him what happened, he says, "Ridiculous. I won't even get *in* that elevator again. Guess what? Your building managers, owners—whatever—they're morons. I mean, just stop paying the rent."

"Stop paying the rent?"

"The same."

She wipes her eyes. "I was so scared, Satch! I could've fallen down the shaft! . . . I don't know; what you said is weird. They'd kick me out."

He runs his fingers through her black curls. "They can't evict you, babe. Get a legal advocate or something. Or, but you know what? That guy Len is one serious organizer. Maybe we can squat in that arts building he's getting."

Ruby stares at him.

"They do it in Holland all the time. Hell, I've done it. Anyway, stop paying the rent until they fix your stuff. Why do artists have to be treated like shit? San Francisco's supposed to be the city that loves us."

Ruby, shopping in the Haight, stops to look at a window full of quirky plastic trinkets on a display of bright-colored silk. As she walks in, a bell rings. A clerk with spiky magenta hair and rubber earlobe plugs asks, "Can I help you?"

She says, "I need a plastic skull about this big." She holds her hands about five inches apart.

"No problem."

"You have one with a hinged jaw?"

"Actually, yes."

She picks it up and says, "Good," holding it in both hands.

Next she's in a small grocery store, choosing a slice of chicken liver from the butcher: "That one."

"Something a little bigger, maybe?"

"No, I need *that* one. I'm not gonna eat it."

The butcher laughs. "Whatever you say, miss." He wraps it in white paper, puts it on the scale and quotes a price.

At home, she sets both objects on her kitchen table. "This piece will be about how much the surgery hurt," she says to herself out loud. "And I need something dark behind it. To throw the colors into relief." She glances toward a square black panel by the refrigerator, near the floor. "Aha," she says.

Ruby arranges a small tableau with the chicken liver, ragged and bloody, inserted into the mouth of the plastic skull. She sets up her piece. As Satchel walks in, she's taking video of it with the camera Gretchen gave her. He surveys the scene before him, planting his fists on his hips.

"Well, *this* is a downer!"

Ruby raises her eyebrows. She responds, "Hey, I'm in the middle of something."

"Yeah? Fine," he says sharply. "Just take a mop to it afterwards, okay?"

Ruby looks up from the camera. "Don't tell me how to use my own place."

"It's stinking, Ruby."

"You know what? I'm making a piece about my illness and surgery. Maybe to you it's silly, but for me this is work. You and your big support of artists, Satch!"

"Well, you look terrible, and the place is out of control," Satchel says grimly. "How come you never rest? That's not helping, either . . ." He's wearing ripped jeans and a stained undershirt. He looks disheveled himself.

"I told you, I'm working. Find something else to do. We can meet up for dinner."

Satchel groans. "It's not just when you're doing art stuff. I'm *never* allowed to be angry or scared. I can't say jack."

Ruby clenches her teeth. "What are you talking about?" Then, making a decision, she snorts, turns the camera on him and starts filming.

He turns away, slapping his hand against the wall. "I'm not used to taking care of somebody. You won't even go to your follow-up appointment." His hands are shaking.

"I never asked you to take care of me!"

"You need a lot of taking care of. I don't care how original you are. You're a pothead drunk and I can't even find my shoes in the morning."

"*I'm* a drunk? Fuck you, Satchel. Get the hell out!"

"What do you mean? You probably can't even pay your rent without me."

"You and your damned artists' crusade! First you don't want me to pay rent, then you threaten me because I'm not doing it. Did you even have plans of chipping in? Go away!" Her black eyes are full of tears. She crouches, still filming him. "I'll be just fine without you . . . you piece of shit. I never needed you!"

"As if *that* was ever true," he mutters. "You're probably AWOL from chemo right now!"

She sits down flat on the floor. "I'm fine. I don't have cancer. They cut all of it out, they—"

"You don't *know* that! Nobody gets to find out until you just—grind yourself out like a fuckin' cigarette. For chrissake. Willya turn the camera off?"

"No way."

"*Ohhh!*" Satchel clenches his fists, lurches toward the kitchen wall, and heaves a full punch at it. A chunk of yellow plaster splatters off. Tearing into the bathroom, he slams the door, splashing water on his hand. Then he bends over the sink, grabs more water and throws it over his forehead. When he straightens and sees his desperate eyes in the mirror, his jaw clenches. He wrenches the water off, seizes a toothbrush and his coat, and careens out the door, skipping raggedly downstairs.

Unable to remember where he parked his car, Satchel walks through a narrow, dank alley in Chinatown with washing hanging from high windows. He pauses for a swig of whisky from the bottle in his coat pocket, cranes his neck to look for the moon, then puts the pint away and strides on. Stumbling over someone lying by a brick wall he mumbles, "Ah, sorry, man." The man lies curled with his head against the wall, and opening his pale eyes he looks up at Satchel, who asks, "You all right?" There's no answer. "So, okay," Satchel says, picking up his pace.

The homeless man mutters, "Bad. Motherfuckers crawlin' up my legs. *Wait.*"

Turning back, Satchel says, "Yeah?"

The man points. "There's some on you too," he says.

"Oh?"

"Turning stuff a wrong color."

Satchel smiles quizzically. "So what color's right then?"

The man pauses. His pale hair, reddish in the night, folds onto his neck. He says sadly, "Blue. Thass how it s'posed to be."

Satchel laughs, then dips into his other pocket for a fiver and hands it to the man. "Be even better if this was blue, right?"

"Gah bless you, man."

"Y'know what?" Satchel reaches into his pocket again, this time for the pint, and hands it to him.

Sitting up, the man takes it eagerly and says, "Buddy. Hey, you all right, bud!" He stares at Satchel's face in the dim light. "Wha's wrong?" he asks.

Surprised, Satchel tells him, "Hm. Just can't forget this lady I used to love."

"She pretty?"

"Yeah. Way pretty. It's her spirit, you know? That I loved. Or love. Can't figure it out."

"Whasser name?"

"Gretchen."

"Whatchoo gonna do?"

"Go to New Mexico. Where I loved her. Try to understand something." The man in the alley sips. Satchel adds, "You only like blue things?" They smile at each other.

"You kinda blue. Yourself."

"How? Baby blue? Prussian blue like the crayon? True blue?"

The other man wipes his mouth. Finally he answers, "Gotta try harder, buddy. For True."

Satchel grins, salutes. And hurries away.

He finds his car and gets in. Looks steadily into the black sky. His eyes glitter and there's some kind of poise in him now. Hands on the steering wheel, he says out loud, "Time for New Mexico." Starts the motor.

Only a sliver of moon over the New Mexico field. A family's pickup truck raises dust on a dirt road in the night, as children jostling in the open metal back call to each other in Spanish. A few lights shine evenly from nearby outbuildings. Satchel walks slowly through a cornfield toward them, a flashlight in his back pocket. He pushes the stalks, tears his way doggedly through. When he reaches a small rectangular adobe building, he nods. He starts poking around in an unlocked shed the size of a closet, finds a ladder. Good. Just where it always was. This gotta be quick. Pulling it toward the outbuilding, he sees no one's looking out close-by lit windows. Silently he sets the ladder so its top rests under an arched, wooden-shuttered attic window. He sneaks up one step at a time. When his foot hits a rung, there's a small metal sound and he pauses, worried, then keeps going. At the top he hesitates and looks down: staring toward his own feet he's scared, unsure why he came. But he peels back the shutters, and as he carefully eases himself in through the window, cobwebs catch in his hair. Standing in the dusty attic, he has to crouch. He runs the yellow ray from his flashlight around, muttering, "I'll recognize the box. I know it's here." And soon: "Score."

Putting the flashlight down, he snaps a brown box's string, crouching under pocked overhead beams, and whispers, "Okay, lid off. Christ. Her papers are so organized. She has this way of holding onto things." He goes to a file section marked "Personal" and then the year. "Yessss. That way of keeping things even when they're lost . . ." He pulls out one of her journals. Chuckling, he says, "She's been after me to send this back for years! I might or might not."

He scans a page and starts reading it out loud to himself: *While we lay together, he talked for hours about Milton, until it was unclear whether we were going to make love at all.* Looking up briefly, he says, "That's gotta be me." Going on, "Ugh, then there's pages about my drinking. Crap." He leafs to another period and reads, *He has beautiful arms.* He shakes his head. "That's not me. See, she *did* look at other guys. I knew it."

But there's a sound, a definite rustle. Sneaking up to the window again, Satchel peeks. There's somebody standing below; a plaid shirt can be made out in the darkening night. A woman's voice calls out roughly, "Hey. Mister. Whatcha doing?"

"Uh, I used to live here. Sorry. Left some papers, so I'm just . . . getting them."

"You say you lived here? You took my ladder. Lemme see your face."

Satchel puts his head out of the window a little, his green eyes feverishly animated. The woman says, "Awright, you. Get down from there right now." She moves up to the ladder and grabs it.

"Hey!" Satchel yells. "Take it easy, I'm coming." He turns around, eases one leg through the window until he finds a rung, and as he gets his other foot onto the ladder he moves too fast—grabs the sill—has the woman shifted the ladder? Satchel tries to start down it and, grappling, he loses his hold. Suddenly he falls, slashing at great speed through the sad and muted night; and a howl leaps out of him as he tumbles all the way onto the ground with a horrific thud.

6. SHAKING, STANDING, NOT STANDING

Ruby, pensive and sad, sits on her floor smoking a joint. Exhaling slowly, she says to herself, "Nobody's buying, so . . . might as well keep the whole stash to myself. Helps with the pain, anyway."

There's a knock on her door. She puts out the joint, gets to her feet and opens. A man stands in the hallway under dim fluorescent light, wearing a dark suit and a fedora.

"Hello. Are you Ruby?"

"M-hmm. Yes. And who might you be?" she says.

"I hear around the building that you were in the hospital. Are you all right?"

"I'm okay. How did you know? You live here? 'Cause I've never seen you."

He smiles. "My family's connected here. Excuse me if I'm bothering. I just heard about you and wanted to make sure you're okay."

"You have relatives here or something? . . . *Wow*, that's a good-looking hat." As she says this, he takes it off, revealing his wavy white hair, and grins. "You have an Italian smile," she adds.

"That's right. Would I be correct in thinking you do, too?"

Ruby laughs and nods. She looks into his face, then at his rather elegant hands. His fingernails are clean and well-cut. Behind her, the last light of sunset shines softly through gauze curtains as if ready for a visitor. Impulsively and rather recklessly, Ruby says, "Do you want something to drink? Tea? Sometimes I make crazy invitations. . . . Maybe it's your hat."

He smiles more deeply and walks in, closing the heavy door behind him confidently. "That's gracious of you. Yes, I'd like that."

Cane-bottom chairs stand around the crowded room, stacked with misplaced objects. "Let's see," Ruby says, going to her cupboard, flustered. "What have I got? Um, Earl Grey."

He stops to stare at the giant painting, which now looks finished, but says nothing. He moves restlessly around the room, looking at its condition.

"Sit down," Ruby says, removing a stack of papers from one of the chairs at the table. There's a half-open tube of oil paint underneath. "Oooh. Sorry. Better sit on the couch."

He laughs. "You're an unconventional girl. I like you." He sits on the couch and puts his hat on the nearest table, an orange crate. "You may put my hat on a statue, if you have one that could use it."

Ruby claps her hands together like an excited child. "You know what? Forget the tea. Let's have a glass. Would you take a little shot of whatever?"

"Sure. I'd be delighted, Miss . . ."

"Ruby. Just call me that."

He stands again and takes her hand in a courtly manner. "Ben. Call me Benny." He does not tell her his full name, Benedict Di Noti, as he'd told Gretchen. He does not mention his true relation to Ruby's building.

She sits down close to him with a bottle, pouring each of them a glass with a practiced hand, and slugs her own in one gulp.

"Whoa, young lady! Are you drowning your sorrows?"

"Actually, yes."

"A man, perhaps? Someone who didn't see your special beauty?"

"One of my sorrows is a man who fits that description. Clever of you."

"Not clever, my dear. It takes years of life to see what's precious in this fleeting world."

"You're that old?" Ruby says archly. Her manners are unpredictable. He hesitates, and she continues, "God, I'm sorry, that was rude. You don't look old at all. Really, you're one handsome guy."

She goes to pat him on the back with her free hand, but he takes hold of it and presses it to his heart. Before she has a chance to think, he deftly puts his tequila on the floor and kisses her. Clearly a practiced move.

"Hey! You're hella too fast. I ought to slap your face." She stares into his eyes. But her loneliness is undeniable, even to her. "Yeah, I should. . . . Though with the fedora and all, you're kind of sweet," Ruby says. Glass still in hand, she wraps her arms around his neck and repeats the kiss. Ruby's stoned, somewhat drunk; and to her surprise, within the hour she and the older man have sex on the couch.

Afterwards, they sit on her balcony in semidarkness. His silver hair brushes her forehead. He says, "You know, dear, that's a sizeable hole you have in your plaster over there by the door."

Ruby clears her throat. "The last guy in my life—he just left. That was his parting gesture," she says, "punching the wall. Crazy!"

He has his arm around her shoulder. "Terrible. Is he a violent kind of guy?" he asks in a raspy voice.

"Not to me. Just to the wall."

"Horrible." He stiffens.

"You're not gonna believe this," she says in a low voice, "but I took a movie of it."

"Well, good, dear. Who knows? You might need it in court sometime."

"In court? What d'you mean? He's gone, anyway."

"Putting a hole in an apartment wall . . . from where I stand, that's a truly disgusting thing to do. Criminal," says Benedict Di Noti.

Ruby sits on her kitchen floor, exactly where she last saw Satchel. She lifts the video camera Gretchen gave her and watches the footage she took that night. There's no sound.

First a skull appears, stark white against black. It has a tongue. Though it shudders as if to speak, instead red meat-blood stains through its teeth. The skull's eyes look worried.

Then the view goes crooked as a large shape swishes past. The frame goes white, lingers shakily, then comes to focus on the head and torso of a disheveled man, whose shirt flaps as he jerks his arms angrily, his eyes bloodshot and furious. When he turns, there's just his back; then he suddenly lurches—and crumbling white pieces of wall leap. He grows small as he moves away. Disappears behind a door. And a short lull's followed by grey snow, as it ends.

Ruby rewinds and watches again. The skull appears: tongue, blood, worried eyes. Big man-shape, angry. Turns away, lunges, white chunks shattering. Goes away. Away.

She puts the camera down and sobs, wiping her eyes with the back of her hand.

Gretchen sits at Ruby's old splintered-wood kitchen table. "How are you doing?" she asks.

"Getting short for rent money," Ruby says. "Being I don't know who's the landlord, I gave a letter to the super to pass on, saying do something about the roaches. That I'm not going to keep paying if they don't. Should've said it a long time ago."

"Hey, good, Ruby. I'm proud of you."

With a self-deprecating smile, Ruby says, "Too bad I'm not dealing lately. I used up my stash, 'cause nobody's buying. A little dope would come in handy right now. Aside from a couple commissions to paint something, for years I made a not-too-horrible living selling pot and keeping some. I also get a windfall here and there from selling a painting, but it's been mostly pot—business is shit. Everybody only wants coke these days. Not into that scene."

"Are you still in pain?"

"Not too bad. I'm doing okay. Even hanging out with somebody. At first I thought just a one-night stand."

"Yeah? Who? What does he do?"

"Retired, I guess. Seems to have money."

"Is he spending any of it on you?"

"Not really. He brings me flowers. Those tiger lilies on the table, they're his."

"That's nice." Gretchen doesn't look sure. "Does he like your painting?"

"We don't talk about that."

"Oh. Well, couldn't he buy you dinner? . . . I hope he's not taking advantage. This seems pretty sudden."

"Guess he could take me out—dinner or a movie. But he, you know, calls me 'dear.' He's like, 'Don't worry, no strings attached.' "

"Do you want it like that?"

"Stupid, but . . . I feel good when somebody with manners wants me. I guess I specially feel an older guy. From way back . . . even when I don't want. When I'm high I can get into it." Gretchen's eyes turn anxious. Ruby goes on, "I know, bad thinking. . . . *God,* I hate that Satch took off. Anything's better than alone right now. What's wrong with me?"

Gretchen hesitates. "Ruby . . . you know that Satchel and I were together for a couple of years in New Mexico?

That is, if you can call it together. He and his wife were separated."

"He told me. Sorry, Gretchen. I didn't know until after I fell for him. God knows why. Such an asshole. But at first he was—"

"—It's all right. Just saying he doesn't do the long haul on anything. He operates like a rock player, grabbing . . . obsessive and angry. But I knew him as an amazing drummer, before he got on this new lead-vocalist kick. . . . Seeing him with you felt weird at first, but you were probably good for him. I hope it took his mind off himself."

Ruby leans her elbows on the table and starts to cry. "Benny cares about me, I think."

"The new guy?"

"Yeah," Ruby says in a small voice. "Benny Di Noti."

"Wait. Did you say Di Noti?" Ruby nods. Gretchen suddenly asks, "What does he look like? Wavy white hair? Does he wear a, you know, a fedora?"

Ruby frowns and nods again. "You *know* Benny?"

Gretchen goes on relentlessly, "Benedict Di Noti? Christ, Ruby. He owns my building! He tried to buy me off with some shared ownership scam so he wouldn't have to spend money fixing anything."

"What?"

"You've got yourself in a nightmare. D-I-N-O-T-I. He's a sleazeball."

Ruby wrinkles her forehead and stares as a dark, ugly fact rolls up against her.

Gretchen says, "He probably owns *your* building, too. This feels to me like that old vaudeville act, 'I can't pay the rent/you *must* pay the rent,' and the predator guy pulls the girl into bed. I think you're having sex with your landlord."

⌗

It's a sunny, affable morning. People jog around the small park fronting Columbus Avenue. A small group in matching T-shirts is doing Tai Chi, their fluid, orchestrated movements led by an older woman in a long, quilted vest. Nearby, Ruby sits, pale and miserable. She pulls her fingers through uncombed curls. A tall young man with dark blond hair walks by; he stops, looks at her and says, "Mind if I sit?" He's dressed neatly in a white button-down with blue stripes. Ruby shrugs and he sits next to her. In the background, one or two people walk their dogs, and the older Chinese woman calls Cantonese instructions to the Tai Chi group; it's peaceful in the park. After an awkward pause, the young man on the bench clears his throat. "Miss, can you tell me where Mario's Bohemian Cigar Store is?" Ruby points across the street indifferently, without looking at him.

"I understand it's a great little café," he says.

Ruby sighs. "In the morning. At night it's like Tosca, the other one. Movie actors, and people who come around to see if they can get something out of them."

"No kidding. Wow."

"Where you from?" Ruby asks, without putting any effort into it. Her hair's frizzed in a way that looks inadvertent, and she's wearing a Satanic Surfers T-shirt.

"New York."

"You don't sound like New York," she comments, a little sourly.

He laughs. "Sorry. I'm only in town for a few weeks, and honestly, I was looking for a pretty young woman to have coffee with this morning. I shouldn't be bothering you." He starts to get up.

"Oh, hell, a cup of coffee sounds okay."

The young guy smiles in an engaging, friendly way, despite her unkempt appearance. Ruby looks at him more closely. Fairly lean and fit, he has an immaculate and obviously costly haircut. Ruby stands and begins to brighten, as they walk over the damp morning grass toward a sidewalk table at the corner café.

In another part of town, the Financial District, there's a large leather-smelling office with a huge chandelier—Ben Di Noti's. He's conferring with the same young man who took Ruby out for coffee. No fedora, no winning smile. He says, "Figure we can broker the Greenwich property for eleven point two mil. You on top of all of your calls, Nick?"

"Sure, Dad." The younger man, in a khaki suit with shoulder pads and dark tie with broad diagonal stripes, stands slightly bowlegged, both deferential and knowing. He says easily, "We have a meeting tomorrow at three."

The father tells him, "Get rid of that crappy sinkhole on Larkin. Nothing cosmetic. It's not worth shit."

"Should we run a quick fumigation?" Nick asks. "The tenants might complain to the buyer."

Di Noti says no. "We'll get forty mil from my pal Chang in Shanghai, sight unseen. Don't bother."

"Dad. I need to check in. You said you're through with that Ruby kid, right?"

"Sure. Why?"

"Yeah, I thought she sounded cute. Sorry, a little confession. Tailed her to the park on Saturday morning. Made as if I was some anonymous tourist."

"What, you like her?"

"She *is* cute."

Di Noti ruffles papers for a minute, then looks up and says, "Ahh, you devil. She's sure got the tatas. What the hell, kid. No problem, you can have her." Nick gives his father a toothy, slightly apologetic grin. "Ahhh," Di Noti goes on, "we could hold off eviction a little longer. But she's nuts. Don't worry, though. She isn't married or anything."

Nick smiles wider. Slicking the side of his short hair, worthy of a Gucci model, he answers, "She's entertaining. I'm her hero. She has no idea who I am, thinks I'm some entrepreneur."

Nick sits on the couch at Ruby's in a tailored shirt and dark wool work slacks with his legs crossed. "Hey, know what? My company decided to locate me here instead of New York."

"Really, Nicky? Amazing." Ruby's looking more stylish than usual in a bodysuit and a big black lace bow over tousled hair.

"You like?" he asks.

"Sure, I do. You're the first guy I dated in years who actually looks at my work."

"Well, it's not like anything I've seen. I haven't been around artists. Hey, here's what should happen. Do a painting of *me*. A portrait. I'll pay you to."

"You're commissioning me? Oh my God, Nicky! I don't know if I can."

"Sure you can, babes. Work from a photo if you want; I'm tied up at work. I'll give you a couple hundred for it. Say, two feet across by three feet high. There's a place in my foyer it'd fit fine."

"Like over a little mahogany table? You're serious? This is your idea of art?"

"Cherrywood. Yeah-yeah. Come on, it'll be a kick. I'm sponsoring you here. Show me a little enthusiasm. You could stand to brush up your marketing skills. Gotta get you some success!"

"Well, I can use the money, that's a fact. . . . You don't have time to sit for it?"

"I'll give you a photo, like I said. C'mon, just rip the job out, something quick. Your impression of me." His eagerness contrasts with the cynicism he flaunts with his father, which Ruby doesn't know.

Working rapidly from the picture, she soon has it done. The face has a sensuous cast, along with a nobility his face does not possess.

Nick, standing in front of the portrait, sees it for the first time. He laughs self-consciously. "It's kind of . . . different. Kinda cool. Looks comfortable in his skin, I think." Suddenly he says impulsively, "You know what? We should go out. Go celebrate."

At this, Ruby's excited.

"Let's go," he says firmly. "I know what restaurant I'm gonna take you to. Come on, get dressed. It'll be fun."

Ruby's wearing a basic black sleeveless dress. She nervously sucks in her stomach to make it fit. The restaurant has a high interior dome, brass fittings and ornate bouquets. A staff person offers to check Ruby's coat, but she declines. The tables are so close it's hard to get into her chair, though Nick pulls it out for her. Conversations on either side are easy to hear. Ruby looks around anxiously. A waiter arrives, and Nick, in a blue suit with a pale green tie faintly patterned with diamonds, orders aperitifs. He says confidently, "We'll start with the sea scallops in tomato glaze."

Dinner with pecan chicken and poached red snapper has a different wine with each course, then tartlets for dessert. Ruby finally says awkwardly, "Can I—can I take some of this home in a doggie bag?"

Nick looks at her, startled. Then he laughs loudly. "You *really are something.*"

Plaintively, Ruby explains, "It's just that everything was so good. . . . But never mind. Thanks to your commission, I actually have money in my pocket. Literally." Thinking she should be grateful, she pushes her plate away, leans in and surveys Nick's face. "You're hella good-looking. Really."

He chuckles complacently.

Now that Ruby's no longer worried about using the wrong utensil, she's more at ease in the role of flirt. She reaches out and taps him on the sleeve with her long, flexible hand. "Do you miss New York? Tell me about your job, Nicky. I want to know *everything* about you."

Nick stops smirking. His forehead curls. "You know what? You're all right." He stares back at her, warmth mixed with irony. "Crazy, but sweet. And your ass is beyond compare." Nick starts to reach out his hand to her, but hesitates. He uses it instead to signal the waitress. "Check, please?"

Ruby says, "Okay. So, you want to go to my place?"

"Absolutely," he says. "I expected no less." A server delivers the check to the table in folded leather. Nick slips his credit card into it and asks Ruby, "Want to visit the ladies' room before we go?" She demurs. "Be right back," he says, striding toward the rest rooms.

Ruby fidgets with the tiny fork from her dessert. She mumbles to herself, "How the hell much is all this going to cost?" Glancing, she says, "Yikes." She idly picks up the credit card, curious, and looks. The name, in platinum-colored letters, is Nicholas Di Noti.

Nicholas *Di Noti?*

She holds the edge of the table with both hands for a full minute, shocked and pale. Her hair hangs over her face. Then she grabs the leather folder, gets up impetuously and hurries over to their server. Yanks the money Nick gave her for the painting out of her pocket and thrusts it at the server, together with the bill.

She marches back to the table and slams the leather folder back down. Nick returns, sits and, without looking at Ruby, signals two fingers. A chic young waitress comes and bends briefly, whispering furtively to him. As she backs away, his expression hardens. He says coldly to Ruby, *"What did you do?"*

Ruby sits smugly in her chair, hands folded in her lap. "I took care of it," she says in a chilly voice. "As you know, I had a few bills on me. . . . You don't own everything about me, fucker."

Nick, caught off guard, flushes angrily. Getting up suddenly from the table, he overturns his plush, expensively embroidered chair.

Next morning, Ruby's asleep in her bed with its threadbare quilt. A heavy knock wakes her. She throws on a rayon wrap without tying it, opens the door partway. Two large men stand there. They wear black company uniforms.

She bursts out, "What're you doing? What's going on?" She's reluctant to open her door wider.

"Building security. You been ordered to leave." The bigger man pulls a folded paper out of his pocket.

"What the hell! We don't *have* security."

"Yeah? We just started." Sniggering, he waves the paper in her face.

"What is it?" Ruby asks, confused.

"Looks like the landlord found out about your little prostitution gig."

"What? That's insane."

"Uh-huh," the imposing man says dismissively. Then he tells her, "You need to get out."

"No," Ruby says, belligerent. "I'm not moving." She tries to slam the door shut.

"You'll do whatever we damn say," the second man threatens with a tight face.

"Stop! Leave me alone!" Frantically, she presses against the door.

The men press back, one calling out, "You got twenty-four hours to vacate." One of them manages to reach his arm in. Ruby leans on the door with her full weight.

"You're nuts!" she hollers.

Against the force of both men the door swings open hard, throwing Ruby sideways—the pink ribbons to her wrap fly wildly, and she lands on the floor. She shouts, "Ow! You trying to kill me?"

"Twenty-fuckin'-four hours. Or whatever's left on the premises gets tossed on the street."

"You can't do that!"

"Shut up," the bigger man tells her, twisting Ruby's forearm behind her back.

"Stop it! You'll break my arm!"

"Yeah? We can break you and take anything you got." Ruby stops struggling. "And we know all about how you're inta drugs, bitch."

She lies with her defeated face sinking into the linoleum.

7. SERPENTINIZATION

Satchel stands in the doorway of Gretchen's apartment, leaning on crutches. "Damn, it's good to see you, honey. You have no idea how good."

Her hands fling to her mouth. "What happened?"

"It's just a sprain."

She shakes her head, folds her arms and says, "There's coffee." She goes to get him a mug, and he sets his crutches against the wall.

"Your kitchen floor is so clean! That oil soap you use on wood smells homey." Gretchen doesn't answer. She looks worried, the same look she had taking care of him in the past. She pours him a cup, brings it to where he stands. The coffee's a deep, flavorful blend. Facing the stove, he takes it and says, "Cool. You still have that white enamel coffeepot! Hey, look. . . . I been thinking about us. You know? . . . While I was in New Mexico I figured . . . we really ought to get back together. We were so good back in the day." He shuffles to the table and starts easing into a chair.

"How did you hurt your leg?"

He laughs and tells her, "It's no big deal."

Gretchen says, "Get back together? Satchel, it suits you when things are just impossible. You know that, don't you?" She's still standing.

Satchel turns sad. "Oh. Okay. You like that Len guy." He stares into his coffee.

"I do, but this is not about that. . . ." Gretchen crosses her arms. "You can't keep showing up saying you want to be with me. Even when I was crazy for how you played drums, I don't remember us being great together. I doubt *you* even thought so. Remember you always said you were going to divorce your wife?"

Satchel sighs. He says earnestly, "She was mean."

"Then maybe it shouldn't have been hard to decide. But you kept going back to her. Did you get divorced? No."

For a little, Satchel sits drinking his coffee, looking at Gretchen's kitchen floor. He mumbles, "Mmf. Nice brew."

Gretchen finally sits down at the table. "What if you picked someone or something and really tried to stay with it? You're a good musician. Do you love it enough? . . . Could you do it every day, without trashing your hotel room or breaking up with somebody? . . . Or getting completely bombed?"

Satchel gapes at her. "So, and I didn't give up my wife. Whaddya want me to do, marry you?"

Gretchen laughs. Then she puts her hand on his arm. "Satchel, I want to see you settle down with yourself."

He looks toward the ceiling uncomfortably. "Settling. What does that mean?" he says resentfully. "Never liked the word! Sounds like settling *for* something."

"I'm talking about paying attention to your music. Also, if you look around, you might see you've been missing out on people."

"People? I guess now you mean Ruby."

"Well, *she* certainly missed you. She hasn't been doing very well."

Satchel looks at Gretchen closely. His face changes and turns grave. "Is she a goner? Because I can't handle that."

"I don't know her prognosis. She's a sensitive woman. Also beautiful and gifted. I guess you know she's staying with me? She's at the grocery store right now. Back in a little."

Satchel twitches his feet under the table. Gretchen waits. He says, "This is *so* completely not how I wanted today to go." He's slipping into a bad memory, and neither Gretchen nor Ruby is part of it: crouching in damp, ugly darkness with a friend beside him. They're reloading their ammunition. There's an immense, excruciating sound. And after the detonation he sees all that's left of his friend . . . filth and chunks of hot fleshy garbage, in the blackness that has turned red, contaminated by obscene lights. . . . He shudders, tries not to move. Nothing to try here, nothing to show. He doesn't tell Gretchen. This part he's never said.

Gretchen finally asks, "Satch? What's going on?"

He stirs. "Uhhh. There's a large serpentinite rock in front of the Oakland Museum. Ever see that? It's huge. Sort of blue and jade."

Gretchen waits. "Rock?"

He speaks faster. "You know every state has a state rock, right? Your State Rock of California is serpentinite." Gretchen inhales, touches her collarbone. He goes on, louder. "Asbestos occurs naturally in serpentinite."

"Right," Gretchen says distantly. She gets up and starts walking to the next room.

"Hey. When I tell you stuff, you don't listen!"

Gretchen turns around then and looks at him. She says calmly, "You change the subject when anything's hard."

His eyes tear up. He says, "Okay, fine, want to hear about hard? Hey, last time I saw Mom I was a child. She put a goddamn pink scarf around her neck when she kissed me good-bye—it had cherries on it, like a tablecloth—I can, like, actually see the little curvy rectangle that on each cherry has a shine. A fake shine."

Gretchen says gently, "We used to talk about that a lot, Satch. I know. I'm saying what about Ruby? Maybe she needs our help."

⊞

Len and Gretchen walk along Fillmore. A dry, gritty wind huffs. His stride is long; he has a stately quality, whether still or moving. Len keeps the pace, slow but purposive.

A strongly-built black man cuts across their path. Unexpectedly he yells, "Fuck you, motherfucker!" Gretchen jumps. As the man moves toward a white man in a suit, Len keeps walking; Gretchen darts anxious looks.

"Yeah? Fuck you too!" the white man shouts back.

"White trash! You white trash!" the first man hollers. They push each other.

"Yeah? You imbecile! Monkey!" The men tussle around the sidewalk. Gretchen, horrified, clutches Len's sleeve, as a few young blacks push into the scene, yelling, *"What* you say? Monkey? Say again?" and cursing. Len pauses, like he's evaluating; Gretchen stares helplessly.

The black man grabs the white one by the arms and bursts out, "Haha! You know you want my ass! Gimme a kiss, white trash!"

"Ha. Been too long, asshole," the other says. They grip each other's shoulders and break into loud laughter. The angry crowd calms slightly, confused, as the two men clap each other on the back.

"They running you ragged at work?" the black man asks.

"Oh, yeah. You're missing it, monkey boy," the white man answers.

Then the black man, sprinting off to catch a bus, calls, "Take care now, white trash." The other man waves and walks off, laughing. The young black men group together, comparing what they saw, arguing with each other.

Gretchen says faintly, "What . . . *was* that?"

"Couple old work buddies, I guess," Len answers in his ordinary quiet voice. "Guess they have a wild sense of humor."

"Really? How is it funny? That white guy said 'monkey,' right on the street, in the Fillmore." Gretchen links her arm with Len's. "I see crazy stuff in my neighborhood, but not that," she exclaims. "Shouldn't we have done something? And also, are you always this peaceful in weird situations?"

"Nah. But if a fight's coming, I look before I jump. Learned that growing up rough. With those two guys, it's not new. And they have some kind of deal about their damn kidding."

"Well, I get why the black kids weren't having it. If I was as tall as you, maybe it wouldn't have scared the hell out of me. But it did."

He gives her arm a squeeze, looks back, and says, "Racism's a bitch. But everybody's walking off now." Gretchen shakes her head over the rifts in her city. The neighborhood fractures among waves of folks who arrived at different times, in such different ways.

Len stops at the corner. Pointing to a chartreuse flyer on a telephone pole, he asks Gretchen, "Know these poets? Want to check out their event?"

Gretchen takes a deep breath. "I wouldn't mind meeting some. But I have to tell you, I don't know about this space at Petta's. What is it to you, really? Why are you doing it?"

"For art openings, theater, multimedia. Music . . . work-space. The place is *so big!*" He makes an eager arc with his arms. "Come on! We can make studios in the basement. Whoever needs to will crash there."

"What are *we* going to do there?"

He laughs. "How about make love all night, paint in the morning, take tickets at sunset. Like . . . like Amsterdam."

Gretchen's thinking. "But artists are hard to organize. What if they just see you as some outsider, collecting photos for your archives?"

"They'll pitch in when they see what a great idea this is."

"But Len, those real estate brokers—what if they try to smash you? They're evil guys. They did a number on my friend Ruby."

"I don't think they're evil. They'll just want something out of it. We can do that. Clean up the joint and stop it deteriorating. But . . . wait—what happened to your friend?"

"It was terrible. The building owners scared her and messed her up. One was my landlord I told you about."

"Holy shit. All the more reason we got to get the space! It should belong to us, not some overseas investor. If we work there, or even live there, it could last a long time."

"How, Len? They'll just hurt us."

"We're hurt now! Gretchen, how many people get to see your photographs? They should *know* what you do."

Gretchen smiles and asks, "Who's going to see it? Is this a community thing? Will it be family-friendly?"

"Not always. I've got eighteen plays never produced, mostly for profanity—we can indicate what's R-rated."

"I have a confession. I was so shocked by the incident back there, I almost fell over."

"Well, they were playing, but I guess they had love-hate street theater going on. They got *your* attention!"

They both laugh. Gretchen asks, "So you're recruiting me to your cause?"

He says, "Only if you want to help. You could find out who actually owns Petta's. Maybe we can convince them to let us in."

"Okay," Gretchen tells him. They link arms again.

⊞

Just before dawn, Gretchen tiptoes across her front room; the two blanket-wrapped shapes of Ruby and Satchel huddle together, asleep on the couch.

Gretchen, leaving the apartment, lifts her head and picks up her steps, swinging her arms. She passes familiar buildings along the street: iron foundry, Mexican restaurant, animal shelter, union hall. By an industrial laundry with papered-over windows, a woman's squealing laugh can be heard. A downtrodden old man in a turban and tattered clothes lumbers forward with a cart overloaded with his belongings; Gretchen nods and says, "Good morning," and the man softly answers. A stocky woman holds two little girls in plaid skirts by the hand—Catholic school uniforms. The taller girl in black braids lags as the woman urges her forward. Other children gather in the school's cement-paved playground. Gretchen leans toward the fence to catch sight of small boys shrieking as they follow a ball. At the next corner, a bedraggled, surly man moves too close and she walks fast, clasping her briefcase, avoiding eye contact.

Gretchen reaches a grey building with battered steps. An older man behind an iron gate sweeps leaves from the sidewalk; he wears a skullcap and leggings. He greets her: "Hello, miss! Good to see you!"

Gretchen smiles. "Good morning! Glad to see you too," she answers. "Still playing your clarinet?"

"Some days. In my room. If you come late to work, you can hear a little. But—you always on time!"

She smiles again, goes in and unlocks the empty office. Takes off her tennis shoes and puts on heels.

A young man with an alert face comes in and gives her a mock salute, saying, "Hey, boss. I can help you with the data base problem when you get settled."

"Thanks, I'll be with you in a few," she answers with a smile. "Got a meeting at ten with headquarters, and we need to start the report." Her phone rings. "Hey, Shana. . . .

Really, BART delay? Can you be here by nine? Let me know." She tells her intern, "The subway's held up, so the others will be late, but we have to finish our report." The young guy nods cheerfully and goes to his computer. As Gretchen fires up hers, she already has her face in Post-its and lists.

Meetings, calls, laughing with the staff . . . when she's thinking too hard she closes her eyes. Sandwich, coffee, quick walk around the Mission for a breath of fresh air, then her face in the computer again. At the end of the day, Gretchen's back at the bus stop where, not long before she met Len, she took the factory picture. Grateful and tired, she hops on. Soon she'll need to see to dinner for three, something she's not used to.

At home, she flops down on the couch next to Ruby, untying her dun-colored shoes and rubbing.

Ruby says, "Hey, I like those shoes." She's up for a little girl talk.

"The color reminds me of a deer," Gretchen says. "I got them for comfort."

Ruby laughs. "I'm vain about shoes; I love boots and a great pair of four-inch heels." Her short black hair is rumpled, and she looks as though she just woke up.

Gretchen looks around. "So where's Satch?"

"He went for a drink, probably to Specs. I don't know what's going on. With us, I mean. Guess it's one night at a time." She stares straight ahead.

Gretchen says, "You know how he intellectualizes? He made a little speech about this State Rock of California, serpentine . . . no, serpentinite—and that ticked me off. But I was curious about it, so I checked."

"What is it?"

"Some ancient seafloor rock. Apparently when tectonic plates grind together, the ocean carries the stuff onshore.

The underwater rock's gradually transformed out of some older rock with magnesium and iron in it."

"Sounds like a vitamin I should take."

"I saw strange references to 'serpentinization.' A whole process. I'm not sure if that means how the rock turns it into serpentinite or what happens to the rock afterwards. I'm imagining things like underwater volcanoes. Because shifting tectonic plates bring the rocks onto land."

"Wow!" Ruby says, her black eyes animated. "Slashing, mad-powered convulsions under the Pacific! Shaping hard rock on the sea floor. And jetting it all over the place." For a moment she looks happy. Then adds dejectedly, "You know what? I feel like one of those rocks."

"It's okay with me for Satchel to stay here for a little, but is it okay for you, Ruby?"

"Of course. For now, probably better than I realize."

Gretchen hugs her. "Tell you what. Let's put on some music. How about Simply Red? I'll see what I can slap together for spaghetti."

Gretchen phones Len to say she found the owner of Petta's Market through City Assessor records. Meanwhile, he's found the real estate broker. They're the same: the Di Notis. Gretchen and Len exchange a long, charged silence. She meets him at his place to craft a letter to Benedict Di Noti, proposing an artist venue at the market site. It's going to stress that local merchants like the idea, because it's good for tourism.

This is the first time Gretchen has seen Len's living space. It's in an old building with rusty fire-escape stairs hugging the exterior. The walls of his studio apartment are pale grey. His curtains, cheap but appealing, are velour drapes of a rich burgundy color. Masks line his walls: an

African giraffe face, a Tibetan Buddha, a grinning Kabuki with lacquered flower headdress. One corner has a group of tall, leafy plants.

Gretchen exclaims, "You have great light. I'm addicted to bright light in a living space."

"Me too," Len says, smiling. He shows her his small 1930s stove, a curtained sleeping area in shades of dark blue, and the miniscule bathroom. Gretchen sits to draft their letter, reading out loud while he makes comments and changes. The back-and-forth flows easily.

Afterward, Gretchen looks at Len silently. She takes a sheaf of her photographs out of her leather bag. "They're for you," she says. Some are black and white, others vibrantly colored.

"Beautiful. Beautiful! Wow. Have you ever done sets? Or puppets? Maybe we could work on something together."

She says, "Not sure I have time. I'll think about it,."

He pours two glasses of mango juice into little champagne glasses and says, "Let me show you the last painting I made. A couple years back." Going to a cupboard, he hauls out a tempera painting of three stylized lizards, their bodies inscribed with interlocking lines of white dots. The background has dense geometric patterns.

Gretchen doesn't speak, but her eyes are bright and happy.

Len asks, "Are you hungry? Want to go get a bite?"

"I should get home, actually. I have more photos to work on tonight."

"Are you sure?" Len says, with his hand on one hip.

After she leaves, Len washes cups and glasses. *Could I get her to Europe with me? But—she seems rooted here. Guess it would be unfair. And I'm chaotic, she's orderly . . . Ah, what am I thinking.* He's unsettled.

Len stands at the front of another LiveWire meeting of North Beach artists. It's not as big as the first meeting, but people shout out opinions on the draft letter to the Di Notis: "Too long." "Take out the three-syllable words." "Use real estate jargon." "Have somebody on the Board of Supervisors send it." "Too short." Len listens patiently and Gretchen, who's taking notes, is disgusted; she watches Len include people's energies and ideas. After a while she says, "Do I hear any volunteers to do a better job than we did?" Suddenly everybody has commitments, sick relatives, demanding jobs, migraines.

"So who's going to revise it?" Gretchen persists.

Len says calmly, "Okay. We'll take the input and revise this." She gives him a look.

Gretchen swabs her red linoleum kitchen counter with one hand as she talks to Len on the phone. When she protests that all the work's falling to them and no one appreciates it, he says, "Don't worry. It's always like that. Just human inertia. They'll do better as we go along. Eventually they'll be claiming credit for every success. Just ignore it!"

"So *that's* the drill," Gretchen says drily.

He tells her, "I called Di Noti, the older guy. . . . He insists they don't need anybody to keep the place cleaned up. We should talk to City Hall, get the Di Notis nabbed for the spray-paint growing on the windows."

"Is there an ordinance?"

"Yeah, and if somebody reports it, the authorities post a warning on the window to get rid of the paint, with a deadline." Len adds, "Just a fly in their ointment, but helps make our point."

"Okay."

"What've you been up to, Gretchen?"

"Work was killer today. On the way home I had fun, though. Some camera crew on my corner shot a movie. They had tripods around these actors dressed like GI's; one had to punch the other one. They yelled and got agitated."

"I love San Francisco for that—all the indie movies shot here. And teens with their hand-held cameras. A guy I know says someday everybody will be doing it. Today I was guest presenter to a high school art class—I'm revved about that. I was going to tell them how my friends and I used video cameras for street theater, but they wanted to talk about politics, which I wasn't supposed to. The kids are great—full of questions, ideas. The teacher's a friend, so if he gets screwed, he can say he forgets my damn name." Len laughs.

"You're a busy guy," Gretchen says lightly.

"Hey. I'm the one always calling you. Sometimes you don't call me back. I think you're the one who's busy!"

Gretchen insists, "I talk to you more than anyone, Len."

"Well, I certainly phone you more than anyone. You can call me any time."

"Okay, I know. . . . I go into my own universe. Well, I did have one relationship where we were in touch a couple of times a day. Now that I think about it, we were practically together twenty-four seven, except when one of us was out of town."

"Exactly! Only way to do a partnership."

"The only way?" Gretchen asks uncomfortably.

Len is silent. "Uhhh. . . . I guess you make me think about . . . I was going to tell you some other news, so . . . well, some new people are interested in what we can do with Petta's Market. A young musician dude, Julian. Some students and an art teacher. Maybe they'll help."

"Good! If we call it North Beach Artists, we need more artists. Oh! I guess I just said 'we.' "

⊞

Another meeting at LiveWire. Ruby, in a beret, crouches by the huge front window. She hands Len a petition she's brought round to some of the local store owners, explaining. "I appealed to them as a fellow Italian. There's only eight signatures, but I'll try to get more."

Len says, "Thanks! It's a great help." Gretchen smiles at Ruby proudly and gives her a thumbs-up.

With uncharacteristic humility, Ruby says, "Gretchen told me I'd be good at it, so I gave it a shot." She gives the thumbs-up back.

Len switches off chamber music he's been playing on a boom box. He begins, "Okay, guys. The Di Notis have control of Petta's Market. Gretchen and I sent a revised letter, from your feedback last time. We used registered mail to prove they got it." He holds up a confirmation notice. "We're saying there's a long history of Italians in North Beach sponsoring the arts—that we'll take care of the disintegrating property until it's sold—and that merchants in the area say it's good for tourism. So it's good for *them*." Len passes a copy around. There are murmurs of approval.

An emaciated-looking guy with an untidy beard and harried eyes interrupts by suggesting that everyone buy his poetry book; he's brought several. Len takes the copies, puts them down on a table, and says, "If anyone wants to check these out afterward, they'll be here."

Satchel moves to the table and pulls up a chair, as though he's the host. He seems to be looking for a place in the efforts. As their gathering ends with plans for next steps, Len goes to Satchel; they start talking companionably about Mozart, local musicians who might want to perform in the Petta's space and—again—quasars. Gretchen stands by, shaking her head with a little smile. Mozart? Since when does Satchel have an interest in Mozart? Apparently Satchel looks up to Len.

INSIDE GRETCHEN

Mother used to cross her arms over her head so her elbows made a square in the air, whenever Dad yelled at her. I couldn't see her eyes but felt her tears in my own face. He never hit me, only her. After a long sweaty day in the auto plant he'd shout at her, "You're bashing me with your nagging. What's your problem!" Furious at our whole life. Two heart attacks and he was gone. When I offered to come home from college and help Mother, she insisted I finish. And as an only kid, my survival's still the top thing to me. . . . Len doesn't make me do anything he wants or needs. Acts like he's where he's meant to be. I like that. And my cat Oscar is all for anything good that comes his way. So: two real friends.

8. QUAKE AND BAKE

It's a hot Saturday afternoon, and crowds roam parks, cafes and museums. Women in belted shorts, men in cut-off-sleeve tees, kids in neon. Len, Gretchen, Ruby and Satchel sit on the steps of Saints John and Paul Church. A young guy with a single dark braid down his back drives up on a yellow motorbike. He has round rose-tinted sunglasses, a missing front tooth, and a fluorescent-painted guitar case strapped to his back.

"Julian, my man!" Satchel yells, saluting. "I see you've got your axe." Julian locks his bike to a pole and joins them. They all stand to greet the newcomer; Satchel leans back and smiles, lounging against the church wall. Gretchen turns to Len and asks, "So how do we start?"

He says, "Well, my style of protest is get musical and go for the goofy. Maybe start by attacking the greedy landlord bastards with something loud."

"A chant?" Ruby asks. "You mean a protest chant?"

Len shakes his head. "I'm thinking electrical and weird. Say, something about unbridled expansion."

"Like slash and burn?" says Gretchen.

Satchel stands up and throws his arms out. "Yeah! Slash and burn expansion!"

Julian smacks out an acoustic chord on his guitar. Len stands too, laying his hand on the young man's shoulder.

Ruby, following the guitar's punk tone, whines in a baby-voice, "It was a rotten day in a pitiful world."

Satchel jumps in with another line. "In a *scag*-gy part of town!" They all laugh. He shouts, "It was a scumbag of a *millennium!*"

"Okay! It's silly and it works," Len says.

Gretchen scrawls their lyrics into a notebook. "What next?" she asks.

Ruby suggests, "Should rhyme with 'town.' "

Satchel's excited. "Down up down!"

"But what goes down?" Gretchen asks.

Julian finally has something to say. "Tears."

"Up and down?" Ruby turns to him, skeptical.

"Yeah, and so, but I like that," Satchel says emphatically. "Your tears go down up down!"

Julian and Satchel throw in a musical chorus, "Slash and burn expansion, slash and burn expansion . . ."

Len says, "Yeah, it *should* sound raucous. The nuttier the better. Purpose of this is to get people to wonder what the hell we're up to. Once we have enough stares, we can get interviewed to explain what we mean. We can also slip the corporate real estate guys into the lyrics."

Ruby asks him, "Can we put in that they mess with people's lives?"

"I don't see why not."

They spend an hour collaborating on the song, and finally Satchel shouts, "Beer call! Let's lubricate the lyrics. Time to go to Vesuvio."

"I want to stop in at the church," Gretchen says. "I'll just take a look. And catch up."

Len says, "I'll be along in a bit, too." As the others dust themselves off and head out, Len opens the heavy, creaking wooden door on its iron hinges. Gretchen wanders down an aisle. They stop at a stained glass window. Len says, "I like to hang out in old churches. Not to pray. I think about how people look here for honest help."

"For answers?" Gretchen asks, looking up at him. When they stand close his height seems extreme, though she's a tall woman.

Len sighs. "Well, the way it is for me is, it hurts. That we have to fight for buildings that should belong to us. To me, they do."

Gretchen walks slowly around a pillar, then says, "I didn't mean to stay long in here. Just wanted a moment."

As they walk toward the door, Len goes on, "Life without beauty's drudgery." Gretchen turns to him. All at once she takes his face in her hands and kisses him on the mouth.

After the group finishes hashing out their protest lyrics at the bar, Gretchen gives her handwritten copy to Len, and he goes home to type it. Julian hugs everybody good-bye, and the others follow Gretchen to make dinner at her place. As soon as Satchel and Ruby finish peeling vegetables, they sit down together on the couch. Gretchen finishes up.

Gretchen says, "Guys? I have something to say. Things are changing. Privacy's going to be more important to me these days. In fact, I'm going to need you two to stay somewhere else."

Ruby sits silently, stunned. Satchel answers for both of them. "Geez, Gretch. Are we eating you out of house and home?"

"I just need it," Gretchen repeats.

Ruby looks at her with a dire face. "But how, Gretchen? Where—"

"Chill out," Satchel interrupts. "We'll crash at Julian's. I'll handle it."

Gretchen's brushing her teeth with gritty blue paste. In the mirror, Len stands behind in her bedroom. He's examining one of her photographs on the wall.

As she comes into the room he says, "Ah. Didn't hear you."

Gretchen laughs. "People have claimed they can't hear me come down a flight of stairs."

"Mm. That's unusual," Len says awkwardly. There's a short pause. Both of them want to get from here to her bed, but neither one is quite sure how.

Gretchen goes on, "I thought it meant something bad. Like it's not okay to be quiet."

Then he says gently, "But there's a kind of light in you." She looks proud, nervous, glad and confused.

"Light?" she prompts him.

"How you move. Not anyone else's way. Like a dragonfly over leaves." That's an unlikely declaration. Gretchen waits for more. His hand presses the back of her head until their foreheads touch and then, his hands on her hips, finally he's clasping her to him.

INSIDE SATCHEL

Heavy sweat's hard on laundry. I expect it during a gig, but man, in the Safeway? When certain memories hit, it's always a long, fast fall with my heart slamming way too fast. It didn't do my marriage good. I also tried telling Gretchen a thing or two about this, but so she only has one way to go and that's physically comforting me, which believe it or not sometimes scares me more than it helps. I don't think it used to hurt her feelings, but I bet she sure as hell didn't get it.

The mud. So fucking cold it's like my hands were encased in it. Actually my hands were wrapped around the rifle. Too dark to see much, but no big difference between tree trunks and moving leaves, all of it this sickening green-brown. When I dream it, the color's lighter.

Vomit. Whole dream gets covered in vomit. I don't remember feeling sick in the brush, just tangled. Endless green night. After a while on patrol, the smell of smoke-maggots-burning intestines just congeals into smell of life. The new normal. Dreaming about a smell that bad.

It's still worse to be asleep than awake. Funny thing, it took a bunch of years before I see this shit in the middle of a conversation. Sometimes a buddy's face shot off, but so it's more the big green or vomit I'm dropped into without a motherfucking signal. Hands might as well be clamped around that piece for good. Cold, mush-frozen air and my heartbeat goes wacko.

Need a joint. Few glasses of Jack. The cruise ship was good for a while. That's all. Miss drumming. Behind the drum I'm good. Hanging with my kit around the clock might be okay, but for some fuckin' reason I can't. Haven't told anybody. Thought maybe Ruby, but she turns out to have this train wreck of a life. I like her but, hell. I'm a bigger pile of shit.

Through the early evening window of Len's apartment, street lights glimmer. He's quietly writing a play. He searches for the right word, can't find it . . . and then there's an odd rumbling sound that's growing stronger. The floor trembles hard; Len drops his pen, hurries to his door. His building's lights go out. He rushes across the hall and bangs on the door across from his. "Hey! You guys all right?" There's no answer, but the rumbling turns into a low roar. Len pushes open their unlocked varnished-maple door; in the small studio apartment twinned to his, a young couple scrambles, naked, for their clothes.

"Here!" Len hollers. Yanking a blanket off the bed, he grabs the girl by the arm, pushes the boy—forcing them into the shelter of rough wool. They shout incoherently and, bundled together, hurry toward the stairs half-stumbling, blanket flapping. Len follows.

Across town Gretchen sits in bed leaning against the wall, her gaze directed to a book. A huge truck-sound storms the neighborhood, followed by a boom like fireworks or a distant cannon. Her body lifts slightly, along with the whole wall behind her, and thuds down, spine banging the wall. Pain rushes out of her mouth. Leaping up, putting herself in a doorway, she plants into it. Her hands push both sides of the frame, and she jams both feet to steady herself against the wood. Something falls and splats on the floor. Objects fly—cascades of splintering window glass— mauled as if by a giant rumbling beast. Her framed photos jump off the walls; most of them tear, as the glass meant to protect them shatters.

As Julian's apartment starts to roll, he and Satchel are practicing "Slash and Burn." Ruby, dreaming on a sleeping bag, flips open her eyes, slides and jerks against the floor. Satchel yells, "Shit! Damn!" The building sways. Satchel slips, falls sideways. Ruby, not fully awake, whimpers, buries her face in the bedding. Julian grabs his guitar and the nearest box of sheet music and careens downstairs, along with a shrieking neighbor. Satchel and Ruby cling together, then get up and hold tightly to the stair rail, following Julian as other tenants smear past.

Gretchen has been calling Oscar. He comes to nuzzle against her worriedly. When the aftershocks finally stop, Gretchen crouches down, surrounded by broken glass. She picks up a scrap of one of her torn photos, holds it in her hand for a moment. Steps over the mess to a file cabinet. Inside, metal boxes of negatives are safe, but her hands are shaking. She goes to find a first aid kit in the front closet, grabs her purse and key. As she walks into the hall and locks her door, Oscar slips out with her. She knocks on doors in her building; most people don't answer, apparently not home or already outside.

Two doors down on her own floor, an elderly Chinese

woman who lives alone answers. Gretchen asks, "Are you okay?" The woman's face is pale against her dyed-black hair. Speaking excitedly in Mandarin, she points to a bleeding cut on her arm. Gretchen walks to a sink in the disheveled apartment, stepping over an upended chair and shoving a smashed vase aside with her foot. She wets a cloth; fortunately, water's running. After cleaning the woman's cut, she puts on antibiotic ointment, then bandages the wound carefully. The woman's still talking and gesturing when a young Chinese woman comes up the stairs. "Mom? Mom?" Gretchen explains and gets an effusive thank-you from the worried daughter. Arm around her mother, she says, "Can we exchange phone numbers?" And they do.

Gretchen asks, "Did you see a white cat on the stairs?"

"There was one in the front hall. But I think it got out when I opened the door."

Gretchen goes down to the street, still carrying her first aid kit; most of the area has no visible damage. The air's dusty. She calls, "Hey, kitty-kitty. Oscar!" He's not in sight. Worried, she keeps calling. Neighbors milling on the sidewalk compare stories. Two Latino men and a small boy in a plaid flannel shirt, a large lady in a muumuu, women in curlers and kerchiefs, lots of nightgowns and pajamas. Gretchen asks, "Has anybody seen a white cat?"

"Sorry, no."

The large lady says, "I know that little cat. I would've noticed."

The boy says, "I think I might of seen him on the steps. He's not here, though."

Gretchen says to them all, "Can you keep an eye out for him, please? I'm in Apartment 302. You can knock any time."

Her friends arrive, all of them trooping up to her place, talking over each other like the neighbors about everything that happened. The apartment, except for a surface wound in the ceiling, is relatively undamaged but full of broken glass. Len, Satchel, Ruby and even Julian go to work with gusto, sweeping and bagging. Gretchen has a camp stove with a small burner, and she's stirring up a huge stew pot with her already-defrosting chicken and beef, canned beans and corn, and any and all vegetables from her nonworking refrigerator.

Len seems galvanized, as though foreign travel and theater sets have magically appeared. He keeps singing choruses of "Slash and Burn" like an ironic refrain. Julian lugs in a generous amount of warm beer. Somehow they're managing fun, working in the midst of the torn expressions of Gretchen's life work. All she says is, "I'm so worried about Oscar. . . . He should have come home by now. It's not like him. Must have gotten really spooked. . . . At least I still have negatives, and my camera looks fine."

Julian says, "Hey, don't worry. Your cat'll show up."

Len has an arm around her. "We'll get it back together."

Julian asks, "Anybody try to crawl under a heavy piece of furniture?—I think we were supposed to."

That night, Len sleeps in Gretchen's bed, and the friends use blankets laid out on her floor. There's not much sleeping involved, but in the dark Len suddenly intones loud, in a deep, sepulchral voice: "Ahhh. Who is it? . . . Who's the landlord now? Nature?" They all burst into helpless laughter.

Next morning, they walk all the way to Petta's. The windows are decimated. Julian slips through one, getting a few scratches he ignores, and heaves open the front door. The exposed-beam interior is a wreck.

Satchel throws his arms wide and yells, "Hooray! Home. I'm home!"

Gretchen says, "Hey, I don't think it's safe to go in. What if there's structural damage? What if it collapses?"

Len tells her, "I'm going to go for it. You could be right, so maybe stay here."

Ruby and Satchel walk in with him; Len finds a broom and starts sweeping fallen debris from the walls and ceiling of the unused market. He says, "Satch, why don't you check downstairs and see whether it looks doable to set up studio spaces." Gretchen stands by the front door while the rest of the gang starts organizing debris into piles. She says, "I should get going—look for Oscar and see if I can get back to my job."

Len goes to her and kisses her good-bye. "Okay, sweetheart. I'll find you later and help with Oscar." As she leaves, he's sweeping energetically.

Gretchen checks some of the storefronts but finds few people; most businesses are still closed. She starts walking alone through the streets, sees throngs of people in front of their damaged buildings. She watches gravely, witnessing their worries. The day's clouds seem tumbled and oddly shaped, wrong. She tiptoes through rubble. It's a long walk back to her place; she passes the stucco façade of a union hall that's partially collapsed.

As she reaches her area, where most of the buildings are in decent shape, an old unkempt man with fuzzy hair stands, bent over a shopping cart. His thin hair trembles while he arranges the cart's contents under a dirty blanket. When Gretchen passes, he starts.

"Are you okay?" Gretchen asks.

"Whattayou want? Get away!" he yells, lunging at her. "Get the fuck away!"

Gretchen holds up both hands with palms out and backs away, jarred by his reaction. When she finally reaches her workplace, she finds it closed, with one of its windows boarded up.

At home, there's no sign of little Oscar.

⊕

Len strides into Gretchen's kitchen with a bag of yams, potatoes and fresh broccoli and tells her, "Got these from a free market." Ruby, Julian and Satchel follow.

Satchel makes an announcement. "Know what? Julian's place is in bad shape. I say we camp out at Petta's. In fact, I'm just gonna move in. I *knew* it'd be a great place to squat! There's just a lot to clean up."

"I'll stay with you again tonight, if it's all right," Len says to Gretchen. "My place hasn't got running water. Tomorrow I'll go back to the art space."

Ruby says, "If we can get brushes and paint, I'll be at Petta's, too. I want to set up a work area."

Gretchen takes Len aside. "If you think it's structurally sound, I'll come whenever I can. But what will the Di Notis do, Len?"

He pauses. "Huh. I don't know."

"You look exhausted. Are you?" Gretchen asks.

"I guess. Feeling kinda wired. A little nuts." Len steps toward the group and, putting on the voice of a science TV narrator, he intones, "And now. Immense shifts under the earth—and their ricocheting forces—leave San Francisco ravaged . . ."

Julian pitches in, "The ferry building and the Bay Bridge totally upheave!" Len and Satchel look at each other and laugh raucously, slaphappy with fatigue. Gretchen, with her hands in a bowl of makeshift salad, shakes her head.

But Satchel narrows his eyes and croons, "Over a huge expanse of time . . . rocks deep in the ocean powerfully pull two ways—kneaded and crushed down, yet also yanked sideways by tectonic faults . . ."

Ruby interrupts. "God, what are you guys doing? What's so funny?"

In a deep, gravelly voice, Julian goes on, "Hidden fissures far below . . ."

Satchel whirls Ruby around and hollers, "Rocks in the water! Deep below! Serpentinite."

Len says, "It's a timeless dance."

Gretchen has been working at the stove. Turning, she says over her shoulder, "Yes. We know. The timeless dance is serpentinization. Hey, I'll photograph you guys in the art space. Dinner's ready, soldiers."

Satchel claps Len on the shoulder and says, "Lennie, come stay with us."

Len says, "Tomorrow. And I'll start a Lost Cat flyer."

Gretchen's taking photos of rubble and trash that the group is cleaning at Petta's. New people show up to help, and a few rolled-up sleeping bags lie stashed in the corners.

Len calls out, "Satch, can you get a ladder and put some plaster on the crack up there?"

Satchel hesitates. "Ahh, man. I'm *no good with ladders*."

"What?"

"Okay, whatever." Satchel, shirtless and in overalls, goes unsteadily up the paint-dappled steps. Gretchen watches as he climbs with a pan of plaster in his hand and a trowel in the other. She shoots photographs of him—and of Julian hammering in loose nails with a cigarette hanging from his mouth. Also of Ruby unrolling canvas to paint and Len gathering trash.

Len disappears for a bit and comes back with a painting in his arms. "I have something for you," he says. "Two lizards wrapped around each other."

She smiles. "Wow! Vibrating with color!"

"Hope it works. Haven't told you I'm color-blind."

"Really? Can you read stop lights?"

"Yeah, the red one's on top. I know my paints by name on the tubes, but mixing them, I'm never sure if it's good. Used to stick to black and white, but I experiment, too. If you like this, it's yours," he says. Still holding her camera, she kisses him.

When he leaves with some of the others for supplies, Gretchen props the painting Len gave her against a wall. She goes in search of Ruby, who seems tired, and sits beside her on the floor.

Ruby says, "You look good. Hey, gimme some distraction. Something unrelated to grime and chaos!"

"Oh. All right. . . . On the way over I was thinking of all our big talk about quasars. Remember that?" Ruby nods. "Well, the computers at work are up now, so I looked up quasars. They're not stars; they just look that way from the ground, through a telescope. Apparently the amount of energy they give off is a hundred times the energy of a normal galaxy."

"Really?"

"Yes." Gretchen glances up at the gritty ceiling. "And this is wild . . . the quasars can drown out light from stars around them."

"Holy shit!" Ruby says, shaking her head. She looks downhearted.

Gretchen goes on, "Come on, you wanted distraction. I found discussions about dark matter, too. That from the laws of physics, gravity should slow down our expanding universe. But instead, it's expanding faster. And these physicists say that dark matter's responsible for it."

"Uh-huh. Yeah. Like Satchi," Ruby says. "His group was called that."

"Ruby! I'm not talking about our love lives."

Indignantly, Ruby says, "You don't need to. *Your* guy even puts up Lost Cat flyers."

Gretchen smiles. "True. He just gave me a painting. We

inspire each other," she says. "It's just happening this way. Like a physics of happening."

Ruby sighs. "Revoltingly mushy," she says. "I've been painting in the basement. It's dirty, and I think it's creepy, but you're quirky, Gretchen, so maybe *you'll* like it. Come with? Here, let's take a flashlight."

They make their way down the stairwell. Gretchen still has her camera. The floor's damp, with large, empty wooden fruit boxes jumbled; unfinished walls are full of thick snaking wires. Gretchen starts to take photos as though she's asking questions of the place, the way one would ask strangers whether or not they have a family or where they're from.

Finally Ruby says, a little sadly, "I'm cold. I want to go up."

Gretchen puts her camera into a bag slung over her shoulder and asks, "Are you all right?"

"No. . . . Listen, Benny Di Noti's gonna come over. This afternoon. I'm scared he'll kick us out."

"Today? He's coming here?"

"Yeah, so I hear." There's a pause. Ruby goes on, "I'm gonna say some things to him."

Gretchen looks into Ruby's fierce eyes. "Okay. Okay," she says, nodding. "I wish I didn't have to go back to work." She adds, "Maybe he's never even seen the place." Suddenly her tone turns hard. "His listing's for his international mogul buddies, pretending it's on Telegraph Hill." Gretchen rubs her palms together, shaking off the dust that surrounds them.

Benedict Di Noti and Ruby stand face-to-face at Petta's. He carries a briefcase and has a tweed overcoat coat draped on his arm. He doesn't take off his fedora. Instead of greeting her, he says, "Where's . . . Luke, is it?"

Ruby's arms are folded tightly across her breasts. Suddenly she shouts. "You sicced your goon squad on me! Kicked me out of—"

"I'm not here to—"

"—my place! Conned me big time! Why'd you—"

"—to listen to this idiotic—"

"—bring me fucking *flowers,* asshole?" Trembling, she takes a step backwards in order to keep from hitting him. "Look at you in your stupid fucking prince-hat. Got *any* excuse, poser?"

He says frigidly, "My wife was in the hospital, with her gall bladder."

Ruby throws up her hands. "*I* was recovering from surgery!"

"You never said. Where's this Luke?"

"Len. Don't *know* where. Why'd you *do* all that to me?"

Di Noti sets the briefcase gingerly on the dirty floor. Nobody talks to him in this manner! Certainly not dutiful Nick, and his wife's too sickly to try. Ruby's intensity's vulgar, yet also a bit exhilarating. "We had a good time, right? You liked talking to me."

"There was no talking, except on the balcony. It was all you."

Di Noti sticks out his chin. "Don't give me that. The way it was? I treated you sweet. You little artist girlies like 'sweet.' "

Ruby bursts out, "You made me do stuff to you I hated!"

Composedly, Di Noti says, "I didn't make you. You got an extra two weeks in the building, right? *Just try* going to court. You dealt drugs and slept around."

"You pimped me to your own *son*, douchebag! I didn't even know who he is!"

"A pimp gets something from the lady's activities. You cost us plenty in back rent."

"Good!" Now that she's had her say, Ruby's rage shifts slightly. "For a little while you seemed—I actually thought you were, like, *kind*." She crumples her mouth.

Di Noti takes a sharp breath. She waits for the next thing. There's a silence that might turn the moment. . . . But without answering or waiting for Len, he swoops up his leather case from the ground and walks away.

Ruby paces the scratched floor. She clenches her hands, shakes her head, and lets out a roar at her many kinds of powerlessness.

9. SLASH AND BURN

Di Noti walks gravely through the doors of Saints John and Paul, removing his fedora. He stops at the collection box, puts in some bills and lights a candle. Makes his way to the confession booth, sits before the screen.

"Hello, Father. Forgive me, Father, for I have sinned."

There's a faint cough from the invisible priest. "Welcome, my child. And how long has it been since your last confession?"

"A long time. Four . . . five years."

"So long! What were your sins? Tell me, my son."

Di Noti crosses himself, his face grave. "I seduced a young woman. It was recent . . ."

"And has this continued?"

"No. It's over."

"Twenty Hail Marys, my son."

"That's it, Father?" Di Noti's unsettled. Even indignant. "For my sin?"

The response comes, quick and efficient: "If there are other sins, continue with your contrition."

Exasperated, Di Noti insists, "She's too free and easy. Loose. So I didn't think she was that good of a girl. Now I'm starting to think more like she was."

The priest heaves a sigh. "All right. *A hundred* Hail Marys."

Di Noti mumbles what he knows he must. "Omigod, I-am-heartily-sorry-for-having-offended-thee I detest all-my-sins . . . lordgod-of-all . . . I-firmly-resolve-through-

thehelpof-thy-grace . . . to sin no more and avoid the . . ."
He hesitates. "Well, but Father . . . shouldn't there be
something else? . . . I take the Lord's name a lot. Didn't
attend Mass all this time." It seems irrelevant to mention
having some guys confront Ruby, more of a professional
decision. He wants to say something about Nick's involve-
ment . . . but discreetly. Allowing Nick to get mixed up in it,
he definitely shouldn't have done. "Another thing, I didn't
give the best example to my son. I—I also boasted about it.
About the girl."

The priest says, barely audibly, "Very well, my child.
Misereatur tui omnipotens Deus, et dimissis peccatis tuis,
perducat te ad vitam æternam, I absolve you from your sins.
Amen."

Di Noti stands, walks awkwardly away, his face strained.
From beyond the curtain, the priest is saying, "Go in peace,
my son." Di Noti frowns. Restlessly, he starts to walk fast,
hands jammed into his pockets, head forward. Then looks
down as if watching his shoes take steps on their own.

In a back corner of Petta's, Len sits on a makeshift corner
pallet, back against the wall, knees bent. The cement floor's
unforgiving, despite some quilts and coats. Gretchen sits
with her back against his chest. Their legs touch, his arms
wrap around her, and her hands rest on his. Gretchen closes
her eyes, and in the early night's quiet, as she smiles Len
does, too, feeling it without seeing. A votive candle burns
on the floor next to them.

He says, "The dark in here moves like prowling. . . .
Circling the room. Reminds me of the slow part of a train
ride. . . ."

"Tell me about one you remember," Gretchen says.

"Mm. I'd get on one in Europe and just ride. Hours,

overnight, days. Yeah, and looking out that window. A full sun overhead. Pale fields, pine forests, lights flickering—trees slashing by . . . or up in mountains they'd be so close it was like you floated through them . . ."

Gretchen sits unmoving except for her breathing. Len falls into synch with it. Finally he says, "But, you know . . . not what I was there for, in the end."

She shifts, lifts her face toward him. "What, then?"

"Looking for someone. A partner . . . for my partner."

Gretchen smiles shyly. "What does that mean to you?" Gently, she moves out of her position so she's facing him.

"Oh! Partners do everything together. Talk in the middle of the night. Make love, make meals, hatch plans, shower, mop the floor. Take walks, make love again."

She laughs softly. "And would these partners, by any chance, be involved in theater?"

"Sure, why wouldn't they? Write plays, find actors, make costumes. . . . Even more fun if they get to hassle the powers that be . . ."

Gretchen looks down. Her upper lip tightens in a certain resolve. She asks, "Is this what you wish you had or what you *have* had?"

Len watches her steadily. "It's come my way a couple times. Adored a few women who liked that way of things."

"What happened?"

He looks away. "Last time I had a partner it went five years. In theater, you separate for weeks or months. So I'd say, 'If one of us has a beer with somebody and spends the night, okay, as long as we tell each other.' But she had another lover. Didn't say."

Gretchen waits.

He brushes some flecks off his jeans. Then continues, "Didn't want to hurt me, I guess. I thought we told each other everything, but she had a secret life. After you find that out, it's not the same."

"That's rough, Len. But now? You didn't give up your ideas about a partner?"

Len looks at her again and shrugs. "Still sounds like the best there is."

Telling the truth has grown between them in a way that lets Gretchen say, "I think any woman who fell in love with you would want to try. Even to see what would happen! Though—uprooting your life when a lot is already in place—I'm not sure what *I'm* capable of. For a long time I've had a steady job with regular hours and health benefits. For me, that might be necessary."

Len nods, almost as if this hadn't occurred to him. He hasn't finished spending the money from his last theater commission as a director.

She's changed position, kneeling in front of him. It makes them closer to the same height. Len puts his hands on her shoulders. "I can't write letters the way you wrote to the Di Notis. You translate things and make sense of them. Nothing can get done right without that. . . . Gretchen, what does a partner mean to *you?*"

She says, "I wasn't looking. But I'm not opposed to changing."

"You're not?"

"I suppose I already have, or I'd be a lot more scared to talk about this. Most of what you are is new to me, though. You hold these dreams about theater so close."

Len sighs. "But there's other stuff I want to do while I still can. Painting. I don't always enjoy trying to pull people together, dealing with everybody's different vision."

"You, Len? I thought you were a born organizer."

"I bet nobody is. It's kind of gritty. With North Beach Artists, we took advantage of an earthquake, but now we have to negotiate with the Di Notis—and we can't stand them. I was late when Di Noti showed up. Wasn't even around. And apparently when he came, he hassled Ruby."

He shakes his head. "Satch-o isn't any better than I am when it comes to rules of the timepiece."

"But Di Noti was *early!* Anyway, Ruby wanted to meet him head-on, herself. She told me. I wish I could have been there, too."

"Well, I'll call the bastard and see him at his office."

Gretchen shifts again to cross her knees, rests her chin on her hand and grins. "You've got me egging you on, here. Very clever, Len."

"Aahhh, if I was clever I'd woo you with a little more financial stability." He smiles, running his hand through her hair. "Enough talking. You have to go to work in the morning, and this pile of blankets is as scratchy as hay, but what do you say we make better use of it?"

Di Noti, behind an immense desk, half-rises, neither standing nor holding out a hand for Len to shake. Len is so tall he towers over the seated man. Di Noti glances at the papers in front of him, then sweeps his hand toward a leather chair. Len sits; Di Noti looks up and steeples his hands.

"Nice place, Mr. Di Noti," Len says. He's dressed in corduroy pants and a sweater.

"Yes. Union Square is the best in the city."

"Been here a long time?"

"Seventeen years. And you, Mr. . . . Consideen, is it?"

"Considine. I grew up in Richmond, but I like to be in San Francisco as much as I can."

"You must be some type of artist," Di Noti says. "I got your letter. It's a bit outdated, since the earthquake."

"Well, Mr. Di Noti, I'm here about that. We'll take responsibility for the mess. We can clean it up for you. In fact, we've already done quite a lot in the past few days."

"I saw."

Len goes on, "We'd like to make something out of the partnership that's developing with you."

Di Noti shakes his head. "Wasting your breath," he says dismissively.

Len sits, recalculating.

Di Noti goes on, "Partnership, shmartnership. I don't like you screwing with the electricity and plumbing. Can't have any substantial work on the building. You know it's for sale."

"Not that your prospective buyers would come over and check. We'd like to negotiate with you," Len says, squaring his shoulders.

"Skip it. The place is under my control."

"And by that, do you mean—"

"I'll tell you what I mean." Di Noti shoves his chair back, stands up and goes to look out his fine, broad window at the exquisitely-maintained palm trees below. Len remains quietly in place. With a little huff, Di Noti turns around again. "I'm not stupid. I'm aware of the fact that the property is in a hell of a state. For now, I'm going to let your people have access. Then we'll see."

"Mr. Di Noti, we can definitely make you happy with that decision."

"Just go. Go and do your . . . your art thing. I'll inspect the premises before you do anything public. Any events and so forth."

Len sits leaning against the brass studs of his chair. He looks up at Di Noti, who has now taken a position; Len decides there's nothing to be gained by raising other issues.

Di Noti says hoarsely, "You can go." He flicks his fingers, sits, and returns to his papers.

⊞

Len reaches out his arm to Satchel in a knuckle-to-knuckle handshake. Satchel yells, "L. You did it! L.! The place is our palace! Man, the music we're going to make. Art! Theater! Oh, God!"

Len surrounds him with both arms. "Those local merchants backed us, man!"

Ruby, flushing, shakes her hands up and down like a little girl. "We need confetti!"

Julian nods. "I'll go get some cheap champagne."

Len says, "It's time to get to work. This means we can *do* our work. I can't wait to tell Gretchen."

Ruby sits in the office of her surgeon, who says sternly, "You shouldn't have been a no-show on your follow-up appointment. But you're one fiendishly lucky woman. Looks like we got it all out. Since you have no new signs, it's not likely to recur. No radiation, no chemo."

"Whew! That's incredible!" Ruby adds, "I guess I had no right to expect this, since I skipped out. It's like the long afternoon of tests today was payback."

The surgeon smiles wryly. "Miss Arena, you're good to go. See me in six months. And get regular mammograms. You'll need them."

Ruby scans newspaper want ads. Suddenly she holds the paper close to her face. The ad says "Professional Clown Needed." She nods with satisfaction. "Damn, yeah. I can fake that."

Two days later, she struggles into a dinosaur costume with an immense head, which has only a little rectangular screen for breathing. Since she's short, the sight-holes and small breathing-screen don't line up to her body. She wriggles to adjust the unwieldy outfit as best she can, sighs, and bravely walks into a corporate cocktail party. It's noisy and bustling. She slowly makes her way in the crowd, alternately lifting her feet and arms.

A young guy with a turquoise tie comes by and says, "This is so fun! Great costume. Hey, I got promoted this morning, woo-hoo! I'm gonna get another drink." Another man walks up to her and says, "Can I tell you something? I had a crap day. I don't want anybody to know, but I stole money from the till at work. I can't even decide whether to put it back." Ruby angles herself into a sort of all-body nod. He wanders away with his drink in his hand. A woman comes close to her and tells her, "I hate parties like this. I'm so fucking depressed. I feel like jumping over that balcony. You know what? You have a sweet face." Ruby repeats the difficult-to-achieve all-body nod. The music shifts from raucous to lazy lounge style.

She starts to sashay carefully around the room. Then she loses her balance—suddenly falls right onto her back, legs waving in the air. People clap and gather around. Someone puts a party hat on the depressed woman and yells exuberantly, "Love the dragon!"

Gretchen asks, "Did you quit?"

Ruby shakes her head. "Not yet. Mostly it'll be working children's parties. I just don't want to do it upside down."

"So it's not bad?"

"Nah. It's silly but bearable. There's nothing remotely creative about it. I did enjoy *meaningful* performance when I was in music—you know, before I was a painter. Right now I've been thinking how I'd really like to get into some performance art."

"Interesting. If you do, I can photograph it."

"What I have in mind is something that takes . . . pain, the strong experience of pain, and makes its memory less painful. Whoever or whatever did it to you isn't there . . . can't do that to you. It'll be kind of an enactment. Take away some memories I don't want."

"Wow, Ruby."

"I don't want to say more until I figure it out."

"I'm sure you will."

"Thanks, hon. So, anything new with you?"

"Actually, yes! This is big. Guess who's sleeping on my bed? It's Oscar. He came back!"

Ruby gasps. "By himself?"

Gretchen nods. "I have no idea where he went or why."

"God, that's fantastic! Let's go see."

The cat, curled in an oval of sunshine on Gretchen's comforter, has a faint but discernable smile. Gretchen sits down beside him, stroking under his ears, as he vibrates prodigal bliss.

At Petta's, Satchel and Julian bang out energetic riffs from "Slash and Burn." Behind them, a crew of several people continue cleaning up.

Len says to Gretchen, "I need to let my Aussie friends know what's going on. And play it up. We like to blow things a little out of proportion. Like, 'Yeah, guys, *very* active times at the moment. We did a whole siege on the place, best corner in the city, and the investment group told us we can squat. This ten thousand square feet of space is ours!' "

Gretchen laughs. "You must miss them."

"Sure. They're like war buddies."

"I'm curious, Len. Why did you leave Australia?"

"I was deported."

The music starts again with a vengeance.

"Really? What happened?"

"The way we hit the Ministry of Arts and the Opera House made us out to be an element they had to get rid of."

Satchel can be heard telling Julian, "Go back to the bridge. Let's try some other chords."

"People could get hurt in this situation. Even if it's bad press coverage about the group or about you."

Len says, "If anybody tries to bust up what we're doing, we can ignore it. When things get polarized, there's news. If we're *in* the news, we point out the importance of the arts. Talk about artists who want and need this, and how merchants love it—because it helps business—and local Italians love it 'cause their history overflows with the arts."

Gretchen says, "Let me be devil's advocate for a second. Do you ever think that the neighborhood might want another grocery more than a haven for the arts?"

Julian lets out hoarse guitar stutters.

Len says, "I don't see a grocery store—Di Noti will probably sell to somebody overseas. And as long as there's been music, theater, imagery, there's always been people who don't feel it. Don't like it. All the same, you can't predict who's with us. I've talked to store owners who love what we're doing, and they're into it. One of the local cops on the beat loves opera—these plumbers fixing one of the stores on the same street as Petta's say they want to come by and see paintings or a show. And artists losing studio space have to get more, if they're going to stay in the city."

"Are you exaggerating?"

"Not too much. Oh, and I got through to the assistant for a guy on the Board of Supervisors who's interested. Good for tourism, see?"

"Ruby got badly hurt and even had to put her paintings in a storage unit, but it's not like any of us in the group have no place to live or stay."

"One of these days North Beach and all of San Francisco will get its artists cleared out through the real estate industry, Gretchen. I'm not sitting by. And bottom line, nobody can convince me that art isn't from the part of us that makes being awake worth it!"

Outside Petta's, a big red and black poster highlights the date, the name Ruby Arena, and her performance "Use Yourself Lose Myself." Inside there's a crowd of students, tourists, local artists and friends. At a table by the door Len sits, alert and efficient, taking the cover charge for Ruby.

Their audience quiets. Ruby, wearing a black bustier and black armbands crisscrossed around both arms, kneels at the center of the floor, her face bent forward, arms crossed over her head. A few distant building sounds mix with muted street traffic. The big space still smells noticeably of mildew. Ruby rocks anxiously for a while. Her short black ringlets are disheveled. She slowly gets up; above the black bustier there's a floppy red bow tied around her neck, reminiscent of recent Mayor Dianne Feinstein's blouses. Ruby's mouth is grotesquely painted black, and her face is grim. She reaches down into the bodice and pulls out a small rubber hammer. Poises it over different parts of her body and, as if choosing the best place, taps the tool against her forearm. She whispers, "Why does it do this?" The tapping becomes more vigorous. It's gradually taking on the intensity of blows. Ruby's arm flushes red. "Why do I do this." Her face contorts painfully, but the words repeat in a monotone, like a ritual statement. At times she paces the room, stopping with her back to the audience or in front of someone in the front row. Hypnotically: "Why bound. Why hostage? Why dressed for who injures me? Why hidden? Hidden. Why dead to the sound of birds? Dead to the sound of children? Why hidden? Why . . . do I do this." (Thunk, thunk, thunk.) "Why does this . . ." (Thonk thonk

thonk thonk thonk.) The blows become more disturbing and repetitive, and occasionally she stops long enough to say hoarsely, "Why do I do this."

A man's loud voice calls authoritatively, "Because you fuckin' deserve it!" He holds his hands around his mouth like a megaphone. Onlookers gasp. Swiftly, he stands—a young man, well-dressed, in a dark suit. He has light, carefully cut hair.

Is it part of the performance?

It's Nick Di Noti.

Satchel's rage rushes him into an immediate lunge from his nearby seat, and swinging broadly, he lands a solid punch to Nick's face. People slip or fall as chairs tumble. Satchel, shouting, yanks Nick to his feet.

In an upswell of noise from the crowd Nick cries out, "No public performances! You *knew* you couldn't do this!"

Len steps up, puts a hand on each man's shoulder and pushes them apart. He says, "Who are *you?*"

Ruby, shaking, is the one who answers, "Nick Di Noti, from the brokers."

Satchel cries, "That fucker! You know what he did to Ruby?"

Gretchen stands by, documenting everything with her camera.

The son of the real estate scion brushes his thighs vigorously with both arms, though most of the damage is to his coat. A line of blood zigzags from his mouth to his chin. "Stop this show!"

"*You're* the performer, asshole!" Satchel yells. He's bloodshot with spitting fury.

Len turns to Ruby. "Get Satch and take care of the front door, okay?" People on the street, hearing the commotion, start trying to get in and see it. After Len's direction, Satchel lowers his head, then says, "All right, boss." He and Ruby start toward the door.

Nick takes that moment to say, "You had your chance. You're washed up!" He rolls up his sleeves to restart the battle. His face and arms are reddening.

Len tells him, "We invited you and your dad to this performance, and we sent letters about the electrical work."

"And we never said yes. The police are coming."

Gretchen moves in to photograph Nick's angry face at closer range.

"Get that away," he tells her.

Noise rises as some people try to leave and others pull back to the walls. Ruby and Satchel try to calm things down. One long-bearded, unkempt man shouts, "My jacket! Give it back!" People surge in different directions—another disheveled guy threatens everyone in sight for no reason.

Three cops arrive, pushing into the crowd around the door and forcing their way through to Nick, Len and Gretchen.

Nick draws himself up and exclaims, "Officer, I was just assaulted." Gretchen continues using her camera. "Our firm owns the building, and these individuals have no permission whatsoever for this gathering." He turns to Gretchen and says, "You get out."

"Okay, keep it calm," a cop with a bushy moustache says. Gretchen moves in.

Nick goes on, "I'm Nicholas Di Noti! Our firm owns the premises and these individuals have no right to be in here and do this." The policeman yanks out a pad and starts to write. Gretchen's camera clicks faster. Nick wheels at her and cries, "Get that motherfucking thing away from me!"

The officer takes hold of Gretchen's arm and says, "Miss, put the camera down." Gretchen ignores him and goes on shooting. He says firmly, "I told you, stop it. Here, give me that." He tugs on her.

Len moves in. "Hands off her!" Gretchen tries to keep hold of her camera. Len and the cop shove each other, and faster than any of them can see it, a nightstick comes down on Len. Kicking, he's jumped to the floor by the other two policemen. One tries to handcuff him, and another clubs Len's legs. Len kicks back hard, and a harsh blow smashes against his kneecap. Throughout the screaming, Gretchen keeps taking pictures. Police force Satchel's arms behind his back as he struggles, shouting, with tears in his eyes. Ruby, wide-eyed, covers her black-smeared mouth with one hand.

Gretchen, horrified and clutching the camera, says hoarsely to Ruby, "I have to get an ambulance."

"Phone booth right on Filbert and Stockton, honey. Or North Beach police station."

Hours later, Len lies in starched sheets in a small vomit-green room, with his right leg bandaged and his left leg in a huge cast. Gretchen strokes his forehead. Smoothing his hair she whispers, "I should have ditched the camera sooner to call an ambulance."

Len shakes his head with eyes closed. "No. You did good."

A few days afterward, Len's propped up in a hospital bed, straight as royalty. Gretchen's with him again. On a night table nearby, his room phone rings. Gretchen answers the call from Len's friend and hands him the receiver.

Len's conversation is short. "Hey, buddy! You heard already? It's been a circus. Pretty explosive." There's a silence. "Yeah, things got a little physical. Don't worry, I'll be okay. We're gonna win, though. Good to hear your voice. Keep the faith!"

Afterward, he grins at Gretchen. "Sweetheart, can you get copies of your photos to the press?"

Gretchen answers, "I'll try." She smiles ruefully. "There's a catch. It looks like you shoved the cop first."

"Oh. Crap," Len says.

"Please don't tell me to get rid of the shot."

He just laughs. "Okay, then a photo show at LiveWire?"

"Sure. I'll do it. *You're* upbeat today."

"Well, getting banged around sucked, but you're here with me, and we're still in San Francisco. Best city in the world!" He's still grinning.

"Yeah? Honestly?" She says doubtfully, "What are you talking about?"

"Arts getting out from under the war machine. . . . Damn, I *love* this place."

"But Len, what'll happen to Petta's?"

"Maybe I screwed up." He looks down. But he can't help smiling again. "At least I got to talk to the power. That slimeball Di Noti. Gotta keep fighting for Petta's. Keep it as long as we can."

"Who's going to? With you in the hospital?"

"Talk to Satch for me. He's pretty erratic, but he's got the heart to make an organizer. You'll have to keep him on track, though. Ruby's good talking to people. Julian has energy to burn. Just a few more people and it flies with me or without me."

"*I* want to fly, and I want it to be with *you,*" Gretchen says, with a worried brow.

"You're the one with the wings, sweetheart," Len tells her. He breathes deep and closes his eyes again. "Ahh, you really send me."

"It's Demerol."

His eyes are still closed. "Funny thing, my chest hurts. A lot."

Gretchen straightens the sheet. "I'll to talk to your nurse. Get some rest." She kisses him gently.

⊕

In a hospital waiting room, Satchel and Ruby sit, arms around each other. She says, "How come you don't carry a flask? We need tequila."

He shrugs. "Yeah, good idea, but not here."

"You know what? One thing still bothers me. When you left, why'd you take my toothbrush?"

Satchel pulls away. "What? *I didn't,* Rube! That toothbrush was mine, right? I *think* it was. You need to learn to trust somebody." He leans against her shoulder again, but stares at the ceiling morosely.

"Hell, forget it," Ruby goes on. "But let's not talk about Len. Something less awful. . . . I need distraction. Uh, there was this thing on TV at Gretchen's . . . a math thing. Geometry."

"And *so* . . ."

"Be nice, Satchi. I'm going to ask you a question. It was about scalability, but I had no clue what they were talking about. What is it about how if you double a line on a square on each side it's more than twice as big?"

Satchel lunges to tickle her.

"No, come on, I mean it."

"You're right—sorry. I'm friendly with math. I'll give it a shot. . . . If you stretch a line and make it twice as long, it's twice as long. But if you double a two-dimensional *square* on each side it's four times bigger." He uses his hands to illustrate. "If you take a *cube* and double the size of the sides, it's eight times bigger. See?"

Ruby smiles. "Actually, yeah, I can. I haven't felt anywhere near this good since before Nick started the fight. And another thing—is it true that if you scale a praying mantis a few hundred times its size, it'll fall over flat, 'cause the skinny legs can't support the weight of its body?"

"Absolutely. True. Muscle fiber strength won't increase just because size does."

Ruby's quiet. Finally she says, "When I was in school I

had some kind of learning disability, or so they said."

Satchel snorted. "Bullshit."

"You think?"

"Look, Rube, I'm pretty much off my nut. You may have a few quirks in your reasoning process, but you're a thousand times more creative than most professionally artistic people I ever met. I can't always keep up with you."

"I can't believe you said that. You mean it?"

"Maybe absence made the heart go fonder. Ruby, your paintings are fierce. They straight up whip me around."

In the hospital corridor a doctor says quietly to Gretchen, "Miss Wilson, we're just bringing Mr. Considine back from another X-ray. There's a complication—he has a secondary lung infection." The doctor explains that he may have contracted it in the hospital.

On a gurney, Len, with an oxygen mask over part of his face, looks up at Gretchen as he's pushed past her into his room. He says shakily, "Hey. Hey, sweetheart." Attendants settle him into bed and Gretchen sits at his side, trying to mask her own upset.

"You don't need to talk, Len. I'll just stay here with you. Does it hurt a lot?"

Coughing, he pulls the mask to spit into a tissue. "I'll be okay." His breath comes fast and labored. Gretchen's face is tight, anxious.

Just then Satchel bursts in with excessive cheer. *"Hey,* Lennie."

Len waves feebly. "Satch-o." It sounds like boys' sports nicknames.

"Awesome, you tricked them, Mr. L. Mr. Considine. Mr. El Con!"

"Let's keep it quiet," Gretchen tells Satchel.

In a stage whisper, but with equal enthusiasm, Satchel goes on, "Australia, huh? You were over there? Hoo, man. Last time I was in Australia I had a blast."

"When were *you* ever in Australia?" Gretchen asks him skeptically.

Satchel says, "We stopped over while my band was on the cruise." He turns back to Len and drops the stage whisper. "Anyways. I was wandering through these caves. Aboriginal paintings, beautiful. But so I met this one guy. This first-class elder. Beard, hair a weird color of chartreuse, telling me stories of their mythology. Fascinating. I asked him what was he doing in the cave. He was then telling me how he'd met this lovely girl a little before, walking through the cave, and how he had just made love with her."

Gretchen says crossly, "Satchel, Len should rest. He doesn't need to hear about kinky exotic encounters."

Len speaks up. "It's okay. F—finish your story," he says evenly, as though it were a straight news report.

Satchel splays his hands and tells Gretchen, "Don't go all priggish on me, Gretch—it's not like I'm bringing him a copy of *Penthouse*. We're here to cheer him up. I mean, we love this guy, right? . . . And *so*, boss, he told me it was the most magic thing. She was just standing there, man, like she was waiting for him in the cave . . ."

Gretchen says disgustedly, "I did *not* hear that."

INSIDE LEN

Ever since I was a kid I couldn't get why the world is so fucked. My mother cried a lot, and I don't exactly know the reason. When I was really small, before California, she had a factory job. My dad worked the Mesabi iron mines, and I guess the pay stank. This was in northern Minnesota. Barely paying the rent money equaled no food, I'm pretty sure. They didn't talk about it. Actually they didn't talk. Weekdays my mom left me with an Ojibwe lady, one of Mom's rel-

atives . . . who had a bunch of kids or anyway took care of us. I was happy with it. She'd take us in the woods, have us listen to birds, and we'd watch trees and plants. She'd say be thankful. I was, man. . . . A total flipside to the cold empties at home.

I wasn't onboard with the move to California . . . but hitting my teens, life was golden. First girl was a woman, foreman's wife at the actual plant where my folks worked shipyard. Auburn hair and tits the size of France. Private experiment between her and me. Also had major fun with high school buddies, and none of us got busted. We boosted cars or hung out at the docks, whatever the fuck made us happy. Too much energy, like over-the-top California sunlight. A lotta girls, beer, loose gladness.

College . . . can't remember what came over me, finally thinking about other people in the universe . . . maybe because I was drawn to theater. Saw extremes of human hurt and denial and noticed it had been around me all the way through. . . . Met kids with pain on a constant basis—top-athlete buddy with this bizarre heart disorder who could never play again. Another guy, math genius whose dad always hit him upside the head. . . . Even one friend whose girlfriend got pregnant from a rape. . . . I hate when people hurt so bad they're not looking forward to much. . . . Had to push on that, like a big rock, road block or something, Needed to push. Still need it.

Theater can change things up. Knock you senseless when it's done with complete heart and focus. I don't like doing it indoors that much, but usually I have to—make cash, then go do it in the streets. In spaces just outside or at the door of some big institution. Power means space somebody stole. Maybe I wanta steal it back.

North Beach makes me think of Van Gogh's stars. People talk, laugh, clap each other's shoulders. Painting, music, performance—to me it's a birthright. If you know I think this, you probably just laughed at me. Yeah, okay. I love theater. I'm gonna keep on, whether I have to sweat for it or scream for it. I also tinker at three a.m. with old plays. How big of an ugly duckling is that? . . . I am big, though. And I have a decently large dick when the mood hits, but in the last few years it comes and goes like fog because part of my deal is I want to *be in love. You can't make it happen. It has to discover you.*

Here I am in a hospital and practically X'd out with pain in my leg that barely improves with the meds. . . . Also, my chest seems to be a field of burning grass. . . . A couple times I saw one of Mom's aunts use sweetgrass for prayer. Is that theater? Weird thought. But we moved, so I didn't get to know them—they might say I'm some wannabe. I should know more . . .

Gretchen sees a lot without saying. . . . Me, I always had to find places that call for slam-and-thunder. With her, I'm pretty sure what I can do is show a hell of a lot of people how to own more of . . . of . . . give them more strength to . . .

Can't make it make sense right now. I don't know why this sort of burning field in me's too much . . . taking me away. Away from everything I love.

Gretchen's contact print of shots from the Petta's confrontation shows:

> *Nick Di Noti, livid, with a skewed, wide mouth, his suit jacket pulled sideways by Satchel's hand*
>
> *Nick Di Noti with half-lidded eyes and flared nostrils, mouth open in speech, as his hands push outward*
>
> *Policeman's eyes and furrowed brow close to viewer*
>
> *Len behind, policeman lurches toward him, back view of policeman's buttocks and thighs, shiny pants*
>
> *Len shoves policeman*
>
> *Policeman's raised arm, holding blurred nightstick as Len leans away*
>
> *Clubs come at Len as he falls*

Len's upraised legs; uniformed arms with clubs kick and strike legs

Gretchen shows the images to Len. The only sound in the hospital room is his rasping, too-fast breathing. As Gretchen hands each photo to Len, he looks for a while, then points with his index finger to the details: nightsticks, grimaces, faces in rage including Len's. He laughs, a bit wheezily, entertained.

Ruby's at Gretchen's apartment, waiting for her to come home from the hospital. She walks around, looking at the place, pleased at how well things got organized after the quake. She was part of that. Along one wall, Gretchen's packing boxes for photographs stand in neat stacks; most of them survived. Ruby picks up Gretchen's lizard-shaped scissors and smiles; the cutting edges form legs, and their hinge is an eye.

Suddenly Gretchen's home. "Oh my God, you startled me!" Ruby flutters her hands. "I didn't hear a thing. Really, you have the quietest walk of anybody. It's spooky."

Gretchen gives her a worn smile. "So I hear."

"What's happening with Len?"

"Now they're saying pneumonia. It happened fast, but it's bad. If he's not better soon, they might even have to intubate him."

"What's that?"

"Stick a ventilator tube down the windpipe. Don't worry, I don't think it'll happen. He was healthy before he got injured. The lung infection popped up unexpectedly."

"Yeesh! Because of germs at the hospital?"

Gretchen, pale and drawn, has two vertical lines between her eyebrows. "They're culturing it. But—you know. It's a hospital. Full of dangerous bugs. I want him out of there, but the broken leg's so bad he'll have a different walk for good. That's what the doctor says."

"You know I don't worship medics."

"I'm tired, Ruby. So-o-o tired."

"I brought tequila. Want any? At least some tea?"

"I want to fall over. But I don't want to sleep yet, just rest—come and talk a bit."

For a while Gretchen lies face down on her bed. Ruby sits by her, then leans sideways with her head propped on her bent arm, watching gauze curtains flutter in the window. Finally she says, "Gretchen?"

"Mm." Gretchen turns on her back and opens her eyes.

"Len has a broken leg, and Satch hurt his leg, too. That seems weird. Maybe . . . do you believe in evil?"

"Not like a magical entity, if that's what you mean."

Ruby tells her, "I had this dream. The Prince of Darkness is there. For some reason I am, too, trying to figure him out. I'm saying, 'What do you do all day?' And he says, 'I have a job.' 'What is it?' And he tells me what you'd expect: leading people to the brink of crime and all. He has hooded eyes, face like Rutger Hauer in "Blade Runner," bald and in a grey thong. So I say, 'What about God?' and he's like, 'What about him?' 'Well, d'you *know* him? You've met?' 'Sure, we talk all the time.' Wow, that gets me. He says, 'See, he's a work colleague. We team together.' 'But why?' What's that about, y'know? And his eyes go all earnest. He says, 'It's a project. We test people's faith. The integrity of their faith.'"

"Sounds like some ancient Gnostic version of religion."

"The only faith I have is in . . . *remembering*, though. I need to remember and gather things in order to make meaning out of them. Then they get dispersed, and it starts over. Without making a painting or a ritual or some film, I can't make it *at all*, Gretchen. You know?"

Gretchen doesn't answer, just reaches up to touch Ruby's hair.

"We moved around so many cities and countries when I was a kid, my dad being in the army. I really think about some of the places we lived."

"Yeah?"

"Like Kathmandu. My dad was stationed in Nepal, doing something behind the scenes. I was a little kid, but I'd get out of bed at night, without my parents even knowing, I guess, and walk around in the street, right in the garbage. I saw a lot of strange things there . . ."

Gretchen pulls back, puts a hand on her own forehead. She says softly, "Please, sweetie. For some reason . . . I want to hear, but I can't do it justice. I'm a wrung rag. I can't handle any more tonight."

Len has a different oxygen mask that puffs air back to his lungs every time he takes a breath. Monitors and computer screens dominate the room, displaying his vital signs and his body's interaction with intravenous medications. He has plastic tubes extending from so many places that Gretchen dreads displacing one; he's been catheterized, and a plastic port on his arm serves as the nexus for large needles delivering liquids through his veins. His feet and hands have swelled, because his kidneys and liver aren't functioning normally.

The nurse says, "We'll try giving you some water now, Leonard. I'm going to take the mask off for a little, to see how you do on your own."

Len leans forward, trying to sit all the way up, but the nurse carefully moves his shoulders back against the bed again. Gretchen tries to look cheerful and casual as he gulps a little fluid from a bent straw. Some runs down his chin. He wipes his wrist on it, then lies back, spent. His face is grey and alien. The nurse quickly clamps his mask back on, and there's a plangent sound of beeping.

"What's going on?" Gretchen asks hurriedly.

"Oxygen level's low. I'll get the doctor."

Gretchen moves in and takes Len's hand. He opens his eyes, trying to speak, and gasps, "At . . . San Jose State I . . . designed a set . . . got it . . . built-in-two-days I . . ." She takes his other hand and shakes her head. He closes his eyes again, remaining that way while blood is taken from him. His breathing's so rapid and erratic that red lights and multiple beeps start to go off on his monitors.

Three people in white coats burst in, surrounding a crash cart. "What's happening?" Gretchen says frantically.

"We need you to step outside, ma'am," a doctor she's never seen barks at her.

"No! What are you going to do?" She sees a large blue tube in the doctor's hand. "Not intubate him—"

"We'll do what's best for him right now," the nurse says kindly, firmly.

"I have to talk to him!" Gretchen bursts out. "Let me talk to him!"

Len startles, face flushed, eyes confused.

"Everything's going to be all right, darling," Gretchen says to him. "Do what they tell you. I'll be here!"

He shows no recognition; his eyes—wild and darkened—settle like embers, and the nurse cries, "Ma'am, you need to leave *now!*"

They make her stay in a dimly-lit waiting room. Once, she strides through the swinging doors of the ICU and demands information. The door to Len's room stays shut. A nurse says, "Sorry, honey. They're working hard in there. The surgeon will tell you when they know more."

After a while a different doctor comes to move her to another, smaller waiting room. She says, "Things don't look as good as we hoped. He has a collapsed lung and his organs aren't working well."

"What does that mean for his recovery?"

"It means his organs are failing. Not good."

Gretchen waits quietly in the side room; in spite of her horror, she understands that she can't do anything for Len. With the sound of her own heartbeat roaring in her head, she walks to an area where she can phone Ruby to come right away and bring Satchel.

The surgeon finally comes to her. He has a crumpled, unhappy appearance. Looks exhausted.

"Ma'am, we attempted everything for your friend."

"What?"

He tries to say it another way. "I'm afraid I have to tell you our efforts were unsuccessful."

Gretchen stares. Then she says, "That's not true. He's not gone. *He's not gone.*"

"I'm very sorry. . . . Very sorry, ma'am." His voice is pinched.

The words "sorry sorry sorry" seem to echo. Then she hears her own voice repeating something over and over. It's strident but seems distant to her, almost underwater. Although the surgeon has taken off his cap and walked away, for a short while medical people surround Gretchen. Has she fallen? She is dizzy. She needs to vomit.

A day later, Gretchen's had no sleep, except for slips into nightmare and jerks out of it. Ruby has gone for groceries, and Gretchen's home alone, expecting Satchel shortly. She wants something normal. Stroking Oscar, she sits on her kitchen floor by a white wooden pedestal with curved, tapering legs. Her favorite plant is her aloe; she's gazing at it, thinking of its powers. If she happens to burn herself cooking, she cuts a piece of aloe to bandage her sore with the plant's medicine, knowing that within a day or two the wound will shape up, leaving no scar.

It's taken her years to understand this aloe. She wanted it to grow straight, like succulent plants she's seen on her walks through the neighborhood; she even weeded out any recklessly-tumbling offshoots. When her cold apartment wounded the plant, she repotted, keeping only the proud-looking leaves with better posture. But over time she's seen new, uprising growths acquire untidy, reckless habits of out-reach. This aloe is not meant to be well-organized.

Oscar slides away to play with a toy, and Gretchen peers at a small spider web on the aloe. It must be the work of a very little spider. Grey-white dots lodge in the web, juice-sucking gnats. So: she has an eight-footed ally in the health of her plant. She sits quietly watching the live insect, visible in its web. There it is, a lord of fumigation, her tiny prince or princess, a spider so different in scale that five of it could fill the span of her fingernail. She sees it coax new strands, repairing others. It rushes at nothing. It just does what needs to be done. "Hey. Hey there," Gretchen says softly.

She gets up, brings a drop of water, and spreads it on the overarching leaf. It glints. Moments later, the spider appears next to it. Completely engrossed, it attaches itself to this watering hole. It crouches, still, and stays taking its drink in peace.

Gretchen knows only a few things for certain. One is that she likes to smear water on a clay-potted plant, in case a little spider comes to drink it. Another is that she herself is thirsty; and the water she drinks, whether sipped or quickly drained from the glass, seems to stream through her body, then escape out her pores or through her hair like air, like wind. Walking around her home, she discovers herself squeezing one hand or the other. "No!" she cries out. "That's wrong. Not here. Not this room." She hurries to another room, a different task. The room is wrong. *No place is right.* That is the third thing she knows.

She's still sitting by the aloe plant when Satchel arrives. He leans down for a quick hug and says, "I'm gonna make salad while we're waiting for Rube. We have some greens from yesterday." He goes to a shelf and starts rummaging among plates and cups. "Need a big bowl," he calls, over his shoulder. "Got one?"

"The low wooden cupboard over here."

She points to it; Satchel comes back, bends to open the door. Sticking his head in, he grumbles, "How the hell you find anything? Pitch dark!" He shoves the door open wider.

"Wait, don't—" Her eyes jump to the plant stand, already leaning. *"Oh!"* Gretchen lunges, almost catching the clay pot on its stand, but it lurches hard and lands on the floor. Gretchen wails, "No! *No!*" She gathers pieces of the wreck into her hands. Her broken aloe lies among shards of its pot.

"What the hell?" Satchel, bowl in hand, surveys the damage. "We can re-pot. No big deal." But Gretchen continues crying. Anxiously, he says, "Sorry, sorry, Gretch. What's so bad about it?"

"A spider. It was important."

"A *spider?* A fucking *spider?*"

"Go away," Gretchen says, sobbing at the floor.

"No. I was gonna make dinner for you. And so, but you're not feeling me here."

"I really like that spider," Gretchen answers sadly.

Satchel stands up with a huff. "Cut it out! You're crazy," he says irritably. ". . . Oops. I shouldn't . . . okay." He adds, quieter and more solemnly, "I'm trying to help, Gretch, take care of you. It never does any good."

She murmurs, "See, I loved him, in spite of myself."

"The spider?" Satchel crouches beside her. She looks up reproachfully. He says, "Yeah. I know you fell in love."

Suddenly she's explaining. "He needed a . . . some kind of beautiful, just, impossible world. And for that he was willing to . . . was he really present to people, even me, Satch? . . . I'm so mad. Mad at him for—"

"Seriously? You're pissed?"

"For leaving! Maybe, did he even use people? But he didn't think like that."

"How, then? No, yeah—what are you saying, though?"

"It's like he worked it, this big dream, in his dreamy way, all . . . all the time. . . . Didn't know it would cost him his life—but what if he'd say okay, fine, I'll give up my life? If it lets artists have their place—a *place* for performance and paintings and sculpture . . . photographs. . . . Aahhh, what's it all been for?"

Finally Satchel's not talking. He puts a hand on her shoulder and says, "What do we do?"

She sighs.

"I'll clean this up, okay?" he offers. "All right?"

"No, do something else. Go ahead with it—the . . . the dinner."

Satchel starts to protest, but instead he gets out the pot and starts to set up pasta. He turns around, sees Gretchen moving the mess of dirt and plant and broken clay with her hands, and brings her a broom. He asks, "You okay?"

"Not really. I'm inside out. I feel so many things that don't match. Mostly, it's . . ." She sobs and wipes her tears with the back of her hand. "I still love him. . . . And I'm not ready to do things yet that have to happen." She stands to take the broom.

Satchel says, "He tried like a son of a bitch to get Petta's. Artists' rights! I don't know, but I like that we've all been hanging out, and that was him. We don't have to give that up." He lays tomatoes and peppers on the counter. "Say, you know what? I'm getting a fucking idea. We could do a fundraiser, show your photos, like pull people together. Kinda fits what he had in mind, yeah?" He laughs.

Gretchen stares at him. "You mean it? That's something you want?"

"Make him proud of me, right?"

"Wow. I didn't see that coming."

"Maybe in a few days we'll talk more."

"Can you ask Julian and Ruby to help?"

"Yeah . . . *yeah*. The new galactic fact is I'm gonna be Lennie's henchguy."

Gretchen shakes her head but smiles through the messy tears. "Right-hand man?"

Satchel nods. "The same."

A crowd at LiveWire spills out forcefully onto the street. Cars honk as wine, laughter and loud greetings circulate. A poster in the window's announcing a new performance piece, Ruby in "Own Up to It: We Own It!" Small groups of artists, neighbors, and tourists move into the street to talk, smoke or argue over the news coverage on Len, his project and Petta's. One contingent of supporters accuses the police of his death and the Di Noti firm of instigating it. Inside, Gretchen's blown-up photographs of the violent incident at Petta's cover three walls. There are no chairs this time, but the standing crowd fills the space.

Ruby's performance starts. The lights dim: against one wall—the only one without Gretchen's images—Ruby's soundless film projects. In front of it, Ruby kneels; she faces forward, as her shadow casts against the lower screen. A grotesque skull appears above her. The skull's protruding tongue shines, menacing. Then a rumpled man's head and torso lean at the viewer; his arms jerk in anger. Furious eyes. Ruby straightens slightly from kneeling and speaks dully.

"What is to win? What is won?" . . . The skull shudders, and blood runs through its teeth. Ruby's voice turns hard. "What does a winner win?" Onscreen, the large man-shape slams past. "What do losers win when they lose? . . . *What do they own? What is mine?*" The man's back as he turns. "Who do they own?" White, crumbling pieces of wall fly. "*What do we own.*" . . . Man grows small as he moves away. Man disappears behind door. "Own . . . my own . . . his own . . . her own . . . their own . . ." The sequence begins all over again, this time mixed with the same actions she did in her first performance—small hammer taps against her body softly, then harder. "Why do I do this. . . . What do I own . . . my own . . . his own . . . her own . . . Why do I do. Why do. What is lost? Why does it do it." Recurrence of skull, man, question, self-hit, arm-jerk—question repeats until the audience discomfort seems almost sweaty. At last Ruby says, "Lost not lost. Yours not yours. Lost . . . not lost."

What has seemed a long time finally ends.

Satchel brings his drums onstage, house lights come up, and during a break he and Julian set up with Ruby for a series of songs, some punk-inflected, others influenced by House music. The crowd dances in place.

For the last number, Ruby calls out, "Here's a song we made with Len Considine about cops and corporate thugs of San Francisco! And what they do to us." Julian launches a wild guitar riff. Satchel jumps in on a heavy bongo beat.

Their crowd lets out a cheer, and the musicians break into "Slash and Burn." Ruby turns up the voltage with her whiny, strident, funny and scary vocal tones:

> *It was a rotten day in a pitiful world*
> *In a scaggy part of town*
> *It was a scumbag of a millennium*
> *Your tears go down-up-down.*
> *Slash and burn expansion*

Slash and burn expansion
Whoa—ohh, wohhh—oh!

It was a rotten game played by what's-his-name
He dismantled your heart
Like a used car part
Your tears go down-up-down.

The landlords and the cops better stop their special ops
They wanta bury our heroes
While they add a few zeros,
Slam us down-up-down.

Slash and burn expansion
Slash and burn expansion
Whoa—ohh, wohhh—oh!

It was a rotten game played by what's-their-name
They tried to kill our art
They'll never kill my heart!
Our fight goes down
    Up
    Down
    Up
    UHHHHHHHHHPPP!

Gretchen, behind her camera, ignores the words that make her wince and focuses on visuals. Satchel's slamming his bongos furiously. Julian leaps forward as his guitar convulses, and Gretchen's camera zooms on his flushed, jubilant face. Ruby dances, the crowd claps, and the roomful of people starts dancing in place wildly. As the music turns intensely heartfelt, people howl and cheer. The line between artists and audience is long gone.

10. WHAT'S WANTED, WHAT'S GOTTEN

It's a dark-gray day a week later, sky smeared with chilly clouds. Satchel, walking along Columbus next to Gretchen, says "My true love is the drums."

"I know," Gretchen says and smiles. "You still want to carry on Len's work, though?"

"An artists' space is a hell of a big project. Might take a long time . . . kinda spooked whether I can do both. I don't know if I can actually carry the spear. God, I hope so. People are scared about the whole country . . . the cold war, defense spending . . . the whole damn world. Hundreds of kids snuffed out in Tiananmen Square, baby! It's freaky. We gotta hang together for something. It's a cool thing, if enough people in North Beach Artists are solid . . ."

"But listen, Satchel. You saw the article in the paper— 'North Beach Martyr in Arts Campaign Killed by Police.' That's not what happened here. At all!"

"Gretch, you know what Len would say. That any coverage we get is a chance for an interview, to plug the value of the arts. But so, hate to say it, tragedy a hero makes. Yeah, I'm game to spin that to reporters. Len's passion for the space? His crazy love for the arts? For me he *was* a hero. I'm not."

Gretchen waits.

Fiddling with his thumb, he finally says. "I used to tell you about my days in 'Nam. Remember?"

"Yes."

"I was a kid when I got fucked up in the war. But ever since, a little bottle of Jack now and then helps."

"Hope you can keep it to after-hours."

He nods. "Yeah. You're not *always* right. On this, yeah. Well, I got music to practice. But I hafta pick up flyers for the memorial. Ruby's coming with. Wanta come?"

"First I need to call Len's family again, the brother. He should be here but doesn't seem to want to. Len was the prodigal son who didn't go back. He made us his family."

Four days later: the memorial. Inside the large, informal and slightly rundown community center, a big side table holds candles with pictures of Len, his art and his performances. Gretchen has on a long, pale yellow dress, faintly marked with flowers, tinted slightly toward the green of a spring day's light. The white cardboard box at the center of the room is Len's ashes. Bouquets, messages, and mementos surround it as an altar.

Gretchen starts to introduce the speakers. In spite of occasional trembling, she's able to do what needs to be done. She doesn't speak about Len.

Heads turn as a uniformed policeman walks in. He goes to the back and stands.

A tall, graceful woman with long black hair comes forward. "Leonard Considine was a great director," she begins. She tells a few stories about the glory days, as his student at San Jose State.

Satchel takes a turn. "Len was the best buddy I've had! Mentor, pal. Goad to perfection. The man was practically a fuckin' god. Wish I'd known him sooner. His example made a better man of me. He had this immense *acceptance*. When I'd start pontificating, instead of putting me in my place he'd say, 'Satch-o, you're a cornucopia of facts.' He never said 'useless facts!' He took what you brought and figured you'd do your best. Didn't he accept *you* the same way? Does it go for everybody here? Lemme hear you." There are cheers.

A thin, fragile-looking young man with soft, curly hair and a striped button-down shirt says, "Some of you might not know I worked with Len on a new nonprofit organization to promote technology in the arts. He gave us fantastic ideas and was never too tired or busy to listen. He wasn't even on the board—he just cared!"

Another man in a dark, careful suit and glasses says, "Len Considine was an outstanding example of community success bred by well-expressed community need. We need fifty Len Considines in San Francisco. The power of local action is what will change the artistic and commercial development of this city." People respond to this agency-speak with respectful clapping.

Ruby, in a paisley skirt and sleeveless navy bodice, says breathlessly, "Thanks to Len, I got to know lots of awesome Italian people in North Beach, especially small-business owners with energy and heart. They were so grateful to us for cleaning up the boarded-up building that was an eyesore even before the quake; they loved the Petta's Market plan and signed our petitions. Len inspired me to find that out. He told us the world needs our art. And that we deserve to be in charge of it, and who gets access to it, and how! And I want to thank my friend Gretchen for listening to me until I had these words for how I feel. Len brought artists together . . . and we still *can* be together." A surprisingly large group of North Beach artists stands, whistling and stomping, and Gretchen gives Ruby a gracious smile.

A good-natured-looking man in jeans and a work shirt, hair past his collar, steps forward. "I knew Len as teenagers in Richmond. Damn, we had great times." He wipes his slightly expansive and pocked nose. "We was pretty bad characters, I guess. But Len would always be thinkin', askin' questions, makin' you get it. I love the guy like a brother."

More speeches and reminiscences follow from groups claiming him. They include Californian anarchists, theater professionals, a couple old hardline Marxists, a painter advancing the cause of public nudity, a dignified art professor, and briefly, a member of the Board of Supervisors—the one who'd had his assistant handle all communications. Gushingly, he speaks of Len as though he had known him.

One of Len's old girlfriends has flown in from Europe. With tumultuous, hugely feathered blond hair, she's wearing a shiny leather sheath, way above her knees, and a lot of crystal jewelry. Sniffling, between frequent pauses she reads aloud an old love letter from Len. Gretchen stands through it stonily, arms folded. She stares down and to one side, and her knees are locked.

After the speeches, Julian gets up from the front row and embraces Gretchen. "I really looked up to the dude," he says gently. She kisses him on the cheek. People start to disperse as the policeman comes toward her. Gretchen whispers to Julian, "He's not one of the regular cops from the Trieste beat. . . . Oh, my God. You think he's here to apologize for what they did to Len?"

The officer takes off his cap and speaks quietly. "Miss Wilson, one of Mr. Considine's associates, a member of the Communist Party, is wanted in San Francisco for arson. We need to learn whether he left the country for Australia."

Gretchen blinks. She has to take a breath. Then she answers abruptly, "Len talked to anybody who'd talk to him. I don't know anything more. Excuse me." She walks away. Ruby and Julian follow her, and as they catch up, they fold their arms around Gretchen while her anguished tears fall.

✠

On an afternoon of somber sky, Gretchen and Ruby sit side by side on the Ocean Beach shore. The wind is up. Both women stare out at churning waves. Ruby wraps her arms close to her own body, knees bent. The curls in her short black hair blow back and forth, sometimes hiding her eyes.

Gretchen says slowly, "Do you ever feel you're not . . . where you're supposed to be?"

Ruby laughs. *"Fuck,* yes. Daily."

"I don't mean situationally. I mean . . . an actual place." Gretchen sits straight, rocking lightly. "I used to kayak a lot. I miss it. . . . Dragging it over the sand, then launching. In the boat I felt like I'm where I belong."

Ruby hesitates, then says, "Painting is a place where I belong, or belong to myself, or something I trust. A physical place? Only place I ever felt comfortable in my skin was Nepal."

"Kathmandu?"

"Yes. I like how magical it is. Love it! Normal life just stinks. One thing I'm sick of is to not know where Satch and I stand. Now he's all about drumming, which is cool, but he and Julian practice until three a.m. And when Satch isn't doing music, he's blabbing everywhere he goes about Petta's. I liked performing there, but I need to be more methodical now. Like you, I guess."

"Hm. Do you want to stay with me for a while again, Ruby?"

"Yeah? Wow, I'd love to. Thanks, Gretchen."

"And Ruby . . . I stopped you once when you tried to tell me about Kathmandu. Do you feel like it now?"

Ruby sits still with the wind pushing her hair away from her face. "When I was little, I used to sneak out, when my parents were asleep . . . walk the streets by myself."

"Sounds scary."

"But see, it wasn't. It was some other kind of universe. Like dreams. I felt surrounded by mythical beings that loved me. Even the trees. Fantastic sand castles that were actual buildings. I want to do things that connect what you can see to what you can dream. It would help if I had studio space again. But for now I'm doing whatever I can."

"I know. Thanks for coming here with me, Ruby."

Ruby puts her arm around her friend. What she doesn't say is that it's never been unusual for her to wake in the darkest hour of night weeping. It was only Kathmandu that had offered her the protection and magic she wished for, as she'd walked dusty streets freely, meeting animals and sometimes old people, who exclaimed over her like she was a little saint.

"How are you, Gretchen?"

Gretchen sighs. "It seems as if I can see and hear every moment of the time with Len. Every word. And random things like when the four of us were together at Trieste. All talking about quasars. Remember?"

"Yeah. At first you said you didn't get it."

"No, I've never been that all interested in science. But one night after I looked up quasars, Len and I talked more about that. About . . . ha, I can't explain why this made me so happy. Their blueness."

"Blueness?"

"They look blue. And another thing. They're probably spiraling away from us. Somehow, talking with Len about things like that made me know his heart better."

Ruby sighs. "You're like one of my paintings! Without even trying."

Gretchen laughs. "Now I wonder what we'll do with our lives."

"Me, I was drinking too heavy and smoking too much pot, so I wanta find out how things go without that. I even go to AA meetings."

"Yeah? I didn't know you needed to."

"It was harder to drop out of tequila than I thought."

"What's it like? The meetings?"

"Different. Okay, one guy in his early twenties says the reason he relapsed is he's 'fostering' a cockatoo. He's over-whelmed by parenting it and wants to find the owners, to make them step up. He seems ticked off all the time. Then there's this girl with pink hair who talks about struggles with her HP. I wasn't sure what it is . . ."

"Her printer?"

"Right. Sounds like Hewlett-Packard. No, I finally fig-ured out she was talking about her Higher Power. She'll also say, instead of God, like, 'I had to turn the whole thing over to You, Big G.' But. There's one guy who recovered from leukemia and now he has it again. And a girl who always cries, because her mother has never been anything but de-pressed. Who cares what they call what helps them? It helps me, too. The more I'm in the meetings, the more I feel like I'm getting my thing together. I still smoke a bud some-times, but that's pretty much it."

"Whatever it takes, Ruby."

"Yeah. I'm getting a more settled job life, mostly temp-ing as a typist, part-time stuff. And I want to do some vol-unteer work. But it has to involve painting."

"Oh. In case you're interested, I know a church where they need people to paint the entryway. The guy in charge has AIDS, and he's painting in exchange for a place to live, but he could use some help."

"Can you hook me up?"

"Sure."

"What about you, Gretchen? What's next?"

Gretchen sits thoughtfully. "I want to spend more time by the ocean. What's hard is I have to figure out what to do about Len's work. What *I* should do in it."

"What do you want?"

"I don't know. I want what he tried to carry on to . . . to happen. First there have to be enough artists who really want that space or some other one for the arts. Maybe a co-op? It might take a long, long time and investors who have money. A monster project to make that vision work. Make a viable place. The question is whether I spend a lot of time on this."

Ruby walks through the doorway of Old First Church with a bucket of paint. Inside the entryway, people on ladders are painting golden stars on the arched blue ceiling.

Suddenly a man calls out to her. She recognizes Ben Di Noti's voice and keeps going. "Ruby! Ruby." She turns and sees it really is him. Although she tightens her face in disgust, he walks up to her. For a minute they stand staring. Then he laughs, takes off his hat and bows playfully.

"What's that supposed to be?" Ruby says with scorn.

"Miss Arena, apparently you still paint. I would like to buy one of your paintings."

"You have a fuckload of nerve. I don't believe you! Besides, your offspring already has one of my things. Pretty sure your damn family has made its investment." Di Noti stands still with a look on his face she can't decipher. "What are you trying to pull, Benny?"

"Maybe something for old times' sake."

"We didn't have any real times, okay?"

"Come on, now. Possibly your art work will hit it big someday."

"You mean Nick's investment in my supposedly big future."

"I didn't make an investment in your talent," he says. "But I could."

Fog has started to sift toward them. Ruby's face is angry and compressed. "Since when do you give a shit? This is making me gag," she says.

Di Noti answers, "Your Mr. Consodeen blabbed about the tradition of backing arts in North Beach. Actually, that's correct. And in fact, I recently acquired the painting you sold to my son. For that, I paid him considerably more than he paid for it."

The air turns dense as fog moves by. Ruby's confused. "I don't get it. Anyway, I don't do commissions anymore."

"Then some work you've already done. Name your price. Up to a grand."

"So you actually think I could make it big? You're going to score off what I do?" She laughs.

"Maybe. With a little help from your friends."

She says nothing and starts to turn away.

Then, in the tone he'd used when he first came to her front door, he adds, "I understand the group you're with claims the arts are your reason for being awake."

Ruby stops, stands still—listening to cars, wind, and fog horns. "You're still a con, Benny. And I hate you. But you finally hit a note I hear. I guess that . . . look. You can take one of my best paintings for a thou. It's still decent after the quake, and I could use the cash. You think you can make a killing off it? Yeah, good luck. But only this once. Let's say I send somebody to deliver it. You give them a check made out to me. That'll be the whole deal. Given your goon squad and the eviction, nothing after that. Now excuse me—I'm gonna help some people paint the entryway to this church. They need heaven and some stars. So the hell do I."

Di Noti bows again with mock-reverence. "Very well, Miss Arena. I'll have an assistant look out for the delivery. It's been lovely knowing you."

Ruby shakes her head bitterly, as he saunters away. She says to herself, "If he even does it, I'll pass on some of the dough to Len's artists' fund."

That evening, Gretchen waits at her bus stop across from an old factory building. Dusk is falling, and her work day is over. It's raining. When the bus pulls up and she climbs on, she sits in the nearest available seat, by a nervous-looking, unkempt man with matted hair. Immediately he shouts, "Don't touch! Get away."

"Sorry," she says, and stands again. "I didn't mean to."

The man starts thrashing his arms. "Too much noise! People! Too much people!" Three passengers get up rapidly and move toward the back. Gretchen sits in one of the vacated seats, center-facing, out of the man's reach but not far away. She remembers how steady Len stayed in situations like this.

"It's okay," she finds herself telling the stranger.

"Okay? Okay?" Now he looks at her pleadingly, like a child. The hair on his sideburns is straight, though the rest of it looks like parched AstroTurf. Acne-pocked face. His chin, sharp and red, pulls back in a worried wrinkle.

"Sure. It'll be okay," she insists.

For some reason the man asks, "What if he doesn't come back?"

Unhesitatingly she answers, "Don't worry. He'll come back."

The man starts to cry, gasping. He throws a chapped hand over his face, then drops it. "My brother left. Why? He won't call. What if he doesn't call?"

"He'll call," she says, as though she's been calming disturbed people for years.

"He'll call," he repeats after her wonderingly. More patiently.

The bus stops and new passengers step in. The afflicted man starts trembling. As people pass his seat he cringes and bursts out, "Too much noise. Get away. Don't touch me!" There's a constricted line bisecting his whole forehead.

Gretchen tells him, "It's all right. They're just walking by. Everybody gets off at the place they're going. Do you have a place to get off?"

"Want my brother to go by. He left! *Why?*"

"He'll call you." Then, kindly, "I'm sure he loves you."

Tears start to runnel down his face. "Loves me?"

"Sure," Gretchen insists. "He must not be able to come right now, but he'll be thinking about you."

"Be thinking about me," the strange man says thoughtfully. Then he leans forward energetically. "I'm gonna go. He'll call!" He heaves himself up and heads for the front. As the hinged bus door whines open, a woman on the sidewalk tries to climb on, just as the man's getting off. He waves his bony unjacketed arms and yells, "No! Get away!"

Gretchen says levelly, "You can get down. No yelling, though."

He repeats, as he thumps down the steps into rain, "No yelling though, yelling though. Okay though."

It's raining heavily. Gretchen shakes her head; there's nothing she can do about the craziness in her city. But at least she got inspiration from Len to offer a little warmth. She leaves at the next stop.

She has no umbrella and arrives with wet hair and dripping coat to the bar, with its huge mirror and wall of bottles, where she'd met Satchel when he first came to town. It looks dingier than then. He's waiting in a corner booth. The place is crowded. Gretchen, shaking out her wet gloves, sits down beside him.

"Let's get your coat off, Gretchy."

"Don't call me that. Let's get to the point."

"Well, obviously the point is, get things going again for Petta's. You gotta do it. I'll help."

Gretchen makes a small uncomfortable *umf* sound like a German word. Then she responds, "Satchel, no . . . I'm not an activist."

Smiling, he says jauntily, "Ah, Gretch, you and your fear of engagement!" Gretchen flushes. "You know I'm right," he adds, nodding at a nearby booth of college kids—Asian immigrants, artists, musicians. They nod back and hail him enthusiastically. There are still people around who remember his band Dark Matter, and a few of them came to Petta's recently while he was on the drums.

Gretchen leans in. "Not true."

Satchel pours her a beer from the pitcher. Then shakes his head. Drops of rain fly off his hair onto the table. "There you go again. You live in here," and he points to his head. "What about Len's, y'know, legacy?"

Gretchen looks at him steadily. Finally she tells him calmly, "You're right to push for what he started. But I need you to see that photography's what I do. Maybe what I am. I'll document whatever we do. But for artists to have a place like Petta's over the long term, there's another thing his legacy depends on. . . . I'm willing to look for donors. Funders. And write grant proposals. Maybe Julian can work with me. We're probably in this for the long haul. But I can't lead the charge—I'm just not that person. *You* do it." She puts her hand on his arm. "Len would want you to."

Satchel's eyes fill with tears. "Crap, I dunno if I'm good for it. By myself? I got music to play. Might, maybe, get Ruby back. I should make the . . . some—the consistent effort, or . . . I guess I—wait! Maybe it's true he wanted me for this. Right?"

"Yeah. I think so."

Satchel sits still again. There's a silence. Finally he says in a halting, uncharacteristically deep voice, "This could take years I don't have, but fuck, I'll try. I *will!*" Then he pulls himself up straight, grins, kisses her on the cheek, and says briskly, "Okay. Two o'clock tomorrow at Petta's. Bring your camera." He gets up and walks over to the booth full of people who had waved.

"Guys! You know me? Satchel Reilly from Dark Matter. Are you musicians or anything? Artists? I have this great, really slammin' project for you!"

All of them look intrigued. "Really?"

"No shit?"

"What's the deal?"

Satchel bends toward them, eyes shining. "It's about a huge, I mean *enormous* art space in North Beach." His hair shakes a little, hands and shoulders moving with his words, lit up. Telling them what this could mean to each one: their new possibility.

Ruby walks in, wearing her grey smock stained with blue paint. Satchel waves her over. She runs toward him. Satchel says, "Damn, baby, you were wearing that the first time I saw you."

Ruby laughs and says, "Hello, Satchel-like-the-suitcase. I'm here to help."

SPECIAL FEATURES

THE TRAILER

[Pretentious male voice booms behind a series of shots: Ruby wakes up in bed clutching her chest, Len pushes a cop, Satchel hands a bottle to some drunk in a dark alley, Gretchen kisses Len in a church, Ben Di Noti says, "She's sure got the tatas," and Nick overturns a restaurant table]:

> *When creative people sacrifice to do compelling, sometimes lasting work, how much power do circumstances have? How stable, safe and healthful are the living situations of artists?* [The voice sounds like a World War II news clip.] *For the strong or fortunate, a work process and what they make of it sustains them through disappointments. For others, pressures and afflictions write their stories. But their thoughts—even when compromised by struggle or defeat—are owned by them, whether at white heat, in reflection or at rest. See their controversial fight for a place of their own in "Landlords!"*

CHARACTERS RESPOND TO THE FILM

Gretchen (smooths her skirt, smiles, looks down): "The thing you missed is that I've got a sense of humor!"

Satchel: "What the f___! I do *not* have a *paunch.*"

Len: "We're so afraid to take a stand, to go against what society expects of us. I think Gretchen has it in her to make the art site her life's work."

Ruby: "As a portrayal of me, the film's amazing! Ahh, just kidding. My weakness is I need a lover. Guess I could use more self-esteem. Anyway, I liked the skull piece, the self-hitting piece, and it was fun to paint sky on a curved ceiling. North Beach Artists helped me bail my earlier work out of storage, and I just did a series of paintings about home-lessness in San Francisco. We plan to do a show at Petta's, with a lot of Gretchen's photographs."

Ben Di Noti: "Got a prospect in Beijing, very interested in the property. I've been letting the art kids stay there awhile, in case they got some press—nice possible hobby for me to invest in a few of their paintings, while I get the right price on the property. Since that Lon Consodeen character has croaked, I looked into buying all his weird stuff with the dots. May still get it off his family, a brother of his that Nick located in Idaho, who's the default heir. Anyway, now some City Hall flunkies and bleeding-heart reporters are raving about the cute little artists.

"I thought about evicting them, but I have another way to go—my guy in Beijing will probably pay up. He could let the place go to hell again, never even know the kids are in there, still get plenty when he sells. Easy deal. My inter-national buddies right now are all about flipping stuff to their buddies, who flip it some more. Turns out they don't check anything. On paper, the property's an upscale Nob Hill investment."

DIRECTOR'S COMMENTS

—By Truss Showalter, Jr.

I tried to make this work funny as well as poignant and telling. Biggest challenge was four witnesses to a process—all artists—without patronizing or diminutizing them. At times we failed. Hard to let them speak for themselves on the power of art and its vital importance to society, culture and personal experience. A lot fell on the cutting-room floor. Why? Too esoteric? Is there really too damn big a difference between people who make art and people who don't care whether they see or hear it? Oh, man. I'm suffering bigtime. The editing room was a hellhole.

At times we couldn't figure out Gretchen's backstory, and eventually I dispensed with most of it. She stayed pretty mum when the others were talking to me. All four main characters had rough early experiences, but I wasn't trying to say that was what made them into artists. Satchel's more of your standard ebullient, clueless, insensitive but ultimately good-hearted guy, like some other drummers I've known—okay, my brother is a drummer—basically looking for his place in life, which doesn't come easy for most vets. Apparently most people find him very irritating. Feedback we got from women viewers was like, "Can't stand the sight of Satchel. Love to hate on him." At the same time, the scenes they talk about are always his. One woman commented after a preview, "I'm glad Satchel left. And I hope he comes back soon!"

I think a lot of Len, although the audience tends to find him sappy, dreamy, even preachy. He pretty much tells or shows Gretchen his backstory, though. Len carries the flag for the ideals here. Though you may not relate. Because, frankly, I struggled quite a bit with how much his crusade was realistic. I knew fairly early on that he wasn't going to make it through.

Ruby's talented and creative, but to say it nicely, she has a hard time finding balance or taking care of her health. Too much like your stereotypical bohemian chick. By the time we wrapped I wanted to see her to get a handle on some of her hassles. And she did!

Also, after this project was finished, I bought both the paintings the Di Notis claim to have bought. They didn't actually do any of that. In fact, I'm not sure she ever slept with the son. But those guys were scum. They're not based on actual assholes living or dead, though! Just inspirations. You know, old-school guys. Actually, they're a hoot. Uh-oh. I'm patronizing them. It's kind of what I do.

Initially I met with the writer, Mia Stageberg, who insisted that corporate expansion affects artists in San Francisco dramatically. She even said, "Let the artists win!" Sorry, that was ridiculous. When it comes to movies, we don't need our writers for much. It's a time-honored tradition to pay them crap, and I'm good with that. Writers slow me down. I don't read scripts, just tell the actors go, once they get their backstory straight.

In the end, the project needed to explore what is "land," and who "owns" the place where we "live." In a Barthian sense. Okay, I don't mean that. My publicist insisted, "Mention Barthes," but I get nauseated when people talk about signs and signifiers. This project was supposed to go complex, though. I still keep footage of my own cut of the material, because one of these days a wider public might get it. The differences give it another slant. Only place I ever got to show it was indie festivals, so I'm going to call it the Indie Version. Weirdly, I kept a lot of the idealistic shit. What the writer wrote. It was more fun than I thought it would be. Market analysts tell me that slow and reflective are in the future for American culture, so sooner or later there's gonna be a backlash against speed and greed.

If you like words in print, you can actually access it right here. In a few more pages, though.

THE MADE-FOR-TV PITCH AND MORE

The original script for "Landlords" was optioned in Hollywood, and a major pop singer was stoked to play Ruby. Script to be redone by her favorite producer's brother-in-law. Ruby becomes the heroine; the action climaxes with her fatally shooting Di Noti and his son. However, a certain hybrid horror movie under production had a similar plot.

Then "Landlords" was slated to become a made-for-TV movie, as a remake of that ancient 1965 film "The Sandpiper." The Elizabeth Taylor character of a warm-hearted, free-love painter would be updated—with an eighteen-year-old Ruby as the heroine—and with Gretchen as a grouchy, unstable, alcoholic older housewife. Instead of those California beaches in "Sandpiper," the location was going to be Hawaii, though actually shot in Portland. Richard Burton's character in the original film—the priest who fell into sin—is now the hero, a priest named Satchel who, after being suspected of abusing children, has an affair with Ruby (now affectionately named Fluffs), and briefly becomes an international rap star. Crushed with disappointment in his new persona and the sacriligious songs he's singing, he desperately goes into politics, and Ruby gives up painting to run his campaign for Senator. The other characters are dropped and the title is now changed to "Maligned and Unsigned." Although the pitch went well, a contract was never reached.

Two years later, a different film star who liked the Len character became interested in the project, and the original writer, Stageberg, was recalled to L.A. to meet with him and his people. She was unaware that negotiations depended on the Gretchen character being renamed Brittany and played by a twenty-two year old actress. At this point the writer left, relinquished any control, and handed off all credit. The actress then turned out to be unavailable.

After another year and a half, the eventual producer of "Landlords," who had known the writer in kindergarten, felt the work could have a substantial following overseas. He made a low-budget version that got as far as the Sundance Film Festival, and eventually a cut and re-edited, limited-release studio version was made. But the master track somehow disappeared. One story I heard was that some dude at an all-night party at the producer's place in Jackson Hole went ape shit—tossed the whole master into a swimming pool. If you've seen that type of party, you almost believe it.

My version, which I, personally, like to think of as the director's cut, remains unseen. It was deemed too introverted. The Studio was vociferous about how people today are too cynical to relate and, besides, artists don't live that way. Some of my best friends are artists! Actually, almost all of them live that way. But everybody said it comes across implausible. This unseen version has been released below for the first time. I'm calling this one, *mine,* the Indie Version because the Jackson Hole version was never seen again, anyway. Only the Hollywood Studio Version you just saw ever made it to production. That was well received in a San Francisco preview, but it tanked nationally.

LANDLORDS

INDIE VERSION

11. HOLDING THE WALL

Night came on in late-1990s San Francisco, streams of fog looping over the hills of Buena Vista Park, Diamond Heights, and Russian Hill. Ocean Beach lay open with flat dun-colored sand, as the waves turned restless. Around the city, tall trees and bright plants from other countries kept company with native dune flowers, pines and sequoias. At bookstores in dense North Beach, rows of people stood raptly reading. On a crowded subway, a little girl began to cry as people crushed in; her mother soothed her, promising they'd soon be home. In Golden Gate Park, groups of the homeless gathered to find sleeping places among groves of foliage. One man bent over and grabbed a penny; heads-up made it "a lucky one," he said out loud, and laughed.

At a bus stop sat a slender woman at the end of her work day. Tall and pale, she had graceful long hair turning grey. She, Gretchen, had delicate features, and she carried herself with a certain pride and peace in experience she kept to herself.

She stared, smiling, at the massive wall of a building opposite. The last afternoon light tried to glimmer toward it through moving fog. Closely paned windows of an old brick factory, its trim stained salmon red, foregrounded the sky turning grey as she watched. A large dark public mailbox stood by a streetlight that looked too old to be of use. Standing, she took her camera out of her bag and started framing. She clicked, reframed, clicked until the bus pulled up. For her, the place didn't need to have a history she knew. She felt it through her eyes. Even after she got on the bus, she continued shooting random images, gazing through the window.

When Gretchen reached home, it was dark. She climbed the stairs, unlocked the battered door to her apartment and threw down her things on a chair. Sharply, she said, "Damn, it's cold in here." She pulled on a sweater. It felt colder in the building than it had outside. She had lived here thirteen years and had never gotten used to the chill. But she was eager to plug her camera into the computer and upload pictures of today's wall. Gretchen usually used an analog camera, but she no longer had a darkroom. When she felt like it, she went digital. She chose an image and, deepening the dark of a tree behind the streetlight, changed the sky's tint to white. Picked out subtle red highlights. Tried blues until they paled and differed. After half an hour, the city's spare objects anchored in its space. She'd lifted something new into it, a resonance she needed. The scene now had a certain Edward Hopperness, in the way he had painstakingly revealed time's uneasy union with humankind.

The phone rang; Gretchen let the call go to her answering machine. She heard a man's spirited voice. "Gretch . . . honey, if you're there . . . man . . . love your phone message. It's great to hear your voice. Okay, well, it's me. Pick up."

She froze; they hadn't talked in a year. What should she say or not say? Maybe not answer? He'd always liked to call late, even though she told him not to. It felt like an intentional way to throw her off balance. But he'd keep calling if she didn't pick up. She did. "Hello, Satchel."

"Oh, you precious angel."

"So you're coming to town?" she guessed.

"Yes, baby, I can't wait to see you." They'd broken up long ago, but his manner suggested a woman in every port. Gretchen didn't like it, even though at around fifty he still had a boyish voice, and her body warmed to it a little.

Fighting this, she said coolly, "If I know you, you figured you could stay here."

"You have a bed for me?"

"I don't."

"Babe, I can sleep on the floor. Floor's fine, Gretch."

"Don't call me that. It sounds like projectile vomiting."

"You're not like this, you know," he went on ebulliently. "I remember how sweet you are, so cut it out."

She sighed. "We can't get into old complications."

"I just want to see you. How's your cat?"

"Don't you remember, Satchel? Oscar died two years ago. I sent you a post card."

"Damn. We don't have to screw, you know? Just wanna see you."

The crude term irritated Gretchen, but she mused, shifted her weight. Should she let him come over? Could she be sure what she'd want? She still remembered the taste of his mouth. *Be firm,* she reminded herself. *No good can come of it.* Behind his voice she could hear either wind or rain. "Where are you?"

"My band played a cruise ship. Kicked out of a hotel in L.A. last night. The singer got drunk and trashed the room."

"The singer?" Gretchen asked suspiciously.

"Okay, me. Meet me tomorrow."

Tomorrow, they sat side by side at the counter of a nearly-deserted dive bar on Jones. "You're leading a harmless life!" Satchel burst out, wiping his mouth on the back of his hand.

It was sudden and grim; Gretchen recoiled. "Yes," she said, "it beats leading a harmful life."

"Bet you just hole up in your apartment. Don't hold the wall. You can't give all that intensity and brilliance to a . . . a *harmless life*."

Flustered, she said, "Anyway, 'don't hold the wall' means let's dance."

He laughed. "Zion's version's better than the crappy original." He starts whooshing, blapping and spluttering an imaginary background track. Then says, "What are you, clinically depressed?"

"That's ridiculous. I have a job. I have my pictures."

"Fuck it, you *are* hiding. I can tell even by looking that you sleep alone. You didn't even replace your cat."

"That's just cruel, Satchel. Are you this mean-spirited?"

"What about changing the world? I thought that was maybe your thing, that I guess you outgrew. You don't care anymore? Are you on a private holy path or something?"

Then Gretchen sat quietly, angrily still as he lit a cigarette in the no-smoking bar. Coughing with a hand over her mouth, she was thinking *Nobody's telling him to put it out. Why do I have to be the one to either say it or hack my brains out?* Finally she said, "You have no idea about my path. And I don't owe myself to anybody or anything. Also, you can't smoke in here."

"Fine, I'm due somewhere in ten minutes. I have a girl to meet."

Gretchen did not want to hear about that. It seemed unlikely but could be true, given his habits of swooping in, capturing, disappearing.

"I'll drive you home," he added. "I'm responsible that way. Never let a lady down." He threw the cigarette on the floor and stubbed it out. Aggravation hit Gretchen and quickly gave way to relief; she wouldn't have to find and pay for a cab.

He turned, hunching over the counter, to ask the owner about the origin of a lacquered wooden mantel above the mirror. With his hooded hazel eyes shining, Satchel said he could always recognize the work of a fellow Irishman. He was laying the last touches to an ale he'd slugged down. The owner laughed happily and contributed history about the craft of the mantel.

Gretchen stood awkwardly waiting. When they left, she asked tersely, "Did you drive to town in your car?"

"The same," he said. "But I haven't decided yet whether to stick around."

Gretchen nodded. He never decided things like that. She felt herself coiled away from his wanton accusations. Though perhaps, even if he'd drawn blood, she should be a little grateful—just because somebody noticed her work? That did tear at her. Gretchen hadn't shown photographs in any gallery for several years. She spent her days at work and evenings at the computer with images. Wounded and taut, she said little until she was delivered to her door. Safely.

She climbed her usual three flights of stairs. The apartment was cold. She shivered. Without even taking off her coat, she strode into her kitchen, picked up the phone and dialed the super. "Hello, it's Gretchen upstairs. I really need your help waking my radiator for the winter. It's bad."

12. ROACH

Ruby Arena, in her twenties, had been the bassist of a band. Then she became a painter. It turned out harder than ever to pull rent money together, so she took on a sideline as a smalltime pot dealer. Now, in her late thirties, she was ill. She'd learned eight days ago that she had breast cancer. Wasn't she still young for news like that? The new worry resulted in many dishes left in her sink—rimed with bits of salad, buttered popcorn or beef stroganoff. Glasses jumbled randomly there, splattered with tequila. That didn't account for all the cockroaches throughout her apartment. They'd always lived there, permanent owners of the darkness in thousands of unseen crevices.

She had laid claim to this apartment with intricate shawls hung at windows, with books signed by poets who loved her paintings and her animated black Italian eyes, and with a small owl skeleton tacked over the door of the kitchen that doubled as her studio. Imagery had become Ruby's life, and she held onto its force.

When she painted she moved vigorously, swaying and reaching. The shapes, as they happened, called to whatever mystery would be revealed to her—through her. At times she didn't realize until she finished that her inspiration had started with specific feelings—a makeshift shrine to a locally murdered woman, the birth of a friend's child, or even a nineteenth-century novel. Her painting "Köln Concert," full of explosive reds and agitated lines, had eventually given way to white coils that looped over each other until, at last, the lightest colors dominated, with stark flashes of the original jumping through the spaces. The San Francisco Art Institute had bought that one, her only major sale.

She had been working about two months on a huge oil painting in wisteria purple. She dealt with her cancer news by pushing deeper into color. Soon the painting changed completely; powerful arcs of parrot green swooped across the canvas, with strokes of rough black. New eruptions of cerulean blue and bright white evoked a forest turned to lightning. Thoughts of what would happen next dominated her even when she wasn't working. Ruby mulled over colors harsh and lush, the force of shapes she created or wanted to try. Proud beastlike and facelike images arrived to mind.

Loading her palette with brilliant colors from tubes, she'd pour in linseed oil, thinning liberally with turpentine as a solvent (despite its vapor, which she knew to be a hazard). She still painted like her friends from an earlier San Francisco age, although she'd heard of ill health from toxic materials. Ruby, juicing herself for the long hours, favored plenty of straight tequila. For a break, she'd go to the small second-story porch and light a cigarette or roll some joints. Perhaps risk had some loveliness for her in its own right.

With her weight on one hip, Ruby stood in line at a counter. A fairly small woman, she had short black curls and flushed cheeks. Wearing a grey paint-splotched smock, she waited for her afternoon cappuccino at Caffé Trieste. Occasionally she forced back a sleeve to look at her watch.

"You know that paint on your clothes is still wet?" Someone tapped her on the shoulder, a tousled man in too-tight jeans. Before Ruby could answer, a young guy jumped up to point at her accoster, calling, "Hey, hey. You're that guy from Dark Matter!"

Facing the man who'd spoken to her, Ruby said, "You should have picked a better name. *I* used to be in a band. Retrovirus."

"Heavy." He had a winning smile, though he looked older than her; despite his strong build, he'd grown a little slack in the middle. "I heard of that band. Cool. You the only girl?"

Ruby smiled and nodded.

"Bet you broke 'em up 'cause of fighting over you, ha. What's your instrument?" he asked.

He has unusually large eyes, she thought, *sea-colored.* "Bass. And a little sax. You?"

"Just voice, baby. Just me. Used to be a drummer, but now I'm more the front man." He hummed a little jazz riff, and Ruby laughed.

She asked, "You between gigs?"

"Aaaah. You could say. Between rocks, hard places and so forth. Between the rock and the roll."

She glanced at his muscular biceps. "And the band?"

"Money-management issues. Hey, look, you wanta jam sometime?"

"Oh . . ." Ruby flashed toward him. "You're kind of obnoxious, but you have nice eyes. No, though." She glanced at her watch again. "I'm late—I'll have to skip coffee."

"But you gotta see me at work, right? Maybe I'll phone the guys, and we'll pull together one of those San Fran shows we cancelled."

Ruby laughed again. She held out her long hand that smelled of turpentine and said, "I'm Ruby."

He took her hand in both of his. "Satchel Reilly."

"Satchel. Like the suitcase?"

"The same. Ahh, Ruby! The name of a jewel."

Eleven blocks away, Gretchen walked through North Beach on the way to her friend's apartment. She'd realized she needed another artist to collaborate on an exhibition, so she lugged a large binder of photos. Why *not* make a stab at it? Her painter friend had suggested that the two of them plan a brief show at a small gallery on Grant Street. This painter friend was Ruby.

Gretchen laughed happily at the oddness of the owl skeleton over Ruby's door.

Ruby said, "I just made it home. Let's get to it, girl! Spread out your photos."

Gretchen took off her threadbare brown wool coat, set it on a chair, and carefully but swiftly assembled a spread of pictures on the kitchen table.

Ruby exclaimed, "God, Gretchen! Your colors are just amazing. Some of these look like they were taken on a different planet. Wow! And the black and white ones—I love those. So mysterious it's giving me chills."

"Thank you, Ruby. Can I see your work?"

"Sure, if you have time, it's all here. Mostly canvases." They were stowed in different rooms, and she began pulling them out. Gretchen slowly moved in front of each one, watching. Ruby stood by. Finally Gretchen smoothed her hair back from her face and asked, "Which one are you closest with right now?"

Ruby flushed with pleasure. "The new one." They stood in front of its arcs of green and fiery ultramarine blue. It had a proud, disturbing intensity, like northern lights, a meeting of solar wind and earth's charged electrical field.

At last Gretchen put away her photos, and they sat down to the table. Gretchen asked Ruby about the LiveWire gallery. They would have to make arrangements quickly. Ruby explained, "I think they're perfect for what we'll bring in. Their new location on Grant is good and will pull a big crowd, but our work will only be up a couple days. We'll have to hang it ourselves. Probably get friends to help. . . . You want a glass of wine? I've got Chardonnay somewhere; I know you don't drink the hard stuff." She swung open the door of a cavernous old refrigerator.

Gretchen said, "Water's fine." But suddenly she drew a sharp breath. "Oh, no! Watch your feet. Under the fridge!" Tiny roaches streamed out onto the floor.

"Ah, that. Babies just keep spawning."

Cringing, Gretchen asked, "Won't your landlord spray?"

"They don't do jack shit." Ruby hauled out a carafe of water.

"But that's not even legal. Write a letter! Maybe other tenants would go in on it." Gretchen shuddered. "Cockroaches carry disease. And it scares me, because you need to take care of yourself, especially now." Gretchen's forehead contracted like these were her own worries.

"I dunno. Ever since I've been here, they're all over the cupboards. I tried roach sprays and traps. Nothing works." Ruby helped herself to a big glass of tequila.

She poured water for Gretchen, who took it in both hands and reflected, "Different sprays probably lead to survival of the fittest. Look, that one's albino!"

Ruby said, "Yeah, mutant roaches. Aliens. They're colonizing my world. Can't think about it. I've got a tumor to get taken out."

Gretchen put down her glass. "You must be scared."

"I work it off. Have to."

"I'd be terrified. You're really not?"

"Only in the middle of the night."

Gretchen reached out to Ruby's arm. "And we're having a show together! I'm glad. Listen, is anyone going with you to surgery?" Ruby shook her head. "Then I'll go."

"God. What a sweetheart! I accept."

Gretchen sighed. "You know, Ruby? I think I'll have that glass of wine, after all."

Gretchen arrived at the Grant Avenue storefront gallery early. When she knocked, a tall, nervous woman, sleek in black, opened the door just a slit and said, "Hi, sweetie—titles, prices—all there. But give me a few, to finish up?"

Surprised, Gretchen asked, "Shouldn't I help?" The show was to start in twenty minutes.

"Just come back in fifteen, will you, doll?" Gretchen could see two of Ruby's paintings still leaning on the wall, unhung. The curator blew an air-kiss and locked the door.

Gretchen walked down Grant Avenue in her short skirt, emerald green jacket and ankle boots in the dark. She pulled out a digital camera and said to it playfully, "Let's go into the market." Giving the counter girl a disarming grin, she wandered through. Choosing an aisle in back, Gretchen went to work photographing frames of zucchini stacked flat against carrots. No subject was beyond her curiosity, and she loved the lines. Baskets of cabbage—stained wicker, gleaming greens and sinuous purple rounds. In a group of beets, she saw a compelling dark red that created a small majestic world. No one came to interfere.

Back on the street, a hair salon's door gaped. Plonked in the center of her view, its amber neon sign in Chinese blinked. Inside, only a vibrantly green wall and an empty, faint-gold couch. Gretchen shot pictures of the silent scene. She had stalked and found an urban moment that touched something in her spirit. With good fortune, maybe its smoky jazz would reach somebody else through her image.

In the long narrow LiveWire Gallery, talk bounced and crackled. Gretchen looked for Ruby among people turning in their circles. She glanced toward her photographs to see who had stopped to look. . . . An almost preternaturally tall man, shoulder blades defined against his shirt, stood with a hand on one hip, absorbed. He moved close to one of Gretchen's images that she especially liked: sun slamming onto a steep cobbled street that shone with rain. Windows of old buildings surrounded and reflected it. The man crossed his arms, looking closely, and stayed there. Gretchen pressed forward. He had grey hair to his shoulders, a thin craggy face, and blue eyes squinting with something interior. Gretchen watched. When someone jostled him, he caught her eye, then went back to his studying.

Gretchen saw Ruby holding court in front of her largest painting. It still looked like a forest, but the background had darkened. Beside her, the bearish, bearded Poet Laureate of San Francisco gestured expansively. Carrying his responsibility as an old-time Beat, he showed special interest in Ruby's work, put a hand on her shoulder. Other North Beach artists had come: a poet serving as co-curator of this show, photographers Gretchen knew, and a woman who organized street festivals; Gretchen had always respected her drawings of local hangouts. There were jazz musicians—one much-loved elderly black guy in a fez and caftan who supported all the local art events. Gretchen also noticed some lithe dancers and an English model being waited on by an older painter in leather pants. She smiled at the spectacle that swirled around her. Witnessing and savoring, Gretchen felt the impulse to photograph.

All at once the tall man with intent blue eyes stood next to her. His skin was brown-tinged in the way of naturally fair people who crave the sun. He held out a large, sensitive hand. "I'm Len Considine. This is beautiful work, a real love feast of the city. I didn't know you're the photographer, but someone pointed you out to me."

She blushed. "Gretchen Wilson. Well, of course you've already found out." She struggled for presence of mind.

"Are you based in North Beach?" he asked.

"Almost. I live at the edge of the Tenderloin. . . . It's my first show in a long time."

He nodded. "I used to hang out in North Beach, but I've been in Europe and Australia. Just got back." He had a quiet voice, higher than she expected, but clear and warm.

"What did you do over there?" she asked.

"Theater. Art activism."

"Art activism?" She was startled. "What's an art activist? I've known lots of activists, but I never heard of that. . . ."

"Well, when you think about it, there's a lot for artists and art lovers to fight for and against."

"What, exactly?"

He ran his fingers through his hair as though he wasn't used to hearing this sincere question. "Like corporate interests. I really feel they have a stranglehold on art. Anywhere. When I was in Sydney, I saw how the Opera House is their jewel of tourism. It's gorgeous opera—which I love—and pretty much every bit's controlled by sponsors. And these huge companies are up to their necks in things I'd call dirty. Hand in hand with American companies like Solexo, tied up in the Iraq war. We wanted to challenge that."

Gretchen asked timidly, "Who's 'we?'"

"Just some friends. We'd dress up as clownish idiots and grab attention like that. It's amazing how a few signs and something said loudly shake up a public scene, in a moment that's not supposed to happen. Finally we started performing in the lobby, and they threw us out. So we moved the whole thing over to their front steps."

"To chip away at corporate interests? I don't think I understand."

"Why not? Couldn't the opera house belong to regular people? We felt like we had a right to suggest it. Rich folks started staying away, and that *definitely* made an impact. 'Cause we hit the house in their fat pocketbook. We kept doing it and got listened to. They finally even dropped their contract with Solexo."

"Wow," Gretchen said. "What you did . . . that's impressive. I can't help feeling sorry for the opera house, though. I guess there's hardly any funding for art when you compare it to banking or big chain stores . . . even movies and sports."

"But corporate-sponsored music *is* a movie business or sports." His voice had turned firm. "The power guys have our arts by the balls."

"Well, you're certainly definite about all this. Me, I worry more about keeping warm in my apartment."

"Oh, Christ. That's terrible. And a lot of artists in North Beach can't even afford to live here anymore. Who's got decent heating *anywhere* in the city? And tonight—this is fantastic, here at LiveWire, but only for a couple days, right? How many people get to see your work in that short of a time? . . . Most of us can't even afford a studio."

"You're an artist?" Gretchen asked.

"Yeah." He reached into his pocket, handed over a simple business card and gave her a big smile, saying, "Hey, we should have coffee." His face was so lean it grooved under both cheekbones. Gretchen liked it.

But she was swept back by a throng of latecomers. Satchel was one. He surged toward Gretchen, seized her in a massive hug and clutched like a lost relative. "Satch, please," she protested. He ignored this and buried his face in her neck.

"I'll buy you a glass of wine if you stop it," Gretchen said, laughing from awkwardness. She couldn't say she felt no pleasure, but she wanted even more for him to quit.

He yanked both his arms away and grinned recklessly, palms turned up in mock supplication. "I'll get the wine and eats. It's your night, baby," he said. A couple of minutes later she saw him talking to a lively girl with lots of cleavage.

He swirled into a cacophonous group of bearded guys in various berets; Ruby stood at the center, talking into a cell phone. Satchel made his way toward her.

After hours of face-to-face greetings with luminaries, hangers-on and interested artists, an overstimulated Gretchen let herself be swept toward Caffé Trieste with the well-wishing crowd. It had started raining and, umbrellaless, she felt the cold wet assault, even with her hands on the crown of her head. She and the others, most of them laughing and shouting, ran into the café, and someone handed her a glass of Chianti. She sipped from it, then held it close to her midriff. Len, the tall man from earlier, sat against a front window surrounded by people, talking to them. Nervously she put down the glass. Time to make a night of it? The show had gone well.

Outside, she hesitated about where to head for a cab. A few people followed her out into the wind and rain by the street light. Len, the tall man, was suddenly there. His hair was wet and he had no jacket. The tan button-down shirt he wore had rolled-up sleeves and was peeled wide at the neck. He had a birthmark about the size and shape of an oval quarter on his chest, partially visible, slightly darker than his skin. Gretchen had an unnerving impulse to kiss it.

He said, "I hope you weren't put off by our gabbing back there. Just a bunch of old geezers, but we don't mean any harm. Come back?" Gretchen didn't answer. She'd rather have been somewhere with just him.

"I'd better go," she said, looking down at her water-soaked leather ankle boots. Perhaps tiredness had seeped into her with the rain.

"Well . . . you have my card." He stood in the doorway looking at her for a moment, leaning his forearm on the frame. When he did that, the rain felt to her like a remembered song. Then he disappeared inside.

Gretchen stared at the wet pavement, smiled and began to trudge toward Columbus. Someone came after her: Ruby.

"Hey, I'm sorry we've hardly seen each other tonight," Ruby called out to her. "Wasn't it incredible?"

"It was great. I'm glad we did this." Gretchen, hands jammed in her coat pockets, didn't feel she could go beyond short sentences. She needed to go home to savor and figure it all out.

"What's up, sweetie? You look flushed."

Gretchen's hands were sweating. Suddenly she admitted, "It's a man." She shook her head.

"Oh, you look like a little girl!"

Gretchen touched her hands to her face. "Don't, Ruby. It feels ridiculous."

"Tell me. I want to hear the story!"

"There's no story. I don't really want to say."

"Wow."

Gretchen had startled herself by her admission. It was a long time since she'd felt drawn to anyone in that way. Something to think through, not to be teased about. "Are you walking home, Ruby? Come on, let's get a cab."

"Thanks, but no—I'm going back. The night's still young! You really want to leave? I can dial you a ride." Gretchen said she'd rather walk a bit and get a taxi off the street. Ruby hugged her. "Let me know if anything happens with the guy."

"I'll—I'll give you a ring, if it does," said Gretchen, wondering if anything would even happen and, if it did, whether it would jinx things to tell.

Next morning after all the rain, Gretchen was hit by a head cold in her chilled apartment. Sitting on her scuffed couch sipping tea, she fingered Len's card. Nearby, the super knelt on her old Persian rug by one of the radiators, checking its valves like a grim physician. He'd finally responded to her pleas, now that her voice had gone hoarse.

Should she wait until her cold subsided before contacting Len? She stared at the phone as if waiting for directions. Then grabbed the receiver—she *would* leave a message with her phone number, even if she was scared of an actual conversation. He picked up.

"Gretchen? Hey, glad to hear from you. What are you up to today?"

She put a tissue to her wet nose. "Got to go back to the gallery to pull down photos from my show." In the middle of her sentence, the super banged the radiator with a crowbar. Laughing, she repeated, "I *need to take down my show.*"

"Could you use any help? Maybe some company?"

She probably didn't need help, but Gretchen heard herself say, "Sure. That would be great of you."

Two bus rides later, she arrived at LiveWire and opened it up with the curator's key. Ruby's paintings still waited for dismantling; she'd told Gretchen she was hung over but had met someone to help her later.

Len came just as Gretchen unfolded a big box. He went right to the photos and started assisting; of course, a fellow artist would, Gretchen thought. Maybe he'd helped dozens of people do this. Lifting one of her framed photos off the wall carefully, he passed it. They fell into an easy rhythm.

"Hey, I want to ask you something," he said. "Have you noticed that abandoned market on Vallejo? Petta's Market."

"I don't think so. Why?"

"Well, for years it operated as a family Italian grocery store. Now it's partly boarded-up and covered with graffiti. I bet it even has rats! If you haven't seen it, you should swing by and take a look."

"Why?" She put Styrofoam corners on a photo and set it upright in the box, with a sheet of bubble wrap around it.

"That place haunts me. Much better things could be happening in there. You know? A prime location in North Beach, the artistic capital of the whole Bay Area, and it's just an eyesore!" He handed over another photo. Gretchen liked the way he treated it like a royal artifact. He went on, "And this old market, Petta's, is enormous. It's going to waste. What if a bunch of us artists offered the owners we'd take care of it until it's sold?"

"You know that many people who'd help?"

"Hey! The city's teeming with talented people, young and old. If even a few of us are game, we can do something. Put in work spaces—because artists who want to trade ideas and do creative work in North Beach don't even have studios. I know *I* can barely afford the rent."

"Maybe it's just a sign of the times."

"But that's not good enough!"

Gretchen wasn't sure. "Why would the owners trust people to take care of the building? What's in it for them?"

Len asked her, "Should I do any wrapping?"

"No, I'm good. I have a packing system."

"Here's how I look at it," he went on. "Let's get visual artists together, and musicians, theater people. People who could enjoy collaborating. Tourists swarm around North Beach every night of the week—terrific plays could happen there! I can see it. Take care of a space that's been producing nothing but rats, clean everything up. The owners might go for the whole thing!"

"You've had successful productions?"

"Sure, yeah. Before I was an art activist I was a theater professor at San Jose State. We made decent money on our shows. Later I produced here in San Francisco. That was before I left for Europe."

Taking down photos with him had been effortless, and Gretchen now had all of them stacked in the box. To her relief, he hadn't interfered with any of her methods.

He stood facing her. His eyes in dusty afternoon light looked markedly blue against his sun-experienced face. He seemed to have just trimmed his grey hair at the bottom so it didn't quite reach his shoulders. Gretchen made a little slicing motion toward her hair and raised her eyebrows.

He got it. "I had a haircut, coming over here," he said, looking shy. "Look, I want you to see the place. The market. Leave your box here for a little? We can eat something at Trieste. If you're hungry?"

Gretchen wasn't used to spontaneity. She said, "I have to get my work out of here in half an hour—then bring it home. And I have a cold."

Len wasn't daunted. "I can put you in a cab by then. Come on, it's only a couple blocks. I'll show you."

As they walked out, narrow North Beach streets reflected the light of fresh sun after two long nights of rain. When they stopped at the boarded-up market, its door smeared with graffiti, they saw cavernous emptiness inside. Silently, Len reached for Gretchen's hand. She kept it in his.

That night, asleep in her room with lace curtains open to the full moon, Gretchen dreamed of herself as a young girl, living at home, with no experience of life. No man was supposed to be alone with her. Suddenly Len arrived, with straight grey hair like a medieval knight or page. Despite the rule, he and Gretchen found places to be by themselves. He had a circular tattoo, like the crest of a Japanese clan, under his collarbone. He explained how knowledge had been conferred on him by a mentor, and this was a sign of it. Longing, admiration, uncertainty—Gretchen felt several things at once and became pensive. Len said, "Don't look sad. Just because I have all this doesn't mean I can't be an ordinary man." Gretchen answered, "I see you have a spiritual discipline. I'd have liked a teacher, a tradition, but it's different for me." Then Len rode off on a fawn-colored horse. She could see him gallop through a valley of children boisterously spanging projectiles at each other with slingshots. Sitting proud, Len good-naturedly drove straight through. Gretchen had the tremulous sense she might not see him again.

But he came back.

The same afternoon Len helped Gretchen take her photos down, in a kitchen several blocks away Ruby's head was deep in her kitchen cupboard. Her backside protruded from it, hips swaying in work rhythm. She had on a high-necked dress from the Haight, patterned with Minnie Mouse in high-button shoes. Over it she had a black and white checkered apron.

Somebody thumped on her door. Sighing, Ruby got up, stretched and answered.

"Hey, Miss American Gothic," Satchel said gaily.

"Hate that pitchfork painting, though," she greeted him.

"Aw, gimme some sugar, babe."

"I barely know you, dude. Watch it or I'll take a pitchfork to *you*."

"What are you, an S&M freak? C'mon, chill, you look adorable. We heading down to the gallery? We need a dolly or anything?"

"If the paintings fit in your car we're fine," she told him.

"You always got an intriguing smear on you," he said, dusting an oval of white powder off her chin. "First paint, now cornstarch?"

"Boric acid."

"Good, baby. Took my advice for poisoning your little cupboard monsters. Bad bugs begone, right?" Their first phone talk had ranged from Michelangelo to mountain-climbing, and finally on to insect invasions.

"God, my whole apartment equals roach spit and roach crap. This better work." She'd poured trails of the powder everywhere. Dishes and glasses sat on all available surfaces, even stacked on the floor. Ruby wiped an arm on her forehead and slid down against the wall. Satchel joined her, and she pulled a joint out of her apron pocket.

"Damn. And so I've got a match for that, princess," he said, snapping a packet out of his too-tight jeans. "Love to light up a lady." Ruby took the first toke. A slithering sort of comfort settled on her. She passed the joint to Satchel, who inhaled vociferously. "Ahhhhh. Yeahhhh," he commented.

"We'll get the paintings shortly," she said.

"Oh, yeah," he responded, cupping the nape of her neck with his free hand. "And first we're . . . y'know, two people redefining Roach for ourselves."

"Right." She nodded. It was good and effective dope. Strong.

"Ahhhh," he said again. "Do I also smell turpentine?"

"I do use it."

"Wow. In Canada they get the essence out of their balsam firs."

Sitting by him on the floor, staring ahead, she felt his belt pressing against her side. She saw a cockroach crawl by on the linoleum, touching tentatively with its feelers. Suddenly its tiny contours looked somehow elegant. Maybe it would be dead soon; she felt sorry. She asked, "Do you think cockroaches deserve to live? I mean I kind of hope not, but who's qualified to decide?"

Satchel went on, "The ancients, in the Mediterranean, got turpentine from a terebinth tree, you know."

She shifted. *"How* would I know that? You're not listening to me."

Satchel took his hand off her shoulder. He cleared his throat. "But now I have to tell you, babe, it's toxic as hell. Guess what? Gonna ruin your lungs this way. You know?"

Ruby frowned. She said saucily, "I just met you, and you're calling me on my shit. You could leave some space for discovery." A little ashamed of her irritation, she wondered if he invited bitchiness like a style of flirting. But she didn't like to be lectured.

He laughed, though. "It's nice you make me smile," he said.

"Okay." She relented. "You can tell me more esoteric stuff about turpentine."

"And, but so, terebinth is in the pistachio family," he went on.

"No kidding. Pistachio's my favorite." She wanted to see him as that guy again with the sea-green eyes, from their first minutes in the café, the one who liked that she'd been in a punk band, who later promised at the show to help her pack and carry paintings. She looked to see if he still was or had been. His eyes were a darker hazel color, but they were shining in a way she could keep looking at.

He waved one arm in the smoke between them. "I'm gonna be your favorite," he said firmly. "You'll see."

13. PIGEON-BLOOD RUBY

The waiting room smelled like carpet cleaner. It looked like any regular doctor's waiting room—magazines, blond-wood tables, chairs against the wall. But it wasn't a normal waiting room. Soon Ruby would have to walk through swinging doors into a small white hospital cubicle. Wire was going to penetrate her breast, marking one of two places. The first one, the tumor, was a self-evident lump, already targeted to be cut out. The second one, to be marked by wire, was prep for the biopsy on a calcified place above the lump. Afterward, surgery would mean cutting out the tumor substantially, and biopsies of both areas.

Gretchen sat by Ruby. She had helped with the forms, making sure the hospital could supply financial assistance; Ruby had no health insurance. Now, Gretchen handed her a *People* magazine. Gripping pages, Ruby buried her face in nine pages with photos of movie starlets wearing the same short green taffeta dress—puffy sleeves, ruched cummerbunds, borrowed diamonds. She kept re-reading the headline, "Who Wears It Best?" along with names, sites and occasions where famous young actresses had been spotted in the dress. Each time she came to the end of the page she started over, unable to take in what she'd seen. Her throat felt dry, and she kept gulping.

Gretchen, who had been watching this, leaned in. "Oh, look, Annette Bening. I love her."

"Totally," Ruby said, and turned a page. Little-boy haircuts, waves, another one rough and wind-distressed.

Gretchen pointed to that. "Who's the actress with the shaggy neon-red hair? Like Raggedy Andy in a tsunami?"

Ruby laughed and read the caption, *Franka Potente in Run Lola Run*. "Actually, it's gorgeous. I want that hair," she said. "But I'm too curly, and you're just trying to distract me."

"Ruby A—reeeena!" a nurse with a chart called from the hall door.

"A-*reh*-na," Ruby corrected her anxiously.

"Can I come, too?" Gretchen asked.

The nurse said, "No. Afterward, you can walk her to surgery," Her tone was officious.

As Ruby got up and followed, she turned back to see Gretchen waving and smiling. It helped. Brisk and distant, the nurse guided Ruby through the heavy door that would lead to the room where they planned to start invading her body. She felt estranged and terrified.

Next she had to change into a navy-blue-pocked hospital gown; she couldn't get her ties right, in front. Before going to the actual surgery she waited, standing, at the center of a small cold exam room full of machines. The technician who came in was a woman. Ruby was glad for that. She had to let her right breast be squeezed between horizontal plates.

"What's this for?" she asked.

"Like a mammogram," the technician said, "only I'm going to put in a wire that will show the surgeon exactly where the calcified area is."

The lengthy process of threading a wire into her seemed delicate, endless, and as tense as defusing a bomb. All of it was coordinated by live camera, which she could not see, since it was in an adjoining room. In that room, a hidden radiologist viewed a projection of what the technician was doing to her, while harsh metal plates hid her breast from her own view. Ruby couldn't believe they gave her no anesthesia. The plates pressed tighter, above and below—

squashing her tumor. It hurt even more than the hand-inserted wire, which snaked toward the calcified place they'd told her was a second site of cancer. She gave a low groan. Her young Asian technician, friendlier than the nurse, said, "Sorry—a little longer. I know it's rough, but we need to get this right."

"Isn't there a better way?"

"We're trying for a new machine, but this one's fine."

Ruby bit her lips as she went through four full-pressure mammograms.

Then she was told to lie down on a gurney in the floppy gown and get pre-medicated intravenously for her operation. Ruby had chosen to stay semi-awake instead of being put to sleep, because she couldn't afford full anesthesia. Gretchen was allowed to come in for a short time. Her eyes looked squinted, loving and worried. Ruby, starting to feel a little buzzed, told her, "Lying around here like this is weird. I have about two ways I know how to be; one is Warp Speed." Gretchen laughed.

A burly black orderly showed up to wheel Ruby away. "I heard that. What's your only other speed, 'Warning, Battery Exhausted?' "

"Actually, yes," Ruby said. She was glad when Gretchen laughed again, instead of using words. Ruby heard herself echo the laugh, and it sounded loud, but she felt glad about that too. Pushing the gurney to surgery, the orderly was adept—and fast. Ruby said, "You always drive this way?"

He said, "Yeah, no worries. You'll be okay in there, young lady."

Gretchen's face looked still, even a little bit timeless, the first thing Ruby had truly seen since they arrived. Gretchen gave Ruby a good-bye kiss on the forehead.

Once in the narrow grey room, she received Versed through her IV. Ruby expected to watch the whole procedure, but the surgeon set up a paper barrier in front of her shoulders so that she couldn't. More hiding. The pain kept slashing, despite locally-numbing injections. While being cut, Ruby had to ask, "*Please* give me something more for pain!" They did. Several times.

Finally the surgeon told her, "Tumor's out."

"I want to see it. Let me see it!" Ruby insisted, breathless. The doctor held up an irregular, gristle-threaded lump like a ripped-off section of raw fatty chicken, the width of Ruby's thumb.

Only two days later Ruby and Gretchen sat across from each other at Vesuvio, Ruby's favorite bar. Ruby held a whisky tumbler with both hands. The two of them sat against the upstairs balcony railing, overlooking an immense wall of varicolored liqueurs. Leaded-glass lamps hung from the high ceiling. And a steady din of conversation reverberated around dark walls encrusted with paintings.

For once, Gretchen wasn't taking pictures. She said, "Isn't it too soon for you to do this after your surgery? I wish they would've kept you in the hospital a few days."

"Hey! Cheapest way was get out the same day, and they let me! Girl, I *need* to be here today."

"You haven't told me much. Is it out? Are you okay?"

"As far as I know."

Gretchen paused, looked out the window to a vivid new alley mural. She had to say it: "What about that other calcified area? Any chance of a second operation?"

Ruby snorted. "They already did! The surgeon with her big man-hands took two giant chunks out of me. Geez Louise! She said she had to. Like, 'Never mind, cutie, it'll save you a lot of other treatments later.' "

"They did *two* surgeries on you?"

"Two lumpectomies on the same side. Even though I didn't want to get cut twice the same day. And it really hurt. I'm extra pain-sensitive."

"Wow. I know they had to take out the breast tumor, but if they did anything more, wasn't that going to be another time?"

"Exactly! With my say-so. They did anyway!" She waved her hands around. Her eyes were a little glassy.

"Hmmmm." Gretchen frowned. "You think they were too quick to cut you that much?"

"Whatevs. She mighta-coulda done it for the hell of it. I been avoiding the medical profession my whole life."

"Maybe your surgeon worried you wouldn't come back a second time?"

"Yeah! Well, no. How the hell should I know?" Ruby shuddered. "I'm fine! But if they want me to do radiation or fucking-anything *more*, I won't! Bastards."

"Ruby, come on. You can't let that get in the way if you need chemo or—"

"I don't! Not going to. So, fine . . . one of my tits is smaller now. I don't care. I'm *glad*, because all crappy cells are out of there; it's over."

Gretchen shook her head impatiently. "We can go back and get answers. We'll write a list of what to find out."

"Why make a big deal out of it?" Ruby's eyes went hard.

"Let's find out what you're facing. I want *you* to know!"

"Don't put bad vibes on me, Gretchen. I'm fine!" Grimacing, she took a defiant slug of whisky, throwing back her head.

Gretchen stared. Then she said quietly, "Will you go to your follow-up appointment? Please?"

"Prob'ly. Today I'm just gonna be glad to be alive!"

"Okay." Gretchen, who didn't drink much or often, put down her lemonade. "Ruby, I have something to give you."

"That's why your backpack looks like you're moving to China?"

"Yes. You told me on the way to the hospital that you wanted to make movies."

"I did? . . . I *do*."

"Well, here." Gretchen's face turned excited as she took out an old video camera. She grinned.

"Oh, God! Yours?"

"I don't need it now," Gretchen said. "You need it." She handed it to her. Surprised and happy, Ruby carefully avoided her cauterized right chest as she held it close.

That evening Gretchen sat at her table, face serious and focused, with her long straight lashes and no makeup. Photos she'd taken of an old stone wall had turned out well. A tree behind a streetlight and a passing woman all stood as dark verticals against the old pocked wall. Only black and white could have delivered the sense of dignity and aloneness in this image. Gretchen smiled.

She heard a loud knock on her door and quickly went to look through the glass peephole. A solidly-built, poised-looking man stood holding a fedora.

"Who is it?" she called warily.

"Benedict Di Noti," he answered behind the door. "Are you Gretchen? My family owns your building." Through the peephole she saw he had a barrel chest, small legs. His tightly wavy hair, poufed a little in front, was completely white, and over his black eyes, thick authoritative eyebrows held their own.

"I'm Gretchen Wilson, yes." She opened the door partway. There was a penetrating attack of aftershave.

"Hello, then. May I come in? I'd like to check with you about something." Was anything wrong? He looked amiable enough, with his friendly smile.

"Okay, sure. Can I get you some water?" Gretchen asked nervously. He wore an expensive-looking brown suit with a tie clip and starched shirt. Gretchen clutched her patched sweater around her ribs, feeling embarrassed in house slippers and old tights.

"No, thank you. I wanted to say you've always been a good tenant. I appreciate it." He remained just inside the door with his hat in his hand, as if there was something to feel humble about. But there was no uncertainty in his stance or his words. He looked her directly in the face.

"Well, thank you, Mr. . . . Denotee. Actually, I'm surprised you said that. I'm desperate to get the heat fixed, and I keep calling your office. Nobody calls back. As you can tell, it's very cold."

Now he smiled oddly, crookedly. What was he thinking? "So sorry to hear that. I will take care of it. The thing is, Gretchen—may I tell you? The building has been a bum investment. I thought it was in much better shape when I bought it. There's no way I'm ever going to get my money back." Now he seemed genuinely disappointed, even sad.

"Really? That doesn't sound good. What if you make some improvements? I could suggest a few."

He nodded. "I can *make* a couple. We can talk about that. The thing is, Gretchen, you've always paid on time. And I notice you're a take-charge kind of person."

Why in the world was he here? "Well, thank you. I wouldn't *not* pay my rent. I just want to be treated fairly."

"That's what I want to talk about. I'm interested in this place being more under control of the tenants. I like my tenants to feel settled. You seem to like the place. I see you look after it." He gestured broadly with the fedora. "Maybe you'd like to get involved in running the building."

Gretchen crossed her arms and took a step back. "I don't want to be a super. I have a job." He looked a bit less imposing. Suddenly noticing the crease under his mouth, a feature she found appealing in a man of any age, she felt awkward. Her left slipper skidded slightly.

"No, I was only thinking whether my tenants have an interest in ownership. Maybe I should cut my losses. Our family feels this way. You could make a down payment, pay a little extra every month, rent to own your unit."

"Oh!" Gretchen was surprised. "I don't know what to say." Haltingly she added, "What about the heat? . . . It's serious, I mean it."

"I'll have it fixed. Think about whether you'd like to buy your place." Maybe his idea wasn't so bad? At least she could look into it. Would it turn out to be a co-op? If the landlords still had control, who would have responsibilities for repairs? Or decide any upgrades to the building? And what if she got caught up in administrative matters and had no real time and energy for photography? As he left, she thought his idea was already challenging.

She spent another hour working. Gretchen had been something of a purist about her pictures from the start. Though she sometimes used the small digital camera, she preferred her old camera and a process that had no use for Photoshop and cropping. The thrill of seeing, of embracing a moment, a person, a sidewalk or tree as it showed itself right then—that was everything. Her camera, its shape in her hands, its sounds kept her company. She still used hard-to-find black-and-white Pan-X film, for its amazing range of tones. Since she no longer had a darkroom, she'd found a photo lab she could count on to develop and print for her. Even without the excitement of what came out of her photo tray in darkness, she'd made herself learn to savor her quiet wait for the lab. Crucially, as her practice strengthened, the prints showed the impact of moments she'd seen.

Time to turn in. She got ready for bed as usual: wash-cloth, brush, floss, mouthwash, pomegranate hand lotion.

But instead of her usual truce with a cold bed in the dark, she floated into dreamy thought. Gretchen began remembering her lovers. She had come late to sexual love. In her teens, she'd been absorbed in wondering about the nature of consciousness and how languages create mutual agreements. She'd worried about what was real, what death meant, how to live in some fully expressive and creative way. She hadn't thought much about men, except to wish for respect and attention. Therefore, physical love had come as a transformation. At forty-five, she saw it had eclipsed so much else in those early years. For a long time it had seemed the essential beauty in life.

Yet with her first, a shy, mystical boy her age, it would take so long to reach climax that she'd cry with relief as well as joy. Later, one of her professors had fallen for her with the yearning of the damned; it had been fearful and glorious, then steady and considerate, and finally too much in service to his grooves of living. Then there was one who moved like a young strong animal; it put her in mind of a leaping horse. He would lie happily beside her afterward, without speech. That one had made her body respond even before her mind discovered him as a gifted, sensitive pianist. It amazed Gretchen how different men were in bed.

One had been difficult—it took hours every time to arrive at an actual sexual encounter, even when they wanted to. Why had she allowed this for so long? Gretchen thought back to when she saw him the first time. He'd been featured at a jazz club, playing a drum solo with an unusually varied kit. He hit everything in it, riffing and blazing with an intensity that somehow seemed beyond any calling she'd seen. His phrasings splashed and spilled, knotted and spread. His sweating face looked devoured by the need to pour an immense force into percussive fact. Some listeners rocked with closed eyes, others let out a whistle or yell, but she had to watch his face.

The program's liner notes said he'd served in the Vietnam War. It still struck her when she thought about him, because for her generation that war's history shaped so much of who they were, who they became. Still were. Was she ever in love with him for himself, or was it indissoluble from his immersion in the war? Beneath his swagger was a heart she wanted to protect. She'd waited for the times he trusted her enough to show what had been done to him. Even though he hardly ever alluded to it.

As her lover, he made passionate declarations or told improbable stories about his own shady dealings in other countries, then professed that the light was wrong or worried extravagantly about possible failure of birth control. They would start and stop sex and start again, not only during the act, but in their intentions between episodes. One theme: had he really finished with his wife, whom he called his ex-wife, or might they get back together? Another theme: he felt she looked at other men—was it true? He kept asking. These constant preoccupations took the place of closeness. Gretchen finally had to conclude—though reluctantly—that he needed his recriminations, tears and complications, no matter how much she wanted to wrap herself around his pain.

That was Satchel.

"Baby, you lit me the first time I looked at you," Satchel said. He and Ruby played with each other's hands.

She laughed richly and asked, "What was it about me? My eyes?"

"Your name."

"What? When you *looked* at me?"

"Quiet. There are two types of rubies, Indian, which are pink, and pigeon-blood, the Burmese rubies. You have to examine their color in morning light to know they're what they *are*. I used to smuggle pigeon-blood rubies in Burma."

"Shut up, you did not."

"At the time I had a restaurant in Rangoon. Please understand that when you do this, you have to deal with the Triad." He crossed his arms under his head, the better to recount his story, and stared at the ceiling. "And, but . . . so you can't ignore them; they own everything and they don't just go away. I had to go into this mine for them, posing as a tourist. I got a ruby down there that was over a carat—damned expensive stone."

Ruby leaned toward him. *"Pigeon blood?"* she whispered.

"It's like this. Rubies are graded by color clarity, carat and cut. The sellers take out a dagger, jab it through a pigeon's heart, and put a drop of its blood on a paper next to the ruby, right in front of your eyes. You can see the color's the same. That's if you have a good eye, which I do."

"Yeah, I'm pretty sure you're full of shit. But you're cute, so maybe—"

He threw himself across Ruby and shut her mouth with kisses.

14. OBJECTS CLOSER THAN THEY APPEAR

Satchel went to Gretchen's apartment to explain the thing she didn't know.

"What do you mean? . . ." Her voice rose, uncharacteristically shrill.

"We're inseparable."

"What are you talking about?"

"No, yeah, it's true. Ruby and I have hardly been out of each other's sight for six days."

"Where? How?" Gretchen sputtered.

Satchel laughed. "See, I stay over there with *her* now, at her pad." It was like him to use anachronisms when he was keyed up. He ripped a cigarette out of his pocket and started to light it.

"Satchel, don't do—"

"Oh, your lungs, I forgot."

In her mind she said *You always did*. He'd invited himself over to deliver this speech. All of it was infuriating. She resisted that feeling; self-possession mattered to Gretchen. So she thought: *How silly. It's not like I actually want him back*. But she wasn't ready to calm down. She said to him aloud, "You had to pick my friend?" Then it came rushing. "Goddamn it. How could you *do* that to me? You—"

He wheeled and grabbed her forearm. "That's . . . that's not right, Gretchen. Saying that—it's not even you."

"Let go!" She pulled away and rubbed her extricated arm as though he'd hurt it. He hadn't, but her outburst had made everything worse. She thought of herself as someone who didn't lose her temper. Now she had. "Just don't tell me any details," she said. Pulling into distance, she went on, "Maybe I can get used to it."

His eyes went harsh. "Will you?" he said loudly, as though he hoped not.

Gretchen's face went awry as a new thought took over. "Do you take care of her? She's recovering from surgery, you know."

"Of course I know!" Then he went into what she thought of as his customary remorseless slouch.

Under her breath she cursed that. That posturing. As though he'd been through enough when he was barely a man that now he could play it however he felt, on any given day. Sometimes he blustered, but with her, when he was caught out he often slouched in this tiresome, fake-looking way. Finally she said, "Satch . . . it's not a good time; I've got work to do."

Satchel turned his back and left impatiently. Gretchen shut the door on his retreat. Shaking, she made herself breathe even breaths. The phone began to ring. That would be Len. Satchel, still standing outside the locked door, started to knock. But she went to the phone gratefully.

Len Considine knew how to take a stance. Any time he went to a new city he'd poke and peek, feel out interests like his. In this way, along with time spent in local coffeehouses enjoying people he met, he'd cultivate whoever might join what he wanted to do: street theater, art shows, media interviews connected to these. He wasn't picky. He believed in room for many approaches to the same ends, and his indifference to quashing any of them gave him resilience.

Big-boned and self-possessed, he was liked by enough people to feel easy entering new domains. He had a certainty that people working together with heart could transform any aspect of life. When directing a play, he let the actors engage strongly in its content. One year he collected actors through a jaunty newspaper ad, drove them out to the country, instructed them to come up with as many funny improvisations as possible, then sat on a barn roof all afternoon nursing a thermos of coffee—waiting. He could hear rumbles of laughter. As soon as it started ringing across the field uncontrollably he grinned, leapt down and started the fine and sweaty work of binding it all into his skeleton of a play. The actors had already fallen in love with Len's adventure.

Gretchen and Len sat outside Caffé Trieste at a small table. "My favorite place," he said. A tall Chinese woman with long hair wearing a black suit walked by, carrying a portfolio. The father of a little girl wiped his child's face, as she stood with an ice cream cone. Two giggling teenagers zipped past with a few energetic dogs on leashes. An entire row of people sat in chairs in front of the windows, watching it all. These chairs let them sit for hours sipping espresso, taking the sun, reading news—one absently playing a banjo—and everyone faced the street. Len and Gretchen's table sat so close to the curb they were practically *in* the street.

"So what do you want out of life, Gretchen?"

Gretchen looked down and smiled. "To keep making pictures the oldtime way. Faces, bodies. Cities behind those moments. Mostly black and white."

"That's all?"

She laughed. "What about you? What are *you* after?"

Len beamed. "Another kind of world! Nothing less."

"Wow, such a modest ambition."

"Yeah. I've felt like this for a long time. Don't get me wrong, I wasn't born idealistic."

"No? Then how did it go?"

"Grew up rough in Richmond. Both of my folks were welders during the World War. Those heavy-lifters working the Oakland shipyards? That was them. I did fine with how we lived, though. A lot of guys whine about how bad it was running around, skipping school and stealing—crazy stuff. I did all that. Got caught sometimes."

Gretchen said, "That doesn't sound so good."

"But I did have it good. My buddies and I spent all the time we could on the beach. Playing ball, goofing off. I had a happy childhood."

Gretchen laughed again.

Len went on, "Your pictures . . . you seem to have a lot of discipline. I'm impressed. Can I see more?"

"Hmm. You could see one right now. I brought it in case you asked," she said softly. It was a spare interior, darkly lit, with paintings or photos on a wall, a single chair. She handed it to him.

Len pored over the image, then looked at her closer, as if trying to place what he felt. "I'd like to see anything you've done. As much as you want to share."

"That's . . . it's great. I want to see your art too."

"Sure. Come over and I'll show you the whole deal. I have all kinds of documentation on what I've done. The theater pieces too. This photo of yours—is it of a gallery?"

"No, a wall of my room. When I'm playing with digital, that's where I work."

"Your bedroom?" Len repeated. "A lot of black and white. It looks austere." Gretchen could have taken offense, but he sounded awestruck, not condemnatory.

"Len, is there a reason you're in the Bay Area right now? You said you'd been in Australia."

"Actually, I was kicked out of Australia for my plays."

"Oh." For some reason this dispelled her shyness. "So now you're going to try them out in wild and free San Francisco?"

"You bet! I'm crazy about San Fran. It's a hub of the universe. All the talented people around. So much we could do! And then when there's an opportunity to go somewhere else on the globe, I'll be hopping that way."

"Wow. You seem to have a lot in motion."

"Damn right." He grinned at her. "I have a friend that just went to India with a project to get some villagers in better financial shape. There's also a group in Prague doing great stuff with puppets, theater and protest against work conditions, and I know them too. . . . Ahh, so much always coming up!"

Gretchen sat thoughtfully. He seemed hungry for all this adventure. Her heart sank a little. How could she fit into it, ever?

Len changed his tone and said, "Are you okay?"

Suddenly she felt natural with him—as when they'd taken down the photos together—enough to open up about other things. "I'm worried about my friend Ruby. She just had breast surgery for early cancer."

Len raised his eyebrows and murmured, "I'm sorry. What's going on?"

"She basically stayed awake for the operation, just light sedation, because being unconscious would cost more. Now she's acting dismissive. . . . She has questions about why they handled her treatment the way they did, but she doesn't want to go back to the surgeon. I'm not sure what happens if she won't."

He said brightly, "That's what we pay doctors for, to do their job. She should let them decide."

"Well, I'm not exactly saying that. I think she should find out why they managed it so aggressively. What they think the deal is . . . what might happen. And the options."

"We have her medical life all figured out for her!"

Gretchen laughed again. "I'd feel better if she'd just return calls. . . . I guess she'll handle it. But it's hard to watch." Gretchen dropped her hands to her lap.

"Yeah, I can tell this is tough." Len sighed and took her hand. Finally he said, "Listen, I'd like to invite you to a meeting. Bring your friend if she wants to come."

They were back at LiveWire—Gretchen, Ruby, Satchel and about fourteen other people, sitting on folding chairs or crouching on the floor. A few fit on a long seat under the large, bright front window. Len stood in front of the same gallery wall where Gretchen's pictures had hung. Now it had an easel with a big tablet. Len said, "Thanks for turning out. . . . Right now we have a chance to get hold of a space on a prime corner of North Beach that has turned into a miserable wreck. If we artists clean up that place, the old Petta's Market, we can do so many great things with it."

Len didn't raise his voice. He didn't have to. Quiet passion was evident in his stance, his face and his inflection. "Petta's Market was a neighborhood grocery for seventy years, and now it's nothing but graffiti and dirt. Someplace to piss on in the middle of the night. It's not just offensive to tourists! It's offensive to us. We work here, some of us live here . . . a lot of us have to do both in crowded circumstances." A young woman eating a plum stopped to listen closely. "This space in the heart of North Beach could be fantastic to work and show our work. All it needs is clean-up! If we get the owners to let us use the place, we'll take care of it and keep it safe for them until they sell. We can do it. What do you say?"

Clapping, people got up to sign their names on the big easel tablet. Len tore sheets off the tablet, and Gretchen taped them to the wall. People chose what to do—researching North Beach history, finding out who owned the building, asking local merchants for support. Almost every person signed at least one. Only one guy, who looked ragged and inebriated, walked out. Somebody added "printing flyers." And they decided to call themselves North Beach Artists. Gretchen was surprised when Satchel pitched in enthusiastically.

After the meeting, they milled around, talking outside the storefront in gathering dark, and loose groups began moving toward Caffé Trieste. Inside, only three tables under the celebrity photos stood isolated. The others had been shoved together, and patrons liked it that way. They could kibbitz, kid around, and test ideas against all kinds of people. Tonight the crowd was a mix of old poets, young travelers, Italian immigrants, and teachers from New College in tight black turtlenecks. By the time Len and Gretchen got there, they found several people holding forth at once. Satchel was already one of them, flanked by Ruby. Pale but beaming, she looked like a recovering woman.

"Two thirds of the universe has Dark Energy," Satchel was saying with broad gestures. "Hey, man!" he called to Len. "Over here." Len indicated a chair for Gretchen and took one beside her. "The other third of the universe," Satchel went on, "is dark matter—which you can't even see with a telescope. Dark matter! All mixed up with the usual atoms."

Gretchen, awkward at having to sit with Satchel and Ruby, said, "How did you come up with that, two thirds of everything 'dark energy'?"

Satchel leaned forward on his elbows, warming to controversy. "It was a ten-year project checking bent light from quasars. Dark Energy's an outer-space idea Einstein toyed with, but even he decided it was a crappy idea—but now there's evidence. See, now, with your gravitational lens, two images of a quasar appear, but they're so close together you can't—you can't even distinguish them. So, but with modern lenses they make images of a *huge* number of quasars."

Len said cheerfully, "Didn't they use radio telescopes?"

"Yeah, dude, yeah. University of Manchester."

Gretchen said, "Sorry, but what's a quasar?"

"So anyway," Satchel went on, "Dark Energy causes the universe to expand—faster, not slower. Nobody knows what Dark Energy is! You can't see it, smell it—you only get radio pictures of the dance it's doing out there—like flashing light in a dance club!"

"I don't know," said Gretchen. "Sounds like science fiction to me."

Satch tapped his forefinger on her head. "Believe, believe, baby! The old Satchmo knows what the hell." Mortified, Gretchen pushed his hand away. In the vivacious coffeehouse scene, all the pronouncements and jostling ideas would have unsettled her even if she didn't have to sniff Satchel's self-absorption.

Len, who knew nothing about their past connection, seemed to take things on their own terms and rise to the subject at hand. Turning to Gretchen, he said earnestly, "The way I understand, the quasar is a starlike mass with a frightful amount of energy, incredibly bright, probably ancient, probably with a black hole powering its center. . . . If dark matter's out there, and if we're reading its effects correctly, you know, on matter that we *can* see . . . well, however *much* of it there is will hugely affect our fate. Our world and our galaxy."

Gretchen was glad he'd answered her, but she felt suspicious of all these shapely notions. Knowledge didn't resonate with her unless she owned it through experience or dreams. She said, "Maybe 'dark energy' is just a term, a marker, for something we hardly have information about. In a few years, there'll be a different interpretation."

"So what?" Satchel said crossly. "There's already different theories to explain it, three of them, that are very strong concepts right now."

"That's cool," Ruby said appreciatively.

Satchel squirmed happily in his chair. "Guess what? The theories," he said, "also have sexy names: Hot Dark Matter, Warm Dark Matter and Cold Dark Matter."

"Out of sight!" Ruby said.

"I haven't heard that since the sixties," Gretchen said. Immediately she regretted her reaction to the live version of Ruby's hand on Satchel's arm.

"I got inspired. Go, Satchi." Ruby smiled.

He grinned back. "Obviously I'm Hot Dark Matter. I have unexplained gravitational effects." He swiped two fingers along the rim of his cappuccino and licked off the foam.

Embarrassed, Gretchen stroked her greying hair.

Len's attention had wandered. If he sensed any petty dynamics, he seemed averse. Putting a hand on Gretchen's shoulder, he stood and walked off to talk to someone about Petta's Market. She heard him say, "We've been talking about an idea for an artists' space near here." Looking at his empty chair, she felt a pang of disappointment.

"I still don't get what quasars are," Gretchen concluded.

Ruby lay silently, face-up in the blackness of her room. Satchel's arm rested on her stomach, a substantial bulwark against her physical pain. She could tell by his breathing that he was already asleep. Sounds in the building twirped faintly. Cars passed, and a line of moonlight showed under the window blinds. "You sure this is all right, baby?" he'd said. She reassured him that it was already a week; the doctor said in a week she could do what she felt up to. "So let's get back to making it," she'd told him.

She felt after-sex sleepiness. Wet salt was slowly drying on her forehead. Between her breasts the sweat settled into a pool, then trickled down. She shifted to keep it on her good side.

Wondering over Satch and his impulsive, commanding moves, she noticed how sweaty she still was. At nearly forty, she felt more attached to sex than ever, and although she'd found Satch was fifty-one, not "a few" years older than her like he'd put it, he never seemed to wear out. The surgeon would probably be horrified, she thought, smiling broadly in the dark.

She ran her hand across her cheeks and between her breasts. Sleep would do her good. She breathed gently, in synch with Satch. Wetness kept tickling her, and she dabbed with the sheet and then pulled it round her, sinking into comfort, heavy and still. . . .

Was she asleep? She had been. Floating? No, of course not. In water? She felt drenched. The bed, the undersheet. Irritated, she woke more fully. Why was she sweating like this? Also her breast hurt badly. She reached to the bed, damp next to her wound.

Why was it so wet? She rolled toward the bed's edge, disengaging Satchel's arm that still wrapped her waist. Slowly she felt her way barefoot to the bathroom. A stream of wet passed down her side. The danger side.

Alarmed, she grasped at the bathroom light. What she saw just could not be. Ruby stood before a mirror and saw her breast hanging!—sliced through. Her whole right side, skinned-rabbit from collarbone to waist, divided in half, knife-hung open. Ruby's hands hit her mouth first but the scream came anyway. Her body was claved inside-out.

"Ruby? What the hell?" came a muffled call from the bedroom.

She grabbed to push her breast back on with one hand and slammed with the other, to shut the door.

"Go back to bed. . . . It's a problem with stitches."

"Let me see."

"No! Oh, my God. Call my surgeon! The number's on my cell next to the bed."

"Damn. What am I supposed to say?"

Ruby's heart beat so hard she nearly fell. "The cauterization's bad. And then go back to bed! Let me be!"

She heard him grumbling, but after a few door-pounds he shuffled off. She lifted and pressed at her breast with both hands, to stick it back in place. It wouldn't. With violently trembling fingers, she raked at a cabinet, grabbed the box of band-aids that jumped from her and scattered on the floor. Paralyzed with unlikeliness, she couldn't fully feel the pain or even her own feet on the floor. Crying and gasping, she pressed a few large bandages against herself with all her might. They weren't enough, so she cut lengths of white adhesive tape instead, and forced the wound back together.

Her breast stayed up.

The cell phone rang, jangling into the old Eagles song "One of These Nights"—he'd obeyed her after all. After a moment Satchel yelled, "She wants to talk to you."

"Pass it through the door!" Her cell phone reached in and she grabbed it, slamming the door again.

The surgeon said sharply, *"Yess!* It's three a.m."

"You told me to call if I need to. My breast is falling off."

"That's not possible," the doctor said curtly.

"Fuck, don't tell me that. It was down to my waist! The stitches opened up and it just fell wide open."

"All right, Miss Arena. I didn't expect that. I've seen it in the literature, but it's rare. You can call an ambulance if you wish."

"Stop it! Just tell me what to do."

"Tape it with whatever you have. Not electrical tape, adhesive."

"I did. . . . Do you have any idea how terrifying that was?"

"Look. Although what you're describing is quite unusual, these things can happen. What were you doing when it occurred?"

Ruby didn't speak.

"I thought so. Stop the extracurricular activities. Tell your partner to stay off it. Come to my office in the morning. We'll work you in and stitch it again. Meantime, tape it. Try to get some sleep."

Ruby felt along the wall on her way back to bed. She could dimly see the outline of Satchel's upturned face with both arms thrown over it.

"Rube," he said thickly. "This is horrible, babe."

"No, the doctor will fix me in the morning."

"It's terrible, I'm covered in bites. You have bedbugs in here!"

"How can you talk about bugs right now?"

"If you don't believe me, turn on the light. This place is serious hell."

Vigorously, she switched on the light.

Satchel swung the sheet over. "Okay, you can't see them now, but they been all over me."

"I know, I know there's something in the bed, but it's just another kind of six-legged thing. Of which there's way more than I can deal with!" She slapped the light off and lay down, not touching him, speechless.

Trying not to sob, she thought about how she'd hurt the wound. Tearing pain had finally begun to settle in. *Christ, I hate letting this happen. Jumping into the sack—wouldn't I know I wasn't ready? Didn't I? Stupid. So insensitive to myself. . . . Ahh. Help me. Something, help.*

15. POINT TENDERNESS

As the day passed, Gretchen's head ached keenly, and her cough deepened. The cold apartment had made it worse; all the radiator-banging by the super had barely warmed the place. Opening her kitchen shutter, she looked at the street, dark and immobile with wetness. Nothing moved but a small glimmer of crawling light-beads where rain joined asphalt. Her arms felt liquid and weak. She stared at chipped white polish on her fingernails. Two pointless bruises on her forearm were spreading. Her body felt foreign and viscous to her, as if melting from the inside.

She tried to rouse herself and do what she had to. Grocery shopping went undone while rain came on in earnest. For dinner she ate low-fat whole wheat crackers and reduced-fat Provolone cheese. The muffled feeling persisted, and finally she took her temperature. A hundred and one, not bad, but enough to make her feel useless.

And for Gretchen, to feel useless was to feel sad. She held her bruised arm and stroked it, like she'd gentle an animal. She fervently wished someone would bring a cup of tea. No one would hear about these hours; she disliked speaking of illness or unhappiness. Meanwhile, she lay on her bed, wrapped in a white flannel afghan, wondering about her future years. *I wonder how many I have in me.* She sighed. Would the rain stop during the night? Her cough rose in urgency and frequency.

Gretchen got up. There was a cup of tea to make, the one she'd wished brought to her. She did that. And while she swirled honey into the steaming mixture, the phone rang, and it was Len.

They talked about the rain. Gretchen said it made her apartment smell like linoleum. He said it reminded him of a cabin in Northern California he'd stayed in a while back.

"What was it like?" she asked.

"Deserted—nobody in the area knew who it belonged to. I was on my own . . . slept on the floor in a sleeping bag. I cleaned the place up, but I liked the spider webs on the ceiling."

"Did you leave them?"

"Yeah. They hung down like looping ropes. There was no electricity. In the evening, well . . . some sort of little field mice would come out and start chasing each other. They were so funny, running and somersaulting."

Gretchen asked, "What were you doing there, Len?"

"I was in a bad way. I'd been in Australia. And I didn't know what I wanted to do with my life. But I'd learned things about painting while I was over there, and I kept drawing and painting. I liked the way the aboriginals did it, and a guy I talked to showed me how he worked. When I lived in the deserted cabin, sometimes a friend or two would visit and bring me art supplies."

After a moment Gretchen said, "Tonight the rain makes me think of things I wished for when I was young."

"Feel like talking about it? What you wished—for yourself or for anything?"

She smiled with pleasure. Suddenly she felt enlivened. She *wanted* to say some things. She sat with a sense of purpose, whether she could tell it well or not. Phone in one hand, tea in the other, Gretchen started.

"Well . . . I suppose when I was young I was reaching out with both arms . . . for love, and not only that. For social justice. Both. Because of the way we came of age in the sixties and seventies. . . . I went full-out for what I wanted to do. If it had harsh consequences, that was all right . . . though sometimes later I'd find out my mistakes when they hurt people or, well, affected them ways they didn't appreciate." She took a sip of mint tea. "I've done what I wanted straight along . . . what I meant . . . like you, I suppose."

There was a pause, and she was glad he didn't fill it.

"Getting to this age that I am," she went on, "I have a different . . . I don't *expect* the same way. I'm not crushed with disappointment . . . except when I am. . . . I'm not trying to get that rush of fulfillment from someone . . ." Her fever insulated her from the need to explain. "I do what I need to, even when people won't know or won't like it."

"You're not still so attached to people? You don't feel that?" Len asked her.

"I *do*. . . . But maybe some light, some beauty shines through different people at certain moments, and it *feels* as though that's these people themselves, but something greater's only passing through them. If you have a friend or lover for a long time, it can come and go." She closed her eyes, trying for words for her feelings. "But after that person, you see it come through other beings or other things." It wasn't comfortable or easy to tell this, and she set down the cup, pulling softly at the ends of her hair. She could feel the cold air around her and that she was still feverish. "People, yes . . . but just as often trees, images, music . . . not the satisfaction I was looking for in a person, thinking that's where the beauty lives. My camera helps me find it. Then I can give it."

There was another refreshing silence.

She asked him, "When you lived at that cabin, what were you painting?"

"Mmmm. Things that intertwined, seen from above. A lizard would have long lines that reached from head to tail, black lines with running white circles, interlaced in patterns.

Meridians, I was thinking. The lizard's tongue would reach out, toward the sun or food or another lizard."

"What colors?"

"Red! Chili pepper, lemon chrome." He stopped to consider the colors, as though they came to him one at a time. "Uh . . . aspen green, sometimes emerald. Bit of cadmium white, leaning towards gardenia."

Gretchen felt a flash. "Favorite colors of mine," she said.

He laughed.

"It's funny?"

"No, it's wonderful," he said. "I ran into your favorite colors without even trying."

"Do you keep on painting like that?" Gretchen sipped at her tea and waited.

At last he said, "I do theater activism and write plays; I've kept on with it. I've even written lyrics to a few songs. But I still have the need to paint. When I can, I just paint whatever I've been sketching."

She couldn't follow the chronology of his travels, but for some reason she didn't mind. "What else did you do at the cabin?"

"There wasn't any running water. I carried it from a stream. Nobody knew I was living there, see. Or they thought maybe somebody might be—a hermit or outlaw. But they kept away. That suited me. I could spend a whole evening walking around, looking at those cobwebs in the rafters or sketching them . . . just sit with those field mice that came in. They played around the place like babies. Seemed to be having the time of their lives. I loved seeing them."

The silence that followed this was long between them. Gretchen came to the honey at the bottom of her cup. For her to feel so comfortable in silence with someone—this was new. She wondered whether or not it was, to him.

At last he said, "You've been coughing."

"I'm sick. My apartment is so cold. The building owner promised he'd fix it soon. He came by to ask if I wanted to rent to own."

"Did he tell you the price?"

"I called back the next day. He suggested I get a loan, because it could be quite a bit more than I pay now. He insisted it would be worth a lot more later."

"Oh, no!" Len said. His tone turned to disgust. "That's the oldest landlord scam around."

"Really? What do you mean?"

"Way too many things can go wrong for the buyer. If you go down that road, this landlord probably still won't cover repairs—you could be responsible for all of them, yourself. Sounds like he's already pushing to rent to you way over market price in the Tenderloin. Then if you miss a payment, you probably lose all of what you thought was your equity. Your initial payment's also non-refundable—tons of ways to get bilked. If it's rent-to-buy, before you even get to the sale the price could escalate. I know more than one person who went through those things. Even if you complete the buy, you now own property that's steadily depreciating! . . . It can be scary to stand up to guys like him. Intimidating."

Gretchen hadn't thought of it that way. With Len, many things surprised her.

Ruby, humming, walked out of her apartment and down the narrow hall, its crumbling walls slick with ancient cream-colored paint. The sound of the elevator, responding to her button-press, had a forlorn clink. She folded back the iron gate in front and went into the narrow cubicle with its high ceiling. It was poorly lit. Despite this outer gate on each floor, there had never been any door on the elevator; the grate afforded full view of passing walls and individual floors, like a freight elevator.

When she pushed an ivory button for the ground floor, nothing happened. She tried again four times, exasperated. Should she leave? Try something else? She started opening the outer grate, hoping any loose wires would wake up from impact, but it hurt where she had stitches. She quickly gave up and closed the grate.

All of a sudden the whole elevator sank about a foot, with a thud. Panicking, Ruby clutched her hands to her chest. She crouched, searching for the emergency button, and leaned her palm on it. She waited what seemed a long time, trembling, before a thin, stooped man showed up, wearing a security guard's uniform.

"What'd you do now, Miss?" he said. How could that possibly be funny? A surge of rage leapt in Ruby. Before she could say anything, *Zhooooop!* the elevator fell another foot, ending with a big clank. She shrieked and grabbed the black gate. The wounds in her breast brought her close to fainting. "Hold on, hold on!" the attendant commanded. She could only see his legs and feet. The elevator started creaking, and her heartbeat somersaulted.

"Get me out! *Now!*" Ruby begged him, frantic. He crouched, fumbled with the gate—somehow pried it open from outside—and reached down to her from above. Before he could get a good hold on her, she wrapped her hands around his wrists like a drowning victim, hauling herself all the way up to ground level.

"Okay then! Stronger than you look. But you better not try that again," he said, like a playground monitor scolding a kid. Ruby fluttered her hands and burst into exclamations of woe. "Nah, take it easy. You're all right now, you're fine." he said cheerfully, turning to leave. Then she let loose a storm of invective, but he walked away, wiping his hands on each other.

Satchel, coming through the door to her stairway, ran into her. After she told him the incident, he said haughtily, "Well, Rube, that's just the last straw. I wouldn't even get *into* that elevator again. Guess what? Your building managers, building owners—whatever—they're morons. Just, I mean, stop paying rent. Be firm. You gotta do that, babe."

"Stop paying the rent?"

"The same."

She wiped her eyes with her hand. "I was so scared, Satch! I thought I'd fall down the shaft! . . . I don't know; that's too weird what you said. They'd kick me out."

He ran his fingers through her short black curls. "They can't evict you! Get a legal advocate, babe. Or, but you know what? That guy Len is a hell of an organizer. Maybe we can squat in that building he's gonna get for an art center."

Ruby stared at him.

"They do it in Holland all the time. Hell, I've done it. Anyway, stop paying until they fix your stuff. And so, why do poor folks have to be treated like shit? Also, we're creative people. San Francisco's supposed to be the city that loves us."

"Just sit here and wait; Doctor will be with you soon." Two weeks after surgery, Ruby had extreme toothache in a long-neglected molar. Was there some kind of domino effect of cancer or surgery on the rest of her body? She was unwilling to go back to her breast surgeon, but the violence of this toothache made her rush to a dental clinic.

Half an hour later a stocky guy in a pale green gown, mask flopping round his neck, stuck his head out from an exam room calling, "Hi there, be right with you." A young woman in a similar gown, a gaping smile, and teeth too white to be real led her into the room, now empty. Ruby, whose hands had turned sweaty, settled into a massive dental chair facing a blank wall. She found nothing to look at except her coat on a hook, where it had one sleeve inside out. That made her nervous, like the clumsy sleeve could make things go wrong. After a few restless minutes she got up, tiptoed around the instrument tray, and pulled the sleeve through.

She sat in the semi-reclining seat, full of shiny white oval surfaces that felt as uncomfortable and anachronistic to her as a porcelain jewel case. Her back twitched. Finally the dentist walked in. After a lot of peering and metallic poking he declared, "This tooth has to come out! —Now, today." After a short interlude for lidocaine to take effect, he came lunging back into her mouth for a messy, loud ordeal. The sounds afflicted most, her own small squeaks lost in whir-ring, yanking, pumping and clacking. Ruby felt the taste, gritty and bitter, sinking into the crevices of her. How much more blood did she have to give? How much could she?

Back home, Ruby slept. By nightfall, sipping a thin milkshake, she had a pressing need: to sculpt a piece about all this surgery. To tell about her tumor. To say it without words or paint. It came to her arrowlike, how it should work.

What she had to have was a plastic skull. Maybe about the size of a small grapefruit. She could imagine its smooth-ness in her hand. It needed a hinged jaw; the action of this jaw would be very important. She'd put something in the mouth. It should be red. Her pain had to represent itself *in* the mouth. Chicken liver!—bloody and solid but fragile, malleable, frayed.

Film—she would make a mini-movie with the camera Gretchen had given her. The only movement should be blood slowly escaping from teeth down the jaw. White, red. And . . . black. Maybe black velvet background, like a certain kind of Mexican painting? No, texture didn't matter. It only had to throw a sort of whiteness and its self-containment into relief, against the action . . . which was that red pain. To get to the *undoing of it*, undoing the pain.

In one of the Haight's trinket shops, it didn't take long to find a plastic skull close to her idea. Chicken liver also happened to be in stock at a market. For the background of the scene, she decided on a black panel. She could arrange everything next to her stove, by the floorboards.

The actual setup complicated itself so much it astonished her. First the light was wrong, then the piece fell over, and when her chicken liver started to wear dry from testing, she had to freeze and flagellate that meat, then run hot water over it. After sixteen takes she got the right one. Ruby had found something to shout about, and she had to finish.

While she viewed her takes in the camera, Satchel walked in. He planted his fists at his hips, surveying the scene.

"Ahhh. Christ, what a downer!"

Ruby raised her eyebrows. "Hey, can't you see I'm in the middle of something?" She remained on the floor by the stove.

"Shit. I'll come back later."

"Good, 'cause I have to finish."

"Yeah. Just take a mop to it afterwards, okay? If you don't mind." His voice had an unwelcome edge.

Ruby looked up from the camera. "Don't tell me how to use my own place."

"It's stinking, Ruby."

The night before, they'd gotten drunk together at Specs bar. Since they seemed to spend all their time getting high or touching each other, Specs seemed like a fresh idea. But first he'd raved about Len's plans for the artists' space. Then he'd complained about Ruby's disordered environment: "You're a complete slob, you know that?" He'd even turned to the person next to him, someone Ruby knew, and said, "This woman's a mess."

Ruby had protested fiercely, even asking him since when his standards got so high. Satchel had leaned forward with his elbow on the sticky bar table—had gone on, "I know what it's like being around a little peace of mind. A bit of organization. One single fork in a place you could locate it." Weirdly, he had then burst into tears. Like a PTSD victim. What was his deal, anyway? And she then shrank into herself, knowing that people around them in the bar witnessed his outburst.

Now, in the apartment, he was complaining again. She gripped her camera. Frowning, he said grimly, "You're way distant today."

"Well, I'm trying to work, and my feelings are worn out."

"So? So how come you never rest? It's not helping . . ." Since he moved in, he'd stopped wearing the too-tight jeans. His new getup was flannel shirts and camp shorts with rumpled, greasy hair.

"I told you, I'm working, Satch. Find something to do. We can meet up for dinner someplace. Just go." She lifted her chin toward the door.

"There's no point in going. Probably anywhere. Probably ever. We can't leave the apartment. We'll just have to stock up on Chinese takeout."

"What?" Now he had her attention.

Satchel groaned loudly. "Thing is I can *not* be myself with you. I'm never allowed to be—to be angry or scared here. Guess what? I can't say jack. But so, like the rule is, uh, No Sudden Movements. And so you know what? It—it's like *aseismic creep*. Yeah. The only way to stay in synch here is aseismic creep."

"What the hell? I don't even know what that is."

"It's—it's the fault weaseling around at the speed of a pillbug."

"What?"

"Of a pillbug!"

"What are you even talking about? That makes no sense. The 'fault,' like the San Andreas fault?" She put down the camera.

"The same."

"Stop saying that!" Although at first Ruby had found Satchel's quirk of saying "the same" endearing, now it annoyed her.

"Jesus." He turned away, deliberately banging his forehead against the wall. "I am not used to taking care of somebody. I can't look after a person whose breast is falling off."

"It's fine! Fuck you, Satchel. I didn't ask you to." She picked up the camera again and held it tightly.

"You need a lot of taking care of. I don't care how original you are. You're a pothead drunk and I can't even find my shoes in the morning."

"I'm a drunk? Get the hell out! Go back to your mother's, or wherever you came from."

"Uh-huh. Yeah, baby. Screw you, too. Your train wreck of a life. . . . You'll be lucky if you pay your rent without me to chip in." He nodded his head wildly.

Ruby let out a squeal. "You and your pretend artists' crusade, Satch! First you don't want me to pay rent, then you threaten me because I'm not. As if you even had plans of chipping in! Go away!" She looked at him from her crouch on the floor, lit up and feral. "You piece of shit. I don't need you. I never needed you!"

"As if *that* was ever true," he muttered with a twist in his mouth. "Damn nonexistent check-up with your fucking doc. . . . You're probably AWOL from chemo right now!"

She tossed her head. The camera shook visibly in her hands. "I don't have cancer. I told you. They cut all of it out, they—"

"You don't *know* that! You're not gonna let anybody find out until you—you just—grind yourself out like a cigarette."

Ruby snorted, stood up, turned the camera on him, and started filming.

Satchel threw up his hands in disgust. Then, stumbling toward the kitchen wall, he heaved a full punch at it. A chunk of yellow plaster splattered off. Tearing into the bathroom, he bent toward the sink and, grabbing at water, splashed it onto his hand and threw handfuls at his forehead, rubbing. His eyes in the mirror looked fright-filled. He shut off the faucet, seized a toothbrush, careened out the door, and skipped raggedly downstairs.

It was three-thirty a.m. Satchel moved through a narrow, dank alley in Chinatown; damp laundry hung out the windows. Or was it extra clothes, blankets? Satchel had four shots of Jack Daniels in him. He stopped to take a swig from the bottle hidden in his inside coat pocket, then craned his neck to look for the moon. He put his pint away and strode on. Stumbling over a man lying against a brick wall he said, "Ah, sorry, man." Had he actually kicked him? He stopped abruptly to see. The man, who lay in fetal position with his head in a crooked arch against the wall, looked up, plaintive. He had pale eyes. He was not an Asian man, yet here he lay. This Chinatown alley contained him and his hopes and heart. As if they'd resided here for decades. "You okay, man?" Satchel asked. There was no answer. "So long then," Satchel said, starting to pick up his pace.

Wait was the sound that Satchel seemed to hear.

"Yeah?" he responded, squinting.

The homeless man muttered about bad motherfuckers crawling up his legs. "There's some on you too," he said, pointing to his own legs and shuddering.

"Some what?"

"Got it in for me. Turning everything the wrong color."

Satchel came closer. "Wrong color? What color do you say is right?"

The man paused. His pale hair, reddish in the night, folded lank onto his neck. He said sadly, "Blue. Thass how it s'pose to be." Satchel pulled out his wallet and handed him a five dollar bill. The man reached up. "Thanks, buddy! It woulda . . . been even better, even, if this was even blue. You got any food?"

Satchel laughed. He welcomed the peculiar color viewpoint. "Wish I had some on me for you."

"Okay. Gah bless you," the man said. Still lying down, he used a crumpled fist to get the fiver into his battered pants pocket.

Satchel hesitated a moment, then reached into his own pocket for the pint bottle. "Uh, here, man. . . . . Have it."

This brought enthusiasm to the prone figure. "Buddy, you all right!" Sitting up a bit, he accepted the liquor. Examining Satchel's face in the dim light, he said approvingly, "Looking bluish."

"No, yeah? I do? So what kind? Baby blue? Prussian blue like the crayon? Or true blue?"

The man in the alley sipped and wiped his mouth fervently. Finally he answered, "You was mostly true. Little bit baby."

Satchel laughed happily and said, "Yeah. Okay then." He saluted and walked ahead, muttering, " 'There but for the grace' . . . huh." High above, a fog-smeared, three-quarter moon appeared. A nervous look came over him as he stared at its beauty. He began to run.

"Gretchen!" he called out for no reason. Words came to him from a song he or someone had written years ago, *Spiral to the ground / Blacked outta my picture / All out of that / the that's-whereness*. "Lousy fucking song," he said, as if it were a person accusing him. His back ached, and he wondered how strong the line was between him and the drunk in the alley. Maybe even the line between Ruby and the alley? He had left Ruby to her denial. He'd gotten by with other kinds of escapes, so this one might work. Might be a keeper. There was a certain rank smell around him, engulfing. Shaking, he hurried away from the words and the smell, toward some long-forgotten bar, before it could get away.

Toward morning, after one last Jack, it was clear what he'd do. *Not* go back and beg Ruby's forgiveness. He shivered anxiously. Drive to New Mexico. There was one thing, just one thing he needed to know about his past with Gretchen. "That's where it's at," he said aloud. Then as an afterthought, "Do I ever go back to the band?" He got up in search of his car, and by sunrise he'd started the long trip.

It took longer than Satchel expected, and he only had dough for gas and a couple hot dogs or a burrito a day. He slept in the car, washed briefly at gas stations. At his destination the dirt road leading to his old place appeared deserted. There was only a sliver of moon. It made sense that no one was around—on Friday night in the South Valley of the New Mexican town, people went dancing or took their kids in pickup trucks to Mexican movies. But a few lights shone evenly from outbuildings near the one he wanted to break into. The air, cooling after a hot day, seethed with summer density. A ladder had remained where it used to be, inside an unlocked metal shed the size of a closet. He'd need to be quick. He scurried to check those lit neighborhood windows; good. No one appeared in any rooms that faced him. Faint radio music had been left on, the usual crime-deterrent when folks went out.

Silence wasn't his habit, but he managed the ladder without struggle, setting it close to the arched and shuttered window of an attic in the long building he remembered. The beer paunch he'd been slowly growing over a couple of decades influenced his agility. Easy now, one step at a time. A nasty metal tap when his foot hit a rung. *Stop it.* At the top, he made a mistake: looking down around his feet. *Jesus, what am I doing? Haha. Know perfectly well.* Mastering dizziness, he peeled back the shutters and, without rousing any local roosters, eased himself in carefully. A cobweb immediately flapped into his hair.

Eleven years ago he had stored one of Gretchen's boxes in here when she left. She'd said all right. Later he left the place, too, and she grumbled, asked him to give the box back. But shit. Let her get her own discarded memories is what he'd said. For years. Maybe he'd give her whatever he found now.

It took time to adjust to the flashlight. He wanted to sit and smoke a joint. *Later! Box first.* He snapped the string with a penknife. With his flashlight resting on the floor, the tininess of the space spooked him. Pocked beams, jags of dust. *Okay, lid off.* Her papers were so organized it was ridiculous. He went to the section Personal and then the year.

Yes. Loose pages of journaling from a time she was too hard up to spring for a blank book. He'd seen her scribbling the pages. She'd do it on buses, even standing in lines. "Why don't you use a drawing tablet or something? You'll lose them."

She'd looked at him levelly. "I won't lose them."

Ugh. . . . She had a facility for keeping things even when they were lost. Like these pages. The handwriting fluid, elegant. Every entry dated. He was searching autumn of a particular year. He scanned through flowers seen on the way to work . . . other things she was grateful for . . . job hassles . . . muddy rains. *Is that it? Shit. No, wait. Here. Here.* "While I was lying in his arms, he talked for hours about Milton, until it was unclear whether we were going to make love at all." *No, that's just me.* The main thing was had she been seeing other guys? A two-line entry in cramped handwriting read, "The ways you express your pain and the world in which you're living it out put my mind upside-down." *Still me? Drinking, throwing things, crying? For a while she was begging me not to. More . . . more . . . here!* "He has beautiful arms." *Fuck, I know that's not me. Mine were rubbery even then. There have to be details here somewhere!*

He hoped he hadn't said it out loud; there was a definite rustle. Satchel peeked carefully. Outside, below, stood a tall, muscular person. Satchel could make out a plaid shirt.

"What's going on, mister?" the tall woman said firmly.

"Yeah, sorry, I used to live here. Left some papers but, so, I came to pick them up."

"Middle of the night, and borrowing my ladder? I'd like to see your face, if you say you lived here."

Satchel put his head out a little. He felt like shouting, "Actually, that's my ladder" but restrained himself. He tried to sit straight, smile reassuringly with his large, feverishly animated, fifty-one-year old, green Irish eyes. The woman moved closer to the ladder, reached a hand toward it. Satchel's stomach clenched. *Spend the night up here—possible raccoons, rodents? And Gretchen's memories?*

He twitched again, reminded of a sound he could never stand hearing. A bomb-bursted sound. His torso did the thinking. "Hey!" he yelled to the woman, "I'm coming out." He opened the window as wide as he could and, turning away from it, bent forward. Stuck one foot and his backside through it until he found a rung. Then placed his other foot there. He backed all the way out as he held the sill and looked down for another step—but the ladder wasn't steady. It faltered and, losing his hold, he tipped into the shock of a long fall. . . .

During the woman's muffled answer, he, Satchel, felt the night air slash at great speed through his suddenly up-side-down hair of misspent years. He fell, howling, to the ground.

16. SHAKING, STANDING, NOT STANDING

It was rent day. Ruby didn't write the check. Instead she handwrote and sent the management a note about cockroaches, bedbugs, and the broken elevator. The business of pot had not gone well since she was laid up. All credit cards had maxed out; even her cell phone service was at risk.

Within a couple of evenings she received a knock on her door.

"Ruby?" His figure looked dim in the waning light of the hallway. It was an older man in a dark suit and hat. He took off his hat and grinned. He just had to be Italian-American; his wavy white hair had probably been, years ago, as black and curly as hers. She looked into his face, then at his rather elegant hands.

"Mm-hmm, yes."

"I've been hearing around the building that you had a hospital stay. How are you doing?" The fedora looked expensive, but he had a distracting shininess to his chin that didn't match. His pleasant comments seemed wrapped in a soothing aroma of aftershave, mixed with cigar smoke.

"I'm okay. . . . Say, do you live here? 'Cause I haven't seen you. How'd you know?"

"My family's connected here. Forgive me if I'm bothering you. I just want to make sure you're all right."

Ruby had barely been out of the apartment since Satchel disappeared. Cane-bottom chairs stood randomly around the room, stacked with newspapers, tubes of paint, a hairbrush and some spoons. But the last light of sunset shone brightly through her gauze curtains. Impulsively she said, "Look, I just made tea. Do you want some?"

He smiled more deeply. "That's so gracious," he said.

He was definitely a senior, but Satchel had left a week ago, without a single phone call or text. Ruby was in the mood to take a chance. She cleared off a couple of her chairs, and she and the older guy drank her tea.

He didn't say anything about her paintings on the wall or the owl skeleton over the door, but he did comment, "That's a sizeable hole in your plaster there."

Ruby cleared her throat. "Parting gesture," she said. "From a guy who's history now. Crazy! He even took my toothpaste!"

"That's terrible." He shook his head. In a soft, raspy voice, he asked, "Was he violent?"

"Not to me. Just to the wall he punched."

"What a horrible thing." He stiffened, as if he was outraged.

"You're not going to believe this," she said in a low voice, "but I took a movie of him doing that."

"You have him on film defacing the place?" His right eyelid twitched over its large dark hooded eye.

"Well, he was cruel. It's thirty seconds of him turning into a bastard."

The strange older guy tsked. He looked upset.

Ruby said, "I don't know who you are, but you're nice. What's your name?"

"Benny. Call me Benny."

How exactly did it happen? She was never able to remember the part between the kitchen chairs and the kitchen sofa. Somehow they went on to drink tequila; she must have had a lot. She did remember sitting on the sofa for a while with the visitor, and him moving closer. Finally his arm around her shoulder. She'd felt his silvery-white hair brushing her forehead and liked it.

The part she puzzled over most later was how he came to be standing in front of her with his pants open. The next day or two she felt uncomfortable looking in the mirror. Especially with one disturbing detail: sore skin surrounding her mouth. Maybe from his zipper? She'd never enjoyed that kind of sex, and she still didn't. It reminded her of when she'd gone through the same thing with her uncle at age eight. Nobody'd ever known or, as far as she knew, guessed. It still scared her too much to tell, but she knew its music. Now that this new situation was on, she had started to answer it.

This guy Benny was temporary, might get her through for a bit. Chewing her lips worriedly, she thought *Anything is better than alone right now.*

He came back Tuesday and brought flowers. Soon she had bunches of tiger lilies on the table, though some had started to look less fresh than others. It occurred to Ruby that he could afford to buy her dinner or take her to a movie, instead of her skinning her knees on the kitchen floor while they went through his standing ritual. Why did she keep doing it? Was she really so depressed that she couldn't think? Perhaps they could have regular sex. Actually, no—that would be giving him more than she wanted. Lately misery pervaded her hour after hour, and she wasn't eating properly. She must need more structure? Maybe the way he kept showing up brought some.

He called her "dear." One night after sex, they sat on her balcony and he smoked a cigar while she had a couple of joints. Stroking her short dark hair, Benny said, "You're young and beautiful. I want you to know this, dear—no strings attached. If you want to see other people, it's fine."

There was a lot of tequila involved, mostly on her part. Once he brought amaretto. Sometimes, while he sipped and she drank shots, he talked. She let him. He sat in one of his fine suits on her rickety chair, forehead gleaming broadly, gesturing with his hands. He used them in a rigid position that could have been prayer when he was a kid, but over time the two hands had separated; he'd slap them up and down like flippers with a jerk at the end, as if he was making an important point, although he wasn't. Ruby watched this peculiar, emphatic gesture he directed toward the slats in her wooden balcony floor. His words seemed to walk around the balcony without engaging her. Watching stars and rooftops, her mind would drift in and out of the places he liked to go with his voice: cars, expensive food, golf.

Ruby felt too unhappy to work on her art. Afternoon light slanted into her kitchen; she sat on the floor, just where she'd been that final moment Satchel walked into the room. For the fourth time that day she picked up the video camera Gretchen gave her and, in its viewer, watched the footage she'd taken of her art piece about being cut. No sound. A skull appeared, stark white against black. It had a tongue. It shuddered like it wanted to speak. But all that came out was blood. Solid shining forbidding red. The skull's eyes showed worry, which she'd wanted in it as an art piece. But then a shift she never planned had occurred: the view went crook-ed, and something large swept past. All became white and shaky . . . slowly clustering around a human head and torso. A disheveled, annoyed man. A man whose shirt flapped as he lifted his hands. Dismissively. His eyes stared, antag-onized and red. His mouth moved. His eyes widened with anger. There were short pauses between movements of the furious mouth.

Then came a sudden lurch—Ruby knew what matched it—remembered the loud thump. She still couldn't believe her reflexes had been fast enough to follow him and zoom in. The whole image became a white mass crumbling, and this image shook, blurred and rippled. It shifted back to his body, growing smaller as he turned from his punch at the wall and moved away fast. Then—there would have been a whack—a door swooped shut: he had disappeared into it. The door stood closed. At last a grey snowstorm of blank footage said good-bye to what just happened.

Ruby rewound the film so she could watch it again.

Gretchen stopped by Ruby's. They sat at her old splintered-wood kitchen table. Ruby said she'd see her doctor for a follow-up soon, though her tone wasn't convincing.

She went on, "I'm okay. And I've been hanging out with somebody. At first I thought it was just a one night stand."

"Well, I suppose we've all been there. Who is he? What does he do?"

Ruby ruffled her dark hair. "His name is Benny. I guess he's retired. He seems to have money."

"Is he spending any of it on you?"

"He brings me flowers."

"That's nice. Does he like your painting?"

"We don't talk about that. It's not anything serious. I wasn't thinking when I got into it. I just find him . . . I don't know. It helps. Satch took off."

Gretchen hesitated. "Ruby . . . you know Satchel and I were together for a couple of years in New Mexico? That is, if you can call it together. He and his wife had separated."

"I'm sorry, Gretchen. I didn't know until I already fell for him."

"It's all right. I'm just saying he can't make up his mind about things. He acts silly and sometimes mean, but he has a harder time than he says. Seeing him with you felt weird at first, but you've probably been good for him. I hope it took his mind off himself."

"Why're you so forgiving? Not just toward me, but . . . why put up with him being such a dick? Even you do it. Are you even more reality-impaired than me?"

Gretchen smiled a little wanly. "I thought I could help him. Always did. I wanted to."

Ruby shook her head dismissively. Then she leaned her elbows on the table and started to cry. "Benny cares about me, I think."

"The new guy?"

"Yeah," Ruby said in a small voice. "Benny Da Noti."

"Wait. Did you say Di Noti?" Ruby nodded. Gretchen asked, "What does he look like? Wavy white hair? Does he wear a, you know, a fedora?"

Ruby frowned and nodded again. "You *know* Benny?"

Gretchen said, "Benedict Di Noti? Christ, Ruby. He owns my building! He tried to buy me off with some shared ownership scam so he could unload that piece-of-crap property."

"What?"

"You've got yourself a nightmare. D-I-N-O-T-I."

Ruby wrinkled her forehead and stared at the new darkness.

Gretchen went on, "Maybe he owns *your* building. I think you're having sex with your sleazy landlord."

Ruby sat on a bench in Washington Square Park. An occasional bird showed up, waiting for crumbs. She stared at them, then at a teenage girl in tights and a lace camisole, who walked past with a boom box playing "Livin' La Vida Loca." It was Saturday morning, and though walkers and resters were sparse, two large groups exercised in formation. Some in mustard-yellow T-shirts practiced Tai Chi, the others in red did vigorous slashing arm motions. Most were elderly. They sidled or lunged around with spirit, even those whose movements seemed palsied. One old man had long, slender fingers he used with graceful swoops and flicks of the wrist. Ruby thought of Benny Di Noti's hands—a man with hands like an El Greco painting—but the way he'd used them had looked mechanical. Whatever he'd meant with her, she would stop thinking about him or any part of his body. At all.

A tall young man with close-cut hair sat down next to her. "Mind if I sit here?" He already had. Ruby shrugged. After a little while he cleared his throat. "Miss, can you tell me where Mario's Bohemian Cigar Store is?" Ruby pointed across the street, still not looking at him directly.

"I understand it's a great little café," he said.

Ruby sighed. "In the morning it is. At night it's full of people like Sean Penn and stalkers who barge in to admire those guys or get something out of them."

"No kidding. Wow."

"Where you from?" Ruby asked without much interest.

"New York."

"You don't sound like it," she commented, with a faint note of disapproval.

He laughed, then paused. "Sorry. Guess I'm intruding. I'll be in town a few weeks, and honestly, I was looking for somebody to have coffee with. I shouldn't have bothered you. Sorry," he said again and stood.

A cup of free coffee sounded good, now that she was definitely going to lose out on it.

"Hell, okay," she agreed ungraciously. Her hair was un-combed, but the young guy smiled like she was a little princess. He was dark blond and well-groomed. He wore jeans and a close-fitting, faintly shiny black shirt that showed his abs. Ruby couldn't help brightening as they walked over damp morning grass toward a sidewalk table at the corner café.

Benedict Di Noti and his son Nick conferred in a large leather-smelling office with an immense chandelier.

"I think we can broker the Greenwich property for twenty-one mil," the real estate scion said. "Are you on top of your calls?"

"Sure, Dad." In a khaki suit and dark blue tie with broad diagonal stripes, Nicholas Di Noti stood slightly bowlegged, both deferential and knowing, with a toothy and easy smile. "We have a meeting tomorrow at three."

Di Noti told him, "I want to get rid of that crappy sink-hole on Leavenworth. Don't even bother doing anything cosmetic."

Although their firm owned seventy-five hundred apartment units around the city, at all times Nick had minute details of his father's plans in his mobile. "Run a fumigation?" Nick asked solicitously. "Tenants might complain to the buyer."

Di Noti shook his head sharply. "We can get forty mil from my pal Chan in Shanghai, sight unseen. Don't bother."

"Speaking of tenants, okay if I spend some time with that Ruby kid?"

"Oh?"

"Well, you know. She's a babe. I tailed her to the park on Saturday morning and got her coffee at the Cigar Store. It went from there. I made like an out-of-towner. She's not too fond of *you* anymore." Nick smiled.

"Ahhh. It's fine. . . . Not like she can make trouble. She's just an artist. Hasn't got a fucking cent. The bitch is crazy. I admit I had fun, though. She's sure got the tatas! You? Sounds like you like the kid."

"Actually, yeah. Hope you don't mind, Dad."

"Nah. I'm done. You getting any? We can hold off eviction a little longer."

Nick grinned with an air of invincible cheer. Slicking the side of his immaculate hair, he answered, "She thinks we're in love because we do it missionary position. It's like big-eyes Japanese anime or something. A blast."

Nick had exaggerated for effect—locker room conversations with his father had always been transgressively fun—but he found Ruby more entertaining than his father's other castoffs. He'd never spent time around an artist before. He gave her the story that he'd found an apartment in San Francisco, that he worked for a data analysis company that had just decided to locate him there instead of New York. After a cursory look through the paintings stacked in her kitchen, he said to Ruby on impulse, "Do one of me. A portrait. I'll pay you."

"You're commissioning me? Oh, God, Nicky. Portraits are not my deal!"

"You can do it, babes. Said yourself that something new might jump-start you. Use a photo; I'm tied up at work. I'll give you three hundred for it. Say, two feet across by three feet high. There's a place in my foyer it'd fit fine."

"You're serious? Like over a little mahogany table? This is your idea of art?"

"Cherrywood. Yeah-yeah. Come on, it'll be a kick. I'm sponsoring you here. Show me a little enthusiasm."

Ruby was in no position to act insulted. Since Nick said he had no time to sit for her, she worked rapidly from a picture, and within a week it was done. The face had a sensuous, noble, somewhat skewed cast to it, like the paintings of Gustav Klimt. Nick wanted to laugh when he saw the portrait, but for some reason he was pleased, even though he had no real use for it.

"You know what? We should go out. Go and celebrate," he told Ruby.

Her eyes dilated with excitement. At the same time, she needed money, so in a way some more cash might have been better. Besides, the portrait wasn't like anything she'd ever done; she hated to part with it. Maybe some of the intensity she'd found in his face came from a place in him she hadn't discovered yet. She stood, shyly uncertain.

"Let's go," he said. "Come on, get dressed."

Ruby wore fishnet tights and a short, black cocktail dress she kept for heavy dates. She hadn't put it on in several years, and she had to wear tight shapewear to get into it. She added extra lip gloss and long, sparkling earrings, in order to direct attention away from her thirty-nine-year-old midriff.

The restaurant had large carvings in dark wood and a lot of mirrors and brass. Arrangements of giant delphiniums and curly willow branches. Ruby touched one to see if it was fake; it wasn't. Someone offered to check her coat, but she said no. For some reason Nick was able to get a good table without a reservation. The tables were so close that Ruby felt uptight, talking. She ate salad with truffle oil, Chilean fish, and sorbet with mango shavings and cracked pepper. She also drank an aperitif, four large glasses of different wines and, following Nick's example, vintage port.

At one point during the meal, Ruby said, "Can I take some of this home in a doggie bag?"

Nick looked at her, startled. Then he laughed. "You really are something," he said.

"It's just that everything was so good . . ." Silently, she reminded herself that she still had the three hundred dollars from Nick in her coat pocket. Why worry? She decided to experiment with her role here, starting with a little flattery.

She leaned in and surveyed Nick's face. "You're a handsome guy. You must have girls falling all over you."

He chuckled complacently.

"Do you miss New York? Tell me all about your job, Nicky." Ruby reached out and tapped him on the sleeve. "I want to know *everything* about you."

His forehead curled. "That's pretty sweet." He stared back with what looked like a complex mix of warmth, admiration, and irony. "You're an unusual girl. Kind of awesome." Nick started to reach out his hand to her, but used it instead to signal the waitress for the check, the sooner to get Ruby back to his apartment. It occurred to him that, given the evening's libations, he should have used a car service instead of his own car. "Can I get the check?" Almost immediately it arrived on the table hidden in folded leather. His cell phone rang. "Sorry," he said to Ruby. Leaving a credit card, he deftly snapped open his phone, stood, and strode toward the bathroom to take the call.

Ruby fidgeted with the spoon in her dessert goblet. Wondering how much their sumptuous meal had cost, she glanced. "Oh, Christ," she said. How was it possible for any human being to buy dinners like this? If she and Nick kept seeing each other, would that be normal? Idly, she took the credit card in her hand and looked at it. The name, in platinum-colored letters, was Nicholas Di Noti. Nicholas *Di Noti?* Her hand trembled so that she almost dropped it. She set it back into the folder.

He came back, sat and signaled again that he wanted to pay. The chic young waitress bent briefly to whisper to him. As she backed way, his expression hardened. He said to Ruby, *"What did you do?"*

Ruby sat smugly in her chair, hands folded. "I took care of it," she said. "Just now. As you know, I had a wad of cash on me. You don't own everything about me, fucker."

"What the hell?"

"I wanna know who your father is. You never even told me your last name!"

"You never asked."

"So what is it? Who are you to Benny Di Noti?"

"You're cuckoo. You'll never get anywhere without a guy like me. Don't you get it? You should be glad for every minute of me!"

"I hope I forget every line of your face, every lousy color in your eyes, your nasty spoiled voice, every rotten fake laugh that ever came out of your motherfucking mouth—"

His face flushed. Getting up suddenly from the table he overturned the chair. He grabbed his coat—and as he left, Ruby picked up an empty glass and threw it onto the floor, where it broke.

Everyone in the restaurant sat silently staring at her. She could feel red heat off their stares, like they were creatures of some evil planet. Then she felt weak. She didn't know how to get up from the table. She had to rouse herself to stand. Staring down at the large jaggedly-broken glass cylinder, she thrust herself up and stamped hard on the glass. "Mazel tov!" she shouted. No one reacted. As Nick exited the front door, she yelled with all her might, "You probably pluck your fuckin' trapezoidal eyebrows!"

A few patrons chewed their food tentatively. Was she about to be kicked out? Or could you call the cops on somebody for this? She pulled her coat off the chair and threw it over her arm, like Nick had done. *Wish I'd tossed the whole table.* What she was hurrying toward now she couldn't think. She only had six dollars left in her purse—take a bus? *Okay, I'll just walk.* Heels or no heels. The enclosed Stockton Bridge had a long pedestrian walkway on either side of traffic. Yes. She had to get back to her studio, with familiar paintings in corners like signs of hope and her owl bones over the door for protection.

⊞

The next morning a heavy knock woke Ruby. She snatched up an old satin wrap, tying it as she opened the door. Two large men in black company uniforms stood there.

"What's going on?" she asked.

"Building security." The larger man pulled folded paper from his pocket.

"What d'you mean? We don't *have* building security. What're you talking a—?"

"*Yeah* we do. Just started." The man with paper waved it in her face.

She stepped back. "What *is* this?"

"Looks like the landlord found out about your little prostitution gig."

"What? That's crazy."

"Uh-huh. You need to get out."

"I'm not moving," Ruby said. She tried to slam her door. "Leave me alone!" Frantically, she pushed on the door to close it.

They pushed back. "Twenty-four hours to vacate. That's it!" One of the men plunged his arm in, around the side of the door. Ruby leaned against it with her full weight.

"You're nuts!" she hollered.

With both men pushing, the door forced open violently, throwing her sideways to the floor. Ruby shouted, "Ahhhh! You trying to kill me?"

"Twenny-four hours!" the smaller man barked, tight-faced. "Anythin' left on the premises goes in the street."

"You can't do that!"

"Shuttup, bitch," said the bigger man, twisting her forearm behind her back.

"Stop it! You'll break my arm!"

"We can break you and take anything you got."

"Oh, yeah," the other man snickered. "'Nother thing? Reports of drug use." He leaned over and shoved her down harder against the floor.

Ruby stopped struggling. She lay with her face sinking into the linoleum.

17. SERPENTINIZATION

Gretchen opened her door to Satchel and took a step back, and he stood there for a moment, as they'd each done often in the past. It was several weeks since he'd left San Francisco for his visit to the attic, which he didn't mention. With a postcard, "Welcome to Socorro, New Mexico," he'd warned her he would be on crutches.

"Damn, it's good to see you, honey," he said. "You have no idea how good." He looked pale and dried-out.

Gretchen said only, "There's coffee." She was wearing a plaid tunic and leggings and had a dishtowel in her hand.

Satchel moved to the counter fairly quickly and helped himself to a mug. Gretchen went toward him to help. She took the mug from his hand, pouring his coffee. Sad as it was to see him hobbling, she couldn't help thinking how he always had a reason for her to take care of him. "Are you okay, Satchel? Is the leg serious?"

"Naah. Be leapin' around in no time. Whassup, buttercup?" He sighed cheerfully, then burst out, "Hey. Cool. You still have the white enamel coffeepot!" Leaning his crutches against the wall, he sat at the table. "Know what? . . . Listen, sweetie, I been thinking about us. While I was in New Mexico I thought we really oughta get back together. We were so good back in the day."

Gretchen, still standing, backed against the counter and pointed the toes of one foot against the floor, a position she'd taken before, when something needed to be said.

"Satchel, it suits you when it's impossible for things to work. You know that, don't you?" She spoke quietly.

Satchel glanced at his hands, which had started to twitch. "You like that Len guy," he concluded, looking into his coffee.

"I do, but this is not about . . ." Gretchen put down the towel firmly on the counter. "Remember when you couldn't decide between seeing me and your wife? And did you ever get divorced?"

He said earnestly, "She was mean."

She crossed her arms. "Then maybe your decision shouldn't have been that hard. Apparently, it was." At this he seemed to sag. Gretchen poured water from a filtered pitcher into yellow-flowered glasses. She said, "What if you picked someone or something and tried to stay with it?" She came to the table, put down water for each of them, and sat across from him. "You're a really good musician. How much do you love it? . . . Could you do it every day, without trashing your hotel room or breaking up with somebody or getting completely bombed?"

Satchel stared at her. "What do you want me to do, marry you?"

Gretchen laughed. Then she put her hand on his arm. "No, Satchel. That's some weird logic! I want to see you more settled in yourself."

He looked up at the ceiling uneasily. "Settling. What does the hell does that mean?" He said crossly, "Always hated that word. Like settling *for* something—"

"You're not paying attention to people."

"Oh. Huh. You mean Ruby."

"Well, she missed *you*. She hasn't been doing well."

Satchel looked at Gretchen closely. "Is she a goner? Because I can't handle that."

"I don't know the prognosis. She's a sensitive woman. And she's also beautiful and gifted. Ruby's staying with me right now. She's at the grocery store. She'll be back in a while."

Satchel shuffled his feet under the table. Gretchen felt better, now that she'd spoken up.

Suddenly he burst out gaily, "You know that every state has a state rock?"

"No . . ."

"Your State Rock of California, that's serpentinite."

Gretchen inhaled and put a hand to her collarbone.

He went on, "There's a big-ass serpentinite rock in front of the Oakland Museum. Huge. Sort of blue and jade colored. That's your State Rock."

"Right," Gretchen said, shaking her head. Why did he always do this? Restlessly, she got up and started walking to the next room.

"Asbestos occurs naturally in serpentinite," he called, louder. "You're not listening!"

Did he blurt out things like this because of old reasons, his time as a soldier? Or was he just born annoying? She turned to him again and said, "Look. I see you, Satchel. For where we are now, it's enough."

"That's so patronizing. You treat me like a kid."

Exasperated, she finally said, "Well . . . here's the thing about Ruby. . . . Maybe you should just man up."

Gretchen's job had downsized, Fridays off, which had advantages. She and Len walked along Fillmore. A dry, gritty wind huffed at them. His stride was long; he had a stately quality, whether still or moving, his natural steps more leisurely than hers. Len kept the pace, slow and purposeful. She held to it.

Suddenly a vigorous black man cut across their path, shouting "Fuck you, motherfucker!" Gretchen jumped. He ran directly at a white man in a suit. Len kept walking, but Gretchen darted anxious looks.

"Yeah? Fuck you!" the white man hollered back.

"White trash! You white trash!" the first man yelled.

They pushed each other. "Stupid black ape!"

Gretchen, horrified, clutched Len's sleeve as the men grappled and lurched around the sidewalk. Most of the sparse crowd walked past as if it was a bad movie, but right away several tense young black men started to move in. Len stopped but seemed to be evaluating; and Gretchen stared helplessly at the scene, not knowing what to do.

The black man burst out, "You! You know you want my ass! Gimme a kiss, white trash!"

"Ha. Been too long, motherfucker," the other said. They gripped each other's shoulders hard. Both broke into loud laughter.

"Running you ragged at work?" the black man asked. He had on a crisp white shirt.

"Oh, yeah. You're missing it," the white man answered.

The black man said, "Take care now, white trash." They nodded and walked off in different directions, smiling broadly.

Gretchen said faintly to Len, "What *was* that?" The younger black guys, who'd been about to intervene, were still agitated. They started talking things over angrily. It had happened so fast.

"Couple old work buddies, I guess," Len said in a quiet, measured voice. Physically, he towered over all those guys. Gretchen wondered, did that make it easy for him to stay calm? She linked her arm with his.

"That made no sense at all," she exclaimed. "And it works my nerves when people fight." Living at the edge of the Tenderloin she saw people hitting bottom, deranged or on drugs; she coped by ignoring it. But the race words, the sudden shift to "work buddies," the mutual laughter—too many weird things. It often took her time to know what she thought or felt, when something happened. The fault lines between people affected her keenly.

He said, "Yeah . . . the way it goes." Did Len hold his feelings close, like she did? They stood at the corner with no particular destination. Why didn't he seem upset by the incident? She remembered he'd grown up in Richmond with shipyard-working parents. Tough behavior couldn't be new to him.

He pointed to a telephone-pole flyer for an event. "You know these poets? We should check them out," he said, scanning the details. Gretchen, still unhappy, wished he'd show her he at least noticed, even if he didn't want to say anything about the men's encounter. His shift into another subject felt too sudden to be right.

She couldn't help answering him, "Last time I went to that coffee house, a rat crawled out of the kitchen."

He kept looking at the poster. Then he turned to Gretchen and said, "I wouldn't mind going to a reading. Want to?"

"I don't know. Sometimes a poetry reading bores me to tears. What do you get out of it?"

"Just enjoy hearing what poets are up to. Get some juice from their thoughts. Maybe even some hope."

"Hope? I doubt it!" Finally he looked at her. His eyes seemed worn, or maybe sad. Maybe the only answer he could think of to fractured relations in the city was to unite some people around a shared project.

All of a sudden she leaned against him. "Are you hopeful about the space at Petta's? Why are you so keen on it, anyway?"

He gave her a smile and brightened. "If only more people could see the potential of that place. I can picture art openings, theater, multimedia. And all kinds of music. That wrecked, deserted place could be something so different.

Gretchen, it's *huge!*" He made an arc with his arms. "People can set up studios in the basement. Whoever needs to could crash there. It'd be great. Making love at night, painting in the morning, taking tickets at sunset. It'll be something like Amsterdam."

"But . . . what if the artists don't *want* to get organized? Or think you're just some outsider? So far, nobody's actually done anything."

"We need this. I don't care what folks who don't need it think."

"But Len, those real estate brokers—what if they try to smash you? They're evil guys, right? They did a number on my friend Ruby."

"I don't think they're evil. They'll want something out of it. We can clean up the joint, stop it from deteriorating. Wait—what happened with your friend?" He turned to her.

"The building owners had guys rough her up at her apartment. Her landlord's the same one I told you about—*my* landlord."

"All the more reason to get the space! For our friends. It should belong to us, not some investor who doesn't even live here."

"How could it possibly belong to us, Len?"

"Gretchen, people would see your beautiful photos. They should!"

They were walking again. Gretchen warmed to his praise, but she asked, "Would this be a community thing? Family-friendly?"

"Uh, no, not if we're censored. I have eighteen plays never produced, mostly 'cause of profanity. Rappers do it! Right? Anything not-okay for kids, the parents can be warned off. But that doesn't mean we can't show anything erotic or out-there. This is Frisco art for Frisco audiences!"

She said, "You're so exuberant about this. I'm not sure I—that I need those things. These freedoms you want. I was actually so shocked by those two guys back there with their extreme talk I almost fell over."

"They did get some love-hate street theater going on. They got *your* attention!" They both laughed. His single-mindedness, even though it seemed a little crazy, made Gretchen oddly happy. There had always been San Francisco visionaries.

"Len, do you know who technically owns Petta's? Whether the Petta family's still even involved in the sale?"

"Looks like the family got behind on taxes. We need to see if we can get them to let us in, if it's still theirs. The City Assessor would have records."

Gretchen said, "I'll check. I want to see what happens." They linked arms again.

Gretchen crossed her front room on tiptoe; in the light before dawn, she saw two blanket-wrapped shapes, Ruby and Satchel, huddled together on the couch. Did this mean he intended to stay?

On the way to work, Gretchen lifted her head and, swinging her arms, picked up her steps. Buildings along the street: iron foundry, bar, animal shelter, union hall. Passing the industrial laundry with its papered-over windows, she heard a woman's squealing laugh and smiled. An elderly transsexual in a turban, tattered skirt, and missing teeth lumbered along with an overloaded cart, singing a David Bowie song; Gretchen said good morning. The local person answered brightly, "Mornin' to *you,* darlin'." A stocky man passed by holding two little girls in plaid skirts by the hand—Catholic school uniforms. Children had gathered at the school's cement-paved playground, small boys shrieking while they ran after a ball. At the next corner, Gretchen turned watchful for her safety. A ragged, surly guy with glassy eyes moved too close, and she walked fast, clasping her briefcase, alert but keeping her gaze diffuse.

Beside her office, a grey building with battered steps, an old man behind an iron gate swept leaves. He greeted her warmly. "Good to see you!"

Gretchen smiled. "Hi, good morning! Glad to see you too." He generally appeared at this hour in a skullcap and leggings, either standing with a cup of tea in his hands or busy with a broom. He was always courtly; despite his age, he stood straight behind the large broom. "Playing your clarinet?" she asked. He had a jazz past.

"In my room, honey. They bang my door to shut me up!" Once, years back, Gretchen had seen him on the street with his music case on the ground, playing for change.

She opened the office; as usual, she was first. Her work days, three times a week, were always full and usually satisfying. As research technician for a university study, she kept an elaborate database, supervised three interns and coordinated with national headquarters. Gretchen worked from her lists on Post-its, dispatching urgent tasks first. Generally, she'd get the hardest work done while she was fresh. She ate lunch in a small side room: coffee in a red thermos, the sandwich she'd packed in a tiny Korean lunch box, and an apple or fresh greens without dressing. Her coworkers claimed she ate rabbit food. She'd point to their stash of doughnuts and say, "When they test your cholesterol, you won't be laughing."

By the end of the day Gretchen felt worn. She took a crowded bus partway home, and to save herself walking eight more blocks she rode a second bus. There was no way to predict the wait, so she felt relieved when the bus came. She'd need to see to dinner for Ruby, maybe even Satchel. She decided not to upset herself about any of it.

Back home, she flopped down on the couch beside Ruby, untying her shoes. "Do you want to listen to music?"

she suggested. "I'm so tired!" Usually this was how she decompressed.

Instead of answering, Ruby said, "Me, too. I could use some pot, but cripes, I'm out of the business. Hey, girl, I like your shoes."

Gretchen took off the shoes she wore for their slight weight. "All I care about now in a shoe is comfort."

"There's a purple spot, though."

"Wolfberry juice," she said. "Drinking it's supposed to help you live longer."

"Gretchen, only you would drink wolfberry juice. No, the purple spot is cute. I'm vain about shoes; I love four-inch heels." Ruby's black hair was rumpled, and she looked as though she'd only been awake for a short while.

"Where's Satch?"

"He went somewhere for a drink. I dunno what's up with us. Guess it'll be one night at a time." She stared ahead.

Gretchen touched her friend's arm. "Maybe you need to take a while to know each other."

Ruby laughed sadly. "How did *you* get mixed up with him? I never knew."

"Well, I saw his drumming. It was like the whole Vietnam War in one guy. He didn't pose, though. No sexy head-tossing or lurching. I'm not even sure if I saw his eyes."

"He has great eyes, right?"

Gretchen smiled ruefully. "Oh, Ruby. Shh."

"I just meant how did he get so important to you? Or maybe because, I mean because you're the one. In *his* head."

Gretchen said gently, "I don't know about that."

"Well, what happened after the show?"

"I went up and told him how beautiful and intense the work was. He had tears in his eyes but kind of staring away. I just knew he was going to say he was a vet."

"You wanted to look after him?"

"Sort of a reflex, I guess. He was married to this woman

Ann, who was in some insurance office. Really self-contained. High-school-sweetheart marriage thing. I never met her, but I saw her at some of his gigs. He'd go back to her when the need came on him. So I'd let him, but then he had this way of showing up at three a.m."

"Geez. That must have been rough on your other relationships."

"*What* relationships?" Gretchen asked indignantly.

Ruby's hair fell over her eyes and she pushed it back, looking embarrassed and sorry. "Oh. Satch . . . he said—I figured—"

"You know he's not reliable?" Gretchen interrupted. Then she sighed, wishing she could take back her sharp voice. She wanted to stay friends with Ruby, even if it brought old feelings of injustice as well as new ones. She gulped back anger at Satchel for accusing her wrongly, for not seeing the devotion she'd had. . . . Suddenly she just wanted patience among them all. She said, "Look. I never knew anybody who took the hit of that war so young. He made a promising start in music, but now he's messed up. And he has trouble holding onto things."

"Or people," Ruby said bitterly.

"I care about him," Gretchen said. "But trying to fix him was a lousy road. He needs to work. The kind you feel, well, summoned by. I think that's why he likes Len."

"Is he really worth all this concern? He talks to *you*, I guess."

"Not exactly. The other day when I thought we were having a conversation, he starts some speech about a—a State Rock of California, serpentine . . . no, serpentinite— and it ticked me off. But during my lunch hour when I looked up things for Len, I checked it out. Serpentinite."

"What's that?"

"An ancient sea floor rock. Over time, the ocean carries it up onshore. There was a lot about magnesium and iron."

"Sounds like a vitamin I ought to take." They both laughed.

"And strange references to 'serpentinization.' A whole process. I'm not sure whether it means how the rock turns into serpentinite. Maybe underwater volcanoes? Because shifting tectonic plates bring the rocks up."

"Wow, yeah!" Ruby said, her black eyes animated again. "Slashing convulsions under the Pacific! Shaping hard rock on the sea floor and jetting it all over the place. San Francisco's still like that!" For a minute she looked delighted. Then she added sadly, "You know what? I feel like one of those rocks."

"Look, is it really okay for Satchel to stay here?"

"Sure. Even if it's confusing. I appreciate it." She put both her hands on Gretchen's shoulders. "But is it okay with you if *I* still care about him?"

Reaching for a hug, Gretchen said, "Why not? . . . Tell you what. Let's put on some music from Mali. It has drumming and wonderful screamy singing. I'll see what I can slap together for spaghetti."

"You got enough garlic? Hey, I better help. I know spaghetti."

Gretchen found the owner of Petta's Market on the city assessor's Web site. She also confirmed the real estate broker. The names for both turned out the same: *the Di Notis*.

Suddenly Gretchen and Len were in constant contact. At his place they drafted a proposal to Benedict Di Noti for an artist venue in the abandoned market. It was the first time for her to see Len's studio apartment: pale-grey walls, a slight bachelor smell of old laundry and dust, and crushed-velvet burgundy curtains. Gretchen guessed some devoted woman had made them.

Len, watching attentively, said, "Friends gave me most of this." Masks lined his walls: African giraffe face, Tibetan Buddha, laughing Kabuki dancer with lacquered flower headdress. In one corner, some aloe and jade plants nestled comfortably.

Gretchen exclaimed, "You have great lighting. It's so bright."

He showed her his 1930s stove, the curtained sleeping area in shades of dark blue, and a miniscule bathroom. He served hibiscus tea, which they sipped while Gretchen worked at his laptop. She drafted the letter, reading it out while he interjected changes. They stressed the local merchants backing their idea because it could be good for tourism.

Gretchen pulled a sheaf of her photographs from a leather bag, offering it quietly. Len held out his hands. They were digital images she'd taken in the North Beach market the night she met him: cabbage and zucchini, a forest of raw beets in their foliage. Most of them double-imaged in the mirror behind. She'd altered solemn close-ups of the beets so their colors deepened. Scale and dimensions disappeared; frosted and pressed together, the various parts transformed into a red forest. "Beautiful," he said. He looked up. "Your forms have this odd dignity. Still and fiery. Damn, they're practically fulminating. Even a little fearful. I love intensity like this."

"They're for you. I know you like color." Gretchen laughed happily.

"We should work together more! The hell of it is I only know how to do theater and painting." He asked whether she'd done sets or puppets.

"No, photography's my thing. I usually work in black and white with an old-style camera." She looked down, shy.

"Hey. But we should celebrate. Do you want a drink? Something heady." Gretchen hesitated. "It's special, you bringing me these. Come on!" He was already taking champagne out of the refrigerator, and he pulled out two small champagne glasses.

"No, really, it's the middle of the day."

He held the glasses up awkwardly. "Okay, now I feel silly. I frosted them—" Gretchen looked taken aback. He said, "Uh . . . how about mango juice then?"

He stood there so plaintively she had to smile. She said, "I'll tell you what I do want. Can I see your paintings, Len?"

"Hey, sure." He led her to a hallway with a vibrant tempera painting of three stylized lizards, their bodies inscribed with lines and dots. Dense geometric patterns overlaid planes of cobalt blue, tomato red, and a sort of muted Naples yellow. "I learned that from a Maori painter who showed me how he sees, and it made an impression on me. Living things interlocking and the highlights of their bones."

Gretchen didn't speak, but her eyes went bright. She was still and glad, yet needing to go somewhere else to take it all in.

Len shifted on his feet and asked, "Are you hungry? Do you want to go out for a bite?"

"I should get home, actually."

"Are you sure?" Len said, with his hand on one hip.

After she left, Len folded into an armchair. He had so little experience of being with her. To know someone, you had to spend the time. He said to himself, *Could I get her over to Europe with me? I have to move around whenever I need to. But— she seems centered here. Rooted. So it's unfair to her? And then, I'm chaotic, she's meticulous. Ah, what am I thinking.* She declined champagne. Damn, why had he made it so clear he was sure they'd share it?

He dried the unused champagne glasses with their formerly ice-kissed rims and set them upside-down in the freezer to re-frost. That was his way with glasses. He didn't notice himself taking great care in these small gestures. Len was meticulous in certain things, but he'd always seen himself as undomesticated by choice.

In spite of his rapport with Gretchen and the help she was giving, she unsettled him. Though he'd had strong partnerships, Len was used to young adoring women, lovers in various countries that still came and went, or he did. They usually had a bit of money. And time on their hands. He hadn't been with a visual artist far along in her life or definite in her sense of herself. This sort of woman he didn't know. It was delicious and thoroughly frightening. He shouldn't tell her this part; he was sure of that.

At Len's second LiveWire meeting, people had opinions on the Di Noti letter. "It's too long." "Take out the three-syllable words." "Use real estate jargon." "Get someone on the Board of Supervisors to send it." "Too short." Len listened, and Gretchen suppressed her dismay. She saw now that Len welcomed and included a lot of people's energies and ideas. Gretchen loathed writing-by-committee, but she took notes on any sensible feedback. The next day she changed the draft during her lunch break.

Ruby and Satchel came to the third meeting. Ruby, in a beret, crouched by the front window after handing Len a petition she'd brought to local store owners, as a fellow Italian. She had eight signatures and apologized for not recruiting more. She was the first painter to accomplish anything useful, so Len said, "This is a great help!" Gretchen smiled at Ruby and gave her a thumbs-up.

Ruby said, "I gave it a shot." She bit her lip. She wanted to get the Di Notis but somehow feel good about it. And talking to older people in the shops had brought back Italian phrases she hadn't used since she was a child.

Len turned off the chamber music on his boom box and started, "Okay. The Di Notis have control of Petta's Market. Gretchen and I sent a letter with your feedback from the last meeting. Registered mail proves they received it." He held up the notice. "We say there's a long history of Italians in North Beach sponsoring the arts, which as Italians they can be proud of . . . that we'll take care of the disintegrating property until it's sold . . . and that merchants in the area are enthusiastic." Len passed a copy.

There were murmurs of approval. An emaciated-looking guy with an untidy beard and harried eyes interrupted, suggesting that everyone buy his poetry book. Len calmly placed the copies on a table, and said, "If anyone wants to check these out afterward, they'll be here."

Satchel moved his chair to the table as though he were hosting it. If he hadn't yet found his place in the artists' efforts, he seemed to be looking for it. Their short meeting ended in plans, and afterward Len went up to Satchel; they talked companionably about Mozart, local musicians who might want to perform in the Petta's space and—again— quasars. Gretchen stood by looking bemused. She had never known Satchel to show any enthusiasm for Mozart.

Len left Gretchen messages daily, wanting her opinions about the project. Usually they talked by phone in the evening, after Gretchen came home from work and had dinner with Ruby—if Satchel was around he ate there, too. With the dishes done and the kitchen put back together, she'd go to her room when Len called.

Len said, "I called Di Noti, the older guy. He was adamant they don't need anybody to keep the place cleaned up. Let's talk to somebody at City Hall, get the Di Notis slammed for spray-paint accumulating on the windows."

"Sure. There's an ordinance, right?"

"Yeah, a notice will be posted on the front windows. Just a fly in their ointment, but it'll help make our point." He asked what she'd been up to.

"Work was killer. My computer problem took an hour and a half to fix. Of course, just when there's a deadline! On the way home I had fun, though. Some camera crew on my corner was shooting a movie—tripods near two actors dressed like GI's. One was supposed to punch the other one. They both had to yell a lot. It was fairly invigorating."

"I love San Francisco for that—all the movies shot here. All the talent. So many young people with amazing energy, teenage kids making murals and little masterpiece documentaries about their lives!"

"Really? Where are all these kids?"

"Well, I met a bunch of them today. I was guest pre-senter in a high school art class on computer-generated images. I'm revved about that. I was told to riff on how my friends and I used video cameras to document street thea-ter, but what's the point? They're way beyond that now. We ended up talking about politics, which I wasn't supposed to, but the kids were great—full of questions and ideas. The teacher's a friend, so if he gets in trouble, he can say he'll never invite me again." Len laughed.

"You have so much going on," Gretchen told him wistfully.

"Hey, when I call you, you don't always call back. You must be the busy one! You can call me any time."

Gretchen protested that she called him more than any-body. "I'm sorry," she said. "It doesn't come naturally. I go into my own universe and, even if I'm thinking about you, I sometimes forget to come out."

"Always? With anybody?"

"Well, I did have one relationship where we were in touch a couple of times a day. Now that I think about it, we were practically together twenty-four seven except when one of us was out of town."

"Exactly! Only way to do a partnership."

"The *only* way?" Gretchen asked, dismayed.

Len was silent. If the world worked the way he'd like, he could steal her away from her job. And her friends and family. He'd gotten by with doing that before. Maybe it wasn't so much that Gretchen was settled, but that he had extra years on him? He rubbed the top of his head to see how his hair was doing.

He changed the subject. "Hey, some new people are interested in what we can do with Petta's Market," he said. "Students, an art teacher . . . a young musician named Julian. Maybe they'll help."

"Good!" Gretchen said. "If we're going to call it North Beach Artists, we need more artists." It was the first time Gretchen had said "we."

As Gretchen hung up, her hand trembled. She felt the stakes were higher for her than for him. He could leave town when he wanted, but she had responsibilities she'd worked hard for. More important, although she wanted him, being wooed with *Call me any time* scared her; it made things go fast, and she needed to know more about what she was getting into. She loved Len's painting and its other-worldly expressiveness, and he'd been quick to respond to the photographs she'd given him. But they talked mostly about North Beach Artists now. She liked the project, but it was his obsession. She thought, *Does he really understand my work and my commitment to it? How much room is in him for what's going on with me?* These were awkward thoughts that rubbed against her, throwing her off balance. Still . . . his painterly way of seeing reminded her of her own, both in the images she'd given him and the paintings he had shown her. What if she allowed herself uneasiness for now? Even trusted something to unfold that could change and overwhelm her?

The next day, it was unseasonably warm. Gretchen took the bus home from work. The intense heat made her squint; she held her briefcase against her chest and closed her eyes. Someone passed her with a wash of penetrating flowered scent. Warmth diffused and lifted the fresh, lilting odor. Gretchen was thinking about Len. Or perhaps not thinking now, but sensing him. As if to change herself through synesthesia, as she sat with closed eyes and a second person went by, Gretchen breathed a surprising blend of cedar, musk and smoke. It began to collide with the smell of sweat, perhaps everyone's. Slowly these odors, flowers and sweaty wood, set themselves to a single delirious smell. She waited quietly while it crescendoed through her body. Gretchen felt lightheaded. In a little while, she had passed her stop. She got down and walked back, smiling. The smile remained for a long time.

18. QUAKE AND BAKE

Walking up Columbus, Gretchen could hear trombone music and a thonking drum. Around the corner, a phalanx of military guys in buttoned black coats and white capes came by, blipping out loud music. A black limo with open top drove into sight. Two Chinese men sat enthroned in chairs propped on its car seats. At the front an imposing wooden placard had Chinese writing on it. The men wore dark suits. Funeral? Gretchen stopped to watch. She had her camera, and she photographed a stern woman in black uniform with a baton, then the enthroned men on the car.

Another car rounded the bend, bearing a tin contraption like an altar on top. Behind, men with traditional instruments stamped and shuffled past as a loose group; whenever the car in front slowed to a stop, they quit playing. One old man with puffy eyes and a worn yet somehow happy expression did keep up his sound, which grated and whined vigorously, like some unique sackbut. Captivated, Gretchen kept clicking, and though she'd have loved to know how his instrument had been made, the name of it, how he learned to play, she had to keep the moment the way she knew and loved—with her camera. She started running along the street to get ahead of the musicians—dodging old ladies with armloads of vegetables—and quickly shot off a series of images, hoping the afternoon's streaming light would settle well on her prints of the musicians' plaintive forward motion. She'd actually *run* through crowded China-town and made it through.

On the way to meet her friends, Gretchen walked quick-ly. She found Saints John and Paul Church and sat on the steps. After a few minutes, one at a time Ruby, Len, and Satchel joined her. It was a hot Saturday afternoon, and people roamed cafes, galleries, and bookstores. Comfortably unnoticed, the group of four had almost as much privacy as if they were on the porch that had so recently been Ruby's.

A young guy drove up on a little yellow motorbike and said, "Lemme park this." He had a chiseled face, round tinted sunglasses and a single dark braid down his back. One of his front teeth was missing.

When Satchel saw the fluorescent guitar strapped to the young man's back, he saluted and said, "Cool, Julian. I see you brought your axe."

Julian waved. "Yeah! I'll be right there." Satchel leaned back, lounging against the brick wall.

Gretchen looked at Len. "So how do we start?"

He said, "Frankly, my style of protest is goofiness. Let's attack the greedy landlord bastards with something loud."

"Like a chant?" Ruby asked. "A protest chant?"

Len said, "How about something wilder and weirder? Even kind of a punk thing. About unbridled expansion."

"Like slash and burn?" said Gretchen.

Satchel sat up fast. "Yeah, no, for sure! Slash and burn expansion!"

Then Julian appeared with his guitar and started smack-ing out an acoustic chord with gusto. Len smiled, stood up and laid his hand on the young guy's shoulder. They all rose and huddled around the church steps.

Ruby picked up the guitar's punk tone. In a babyish voice, she whined, "It was a rotten day in a pitiful world."

Satch jumped in on the beat with, "In a *scag*-gy part of town!" They laughed. Satchel let out a snorted giggle. He shouted, "It was a scumbag of a *millennium!*"

"It works!" Len yelled back.

Gretchen, who had taken pictures of Julian arriving, put away her camera and took out a notebook to scrawl their lyrics. "What next?" she asked.

Ruby pitched in, "Something that rhymes with 'town.'"

Satch looked excited. "Down up down!"

"But what goes down?" Gretchen said.

Julian stopped playing. Quietly, he responded, "Tears."

"Up and down?" Ruby turned to him, skeptical.

"Yeah, and so, but I like that," Satchel said. "Your tears go down up down!"

Julian started playing hard, and soon he and Satchel teamed on, "Slash and burn expansion, slash and burn expansion . . ."

Len joined in with a fake-pop-music moan, "Whoa-oh, ohhh-oh . ."

Ruby burst into raucous laughter. "I love it," she said. "You look like John Denver covering The Clash. It's hilarious. Totally."

Len smiled back. "But it's okay! We can be silly. The Clash did a lot of posturing. Quirky rebellion's been huge in British rock, right? Did the job. We need attention! We can even write corporate real estate guys into the words."

Ruby asked, "And how they screw up people's lives?"

"Sure," Len said.

Over the next hour they added lyrics, though it needed more work. Until next session came around, Satchel, Ruby and Julian decided to adjourn for beer. Len stayed with Gretchen, who wanted to duck into the church for a look.

The place smelled thickly of old incense. Gretchen went down an aisle. Len followed, and they moved toward a stained glass window. "I like to hang out in old churches," he said. "I don't pray, but I think about how people have turned to God for help. Even answers."

"Answers to injustice?" Gretchen asked. When they stood close she had to look up, feel his unusual height.

"Sometimes if you want it, you have to fight for it."

Gretchen walked slowly around a pillar, then said, "I didn't mean to stay long, but I wanted a moment." They passed the tray of visitors' candles, flames inside the glasses.

As they moved toward the door Len mused, "Painting, music, literature—they give people hope. Then he said sharply, "Life without beauty's drudgery. It's crap." As they walked out onto the street, his eyes held longing. Gretchen was not hearing his words. What she heard was his heart.

All at once she stopped and kissed him on the mouth.

The next day Gretchen had something to say to her friends Satchel and Ruby on the couch. "Guys? Bear with me here. It's really sudden; I need you to stay somewhere else."

Ruby sat dumbfounded and Satch answered, "Geez, Gretch. Are we eating you out of house and home?"

"I just need it," Gretchen repeated. She couldn't imagine any other way to be intimate with Len, but that was too private to say, especially before anything had happened.

Ruby looked at her with a dire face. "How, Gretchen? Where?"

Before Gretchen could get a spasm of guilt, Satchel stood. "Chill, Rube," he said calmly. "No, yeah, no problem, we'll crash at Julian's. I'll handle it." It seemed to Gretchen he knew the reason and that, in a way, he was even taking care of her.

Gretchen brushed her teeth with gritty blue paste. She mixed mouthwash meticulously with a little water, holding it like an aperitif. This would be their first time, and she also hadn't been with a man this way for at least two years. It was like being a scared teenager. In the mirror she could see

Len standing behind in her bedroom, examining one of her photographs on the wall.

He turned as she came back. "Ah, I didn't hear you."

Gretchen laughed. She felt giddy. "People say that. A tough Cree guy I used to know said he could barely hear me when I come down a flight of stairs. Like, 'I hear anything's steps, but you, I guess not.' . . ." How had her friend phrased that, exactly? Maybe it wasn't even those words. She wanted to warn Len about her inwardness. Did he know? Could he understand?

"Wow," Len said. "I don't know what it means." He paused. Then he said, "But I see how light shines at the back of you." Was she being praised for a gift she didn't know she had? Gretchen felt a little proud, but still anxious.

"Light?" she prompted him.

"I see the way you move. No one else's way. Like a dragonfly moves over leaves." It was an unlikely declaration, but all at once Gretchen gave over thinking and worrying. His hand pressed the back of her head until their foreheads touched, and then, his other hand on the small of her back, finally he clasped her to him.

Around ten-thirty the next night, as Len worked at his apartment, his laptop fluttered and fainted. He felt the floor tremble hard—exceptionally so, even for San Francisco—and he called out to the young couple next door. Thunderous racket and the floor's forcible bucking got stronger. The kids didn't answer, so he ran to open their varnished maple door; they were scrambling naked in the dark, trying to find clothes. "Here!" he shouted. Yanking a blanket off the bed, he grabbed the girl by the arm and pushed the boy—forcing them into the rough wool. They shouted incoherently and hurried toward the stairs. Len ran behind to make sure they got out.

Across town, Gretchen sat in bed leaning against the wall, her gaze aimed at a book. She heard what sounded like a huge truck storming by. Suddenly her spine jabbed at the wall, and a boom followed like fireworks or a distant loud cannon. She felt her body lift with the whole wall behind her, then thud down. She gasped, jumped up, ran at a doorway, sat on one side of it with her feet against the other—planted herself steady. Something fell and splatted against the floor. Objects were flying—cascades of splintering and leaping broken glass—mauled by the clashes of broken slabs, deep belowground. Her framed photos leaped off the walls, and their glass shattered.

Ruby, restless at Julian's on a sleeping bag, flipped open her eyes, slid and jerked against the floor. Satchel, in a battered armchair, had been mid-phrase playing "Slash and Burn" on an old drum set, with Julian and his guitar, when the apartment started rolling. "Shit! Damn!" Pointlessly, the musicians stared at each other as the whole building started to sway. Satchel fell back in his chair. Ruby moaned and wrapped into her sheet—mummying herself.

Julian shouted, "Get under the table!" There was no heavy furniture, though. Suddenly Julian grabbed his guitar and a box of sheet music, ran out and careened down the stairs. They were full of shrieking neighbors.

Satchel and Ruby rushed to each other clinging, then grabbed onto stair railings. Their vision blurred as other tenants smeared past.

Len stood on his street surrounded by neighbors. Even before he was sure the quake had stopped, he ran back up. His bookcase lay sprawled across the bed. Swirling dust hovered over hardbacks, lying where his head should be.

Aftershocks had started to settle. Gretchen crouched in the broken glass. Her photographs! In one shaky hand she held part of a woman's face. A glossy torn piece. Her tears fell. When the tremors seemed over, she went to check on her neighbors.

Len went straight to Gretchen's, leaving his books with their mashed pages all over his floor. Her apartment, besides all its broken glass, had a ceiling surface wound. Satchel, Ruby and Julian showed up, all of them eager to help by sweeping. Gretchen loaded a big stew pot with vegetables from her unworkable refrigerator, as well as frozen chicken, beans and beef. She could still use a camp-style cooker. Singing took over, while Julian lugged in a generous supply of warm beer. He said, "Going flat, so get it down."

Len was beside himself with excitement, as if all the travel he'd ever launched or theater sets he'd thrown together had come to life in one night. He kept singing "Slash and Burn" with a hoarse, ironic twist. Every time someone heaved a tired sigh, he started the refrain again, and it turned into a code for helpless laughter. Somehow, they managed wild fun in the midst of the terrible, torn state of many of Gretchen's photographs. Her computer wouldn't start, and she looked pale but only said, "I've got negatives, and both my cameras work. Thank God my neighbors are okay, too. One of them's elderly, and her daughter's taking her in."

Julian said, "Good. Tell you what—I know someone who can fix your computer."

That night, Len slept in her bed, and the friends camped on her floor. There wasn't much sleeping, but around three-thirty a.m. Len said loudly, in a sepulchral voice, *"Who* is it? Who's the landlord now? *Nature?"* They all started laughing madly. Yes: things had changed, and they needed something besides the quake.

Next morning they walked together to North Beach. First they asked around to see how people were doing or whether they needed help; then they went to see about the condition of Petta's. Its windows, fully decimated, appeared vandalized. Julian slipped through one, sustaining some scratches, and heaved open the front door. The rat-smelling, exposed-beam interior looked wrecked. Satchel threw his arms wide and yelled, "Yeah, home! Honey, I'm home!"

Len got a pail, broom, and water to clean pieces of wall from the floor of the unused market. He swept with rhythm and vigor. Gretchen was glad for that, but she needed to leave North Beach to see what had happened to her office.

It was slow, uncomfortable. Making her way through groups of people thronging streets in front of their damaged buildings, she felt hesitant—sluggish and uncertain—not charged or excited like her friends. Some streets were blocked by police; they diverted people on their bikes riding around town to see what had happened. Groups of people gathered to share stories or help each other. Gretchen worried how many might have been injured and what they lost; it throttled her sense of reality. And was there any way to get back to her job?

Walking all the way to Mission, she noted the tumbled clouds. They looked painted. On a street where the sidewalk grade increased, she picked up her pace—setting down her feet carefully and walking around rubble. After a long while she passed the powder-green stucco façade of a former union hall. Part of the crumbling building had collapsed. Past that, rows of nineteenth-century rowhouses and shops stood relatively undisturbed.

A wiry man with matted hair stood bent over a shopping cart. All Gretchen could see of him was the back of his threadbare blue jacket, a sort of smock, and his trembling hair as he worked intently, rearranging whatever possessions he had in the cart under its dirty blanket. He turned to her slightly with an anxious grimace.

"Hi. Are you okay?" Gretchen asked, stepping forward.

Unexpectedly, the man lunged toward her in one bound. He raised his fist: "Get the fuck away!" His arm slammed air as Gretchen jumped back nimbly.

Retreating, she held out her hands. "Okay. Okay."

"The both of you. Get away!" he snarled, moving close. He lunged with his arm again.

Both? Instinctively, Gretchen repeated, "It's okay." She escaped into the street between two parked cars. Then she saw a young man coming briskly toward her. Julian.

He asked, "Gretchen, you all right?" They started walking away together.

"He didn't hit me. Just startled hell out of me."

"He swung at you—I saw that. Glad you're not hurt. Did it come out of nowhere?"

"Yeah, I was only passing by."

"Even though there's folks helping each other, some dudes out here are going crackers. On the way over I saw a lot of shouting. Old ladies keening and crying, guys fighting, kids raiding shops. Wanta call a cop?"

"No, it's not worth it." Gretchen looked over her shoulder. The angry man had bent over his cart again, furiously bundling belongings or loot under the blanket.

"He'll have to sock somebody else then," Julian said. "Len told me to check on you. He thought I'd run into you, and I'm glad I did. C'mon back over to Petta's."

"Thanks, no. . . . I need to find out what shape my workplace is in."

Julian shrugged. "I'll walk you." They went along the uneven pavement in silence.

Gretchen finally said, "I never caught your last name?"

"Aubry," he said. "Nobody uses last names."

"I find that odd. To remember somebody, I need to see their whole name written down at least once."

He laughed. "Well, not that *that's* weird."

"But maybe it's dismissive if people have to be identified by a syllable or two."

Julian shook his head. "My last name reminds me of the old man. Always hounding me because I don't do much with my fucking Princeton B.A. Supposed to be an A-list doctor or architect, y'know? He didn't even back me up on my summer internship in France."

"What did you do there?"

"Comparative Lit." Julian fished in his pocket. "Got into the grad school grind, but the pressure sucked. I did intern in my dad's firm a while, though. I was too Frank-Gehry for them. Dad finally told me I could take my fuckin' French philosophy and airy-fairy designs and stick 'em up my ass."

"Wow. That's harsh, Julian. My father didn't spend very much of his life with us, just came and went every few years. I hardly know him."

"Huh! Nasty. Screw fathers then." Gretchen stopped talking, so he added, "Okay, just mine? Last time I saw him, things got physical. Hence the removed tooth. Maybe I'll keep the hole to remind me of, y'know, all my bravery and self-sufficiency." He saluted to the sky.

"I don't really . . . look for my folks to understand me," Gretchen said. "For the record, I had a dad who slapped my mother around plenty. Me, I've got photography. That's probably what I was meant for."

"Meant for? You—"

"It sees me through anything. In spite of old bad things, I guess I've got a path."

"Sorry, I get a little bitter. But I get it . . . pretty much live for my guitar. . . . Want a joint? Nobody's looking."

"No, thanks."

"Gretchen, you're so straight-arrow. I dig it, though."
Julian lit a tiny stub with a practiced hand. "Lately I decided
I don't need to drink water, just toke every couple hours.
Gotta say, sometimes I wonder why you hang with us
struggling soul-seekers."

"I can't spend *all* my time in my room," she said. "Or
on the job. What about you? You seem to be jamming with
Satchel a lot."

Julian breathed and walked. "Yeah, Satch. I relate. Slated
to be this physics star, then he gets spirited away by rock 'n'
roll. Smart guy, entertaining. Good musician. You should
get to know him." He paused for a big toke.

Gretchen didn't respond. Satchel hadn't spoken about
her; okay, this was easier.

Julian went on, "I'm a music bum. All I actually want
now. Been working the kitchen sometimes at this hip new
restaurant that might lead to a gig. Satch gets me going
when we jam. And I think the Petta's scheme is cool.
Needed. Don't know why you guys go to Trieste so much,
though. This stifling hangout for old farts, chewing their
days o' glory. What kinda recreation's that? San Fran has so
many great places to go. You should try where I work. It's
this organic restaurant that's practically on your doorstep,
Magnifique."

"I've been there, Julian. I like the black lacquered walls
and aluminum stools." She smiled apologetically. "But I
thought the food was stringy, and it looked like pastel
weeds."

Julian laughed. "Seriously, though. Billions of places."

"Well, bottom line, even old farts need a place to hang
out. Trieste reeks of history. North Beach Italian, music, the
Beats. The front windows are world-class people-watching.
And it's friendly."

Julian crushed the last of his joint underfoot. "Well,
time to go make history then. Back to Petta's. We're putting

stalls in the basement, space for studios."

"I'll come tomorrow."

"Counting on you!" Julian said with a smile, waving and sprinting away.

Gretchen unlocked the door to her workplace; except for a few things fallen to the floor, it seemed fine. No one else was around. The conversation with Julian had cheered her; she liked to talk to young people, especially artists. She wondered whether he'd settle into the city the way most people did; within a few years they found a small world of kindred people and places, and after that it took a lot of energy to manage new explorations. Well, Petta's Market would be an adventure for everybody involved.

Back at Petta's, now a fledgling art space, the gang of friends had managed to clear the main floor and organize rubble into piles. When things lagged, Len would suggest a new activity.

It wasn't until nightfall that, ravenous and worn, they all decided to look for an operational bus line to Gretchen's. By the time the others arrived, she had gone all the way home and checked the soup to make sure it was still good. It smelled and tasted all right, so she started boiling it steadily. While she worked on her emergency stove setup, Len strode into her kitchen. He had an armful of new vegetables; as he kissed Gretchen, Ruby and the guys came in behind him. They stood around boisterously retelling their adventurous day.

"Is anybody staying over?" Gretchen asked.

Satchel answered, "Julian's place is in bad shape, so we're camping out at Petta's!"

"I'll stay with you tonight if it's okay," Len said quietly to Gretchen. "My apartment's still in trouble with utilities.

Even running water. Tomorrow I'll go back to the art space and help them set up. You can, too, if you have time."

Gretchen answered, "I guess you can tell I'm antsy to get back to work. I didn't get much done there today." He smiled; he'd learned a lot about Gretchen's needs in a few days. She said, "What do you think the Di Notis will do?"

Len looked tired. Instead of answering, He cocked his head, looked up toward a corner. A goofy smile came onto his face. In the voice of a science narrator, he intoned, "Immense shifts under the earth—and their ricocheting forces—have left San Francisco ravaged . . ."

Julian bent to the skewed moment, adding, "The ferry building and the Bay Bridge totally upheaved!"

Len and Satchel stared at each other and laughed raucously, exhausted and slaphappy. Gretchen, cleaning vegetables, shook her head, but Satchel widened his eyes and crooned, "Over an immense expanse of time . . . rocks deep in the ocean pull two ways—kneaded and crushed down, yet also yanked sideways by tectonic faults."

Ruby said, "God, you guys. What's so funny?"

In a deep voice, Julian went on, "Hidden fissures far below . . ." He held his hands up like claws.

Satchel whirled Ruby around twice and hollered, "Rocks in the water! *Deep* below! Serpentinite."

Len nodded and said, "It's a fact. That's a timeless dance."

Gretchen had gone back to the stove. She said over her shoulder, "Yes. We know. The timeless dance is serpentinization." Her voice was playful but warm. "Hey, I'll come over and photograph you guys in the art space. Dinner's ready, soldiers."

People convened in the new art space at Petta's. Satchel started squatting there. Len, his apartment plagued by erratic electricity, soon joined Satchel, for the time being. Ruby said she'd only stay briefly, but someone had brought paint and brushes—as the most experienced painter, she got yanked into a canvas-stretching project. Late into the evening, marijuana was passed around, but during the day it was all cleaning and clearing of rubble and trash. To rest, they sat on rolled sleeping bags in corners. Before long the friends had bundled drawing and painting into their days.

Gretchen didn't mind Len's relocation to Petta's. She was used to living alone and following her own rhythms. Maybe she could even feel him better at a slight distance. She showed up to take pictures in the new space. At first, crouching, she focused on the refuse they were collecting, absorbed in it—unaccountably, to anyone who hadn't seen her relationship to patterns, shadow, and their mysterious ability to convey states of mind and being.

Len called, "Hey, Satch. Can you take the ladder and plaster that crack up there?"

Satchel was heaping boxes. He hesitated. "Ahh, crap, man. Yeah, no, I'm not good with ladders!"

"What?"

"Okay, that's old history. Whatevs."

"Is it bad on your leg?"

"Hell, I can do it." Shirtless and in overalls, Satchel started unsteadily up the paint-dappled steps. He managed well enough. Gretchen watched as he slowly climbed with a pan of plaster in his hand and an implement in the other; he managed to make it. She snapped photos of him craning his neck toward the ceiling. Then she took photos of Ruby priming her first canvas in the new place—Ruby was the only one who smiled for the camera, but Gretchen waited until she forgot. And Julian stood right in the center of it all, a clove cigarette hanging out of his mouth, strumming an acoustic guitar, his long dark hair spiking down in back. Mostly she photographed Len, as he hammered loose nails to make them safe, covered up windows, gathered trash, gestured where they should put boards or pile them to discard, wiped his brow, or turned to tell a joke. He paid no attention to the camera. She captured the way he did tasks and the energy in his face.

After Gretchen had taken a great many pictures, Len came up to her. "Dear heart," he said. Gretchen, even if she was surprised by the archaic expression, smiled back at once. "I've been holding something for you. For a while."

She waited.

Len went away, apparently downstairs; they were storing some things in the dark, forlorn underground. When he came back, he carried a canvas. It was his lizard painting, the same one he'd showed her—the one she loved. Three undulating lizards vibrated with bright color weaving round their bodies. It matched their visible cells. All three had been outlined in white dots that seemed to thinly separate them from heat, land and air, like skin. He held it out and said, "I want you to have it."

She leaned forward, kissed Len over the top of the painting, and took it in her arms, holding onto the painting like an anchor. As though it settled something in her.

Characteristically, Len soon went with the other men on a supply errand. Gretchen propped Len's painting against a wall and sat down by Ruby on the floor. The younger woman looked worn. Gretchen tried to think of something they'd all touched on. She said, "You know when we were talking about quasars?" Her voice was animated. "The computers at work are up again, so I googled quasars. They're not stars; they just look that way through a telescope from the ground. Apparently the amount of energy they give off is a hundred times the energy of a normal galaxy."

"Really?" Ruby smiled a little.

"Yes. And what's strange about it . . . the quasars can drown out light from stars around them. It's like they *feed* on their light."

"Oh. God."

"What?"

"Holy shit!" Ruby said, shaking her head. "That's what the *Di Notis* are like." She looked downhearted.

Gretchen ignored this. "And I saw discussion threads about dark matter. Remember we talked about that? They seem to be powering quasars. In the laws of physics, gravity should be slowing down the expanding universe. Instead, it's expanding faster. And these physicists were saying that dark matter is why."

"Yeah. Like Satchi and his band," Ruby said grimly. "I remember *that* discussion all right."

Gretchen felt disappointed. "Ruby . . . I'm not talking about our love lives."

"Come on. Like Len doesn't inspire you?" Ruby asked irritably.

Gretchen laughed. "Okay, that's true. We're inspiring each other," she said. "It's just happening. Like a physics of happening."

"But tell me," Ruby said, still challenging. "When you came in, I saw you look around at things that are old and messed up. You relate to that?"

Gretchen was silent. Finally she said, "I do. Yes."

"Why?"

"Well, when a building is shut out from human life, it holds parts of time that are dark and even hideous, but that's because the building has been thrown away. It almost has a kind of majesty. And feels as though it's hurting."

As if Ruby had needed to hear the happy Gretchen say that she hadn't forgotten isolation, she asked lightly, "Do you want to see the basement? It's dirty and I think it's creepy, but maybe *you'll* like it. Here, let's take a flashlight."

They inched down the stairwell carefully. Gretchen had her camera in hand. The underfloor of the building held a rich, heavy smell of old water and accumulations of grime from past years. There were still large, empty wooden fruit boxes, some falling apart. Thick wires snaked around the unfinished walls. For a good while, Gretchen stayed taking her photos. She was interrogating the history of the place like she'd ask strangers whether they had a family, where they were from—not so much for details as to feel it.

Finally Ruby said urgently, "I'm cold. I want to go up."

Gretchen looked at her. "Are you all right?"

"No. . . . I'm scared, Gretchen. Really scared. Benny Di Noti's coming here this afternoon. I think he'll kick us out."

"Today? Coming here?"

"What I heard." There was a pause between them. "I'm gonna say things to him," Ruby said, fierce and anxious.

Gretchen watched Ruby's eyes gleaming in the semi-darkness. "I see," she said, nodding. "I wish I didn't have to go back to work. I should be here to help." They were both quiet. Finally Gretchen said, "Maybe he's never seen the place." Suddenly her tone turned hard. "The real estate listing is for his international mogul buddies. He pretends it's on Telegraph Hill. Making it more expensive." Gretchen rubbed her palms to clear off powdery dust. She wanted to go back to the painting Len had given her.

19. SLASH AND BURN

Benedict Di Noti and Ruby stood face-to-face at Petta's. He had a briefcase in his hand, a trench coat draped over his arm. It looked comical in the cavelike, chaotic space. Ruby held her arms tightly folded across her breasts.

"Where's Len Consodeen?"

All at once Ruby started shouting. "You! First you bring me flowers, then you send over your goons? What are you, a *thug?*"

Di Noti looked incredulous that his expected business meeting had turned into this confrontation. He said, coldly angry, "Is Consodeen even coming?"

She ignored the twist in pronunciation. "He'll be back when he's back. Answer me—why me? Why'd you do that to me—screw me and pretend it was nice?"

"My wife had surgery."

Ruby threw up her hands. *"I* was recovering from surgery! God."

"Well . . . you never said."

Di Noti took a step back and put the briefcase down gingerly on the dirty floor. As if the act gave him confidence, he added, "We had a good time, right? You enjoyed talking to me?"

"What talking? Except on the balcony—even that was all you."

Bristling, Di Noti stuck out his chin. "Don't give me that." Suddenly his face compressed into contempt. "How it actually was? I treated you sweet. You cute little artist girlies like 'sweet.' I know that."

Ruby shouted, "You made me suck your dick!"

Unaccountably composed, Di Noti said, "I didn't make you. It gave you an extra two weeks in the building. *You try* going to court, toots. Go ahead. You dealt some drugs, and we both know you sleep around. Not exactly credible."

"You pimped me to your son! And I didn't even know who he was!"

"A pimp is somebody who gets something from the lady's activities. You cost us plenty in back rent."

Ruby's face changed. The rage in her eyes seemed to have moved to somewhere else in the universe. Her mouth crumpled. "I never figured you for an asshole," she said, her voice quiet and grave. "I saw you as a decent man."

Di Noti took a sharp breath. There was a silence, as though it might turn the moment. Then he puffed the breath away. "I'm not waiting for your guy in charge." Looking at his wrist as though the watch could explain all, he swooped his leather case from the ground and strode out, banging his shoulder against the doorway.

Ruby paced the floor. Maybe she had hoped to fight him until she could recognize something. Until she could see a man in place of a demon. She still wished she could.

The way Benedict Di Noti used his hands in tandem to punctuate a statement seemed like a learned substitute for a more vigorous movement. His face looked somewhat grey or silvery in artificial light. In the sun it acquired a red cast. He could appear to be still while in the midst of a slow and deeply purposeful undertaking. He had other people to say things he didn't care to say, as if the use of too many words would deplete his store.

On this day he had words of his own. Removing his fedora gracefully, he went into the church, Saints John and Paul . . . Santi Giovanni e Paolo, same as the one in Venice. It was also the name of a Basilica in Rome. The one here wasn't by any means the largest congregation in the area; but he had at one time been a regular parishioner. His family had been part of it until his father's death. Their surname Di Noti was an Americanized version of the old Sicilian word for "unknown parents." Sometimes he wasn't even sure he was his dad's kid. Somehow, that name was so out of the ordinary, so tinged with stigma, that his suspicions had made him feel okay to do things he might not otherwise have done. For instance, bringing his teenage son to a so-called lady of the night. Nick had asked him for advice—how to do it right. So he'd schooled him, and he'd been handing him young ladies ever since, after he, himself, got bored with them.

The Ruby thing was weird, though, because it seemed Nick felt sorry for her. Nick was a good son, a great kid. He was young, but he looked to his dad's rules and practices, followed them. One day the boy would be sure to choose everything the best. . . . But the Ruby thing hadn't turned out much of a present to anything or anybody. Seemed like sort of a mistake.

Time to stop at the collection box, put in some bills and light a candle. There was a dank smell of leftover incense at the cool edges of the long nave. He made his way to the booth and sat before the screen. No one else happened to be in line.

"Hello, Father. Forgive me, Father, for I have sinned."

He heard a faint cough from the unseen priest. It wasn't the man he'd known, the family one. Would that be good or bad? "Welcome, my child. How long has it been since your last confession?"

"Uhhh. A long time. Four . . . five years."

"That long! What were your sins? Tell me, my son."

Di Noti crossed himself and, from memory, sputtered that he spoke in the name of all three personas of God. To the unseen, authorized man he then said, "I seduced a young woman. This was a recent thing. . . . I never meant anything more by it."

"And has this continued with the young woman?"

"No. No, it's over." Actually, she wasn't so young. He had maybe used the word to show wrongness. Di Noti remembered how, at this point in the proceedings, the priest would counsel him, and he expected to hear lengthy passages of scripture intoned, to bring matters toward reconciliation. He steeled himself. But nothing of the kind happened.

"Ten Hail Marys, my son."

"That's it, Father? For my sin?"

Di Noti heard the quick and efficient response, "If there are other sins, continue with your contrition."

Exasperated, Di Noti insisted, "She was a good girl, I think. I thought she wasn't, but now I'm starting to think she was. Is."

The priest could be heard heaving a tired sigh. "All right. *Twenty* Hail Marys."

Di Noti mumbled what he knew he must. "Omigod . . . I-am-heartily-sorry-for-having-offended-thee I detest allmysins . . . lordgodof-all . . . I-firmly-resolve-throughthehelpof-thy-grace . . . to avoid the near occasion of . . . to sin no more and avoid the . . ." He hesitated, numb. The Sacrament had speeded forward so quickly. "Well, Father, there should've been more here. . . . I've, you know, taken the Lord's name in vain. Pretty much daily, I forgot to mention. And didn't attend Mass. Or give the best example to my son. Again, pretty much daily. I, I boast about my various sins . . . boasted about it. About the girl, I mean."

The priest, barely audibly, replied, "Very well, my child. Misereatur tui omnipotens Deus, et dimissis peccatis tuis, perducat te ad vitam æternam, I absolve you from your sins. Amen."

Di Noti, unable to finish, stood up painfully and stumbled away. He thought he heard his absolver say, from beyond the curtain, "Go in peace, my son." His face was stretched. He had a restless need. Do something, but . . . do what sort of a thing? Should he tell Nick? No, of course not. Nick was the one who had overcome their heritage completely.

The name, the damned name D'Ignotti, his dad had changed at Ellis Island. Terrible fucking name! *D'Ignotti,* meaning from who knows what parents. Not just a bastard but a double orphan. Well, Nick was no damn orphan, and his loyalty to his father was as good as any dynasty around. And he'd treated him right! Gave him everything! Even got his first whore for his fifteenth birthday, one of the most beautiful girls around. Plenty women, plenty of cash, all the business opportunity a kid could ever want, and Nick paid him back as the best kid, best soldier he could have wanted.

Except this thing with the girl—how it turned out bothered him. . . . She didn't want Nick's money? She was kind of a kid herself. Strange kid, sad kid.

He jammed his hands into his pockets and strode away, his head pugnaciously leaning forward, as if watching his shoes take footsteps on their own.

Knees bent, Len sat in a far corner of Petta's on a makeshift pallet; Gretchen sat in front of him with her back leaning on his chest. Their legs touched, his arms wrapped around her, and her hands rested on his. Gretchen closed her eyes. A lit utility candle burned in a glass ashtray on the floor.

"Tonight the whole place looks like a cellar," he said softly. "Reminds me of some other places. Like Europe. Know what I mean?"

"M-hmm, I think so. I visited friends in Berlin for a couple weeks."

"I was in Berlin awhile too. Just after the Wall fell."

"Amazing!" she said. "I was there for a few days of it. I wonder if we saw each other?"

"I guess it's possible." There was a quiet pause. He adjusted his arms a little and said, "Sometimes it feels like I could have met you anytime I used to ride the train in Europe. I'd have remembered you, though. . . . I would ride for hours or for days. Looking at the sky. Going through mountains, and when the moon came up it'd look very close. Almost like you could float through it . . ." Gretchen sat absolutely still, except for her breathing. Len fell into synch with it. "But that's not what I was there for," he said, "in the end."

She shifted, turning her head toward him, lifted her brows and asked, "What, then?"

"Looking for someone. A partner . . . to find a partner."

Facing away again, Gretchen asked, "What does a partner mean to you, Len?"

"Oh! Partners do everything together. Talk in the middle of the night. Hatch plans for changing the world. Make love, make meals, shower, mop the floor, take walks, make love again." The immediate, yet subtly formal way of saying his piece . . . it was him.

"And would these partners by any chance be involved in theater?"

"Sure they would. On the barricades against corporate power, that's how things happen."

Gretchen laughed. "I can never quite get in your mood when you use those words. You mean hassle the powers that be and glory in it?"

"Yeah, yeah, you said it better. I mean write plays, find actors to perform them, make the costumes. . . . My kind of life."

Gretchen turned around fully, coming out of his embrace to sit so she could see him. "Is this what you wish you had or what you *have* had?"

He looked away, as if suddenly uncertain. "It's come my way once or twice. A couple of women I adored, who were onboard with that way of things."

"What happened?"

More slowly Len said, "Not that I never cried when I lost someone. Last time I really had a partner, it went for about five years. In theater, you can end up separated for weeks or even months, and I'd say, 'Hey, if one of us occasionally has a beer with somebody and spends the night, okay, as long as we let each other know.' But in the end it turned out she had another lover."

Gretchen waited.

He picked up a piece of grit off the floor and flicked it away. "Probably didn't want to hurt me by saying. We were supposed to tell each other everything, but she—she had this whole secret life. . . . Once you break that trust, you can bust your ass to get it back the same way, but it's not."

She hadn't expected to hear Len, the still-handsome theater director, say he'd been on the hurt side of unfaithfulness. "Did it make you give up? Your ideas about the right partner?"

"I don't know. Should have, I suppose. But a life like that still sounds like the best."

Gretchen waited a minute. "Any woman who fell in love with you would want to try. But I'm not sure what it would take to uproot a whole life for you. —I don't know, but . . . I really like my job and regular hours and health benefits."

Len nodded.

"And when it comes to your politics, I'm more the captivated observer than an armed lieutenant, right?"

Len put his hands on her shoulders. "You help me in more ways than you know, Gretchen," he said. "I can't write letters the way you wrote to the Di Notis. You translate things and make order. Without that, there's no action."

It occurred to her then that his partners, even if they were young and malleable, must have had some of her skills.

He leaned back against the wall again. "What does a partner mean to you, Gretchen?"

She looked sideways. "I hadn't been looking for one. I'm fine by myself. . . . But I can't say I'm against changing."

"You're not?"

"I guess I already have, if I can get at all excited to think of gallivanting around the world in the spirit of activism and maybe theater! It's new. I don't know if I'm cut out for it. You hold these dreams very close."

Len stopped to consider. "But then," he said, "sometimes I think I'm near the end of that." He straightened his back. "Maybe at heart, I'm a painter. Trying to pull people together makes a person struggle with *everybody's* vision. Their conflicts. Sometimes I've had enough."

"You, Len? Your appetite for organizing seems huge. And you're so good at it."

"Not so sure. We've taken advantage of an earthquake, but to make anything more of the situation, we have to negotiate with the Di Notis. I wasn't there when Di Noti showed up, and that was some fiasco. He bullied Ruby. I was even late. Satch-o isn't any better than I am when it comes to obeying the timepiece."

Gretchen shook her head. "Di Noti was early! Anyway, Ruby *wanted* to confront him. She told me. I wish I could have been there, too."

"Well, I'll get in touch with the guy and see him in his office. He's a piece of work, but I've dealt with worse."

Gretchen rested her chin on her hand. Len had said nothing about how these partners he talked of would make their living. Most likely women with trust funds or rich husbands had been a support to him. What a boy he was about that. And the acceptable one-night stands? But something in her said that if he wanted, he could learn. As she could.

"Enough about them," Len said. "Come to bed."

"Mm, I want to, but I'd better get back. Work tomorrow." She lifted herself and stood. Len moved toward the pillows on the pallet, his eyes resting on her. She loved the way he just gazed. As if he had years to wait for whatever was right for them. Perhaps that was the cause of what happened next. Leaning down again, she dived at the pallet of coats and clothes, managing to land with surprising agility right across him.

He laughed loud and fully, a rare thing for him.

"Len! Sh, you'll scare them upstairs."

"Oh, poor Julian, the youngest of all," he said, carefree, and slid his arms round her.

Satchel took Len to The Black Hart, the same dive bar where he'd argued with Gretchen when he came to the city. He and Len played pool in a side room—Satchel carelessly if well overall, Len slowly, with occasional deadly accuracy. The floor was made of large wooden shipworthy planks, the walls emerald green. Late-night air gave the room a smoky feel, though nobody smoked—this had been banned in California a year ago. Though it was sometimes tolerated, Satchel didn't want to push his luck in front of Len. A jukebox cycled continuously—Motown, fifties classics, early rock and jazz-inflected soul. Satchel had more experience at pool, but his intermittent drinking had started to show.

A sudden car backfire went off. Satchel slammed the table with his cue and yelled as if he'd been hit.

"What the——?" Len put his hand on Satchel's shoulder.

"Fuck, man. Fuck. That kinda stuff takes me right back to 'Nam. Right back, man. Oh, Christ." Satchel stared wildly at the far wall. Some of his hair dangled over one eye like a tiny broken appendage.

"Okay, let's sit," Len said, taking his elbow and steering him to the bar. He located them each on a stool, side by side. "You okay?"

Satchel moved his stare upward, toward the ceiling. "I guess."

Len ordered for both and started nursing an ale. "Feel like telling me?"

Satchel quickly downed two whisky shots. The place was starting to fill up, and glasses clinked around them. Satchel hesitated; he rarely spoke of Vietnam. All the same, Len's calm allowed him to talk. "Yeah. . . . Okay. This is when I'm eighteen . . ." He stopped, clutched his glass, looked sideways at the ceiling. "Crouching in some dirty trench, and we got Cong in the area. We have to go find 'em. 'Cause there's ammo at the station, a whole *massive* ammo dump. An' I'm just deployed that week, barely got there. Y'know? It's two, three in the morning and now this *bone-splintering* sound. That you think you're already in hell."

Len had never heard this voice from Satchel. He sat listening closely to eighteen-year-old Satchel in the army.

"The sound is 'cause the Cong got in, get into our dump and sabotage. See? Like July-fourth-to-the-thousandth-power *insane*. And I don't even know if I can shoot this piece they issued—didn't train us for shit. Red light going off up sideways an' under me, and I'm very fuckin' scared!—and then. Then. Y'know." Satchel had a thin line of spittle on his lower lip.

Len took one sip of his ale and nodded.

"The guy next to me. Right there, man. His forehead blows off. That's what I see. My friend, man! My friend *peels* into this . . . this . . . awww." It sounded like a boy. He squirmed against the counter. Len waited again.

A harsh gasp came from Satchel. "Okay, well. They put us there at the *start* of 'Nam. Yeah, no. I don't want to say about it. Just, it didn't take long to figure we should never have dragged our asses there. My first week! My fuckin' hello to the glory of conquest, man. Like if we had a chance. The whole village turns out to be in on it. Grandmothers, even. My Sarge rags on me, being I don't want to take an order to bayonet this woman in a church. This old lady that somebody had *already practically done.* Hardly breathing. He says, 'Since your friend *got it* yesterday, you should be up for this.' Yeah?" Satchel pulled his arm over his mouth. "I didn't even *do* the damn . . . couldn't. Huh? And everything so—was just so disorganized he doesn't even react, just gives the job . . . some next sucker. . . . Aaaaahhhh . . ." He banged his face at his hands.

Len continued to sit.

After a short, heaving pause, Satchel went on in a higher voice. "Later I *did.* I mean did do things!" He stared into Len's eyes. "Like were you there, man?"

Called to account, Len shook his head. "Not me," he said. He sipped. Now it was Satchel who waited. Len flexed his wrist. "I've got a good ten years on you, but still of age to get drafted. When I got my notice, I took off."

"Took off? Where, man?" Satchel looked astonished. He clearly had not pictured Len as a draft-dodger.

"Europe for a while. Naples . . . France." Len chuckled. "I was broke, though."

"You weren't a conscientious objector?"

Len shifted in his seat and said more firmly, "Just up and left. I had no plans of getting mixed up in that war. I was definite about it."

"Prescient," Satchel said, more in his usual mode. Finally, aware of the dangling clump of hair in his face, he blew air at it with his lower lip. When that didn't work, he swished it back with his hand.

Len didn't choose the time to bring out what he hadn't liked about that war. He sidestepped by adding, "I tend to move around."

"Shaking off the fetters?" Satchel asked him curiously.

"Well, I don't know. Like now . . . have to see if I stay here longer than I thought. I might." He smiled, grabbed the back of Satchel's neck and roughed up the already-tangled hair.

"Hey," Satch said, as though objecting. But his face changed. He wiped his mouth with the back of his sleeve. "You know what? I guess I should have mentioned. Uh . . . ha, um, I'm drunk. . . . I should have said before, but . . . I know Gretchen . . . ? . . . from old times. Like way back."

"I could see you know each other fairly well."

It had always seemed Len cultivated oblivion to the facts of this. "No, yeah. But . . . I'd never muscle in on you, see? That—y'know, *that* was a way differ'nt . . ."

"I'm cool, Satch-o. This is now," Len said evenly. The stiff set of his shoulders didn't match, but he didn't seem to want more. Satchel sat silently, looking down. His face sagged slightly. Then he roused himself, crushed a napkin in his fist and said merrily, "One more exquisite down-to-earth brew for the road. I'll get it." He stood slightly and raised a finger for the bartender.

Len sat up straight on his stool, letting out a careful breath. He looked like a martial artist who knows what a step implies, with ideas about what and whether to commit.

Satchel glanced at his friend and noticed this might be all they'd ever say about Gretchen's past. Because Len didn't want to know? Or he thought it was bad form? Maybe it was a weird kind of privacy. Or dignity.

Gretchen took many of her photographs standing still, effaced, almost melting into the background. If she had to walk around investigating a possible shot, she suddenly acquired physical grace. It was impossible to tell whether it came from years of experience or from eager attention. She couldn't have explained, and she wasn't aware of it. She found it comfortable examining leaves on the ground or insects or refuse on a floor; she could hunker down without strain. If she had to tip her head back to capture images of the sky, her flexibility came easily.

Gretchen had asked, as a child, why people would want to do bad things, if it means they can't spend eternity in such a safe and lovely place as heaven. When her mother answered that heaven might be boring, she felt her first deep and embarrassing disappointment. She expected people to live from imagination and absorption—to thrive on their dreams. This had resulted in much diminishment of happiness. It hurt deeply when Satchel accused her of letting her own execution of hopes and dreams die of malnourishment.

When Gretchen felt let down, when she feared she had fallen short, or when people didn't deliver to themselves what she'd wished for them, she had a reflexive and almost invariable response. Go out and capture, in black and white, a living being or face in the instant when character revealed itself. If she had to be at home alone, she'd go to her computer, open a digital file of sky or water, and colorize it. Change all the colors. She never knew what she might discover by transforming her photographs this way, but sooner or later it would astonish her. Or become incredibly beautiful. In these ways, she had a kind of stability in her heart that was not easily overcome. It would take a great deal to overcome her.

Di Noti half-rose to lean across his immense desk and shake Len's hand. Len—so tall he nearly had to crouch to meet the gesture—was surprised that the other man gripped his own in a squeeze that pinched. Di Noti, without actually making eye contact, made a hand-sweep toward the bulky maroon leather-backed chair in front of him. As Len sat, Di Noti looked down at a sheaf of papers on his desk. After some moments, he looked up from the papers and steepled his hands.

Len wondered what was coming. He felt the best thing would be to play to Di Noti's demonstration of kingly domain. "Nice view," he commented.

"Yes," Di Noti said confidently. "Union Square's the prime location in town."

"How long have you been located here?"

"Seventeen years. What about you, Mr. . . . what is it again?"

"Considine. I grew up across the Bay, but I spend as much time in San Francisco as I can. Love the place."

"You must be some type of artist," Di Noti said. "I received your past correspondence. It's outdated, given the state of the property since the earthquake." He gathered his mouth in a subtle indication of distaste.

"Well, Mr. Di Noti, we're making good on our promise. We're taking responsibility for the mess. We can clean it up for you. We've swept and washed quite a bit in the past few days."

"I saw," Di Noti responded without inflecting his voice.

Len didn't mention their missed connection, but he went on pointedly, "There's such a long Italian tradition in North Beach of supporting the arts. And we'd like to make something out of the partnership that's developing with you."

Di Noti shook his head. "Wasting your breath," he said coolly.

Len sat recalculating.

But Di Noti went on, "Skip the pretty words. Partner-ship, shmartnership. I don't like your friends messing with the damn wiring and plumbing. You know it's for sale."

"Not that your prospective buyers would be coming by to check up on that."

Di Noti gave a sly little chortle. Then he said, "I've never hidden the fact that the property is an investment, or that interested parties are residing abroad. I just don't want any trouble."

"We'd like to negotiate with you," Len said, squaring his shoulders.

"The place comes back under my control when *I* de-cide." He glanced at his watch.

"Do you mean—"

"I'll tell you what I mean. . . ." But now Di Noti shoved his own chair back, got up and turned to look out his fine, broad window at the exquisitely-maintained palm trees below. Len wisely remained quiet and in place. With a little huff, Di Noti finally turned around again. "Let's have nobody stupid, here. The property is in a hell of a state. I've decided that for now, you guys can have access. Can deal with it, I mean. Then we'll see."

Len kept as steady as possible. "Mr. Di Noti, that's wonderful. I think we can make you very happy with that decision. We'd like to be able to—"

"I'll give you the cell number for a kid who'll make sure anything you do to the building is easily taken apart. Just go. Go and do your . . . your art thing. But before you display any pictures to the public, I'll have to see." He remained standing. "Make sure nothing fishy's going on."

What did he mean? Len felt the brass studs of the chair pressing his shoulder blades. He looked up at Di Noti. Since the man had already taken a position, at this moment there was nothing to be gained in making pledges to him. Or in revisiting his ghastly treatment of Ruby.

The broker said, "You can go." From his vest pocket he swiftly pulled a small folded note with a phone number and set it down within reaching distance of Len. Then he flicked his fingers as though gnats were agitating him, sat, and went back to his papers, which Len suddenly realized had nothing to do with Petta's.

When Len got back, the group hurried to meet him at the market door. Len nodded yes, and Satchel rushed to give him a high-five, yelling "L., you did it! L.! The place is our palace! Man, the music we're going to make. The painting. The theater! Oh, God! We're gonna remake gorgeous San Fran!"

Len surrounded him with both arms. "We had the local merchants on our side. Good old Yankee indignation against injustice."

Ruby, flushed, shook her hands up and down. "Wow. We need confetti!"

Julian nodded. "I'm gonna go get tequila." The missed-tooth gap, front and center in his mouth, gleamed darkly exuberant.

Len said levelly, "And it's time to get to work. This means we can do our work." Turning away slightly, he pulled out his cell phone to tell Gretchen.

Long since, Ruby had skipped out on her doctor's follow-up appointment. Finally she sneaked back to find out the state of her breast cancer. After a few tedious tests and an afternoon of waiting, she sat in front of the disgruntled lady, her surgeon, who said, "Well! It took you long enough."

"C'mon, Doc. I'm here now. Can't go back, only forward. Right?"

The woman in the white coat sternly told her, "You're one fiendishly lucky woman. Looks like we got it all out. Without new signs in all this time, it's not likely to recur. So no radiation, no chemo."

Ruby's face went blank with astonishment. "That's incredible!" She added, "I guess I had no right to expect it, after waiting so long."

The surgeon seemed glad to hear Ruby admit it. Smiling, she said, "Cut down on your stress. A moderate lifestyle will help you stay healthy."

"Um, never exactly tried that," Ruby said sheepishly.

"Take a chance. You're good to go, Miss Arena. See me in six months. You need regular mammograms. And don't forget your vitamin E."

Ruby now decided to settle some things. First she looked for work. Without office skills, she had no chance of a job like Gretchen's, but after a hard week of search on Craigslist, she got a job as a professional clown. Normally they would have hired someone with experience and training, but she scored gleeful applause in an impromptu audition. The work consisted of stalking around parties—children's birthdays or corporate cocktail events—in heavy, elaborate outfits representing action heroes or large animals. Sometimes food, like a giant banana or pickle. The costume confined her completely, except for a small rectangular screen for breathing. This anonymity felt comfortable, like a way of bypassing old shame. All she had to do was to navigate a crowd and alternately lift her feet and arms. Sometimes people came up to tell her things they wouldn't normally say. A man confided that he'd made a terrible mistake at work that day, underestimating the length of a building. One woman said, "Those teeth—they remind me of my stupid brother-in-law. He inherited my dad's money, just by sucking up." Another woman confessed that she was embarrassed and worried about postpartum depression. Ruby didn't respond to what was blurted out to her, just waved her hands or went for a nod. Physically, all of it was vigorous; she could do it.

One night she had to fill in for some very tall fellow hired to walk around a museum lobby as a dinosaur. What she hadn't expected was the size of the costume, meant for a tall person. Her screened facial panel for air hung nowhere near where she needed it. In fact, the breathing screen was above her head. Ruby, five feet four, was in trouble.

For a while she sashayed slowly and carefully around the room. But then, with a slow but loud swoop she fell on her back, legs waving in the air. The crowd loved it. People clapped and gathered around Ruby. Her muffled cries for help couldn't be heard over the din. Finally an Armani-suited man, clutching a Manhattan with a fancy napkin, bent forward a bit and asked, "Doing okay down there?"

"No! Help!" Ruby answered. He quickly organized three others to pull her to a standing position. The dinosaur getup was so heavy that it took a while. Perhaps her viewers were more drunk than she had realized, because they seemed to find this struggle the most entertaining part.

Later, Gretchen listened to Ruby's story of the evening and said, "Good God. Must have been so humiliating."

"Well, not so much the job, but I don't want to be an upended beetle. Unless I can control the experience. If I was planning the action, I'd do something intense."

"What do you mean?"

"I like that song we've been working on for Len. I miss performing. Even before that, I was starting to think about performance art."

"Interesting. I can document it, if you like."

"That would be terrific. What I have in mind is something that takes . . . pain, the strong experience of pain, and makes its memory less painful. Whoever or whatever did it to you isn't there now. Can't do that to you anymore. It would feel like an enactment. One from a space where I'm the one who presents what happens. Like taking away some memories I don't want."

Next day at Petta's, Satchel and Julian banged out riffs from "Slash and Burn" and some other new songs. None were quiet. Behind them, a crew continued the cleanup.

Len had his cell phone in hand. He raised an index finger, signaling Gretchen to wait a second. He was saying, "Yeah, *very* active times. We did a whole siege on the place, best corner in the city, and the investment group basically told us we could squat." There was a short pause. "Don't worry, man. We're rocking that six thousand square feet of space. Talk to you later." There was a lull in the music, while Julian used a new electrical setup to hook up a guitar.

Gretchen said, "You must miss them."

"Sure. My Aussie guys are like war buddies."

Thoughtfully, she asked, "Why did you leave Australia, Len?"

"I was deported."

The music started again with a vengeance.

"Really? What happened?"

"Well, we hit the Ministry of Arts and the Opera House. Somebody figured us for an element they had to get rid of."

Gretchen nodded without comment.

Satchel told Julian, "Go back to the bridge. Try some other chords." The music receded.

"Ever get involved with any politics like that?" Len asked her.

Gretchen answered, "A little. Even as a teenager I was against the Vietnam War. And I joined protests after Kent

State. Remember how devastating it was that cops killed those kids? How overwhelming?"

Len said, "You bet I do."

"When we demonstrated, a big ring of local people crowded around and threw things at our faces. Mostly oozing rotten vegetables. . . . One guy picked me. 'Get her! The blonde! Miss Hoity-toity. What a bitch!' Just pure hate. But nobody got hurt."

Len took her arm. "Did you stay?"

"Yeah, but some other demonstrators showed up with these awful signs—curse words and slogans implying that *we* wanted to kill someone, and they'd carry those. That's what the media captured and printed. Those images were ruining everything."

Julian let out some hoarse guitar stutters.

Len said, "If anybody tries to bust up what we're doing, don't react. Best way to diffuse them is be open to different approaches and let stuff run its course while people put stuff in the mix. Even if things polarize, it gets us some news. Then we get to be *in* the news, point out the importance of the arts. And we talk about a whole renaissance of artists who want this, and how the merchants love it— because it's been a major eyesore—and local Italians love it 'cause their history overflows with art. Oh, and I finally got through to the assistant for a guy on the Board of Supervisors who's interested. He's courting the arts community. Good for tourism, see? We're hopping!" Gretchen was about to ask him why he was so positive they deserved to inhabit this market a family had lost because they couldn't afford to keep it. But Len dipped Gretchen like a teenager and kissed her.

The back of Gretchen's hair touched the floor as she laughed. "You're irrepressible!" she yelled above the din. Part of her had just made contact with the gritty bottom of the building, and she'd actually liked it.

A large poster outside Petta's highlighted the date, the name Ruby Arena, and her piece "Use Myself Lose Myself." On this night, the first public performance there, the paying crowd included more out-of-town students and tourists than North Beach artists and friends. Len stood by the door collecting a pay-as-you wish cover charge, to help reimburse some of the supplies to fix the space.

About fifteen minutes after start time, Ruby walked gracefully, barefoot, to the end of the central area. Already in character, she didn't look at anyone, and though she wore unglamorous long black underwear, her fluid movements gave the baggy garment authority. She knelt at the center of the floor, face bent forward, arms crossed above her head. The audience quieted. Distant, aching old-building sounds could be heard, with an overlay of street traffic. Ruby rocked anxiously. It looked like a modern dance perform-ance, but occasionally she twitched, and once she sneezed. No one laughed. There was clear gravity in her rocking as she went deeper in feeling what she had to do. A few people at the end of rows stood up and moved against the wall to see better or make room for latecomers.

Then, slowly, Ruby got up, unbuttoned the top buttons of her floppy underwear, and reached inside to draw a small object out: a rubber hammer. She poised it over different parts of her body, bending in slow darting motions, and as though choosing the best place for the purpose, she tapped the tool lightly against her forearm. She whispered, "Why does it do this?" Then pulled her long sleeve up to her elbow and continued, as though listening to a faraway sound. The tapping became vigorous. It gradually hardened until its impact took on the intensity of blows. Ruby's arm flushed red. "Why do I do this." A kind of statement? Her face became contorted, but the words repeated in a monotone, like a ritual. At times she paced around the room, stopping with her back to the audience or before the front row. "Why do I do this." (Thunk, thunk,. thunk..) "Why-does-it-why-is . . ." (Thonk thonk thonk thonk thonk.) The blows became more disturbing and repetitive, and occasionally she stopped long enough to say hoarsely, "Why do I do this."

From the audience, a man's voice barked, loud and aggressive, *"Because you deserve it, bitch!"* Onlookers gasped. Quickly, he stood—a young man, well-dressed, in an expensive navy suit. He had light, carefully cut hair. It was Nick Di Noti.

Satchel lunged toward him from his nearby seat and landed a solid punch on the younger man's throat, another to his face. Several people slipped or fell as chairs tumbled. Satchel's shouts couldn't be distinguished from an upswell of yelling; but he yanked young Di Noti to his feet, and Nick's voice cut a sharp swath through the noise—"This event was not approved! You're not getting away with that!"

Len stepped up and pushed them apart. He said, "And you are . . ."

Ruby, shaking, had remained quiet, but now called out, "Nick Di Noti, from the brokers."

Satchel cried, "That fucker! You know who he is? What he did to Ruby?" Gretchen stood by, snapping with her camera.

The son of the real estate scion brushed his thighs vigorously with both arms, though most of the damage was to his coat. A small line of blood zigzagged from his mouth to his chin, and he held his throat with one hand. "Stop this performance," he said hoarsely.

"You're the performer now, asshole!" Satchel yelled.

Len turned to Ruby. "Get ahold of Satch and man the front door with him, okay? Too many people coming in off the street. And get the cash box."

Satchel, head lowered pugnaciously, clearly didn't want to back down, but he and Ruby went to the door.

Nick chose that moment to say, "You had your chance. You're washed up!" He rolled his sleeves to resume the battle. His face and arms were scratched.

Len said, "We called the number your dad gave us, but nobody ever answered. We asked you both to this performance, we described it—sent two registered letters about our electrical work. Nobody responded."

"And we never agreed. The police will be here." Gretchen moved in to photograph Nick's furious face at closer range. "Get. That. Away," Nick told her.

Some people left, others came looking into the front door, and a crowd blocked the sidewalk. A long-bearded, unkempt man yelled, "Hey! My jacket, give it back!" A burly guy shoved into Petta's, tried to grab the cash box from Satchel, and when he was pushed back out, a young boy lifted a skateboard over the intruder's head, trying to smash him with it. Just then the police arrived in thick belts and bulletproof vests. They suddenly were right there with Nick, Len and Gretchen.

Nick began, "Officer, I was assault—"

"Shut up. Sit down," the cop yelled, while he spun around to Gretchen. "You! Gimme that fuckin' camera!" and grabbed Gretchen's arm. Gretchen ignored him and continued shooting. The cop grabbed both her arms hard, as Gretchen grappled to keep her camera.

Len moved in, yelling, "Hands off her!"

At the same time, the cop shouted, "All of you *sit*—"

Len and the cop shoved each other, and faster than any of them could see it, a nightstick came down on Len. Two other policemen rushed over. While the first cop yanked out handcuffs, the other two slammed Len to the floor, cracking his legs with a nightstick. A vigorous kick from Len was met with a blow to his kneecap. Throughout the shouting, screaming and sweating, Gretchen kept taking pictures. Ruby looked wide-eyed, a hand covering her mouth. Gretchen handed her the camera and said, "Keep this for me. I don't want the cops to get it, so don't let anybody see. I'm getting an ambulance for Len."

In the ambulance, Len resisted the extreme pain in his legs. Holding himself taut, he struggled to lie still; whatever the paramedic had put in his IV should soon start to help. He had a keen desire to get up and bludgeon the cops to smith-ereens. Although he knew several regular, friendly North Beach patrol cops, these were different. Though they let him go in an ambulance instead of taking him with them— one of his legs seemed definitely broken—they didn't let Gretchen come along. Damn cops could have killed him! It would have meant a lot if he could just see Gretchen's face right now.

Ah, with the drip in his arm he was finally starting to slow down. He took deep breaths, then tried to breathe evenly and *make* himself think of something else. . . . Remembered the horseback rider in the dream she had told him: where he had some kind of quest. A sign or tattoo under his collarbone, she said. He'd ridden away into his journey, then come to her again. That was the right way. Always back to her. . . . The ambulance lurched and, against his will, he groaned at the pain. City lights soared past, cast-ing beams against the walls that narrowly surrounded him. He was almost there, the paramedic told him. *To where?* he thought. No, no. He knew. Soon, depending on what they had to do to him, it would hurt less . . . or much more.

Len, in a tiny room of institutional pastel green that reeked of hand sanitizer, lay full of painkillers. His leg was in a huge cast. Gretchen ran her hand over his forehead. She whispered, "I should have gotten the ambulance faster. Instead of taking pictures."

Len shook his head once with eyes closed. "You did good."

In the hospital bed the next day, Len had arranged himself so that, in spite of his heavy leg cast, he sat up as straight as royalty.

"My cell phone's in the drawer, sweetheart. Can you get it for me? I want to fill in a friend."

"The nurse said not to use cell phones on the ward," she said awkwardly. "It interferes with their equipment."

Len just grinned. Taking it from her hand, he quickly tapped in a series of keys.

> Hey buddy getting back to u. Yeah been a circus. Xplosive. Landlords blocked gallery/ got a little physical.

Gretchen waited while he paused. Then he texted,

Dont worry. Fine
arts under thumb of
big guys but we're
takin em ON!

He handed the phone back to Gretchen and said, "Just updating a friend—Julian scored me a phone card. My Aussie pals heard something happened. Baby, can you get copies of your photos to the press?"

Gretchen gulped. "I'll try. There's a catch, though. It looks like you shoved the cop first."

"Oh. Crap." Len made a face.

She was afraid he'd say to get rid of the telling shot, but he just laughed and said, "Okay, then how about a photo show at LiveWire?"

"Sure. I'll do it. You're awfully lively today."

"Well, I hated to get bashed up, but I'm having a crazy rush 'cause I'm still alive. Bottom line: you're here. And I'm still here. I still think San Francisco's the best city in the States! We're gonna make it the best in the world. Public health planning . . . a decent chance that gays will have marriage. Women police chiefs and district attorneys—women of color. Getting art out there . . . not just billboards for corporate bullies chained to war machines!"

Gretchen raised an eyebrow and looked at him skeptically. "Now you sound high as a kite. And after what just happened?"

Ignoring this, he continued on in a fast, wobbly voice, "Damn, I'm even kind of impressed with the Di Noti boy.

It takes balls to charge in with all those people surrounding him."

Gretchen said wryly, "Maybe he doesn't think of us as people. Really, Len, I don't get why you're even *trying* to sound so cheery. And saintly." She looked out the hospital window and sighed. "What do you think will happen to Petta's?"

He lay back and folded his hands loosely on his chest. More calmly now, he answered, "Well, even if I screwed up, I got to talk to the power. Men like Di Noti. And guys on the Board of Supervisors that can cramp the Di Noti style if they want. We're not finished fighting for Petta's yet."

"Who's going to do it, though? Until you get out of the hospital?"

"Well, can you talk to Satch? He's a little erratic even for a middle-aged musician, but I think he has the makings of an organizer. He'll need you to keep him on track. . . . Ruby's good at talking up those Italian merchants who like us bringing them tourist business. And Julian, young Julian. He has more energy than he knows what to do with. Just a few more people and it flies with me or without me."

Gretchen put both her hands on his. Her brows were raised plaintively. *"I want to fly and I want it to be with you."* She gave him her lovely smile that curled almost imperceptibly on one side.

"You're the one with the wings, sweetheart," Len told her. He took a deep breath and closed his eyes. "Ahh, you really send me."

"It's Demerol," Gretchen said.

His eyes were still closed. "Funny thing, my chest hurts. A lot."

Gretchen smoothed the sheet. "I'll go talk to your nurse. Get some rest," she said, kissing him.

⊞

In a hospital waiting room, Satchel and Ruby had their arms around each other. She said quietly, "One thing bothers me. When you left, why'd you take my toothbrush?"

Satchel pulled out of the embrace. "What? I did *not,* Rube! That was mine."

Ruby said, "Ah. Yeah. You would say that."

He sighed, then leaned against her shoulder but stared at the ceiling, muttering.

"Okay," Ruby went on. "I don't want to talk about what happened to Len. Let's talk about something else. There's this compelling TV thing I saw—math. Geometry."

"You and math? And *so . . .*"

"Be nice, Satchi. It was about scalability, but I couldn't understand it for shit. What's that about how if you double a line on a square on each side it's more than twice as big?" Suddenly, Satchel lunged to tickle her. "No, c'mon," she said. "There's a gap in my education, but I want a way back in." Two little boys nearby in baseball caps and smeared jackets stared at her.

"Sorry, Rube. I'm friendly with math. Here goes. . . . So stretch a line and make it twice as long, then it's twice as long. But if you double a two-dimensional *square* on each side it's four times bigger." He used his hands to illustrate. Ruby forced herself not to imagine the choppy way Di Noti did that. Satchel went on, "Take a *cube* and double the size of the sides—eight times bigger. See?"

Ruby smiled. "Ha! Weird, but I can. Can finally see it." She hadn't felt anywhere near this good since Nick started the fight. "They said on the program if you scale a praying mantis a few hundred times its size, it'd fall over flat, 'cause the skinny legs couldn't support its weight."

"Yeah. Muscle fiber strength won't increase because of size increase."

"The strength of . . . okay, this is exciting. It's making me think about scalability in architecture—like if you lean things against each other at the top it would stand better. A cone, like a wigwam or yurt thing."

"Or pyramids, Rube. *But* . . . if you use that model, there's other limitations. Like a mountain or an Egyptian pyramid stands 'cause of this enormous stone density, but if you make it hollow, it won't be anywhere near as stable." He started glancing at the kids, who were trying to get candy out of a vending machine with insufficient change.

Ruby stayed silent. She often felt drawn to Satchel's excessive philosophizing, although—or perhaps because—she didn't think that way. But when he declaimed, his tone made her feel childish. It shouldn't be like that, she thought; after all, she made her own discoveries. She had to think in clusters and from instinct. She could visualize hollow pyramids, then other hollow shapes. She decided to say so. "I'm seeing these chambers in front of me. It's like they're rooms of stored experience."

"Rooms of stored experience. Not bad. But lemme guess. You're gonna apply scalability to it."

"Oh. Well, maybe you *could.*" That made her feel stupid. Most of the way through school, she'd had trouble with the way math and science were presented in class; her own insights about color and shapes weren't valued. A few years back, a physician had claimed she probably had a learning disorder, and he was sorry there'd been no Adderall around when she was a kid. As though she should have grown up using it. That triggered her fear of being an outright freak, which sometimes made her words lurch. She blurted, "Like if you applied scalability to the workings of a mind, synapses, you know, there's some clue about—"

"—About what, now?"

"—bypassing the frustration of a person who has trouble taking in new experiences."

"That's totally random, Rube."

"Well, I'm losing the thread, but new experience is

threatening!" She meant the present. Satchel stood up and handed a quarter to one of the boys. They finished their transaction and left with the candy. At the last moment the taller one threw a thumbs-up to Satch.

He sat and said, "What threatens me is expectations. Not so much what other people expect, but if you have huge expectations, it wallops you when life doesn't deliver. Ever read Goethe's *Young Werther?*"

"Banned in Europe, right?" As a young girl, she'd been a voracious reader.

"So, yeah, all these youngsters started offing themselves after reading it. *Pain,* Rube. Of expecting so fucking much."

"Were you born into wealth or something?" She rubbed her forearms.

"Huh. You don't get it, Rube. So, but here's an example. Like—Dad told me Mom was just visiting an aunt. *When is she coming home, Daddy?* 'Your aunt says she'll be back soon.' *Can I talk to her on the phone?* 'Sorry, Satchie, there's no phone there.' Years later come to find out she was a lush. And also humping some friend of Dad's."

"Holy shit. Then what?"

"She lands in some Ohio asylum where she croaks a few years later, and Dad follows her into fuckin' eternity after awhile. So no way to ask who put Mom in the nut house. Anyway, she sure paid for not stepping up."

"Satchi . . ." His eyes looked too big for his face.

"No, Rube. It's like . . . Gretch knows the deal. I'm like, like . . . ha, The Can't Do guy."

They sat unmoving for a while. The room continued its coughing, muttering sounds. Then Ruby said, "My father was an army corporal. We lived in Asia when I was small. Then Italy. Finally on the East Coast, where he sent me to boarding school. *My* mother was a nut case. She had reason to be."

"Seriously? And you—you went to boarding school?"

"I flunked out."

"That's incredible. I almost got kicked out," he said.

"For?"

"Cheating. I didn't cheat on my exams, though. Just sold answers to my buddies. The usual way to get extra cash for weed. Just happened to get busted out by this asshole who hated me. My father fixed it up. Corrupt, yeah? But in spite of all that, music got me. Dad's groaning in his grave, but music is hella better to me than anything. You? Why'd you flunk out, Rube?"

"Didn't study. When they were teaching us crap or re-writing history to fit their agenda, I couldn't get into it. I was busy sketching."

"Then?"

Ruby squirmed. "Pregnant by a tattoo artist I met when I was in the band. I wasn't even twenty, he was older. . . . Shacked up a couple months, I miscarried, and he got drafted. Left for Vietnam. I loved the guy, but he went all ballistic after he got back. And was on some serious shit. Not just meds. Heroin."

"Get out! Really?" Satchel sat back in his chair and dropped his jaw. "You never told me any of that."

Ruby didn't answer.

"I served," he said.

"Thought so," she told him. "It shows in . . . you get worked up in your sleep. Everybody I knew was older than me. Protesters, soldiers. Everybody alive then's messed up. You can't always see the scars."

"No shit."

Ruby said, "Sometimes I think depressed people try to keep their lives small in scale so they can reduce their pain."

"Smart thought. It figures."

It made her feel carefree to hear "smart" from Satchel for the first time. She laughed. "Ohhh. God. That's both of us. We should make our lives smaller."

Now Satch threw his arms around her again. "Hahaha. Not a chance, babygirl."

By the next day, Len had a clear-plastic oxygen mask over his face. Because it was hard to breathe, he tried to focus on things that calmed him. Waiting for Gretchen to come back to the hospital, he thought of what it was like to run his fingers through her hair.

He could always find a small place at her temples that grew paler and whiter. On one side was a silvery flow. On the other side one small area had a certain stiffness, more tangled and yet oddly soft. Maybe only he knew where this different place was. *Another thing,* he thought: when Gretchen went behind the camera her body crouched slightly, with an animal-like litheness. When she spoke, even when the words came haltingly, she meant what she said. The way she avoided grand statements, which might falsify her thought or feeling, made him happy. Gretchen would tell about a past formative experience once, and that would be it. This fell to him like a sweetness of new snow—the once-ness and also the not-again-ness. With other people, she'd hold to a message . . . "You need to see your doctor;" "You need to follow through on your promises." With him, no. It came to him clearly: for however long it could last (he was exultant to know this) he was going to ride it. . . .

His eyes were closed when Gretchen came in. Thinking he was asleep, she sat down silently in the bedside chair. She kept imagining, over and over, the phone call she'd had an hour ago: "Miss Wilson? The doctor wants you to know that Mr. Considine has a complication. He has a secondary lung infection." Her body had felt heavy ever since.

Len turned his eyes to her. Even with the hospital gown bunched around his neck and his face half-covered by a breathing mask, he had composure. "Hey, sweetheart," he said shakily.

She touched him gently with both hands and said, "You don't need to talk. I'll just be here. How bad does it hurt?"

Coughing, he pulled the mask away for a moment to spit into a tissue. "I'll be okay." His hands shook, and his breath came so fast and labored that Gretchen stiffened in a quick-freeze of worry.

Then Satchel burst into the room: *"Hey,* Lennie."

Len waved feebly. "Satch-o." It sounded like boys' sports names.

"Awesome. You tricked them, Mr. L. Mr. Considine. Mr. El Con! Adventures in Frisco and Australia. Hoo, man. . . . Last time I was in Australia I had a blast."

His excessive cheer was too loud. *"You* were in Australia?" Gretchen asked Satchel skeptically.

"No, yeah. The band had this stopover on that cruise. Anyways. I'm wandering through these caves. Beautiful, amazing paintings. Bushmen. I mean aboriginal dudes. But so I met this one guy. This first-class elder. Beard, hair a weird color of chartreuse. Was telling me their mythology. Fascinating stuff. I ask what's he doing in this particular cave. Then he's telling me about how he just met this—this lovely young woman a little while before, who happened to also be walking through the cave, and how he had made love with her."

Gretchen said, "Satchel, Len should rest." *Made love?* Suddenly very aggravated, she felt like making an angry outburst—*Is this a rape story? Or a claim that prostitutes in Australia work in caves instead of on the street?* The intensity of her anger surprised her. She held it in. But what was the point of Satchel's posturing? She looked at Len to see how he was taking it.

"It's okay. F-finish it," Len said. He listened as though it were a straight news report, neither eager nor bored, but absorbing the story. Gretchen watched Satchel's mouth move without hearing the words. Maybe there was a point; actually, what if Satchel was frightened? And he wanted to entertain and distract Len. Maybe that was his idea of loving, right now.

It didn't entertain or distract Gretchen. "I'll be back," she muttered. She stumbled toward the bathroom. In the round, swing-out mirror her eyelids looked swollen. In fact, she felt a mighty siege of tears wanting to explode. Instead, she splashed her eyes and forehead with cold water in the small porcelain sink and gasped against the necessary chill.

Ruby had taken care of the camera. Gretchen retrieved prints from the confrontation at Petta's, which showed:

Nick Di Noti with skewed mouth and livid eyes, suit jacket pulled sideways in Satchel's grasp

Nick Di Noti with flared nostrils and wide-open mouth, hands held out as though pushing air

Policeman with furrowed brow and wild eyes, leaning pugnaciously toward the viewer

Policeman from behind, buttocks and thighs straining, pants shiny—wheeling urgently on Len

Len shoving policeman, his mouth anxious

Policeman angrily pulling out blurred nightstick

Two policemen whacking on a falling Len

Upraised legs of Len surrounded by uniformed men kicking him

Gretchen showed him the pictures. His room smelled profoundly of hand-disinfectant. As Gretchen handed over each photograph, he looked, then pointed with his index finger to telling details: nightsticks, grimaces, eyes of self-righteous rage. Both of them stared into the dark ugliness of unanticipated violence. Frozen into those black and white rectangles, it sucked away words.

The only sound in the room was Len's rasping, strained breathing. Gretchen held Len's hand. Slowly they came into a silence without their cares and struggles, where they simply breathed in unison.

Waiting for Gretchen to come home, Ruby walked around the apartment, marveling at what an orderly space had materialized after the earthquake. She had been part of that. Along one wall, Gretchen's boxes of photographs stood in neat stacks; most had survived the quake. Ruby picked up Gretchen's lizard scissors and smiled; the cutting edges formed legs, and their hinge was an eye.

Then Gretchen was beside her.

"God, you startled me!" Ruby fluttered her hands. "I didn't hear a thing. Really, you have the quietest walk of anybody. It's spooky."

"So I hear."

"What's happening with Len?"

Gretchen had triple lines around her mouth, which looked tight. "If he's not better soon, they might have to intubate him. I'm pretty sure they won't. He was healthy. The infection hit him because of his injuries."

"Because of germs at the hospital?"

Gretchen, her face pale, said, "They're culturing it. But—you know. It's a hospital. Full of bugs. I want him out of there, but the broken leg is so bad he'll have a different walk for good. That's what the doctor says."

"You know I don't always trust medics."

"I'm tired. I'm so tired."

"Do you want tea?" Ruby had familiarized herself with Gretchen's stash of boxes: fennel, apricot, dandelion root, licorice, lemon ginger.

"Honestly, I want to fall over. I'm going to lie down; you can come and talk. I can't do it standing up."

For a while Gretchen lay face down on her bed. Ruby sat by her, then leaned sideways with her head propped on one arm, watching gauze curtains flutter in the window. Finally she said, "Gretchen?"

"Mm." Gretchen turned and opened her eyes.

"The way it happened to Len. . . . Do you believe in evil?"

"Not like a magical entity. In a way, sure."

"I had this dream. The Prince of Darkness was there. For some reason I was, too, and I kept trying to figure him out. I was saying, 'What d'you do all day? What's your job?' And he told me what you'd expect: lead people to the brink of crime. So I said, 'What about God?' and he's like, 'Yeah, what about him?' 'Well, do you know him? You've met?' 'Sure, all the time.' That got me. So I said, 'How?' And he answered, 'See, I work with him. We work together.' 'But why?' Um, what was that about? And he said, 'It's a project. We test people's faith. The integrity of their faith.'"

"Sounds like some ancient Gnostic version of religion."

"The only faith I have, though, is in . . . *remembering*. Like I have to gather things to make a meaning. Unless I make a painting or a ritual or film, they get dispersed. . . . And then I can't manage *at all*, Gretchen. You know?" She flopped down onto the bed on her back.

Gretchen didn't answer, just stroked Ruby's hair.

"We moved around so many cities and countries when I was a kid, my dad being an army officer. I really think about some places we lived."

"Which ones?"

"Kathmandu. I was little, but I'd get out of bed at night, without my parents even knowing, and walk around in the street, right in the garbage. I saw strange things there . . ."

Gretchen cringed. She said in a soft, worn voice, "I'm feeling torn up. Please, I don't think we should talk about this now. Sorry, Ruby. I can't." They lay without finishing. In the curtained window, night changed the sky.

Early morning, Gretchen was alone. She crouched beside a white wooden pedestal with curved, tapering legs, on which there was a plant—a fairly large aloe. It had long been her way, if she burned herself cooking, to cut a piece of aloe and bandage the sore with this plant as medicine. After a day or two, the wound would shape up. Over years she'd grown close to this aloe. She kept it growing straight and proud, weeding out reckless offshoots. When the cold in her apartment wounded the plant, she got new soil and re-planted, keeping only the spears with good posture. But as time passed, she saw how the new uprisings thrived on untidy habits of outreach. This aloe was not meant to be well-organized. She'd come to love it that way.

Gretchen peered at a small white filmy area on the plant; it turned out to be a spider web. Must be the work of a very little spider, she thought. Miniscule grey-white dots lodged in the web. Aha, juice-sucking gnats. So! She had an eight-footed ally in the health of her plant. She sat quietly watching. At last an entire live insect became visible to her on the web, small but recognizable. There it was: the lord of fumigation, her tiny prince or princess, a spider so different in scale that several of it could fill the span of her fingernail. She saw it work, coaxing new strands, repairing others. It rushed at nothing. It just did what needed to be done. "Hey.

Hey there," Gretchen said quietly. She wondered if it could feel her breath. She thought of how Len had said, a few hours ago, "Hey, sweetheart."

She went to bring a speck of water on her forefinger and set it on the plant, watching the spider hesitate before the water drop that glinted, a tiny blue oval. Soon the spider came beside it. Gretchen looked closer. The spider, completely engrossed, leaned up to this tiny shimmering watering hole. It crouched, quite still, and stayed taking its drink in peace. Gretchen found her eyes filling with the tears that slowly worked their way there.

Len's oxygen mask had been switched to one that puffed air back to his lungs every time he took a breath. Monitors and computer screens dominated the room, displaying his vital signs and other levels of his body's performance. He had plastic tubes extending from so many places that Gretchen dreaded displacing one; he'd been catheterized, and a plastic square on his arm served as the nexus for large needles delivering many medications through his veins. His feet and hands had swelled; his kidneys and liver were not functioning normally.

The nurse said, "We're going to try giving you a little water now, Leonard. We'll take the mask off briefly. See how you do on your own."

Len leaned forward, as though trying to sit up, but the nurse put him back, semi-reclining. Gretchen tried to look cheerful and casual while he gulped fluid from a straw. Some ran down his chin. He wiped his wrist on it, then lay looking spent. His face was grey and alien. The nurse quickly clamped his mask back on. There was a plangent sound of beeping.

"What's going on?" Gretchen asked hurriedly.

"His oxygen level's lower than we like to see. The doctor's going to want to look. We can draw blood to get a more accurate reading. I'll be right back."

Gretchen moved in and took Len's hand. He opened his eyes then, trying to speak, and gasped, "One time at . . . San Jose State I . . . designed a set . . . built . . . it in . . . two days I . . ." She took his other hand and shook her head. He closed his eyes again, and remained that way while someone extracted a blood sample. His breathing had become so rapid and erratic that red lights and multiple beeps went off on his monitors.

All at once people in white coats burst in, surrounding a crash cart.

"What's happening?" Gretchen asked frantically.

"You need to step outside, ma'am," a doctor barked. She'd never seen him before.

"No! I have to know what's going on." She saw a large blue tube in the stranger's hand. "You're not going to intubate him—"

"We'll do what's best for him," the nurse said kindly and firmly.

"Then I have to talk to him!" Gretchen burst out. "Let me talk to him!"

Len started for a moment, face flushed, eyes full of confusion.

"Everything will be all right, darling," Gretchen told him. "Do what they tell you. I'll be right here!"

He showed no recognition; his eyes—strangely wild and darkened—flamed like embers unable to settle, and the nurse cried, "Ma'am, you need to leave *now!*"

They made Gretchen stay in a waiting room. Once, she bristled through the swinging doors of the ICU, demanding

to know what was going on. The door to Len's room remained shut. A nurse said, "Sorry, honey. They're working
hard in there. Surgeon will let you know when there's something to tell you."

The doctor came to her after more than an hour, saying
softly, "Things aren't looking as good as we hoped. He has
a collapsed lung, and his organs aren't working well."

"What does that mean for his recovery?"

"It's not good. His body's failing."

Gretchen waited quietly in the side room. In his mid-
fifties, Len was in good health; why did this have to happen? Surely he'd get through it? With the sound of her own
heartbeat careening through her head, she phoned Ruby to
come right away and bring Satchel.

After another forty minutes the surgeon finally returned,
looking slumped. He hesitated, uttered a few confusing pre-
liminaries, and Gretchen tried to hold onto her patience. In
a strained voice he said, "Ma'am, we attempted everything
for your friend. But I'm afraid our efforts were unsuccessful." He seemed exhausted.

"What?" Rigid, Gretchen stared at him. "Then she said
harshly, "That's not true. He's not gone. *He's not gone.*"

"I'm very sorry. Very sorry, ma'am."

The words *sorry sorry sorry* seemed to echo. Trembling,
she heard her own voice repeating something. It was strident, but it seemed distant. Although the surgeon had taken
off his cap and walked away, for a short while medical staff
surrounded Gretchen. Had she fallen? She was dizzy. She
had to vomit.

Gretchen stood still in her apartment, arms limp at her
sides. She knew a few things for certain. One was that she
wanted a medicine dropper to put water on the rim of a
clay-potted plant, in case a little spider came out to drink.

Another was that she was thirsty; and water, whether sipped or quickly drained from the glass, kept disappearing: as though it floated out through her pores or her hair to another universe. Walking around her home, she discovered something squeezing her hand when she tried to do a task. It was her other hand.

"No!" she burst out. "That's wrong. Not here. Not this room." She hurried to another room and a different task. The room was not right. No place was right. It was the third thing she knew.

Ruby had gone for groceries. Gretchen sat by her aloe plant, dripping water into the tray under its pot. Satchel, rummaging in the nearby kitchen, called out, "I'm making dinner, Gretch. Let's have salad. I need a big bowl. Where's that?"

"The wooden cupboard. I'll get it." She got up.

Satchel didn't wait; he hurried over and grasped the knob, grumbling, "How the hell can you find anything? Too dark!" He shoved the cupboard door open and plunged in.

Gretchen had forgotten his impetuous cooking behavior. "Wait, don't push the—" Her eyes jumped to the plant stand. *"Oh!"* Powered by fear she jumped forward, nearly catching her clay pot, but it capsized—stand and plant slamming to the floor. Gretchen wailed. "No! *No!*" She gathered pieces of the wreck into her hands. The broken aloe lay among shards of its pot.

"What the hell?" Satchel looked around him. "We can re-plant it, no problem." He found the bowl he'd been searching for. Gretchen kept crying. "Sorry, sorry, Gretch," he said. "What's so bad?"

"There was a spider that's important to me."

"What? A *spider?* A fucking *spider?*"

"Go away," Gretchen told him, sobbing toward the floor and slumping back down on it.

"You must be crazy," Satchel said. "Certifiable." He didn't know what to do. "Yeah, no," he added grimly. He wanted to call her an observer of life, but he had told her that so many times, and it had done no good.

Gretchen, hunched over, murmured finally, ". . . Listen, Satch. I think . . . I loved him in spite of myself."

"The spider?" Satchel knelt beside her. She looked up reproachfully. "Oh," he said. "Okay. Like, I know you're in love with Len."

Suddenly she began to talk. To tell him. Through her tears she said, "He needed a beautiful and just world so badly. And for that he was willing to . . . he *only* thought about making the world just. And beautiful. He worked at it all the time he was awake! I mean he didn't know it would cost him his life, but . . . he'd have let it—if that led to artists having their place. Not just *a* place. Someplace giving a home to people's souls . . . pouring out their paintings and sculpture . . . performance, ph-photos . . . photographs . . ."

It might have been the largest number of Gretchen's words Satchel had ever listened to. He was surprised how something shifted, maybe not from the inchoate words but her need to say them. She put the broken clay pieces down. Gravely, he asked, "What d'you think you'll do?"

She sighed. Then she squared her shoulders and finally, avoiding the mess of dirt and plant and broken clay, she stood up. "Well . . . I can take the lead on getting the photos out. It'll be hard right now, but that was important to him."

Satchel, standing beside her, warmed to this. "Now you're talking. Get back Petta's! Artists' rights! We could have a fundraiser."

Gretchen stared. "You know, Satchel? That's actually a good idea. Would you—will you work on it? Make calls and get flyers out? Maybe with Julian and Ruby?"

"*Oh* yeah. I mean Len, man. Like one of us musta copied the other one's screwed-up leg? First I wreck my leg, then he cracks . . . uh, no, that's not what I meant. But how many signs does a guy need? I'm Lennie's henchguy."

Gretchen laughed. "You'll be his right-hand man?"

Satchel thought that was good; he knew what to call himself. Now that he knew, he felt safer and more solid. He nodded fiercely. "The same."

The crowd at LiveWire spilled into the street with force; laughter and loud greetings ricocheted around. Cars honked as small groups talked, smoked or argued with a plastic wine glass in hand. Inside, Gretchen's photographs of the incident at Petta's filled three walls. Many of them hadn't seemed to her good enough to show Len; she let them be printed and shown, in the context that he had died. News coverage about Len, his project and Petta's had also incited a vociferous contingent of new supporters. They accused the police of his death and the Di Noti firm of instigating it. Gretchen didn't agree or care, just wanted to honor Len.

At nine o'clock, Ruby launched into her new performance piece: "Own Up to It: We Own It!" She stood casting a shadow in front of a projected loop of blurry film clips from the night she documented Satchel's outburst (his face edited out). As in her first performance piece, she asked questions in a detached voice, increasingly hard and aggressive. "What is winning? Who's winning and what's won? . . . What's won in winning? . . . What do artists win when they win? What do owners lose when they lose? *What do owners own?* What do I *own?*" She went into a brassy, rock-singer voice, leaning on one hip. "Whadda they own? Own it don' own it. Own it don' own it. *We . . . own . . . it. . . . We!*"

The house lights went up, and Julian burst into an explosive guitar riff. Even with their rudimentary electronic resources, it made a strong segue. Satchel threw in a heavy bongo beat, and then they pulled back as Ruby announced, "We have a little number for you here. I think you'll like it. It's about what some powerful cops and corporate thugs of San Francisco do to us every day."

Gretchen, behind her camera, winced at the exaggerated language. But the crowd roused to it, giving a jubilant cheer. The musicians broke into their long-planned rendition of the anthem Len had inspired, and Ruby used her whiny, strident, silly but scary vocal tones to turn up the music's emotional voltage:

> *It was a rotten day in a pitiful world*
> *In a scaggy part of town*
> *It was a scumbag of a millennium*
> *Your tears go down-up-down.*
>
> *Slash and burn expansion*
> *Slash and burn expansion*
> *Whoa—ohh, wohhh—oh!*
>
> *It was a rotten game played by what's-his-name*
> *He demolished your heart*
> *Like a used car part*
> *Your tears go down-up-down.*
>
> *Slash and burn expansion*
> *Slash and burn expansion*
> *Whoa—ohh, wohhh—oh!*
>
> *The landlords and the cops better stop their special ops*
> *They wanta bury our heroes*
> *While they add a few zeros,*
> *Bang us down-up-down.*
>
> *Slash and burn expansion*
> *Slash and burn expansion*
> *Whoa—ohh, wohhh—oh!*

It was a rotten game played by what's-their-name
They tried to kill our art
They'll never kill my heart!
Our fight goes down
   Up
   Down
   Up
   UHHHHHHHHHPPP!

Julian leapt forward and convulsed his guitar, Santana-like. Satchel escalated the bongos furiously. Gretchen's camera zoomed in on his sweating, ecstatic face. Ruby gyrated, people clapped to the beat, and in spite of the crush, their audience started to dance. The goofy song Len had asked for turned into a long impromptu wordless set. As the last note finally launched itself and echoed away, Satchel shouted out an old 1960s taunt—"Up against the wall, motherfuckers!"

The crowd howled with laughter and cheers. The night at LiveWire ended in jubilant hugs.

20. THROUGH THE NARROW CHANNEL

A few days passed before Gretchen said, "Satchel, you didn't have to yell 'up against the wall' at the performance. I remember back in the day when we demonstrated. Even more now, public perception gets skewed by a nutjob message."

Satchel just laughed. "Len wouldn't care. He said get their attention first."

"Huh!" Gretchen said. "You're probably right."

"I learned a lot from Len," Satchel went on. "Whenever we yakked about the way the arts are funded, and that top sponsors are always in league moneywise with some kinda war, like Korea, Vietnam. Iraq. He called 'em 'war pimps.'"

Gretchen shook her head. "But you know, there's a difference between a little bombast between friends and a public message."

"You're a prig, Gretch. Is any beer handy?"

"No. This is important. What Len was working for has to be separated from extremism. Don't let people think you're part of that. It'll mess things up."

"Okay. I'll go easy on the bombast. Me carry spear. No yell."

"Only way to carry the spear is to lead. Be a leader."

"Whadda you want me to be? Lennie?"

"Satchel, didn't you like big events—always? You were a teenage music producer launching bands?"

"So?"

"You *love* being in the vortex. Even when you're fascinated by obscure facts and telling them."

"How is that about Len?"

Gretchen smiled. "Satch, maybe think about what Len's work means to *you*."

He fiddled with his thumbs. "Hm. Hmmm. When you and me first knew each other, years back, I told you about fighting in 'Nam. Remember?"

"Of course."

"I don't wanta say about it anymore. I was a kid-got-fucked-up-in-the-war. If there's no help from a little bottle of Jack now and then, I gotta . . . I need . . . naw. I mean it's like a whole overwhelming. . . . huh!—I probably wasted myself singing." Gretchen adjusted her scarf and waited. He went on, "Yeah. Yeah. You're not always right. But so, on this you're setting me straight. Like you said a time or two, my true love is *drums;* just never thought I was good. I—I'm gonna make up for lost damn time." He sighed, then grabbed his jacket. "So babe, gotta pick up flyers for the memorial, then I got music to practice."

At the funeral in a community center, a large side table with candles held pictures of Len and his art and performances: also his ashes in a white box. The many flowers, messages on paper, and little mementos turned the table into a colorful chaotic altar. The program, emceed by Gretchen, gave many people a chance to read poems about Len or share memories. Except for a brief announcement about the strength of Len's vision and achievements, she didn't speak about him. Later, people would say they were astonished by her composure. In spite of occasional trembling, she was able to do what needed to be done.

No blood family of Len's represented him—parents and a sister had died, and his brother, a few faraway cousins or their parents who had been located had said they "admired him" but "couldn't make it." A uniformed policeman, middle-aged and solid, was present; Gretchen wondered if he was there for security.

One of Len's former students, a tall elegant woman with wavy black hair, came to the front. "Leonard Considine was a great director," she began. She told about the glory days at San Jose State. Some of the others he had taught or worked with in theater came forward, full of praise and sorrow.

Then Satchel took a turn. He held his hands out in front of him, splayed his fingers and tapped the podium anxiously, as if it was the wrong kind of drum. After taking a deep breath, he started. "Hey. Everybody doing good out there? . . . Yeah. Len was a hella incredible friend! Mentor, pal . . . like . . . goad to perfection, I mean, the man was practically a fucking . . . well, I wish I knew him when I was a major screw-up. He made me better by example. Guess he thought of me as a weirdo younger guy with—like verve. Which, y'know, he loved any kind of verve." He opened his eyes wide. "And had this great *acceptance* of people. When I was pontificating, he never put me down. Told me . . ." He stopped here and brushed his forehead with one arm, then finished. 'Satch-o, you're a cornucopia of facts.' He never said 'useless facts!' No, yeah. He took what you brought. And believed you'd do your best. That goes for everybody here, right?" He nodded. There were cheers.

A thin, not very robust-looking young man in thick-lensed glasses said, "I worked with Len on a new nonprofit organization to further technology in the arts. He gave us fantastic ideas and was never too tired or busy to listen to ours. He wasn't even on the board, just cared about what we're doing!"

A heavyset man in a black suit and vest spoke in a practiced, ringing voice, like the head of some local agency. "Len Considine was an outstanding example of community success bred by community need. We need fifty Len Considines in San Francisco. The power of local action is what will change our government. Is what will change the creative and commercial development of this city."

Ruby was dressed in black tights, a herringbone skirt and bright orange sneakers. She took her turn somewhat breathlessly. "Hi. Hi. Um, here goes. Thanks to Len, I got to know a lot of wonderful Italian people here in North Beach. Mostly small-business owners. Some great folks. Full of energy and heart. . . . And most of them liked the Petta's Market plan right away. They were backing us. And they signed our petition, too. Len inspired that. And he got *so* many of us believing that the world needs our art. And that we deserve to be in charge of—of our content. And who should know about it. And how." People clapped respectfully for the tribute, and Gretchen beamed at her.

A sinewy man in old jeans and a work shirt loped forward. "Ahhh. I knew Len when we were Richmond kids. Damn, we had good times." He wiped his nose. "He always acted happy. We'd bitch about school, our families . . . that there wasn't gonna be anything *for* us down the line except drivin' a truck or doin' time. We lifted a little bit of small-time stuff back then, y'know? But Len, he would always be thinkin', thinkin.' He had this monster curiosity, askin' questions, makin' you think along with him. I love the guy like a brother. . . . Yeah, he's my *brother.*"

A muscular guy in a motorcycle jacket with lank hair and glasses stepped confidently up to the podium. He grabbed it with both hands, standing erect and at ease. "Okay. Okay, everybody. We know that Len got sick in the ICU. Sick to his death. That makes *me* sick to death. It's bad enough that the pigs slugged him to hell, but this ICU business makes grounds for a lawsuit against the hospital. I say we go for it!" His exhortation lasted about fifteen minutes. A young Asian man started passing out flyers. They were from a group of volunteers, Medical Professionals Against Injustice. Since their stated mission was to enlist people in the profession to contribute to anti-poverty organizations, it was unclear how this could be related to the memorial or even the angry exhortation.

More speeches and reminiscences followed. Among the groups who claimed Len were Californian anarchists, theater professionals, a couple of old hard-line Marxists, a painter advancing the cause of public nudity, a dignified art professor, and briefly, a member of the Board of Supervisors—the one whose assistant had handled all of his communications.

One of Len's old girlfriends had flown in from Europe. With tumultuous hair permed as a blond Afro, she'd chosen to wear fishnet tights and a thigh-length, skin-tight snakeskin sheath. Snuffling, between frequent pauses she read an old love letter from him in its entirety. Gretchen stood stonily with her arms folded.

For hours, people came forward to speak what they chose. Finally Gretchen announced in a clear, calm way that donated food waited in the adjoining room. As people started to mill around, Julian, who'd sat in the front row, got up and embraced Gretchen. "I really looked up to the dude," he said gently.

She stared at him for a moment, then told him, "You know, Julian, I've gotten to like the blank place in your front teeth."

He laughed. "Actually, I'm thinking of having it fixed. I like your dress." Instead of black, Gretchen wore a soft yellow gown with a flower pattern, Len's favorite.

Others came toward them. The policeman made his way to her, taking off his cap, which showed his buzzed hair turning grizzled. Gretchen whispered to Julian, *"Could it be possible he wants to apologize for what they did to Len?"*

The officer identified himself and spoke quietly. "Miss Wilson, one of Mr. Considine's associates, a member of the Communist Party, is wanted in San Francisco for arson. We need to learn whether he left the country for Australia." He named some aliases. "What can you tell us about that individual?"

Gretchen blinked. "Nothing at all. I never met anybody like that. I don't know anything about Len's old friends or connections."

Len's slinky former girlfriend came up, handed her a slip of paper with her name and Berlin contact information and burst out, "I'm starting a Web site to honor Leonard. Send me digital files of his paintings for the site. Okay? As soon as possible!" Staring toward the ex-girlfriend's fishnet tights, Gretchen took the paper and muttered something in reply.

Her next arrival was the eager lawsuit-monger with the motorcycle jacket. "Just say the word," he said eagerly. "We'll bust these fake medical experts at the hospital and take them for a bundle!"

Gretchen roused herself. "Actually, no," she told him firmly. "I'm not supporting that. Tests were inconclusive on exactly what the infection was. It happened, and money won't help."

"It could help the cause plenty! Not only taking back Petta's, but getting even."

"I wouldn't be part of that. Excuse me," Gretchen said. She went outside, walked down some steps, stood by a fruit tree. She leaned a hand against it, as sobs caught her and carried her with them. There she stayed until people came looking.

⊞

Gretchen held a large paint brush in her hand. She was painting both her bedroom window trim and door fire-engine red.

"Wow. That's a really different effect," Ruby said. She plopped down in the secondhand wicker armchair Gretchen had just bought. It had a washed-crimson cotton blanket draped over it, patterned with birds.

Gretchen didn't look away from her brushstrokes. "I wanted 'different,' so that's good."

"Freshening things up, like?"

Gretchen stopped then and looked at Ruby. "Len said something about my room—that it looked austere. That's what he told me," she said.

Ruby gulped. She didn't have anything soothing to say.

"I have a tin suitcase full of photos I can set up at the foot of the bed. I'll find a little beveled mirror. It'll be . . . warmer," Gretchen said. "More inviting."

"People will love it."

Gretchen shook her head. "It's not really for them. It's for him. He's just not *in* it."

"Oh, Gretchen. Oh, honey . . ." Ruby bit her lip. After a few minutes she left.

Gretchen kept on painting. Her thoughts roamed like a voice inside her, speaking to herself: *A lover's hair falls to your face like an avalanche of flowers. . . . A lover stains your bones. Trying to get rid of that is nothing but a child's drawing.*

Gretchen and Ruby sat side by side on the shore of Ocean Beach. The sky was somber and the air had turned windy, but the two women stared out at the waves, making no move to leave. Ruby held herself, arms around her ribs, knees bent. The curls in her short dark hair snatched up with every gust of wind. Gretchen sat straight, rocking lightly back and forth.

Ruby said, "I have this need to sing again. Other things are bubbling up. I want to do performance work and video and maybe more. I thought painting was all there is for me, but . . . I don't know. Maybe five years from now I'll say, 'I used to paint' or 'I used to sing.' Or maybe painting will hold all my attention."

Gretchen stared at the water. She said, "I used to . . . kayak a lot."

"Yeah, you did that?"

"I miss it. In the boat I felt like I'm where I belong."

Ruby said, "Wow. Knowing that is important. Me . . . the only place I ever felt that comfortable in my skin was Nepal."

"Really? You mean Kathmandu?"

"Yeah." Throughout her life, Ruby had often waked from a dream at the darkest hour of night weeping. The memory of this childhood place offered her solace and protection along with magic. Brushing tears away with her hands, she'd imagine herself freely walking dusty streets again, partaking in their familiarity. Now she told Gretchen, "I make an actual effort to dream about it. You know how some people try to direct their dreams? I try to dream I'm meeting giant birds or sages. Once or twice I did see them." In the dreams, they caressed her and exclaimed as adoringly as though she had been born to them. Then she would feel lost and baffled by finally waking to the dark and her sorrow. She went on, "I can't do it now. There's no time to dream. I don't sleep well at Julian's. The guys practice until three a.m. Lots of great stuff, but all the drumming keeps me up."

Gretchen said, "It would be fine to stay with me again for a while. Want to?"

Ruby looked at how the wind took her friend's hair into her face and then away. "Thank you, Gretchen! I would love that."

"It'll be good to have you. You know, Ruby . . . I'm sorry I cut you off the night you tried to tell me about Kathmandu. Can we do it now? What did you want to say?"

"Well . . . okay. Let me think." Nearby waves surrounding the two women did the speaking for a while. Then Ruby went on, "When I was a little girl, I used to sneak out when my parents were asleep, and walk the streets by myself."

"Mm. Sounds scary."

Ruby became animated. "But see, it wasn't. I was surrounded by a lot of things you'd think would shock me— garbage, all sizes of animals, and strange interactions among people that I didn't understand. But it was like I was safe. It was some other kind of universe. That's what I remember. The strangest thing was that the streets ran with blood."

"My God. That's terrifying. *Blood?*"

"No, though. It wasn't frightening. It was holy. The blood was from sacrifices. See, they'd been done with a feeling of reverence. People used to reach out a finger and touch the blood to their foreheads."

"How extraordinary. That you don't remember being scared by it."

"Well, there's also the fact that other things going on for me were *more* scary."

Gretchen waited. The sound of the water slowly hurling, then folding on itself kept a steady beat.

Finally Ruby went on, "That whole thing with Di Noti? There's a part of me that got used to doing what a man wanted sexually, that I had to do, from when I was just a kid. My uncle."

"Oh, Ruby. I'm sorry. I'm sorry you went through that."

"Nobody knew. Nobody figured it out." She had been small. "You were supposed to respect an uncle. He would start by saying *Take off your underpants.*"

Gretchen said, "I didn't know that happened to you. It's horrible."

"I'm not sure if it was as bad as the shrinks say. Probably. I have this thing that wherever I am, I want it to be somewhere else. Some other lover, other city. Different day. Some other boyfriend or time in history would be better. Been clean and sober for two and a half months, though. I don't know if I'm a real addict, but maybe, because getting along without any mood-altering smokes or drinks is a huge effort. And I was pretty tired of waking up and not liking what happened the night before. Besides that, it's good for keeping a job. . . . But I haven't decided who I am in the daily grind."

Gretchen smiled at her. "You'll figure it out. And you have people who love you." Ruby smiled back and they sat still, side by side. Gretchen took Ruby's hand.

"What about you?" Ruby asked. "Do *you* think about anything you remember that comforts you?"

Gretchen sighed. "I don't know," she said. "Changing my room a way I think he would have loved absorbs me, like an art project. Sometimes I don't see how I could end up loving an activist; I feel like at times they use people, so sure they're right that they force it on you. Still, it seems as if I can see and hear every minute of Len, and I don't want to put it away. His voice. His hands. The birthmark on his chest. Even times when all of us were together at Trieste. Even about quasars, remember?"

"Yeah, Satchel was holding forth, and after, you looked them up."

"Later, Len and I mentioned quasars, too. . . . ha, I can't explain why this makes me happy. About their blueness."

"Blueness?"

"Just that they look blue. Another thing . . . probably they're spiraling away from us. . . . Talking about things like that with Len made me know his heart better."

"I like spiraling away," Ruby said. She laughed. "Is that what we're doing right now?"

"No," Gretchen said thoughtfully. "I think we're exactly in front of this ocean. On sand that's getting fairly damp and cold." She stood up, dusted herself off, and they started walking. "What's hard for me is that I need to figure out what to do about Len's work. What I should do in it."

"What do you want to do?"

"I don't know. Not yet. I do want what he tried to carry on. I expected that Web site they've started in Germany to be kind of a hindrance, full of heavy political rhetoric making him sound like a weirdo. Actually, it's just pictures of his paintings. I decided to send some myself, so people can see the beautiful work he did." They reached drier sand and started trudging through it. "The question is whether I'm going to spend a lot of time trying to pull people together about Petta's."

Ruby was glad she wasn't Julian's lodger any more. She'd learned about an artist with AIDS, who was painting the entryway to a church in return for a place to live. Ruby volunteered to help. Early one afternoon, she found herself walking toward the heavy front doors, carrying a bucket of paint. In the entryway, several people on ladders daubed precise golden stars onto cyan-blue arched walls. She could see a tall, bald, fragile-looking man with a big Adam's apple on a ladder, leaning toward the curved ceiling as he painted white doves.

Just before she reached the steps, Ruby heard a man calling her name. She recognized Ben Di Noti's voice and kept going. As he called louder she turned, saw it really was him and closed her face away. But he walked up to her. For a minute they both stood staring. Then he laughed, took off his hat and bowed playfully.

"What do *you* want?" Ruby asked scornfully.

He said nothing about her bucket of paint, simply announced in a courtly way, "Miss Arena. I would like to buy one of your paintings." He tilted his head coyly.

Ruby set the paint down on the sidewalk. Her voice went sharp: "Your son, the great Nicholas Di Noti, has one of them already. So I believe the family already made its investment." Thrown off guard, she stared him down with her hands on her hips.

Di Noti drew himself up more seriously and said, "I haven't made any investment in your talent." With a touch of dignity he added, "But I could. I could do that."

Fog had started its afternoon shift toward them. "How do you even show me your face? What gives you the right?"

Di Noti said, "Your friend Mr. Consodeen said there's a long tradition of supporting the arts in North Beach. That was correct. In addition, I've acquired the painting you sold to my son for considerably more than he paid you for it."

The air turned denser as the fog moved by. It was hard for Ruby to believe any of this. "I don't do commissions."

"Then some work you've already done," he said quickly. "Name your price. Up to a grand."

"What, so you think I could make it big?"

Wryly, he answered, "With a little help from your friends."

A plan formed in Ruby's head. "Hmmm. You know what? Benny, you can have one of my best paintings that's still decent after the quake, for a thou. But only once. If, uh, someday you make a killing on it, good for you. My . . . my agent or whoever will deliver it to your office. And you can give the check, made out to me, to him. That'll be it. The whole deal. Nothing after that." She felt thrilled and a little astonished that she'd made a fast enough recovery to come up with all this.

Di Noti nodded. Once again he'd taken on an air of mock-reverence, but his eyes looked newly tired. "Very well, Miss Arena. My assistant will look out for the delivery. It's been lovely knowing you."

Ruby smiled crookedly as he sauntered away. Could her intermediary be Satch? No, Julian would be more level-headed. After the money came in, if it did, she knew what she'd do: pass half of it to the artists' fund that had started at Len's memorial. She picked up the heavy bucket of paint and walked up the steps to be greeted by new friends.

Gretchen stood at her bus stop, looking at her watch. It had started to rain. She shook her head, pulled a dark scarf closer around her neck, and opened an umbrella. One hand held it, while the other went deep into her pocket for warmth. She was pensive.

She thought about this challenging San Francisco she loved, which Len had adored. All over the city people were getting by or not. At Sixteenth and Mission, women with haggard eyes, ill-dressed against the cold, swaggered their hips to signal they were free for a "date." Two miles away in the Tenderloin, wandering men with white spittle at the corners of their mouths cursed at the sidewalk, or seized others by the arm and threatened to hit them. Executives in glossy ties sat in plush Financial District restaurant booths, laughing with convivial pleasure about gains of the day. Mothers in the Outer Mission nursed their babies and were glad if they had a hot dinner on the table for husbands without immigration papers.

Gretchen felt Len's presence. The thing was: she didn't

want to be an activist. Who was going to lead the charge? Would Len have wanted *her* to do it? (Was she even capable?) Surely the mantle of activism made the question of whether you wanted to, or felt you could, irrelevant. Had taking care of his vision been conferred on her?

The bus pulled up, and she sat in a center-facing seat, the only one left. She soon realized that its vacancy had to do with the matted-hair guy beside her.

"Don't touch! Get away!" he bellowed. He smelled like urine. She figured it would be better not to point out she hadn't touched him, not even with her folded wet umbrella. She stood up nervously.

The man shouted, "Too much noise! People! Too much people!" Three passengers got up and moved stiffly away toward the back, their feet dragging mud and rearranging it. But then Gretchen remembered the time she and Len threaded their way through a street disturbance—his steadiness in it. Though her way with public conflict was to withdraw, she had a surge of need to speak to this grossly twisted soul.

"It's okay," she told the stranger gently.

"Okay? Okay?" Now he looked at her pleadingly, like a little boy. His chin, sharp and red with scaly skin, pulled back in a worried wrinkle.

She sat down next to him again. "Sure. It'll be okay," she insisted.

"If he doesn't come back?" he asked inexplicably.

She found an answer. "Don't worry. He'll come back."

To her surprise, he started to cry. "My brother left. Why? Won't call. What if he doesn't?"

"He'll call," she said. She didn't know where this came from.

"He'll call," he repeated more calmly.

The bus stopped and new passengers stepped in out of the rain. The afflicted man started trembling. As people passed his seat he cringed and burst out, "Get away. Don't touch me!"

"It's all right," Gretchen continued. "They're just walking by. Everybody gets off at the place they're going. Do you have a place to get off?"

"Want my brother to go by. He left! *Why?*"

"He'll call you. He'll call." Then, kindly, "He loves you." For some reason the words came, as if she *had* to say them.

The man asked querulously through his tears, "Loves me?"

"Sure," Gretchen insisted. "It's all right. He does, and he must not be able to come right now, but he'll be thinking about you."

"Think about me," the stranger repeated thoughtfully. He sat forward with purpose. "I'm gonna go. He'll call!" He heaved himself up, brushing Gretchen's knees with his legs, and headed for the front. When the hinged door whined open, a woman in the cluster of those waiting on the sidewalk tried to climb up from the damp street as he climbed out. He thrashed his arms and cried, "No! Get away!"

Gretchen called to him, "It's okay. You can get down. No yelling, though."

As he thumped down the steps into rain, she could hear him repeating, "No yelling though, yelling though. Okay though."

By the time Gretchen reached her stop, the rain struck brutally. She was to meet Satchel at Caffé Trieste about finding and documenting "a local renaissance that embodies artistic force," as Len had put it. He'd lived as if to stir people into awakeness-his-way. In the window of the coffee house, always his favorite, was a new hand-lettered, unpunctuated flyer, *FIGHT FOR PETTAS RECLAIM OUR*

ARTS. Inside, she saw Satchel holding court in a corner. The place was moderately crowded; there was a doggy smell, permeated by espresso. Gretchen, shaking out her wet gloves, quickly got an espresso at the counter. Satchel, demitasse in hand, greeted her: "This'll be great, Gretch. We're in North Beach to observe talent. Two volunteer journalists who go around as a team, like Siskel and Ebert."

"The movie critics?"

"The same. We're creating a stereophonic view of North Beach and its artistic needs."

Gretchen set down her cup. "But not just looking for talent, right? We'd be finding artists hungry for vision. By the way, the flyer could have used a proofread."

"And. And so. All this is affiliated with valuable real estate," Satchel added.

"What?"

"Well, obviously the point is to get back Petta's."

"Satchel! Now you're making me struggle with why I came." She had just taken off her coat. Others at the table got up and began to drift toward another corner.

Satchel laughed and responded jauntily, "Ah, Gretch, you and your fear of engagement!" Gretchen flushed. He added, "You know I'm right," while nodding to a nearby table of literati. They nodded back and hailed him.

Gretchen didn't care who was listening. She took a few sips of coffee and, dabbing the saucer with a napkin, stared him down.

"I'm going to explain this, Satchel," she said firmly. "And I want you to hear me."

"Hit me with it." He grinned.

She leaned in. "It's not complicated. I've been sitting with this. What it amounts to is that *I don't want to be the opponent of anything.*"

Unexpectedly, Satchel was silent. Then he closed his eyes and put his hands to his temples. After he knew what he wanted to say, he shook his head abruptly. Drops of rain flew off his hair onto the table. With low-voiced anger he responded, "You're the worthy opponent of yourself. You live in here," and he pointed to his head. The group at the next table started drifting away.

Gretchen slowly pushed her cup and saucer away. She didn't seem intimidated any longer by The Speech. "No, Satchel." She didn't look angry. "You never did understand. What happens with the camera needs me to keep things a certain way. A way you don't know."

"Meaning I'm ignorant?"

But in her level tone she was telling him, "No, Satch. . . . You go ahead and be restless. It's good. Bring people with you. Like Len did."

"Gretchen, don't. I don't want you to be this way."

"I know."

"Because I love you!"

Gretchen smiled sadly. "The reason we're saying all this is because we lost Len. It hurts us both, but it doesn't come out the same." She paused. "By the way, those false accusations you used to make to me about infidelity? That was ridiculous."

Satchel's eyes filled with tears. For a moment he resembled the man on the bus. "Shit. Let's get out of here. Let's go eat."

Gretchen said, "I'm sorry, Satchel." She gathered up her bag, scarf and umbrella.

His face changed. He said, "Yeah, no, fine. I have to piss anyway." Then, looking worried, he pulled her sleeve, erupting in a high-pressured voice. "FYI, last time I ever saw Mom she had a pink scarf on with cherries like a tablecloth. Fucking cherries. Haha. I never sat still like a decent kid, and probably an overactive curious brat like me drives anybody to leave. She kissed me good-bye, though. You could do that at least, right?"

Gretchen got up. She looked at him with her serious eyes. "Okay." She delivered him a kiss on the mouth, calmly and gently.

Soon afterward, when he stood at the rest room sink washing his hands with Italian hand soap, he felt confused. *Gretchen used to say my 'home' problem wasn't my fault, but what did she know? She wasn't there. Is she even here? Or anywhere, come to find out. Oh, hell. She's just Gretchen, impossible to figure.* Was it really time to stop trying?

Well, he still had music. Creatively bamming, twanging and socking it to the song with his drums. He'd finally gotten that. It was worth a lot of future fucking years!

And he still had Lennie. Lennie'd believed he was good for something.

Someone banged impatiently on the battered, rest room door, which was covered with messages: *Abby loves Otis. Bush Must Die. Vero & Kiki. Call me for Seconds.* Satchel pushed it open and walked straight to the nearest people. He clapped one on the shoulder. "Dude. Hey—Satchel Reilly, from Dark Matter. Are you an artist or a musician or anything? There's a great project with other North Beach artists that you can get into."

Rain had taken a break, and Gretchen walked slowly along the street. She stopped to watch a bird hop down the sidewalk, carrying lint. The fuzzball, larger than the bird, had tangled with a string in the bird's beak. After it bounced the fuzz along for a while, it forced the whole bundle over a curb into the street. Then it leapt with piercing suddenness into a tree.

Gretchen walked on, but after a bit she looked back, wondering. That same bird darted from a red overhang of tiles above a high window. String and fuzz stuck out under one of the tiles. As soon as Gretchen got out of the way, it had recovered its hidden prize: building materials for home! She laughed out loud.

Ah, her own eyesight was a home. What she had most to do was to *see*. People had different ways with pain, finding solace. Discovering beauty. So long as she had a way to record and share images . . . ! Len was lord of her heart, but she had to be a watcher. Not his soldier.

And she knew where to go.

Gretchen paddled her kayak evenly, one side then the other. Toward the caves, uncertain sea caves. In darkened light, a crack she could see denoted some passageway, and she wanted to go in. Probably a park ranger should have taken her. But she pressed on. She shone her cave light and saw she'd have to lean back, away from low overhanging rock. As she came to the entrance and bent her neck, it felt stiff, even sore; she set herself to ignore it.

The hard, pocked surface was of lava that had surged through the sea in time before human thought. She paused to savor hard overhanging edges, close enough to lay her mouth against. Then she glided through into the crevice. A water current helped; only light use of her oar was needed. The darkness startled, purple at first, then just an engulfing presence of cool air. She felt herself losing gretchenness and coming to a vast quiet that brought her joy.

Reaching a dead end, she slowly reversed course, effortfully, to move out of the crevice into known space.

One cave and then another. There were a hundred and eighteen; she'd never been inside any of them. And she understood that she wouldn't leave today until the last moment to avoid nightfall.

When she came out from each cave, aquamarine water and sky met her. In the next cave, silkened by gold sun, she'd find an anteroom. It became a day of darkness loved by light. Patches of white calcite stretched across walls like maps. Ceiling algae gleamed in geometric patterns, loops. Pale green, bright orange. Sometimes she heard or smelled sea lions resting on ledges at the back of a chamber. She had come to the place in California said to be, in its entirety, the longest cave on earth.

Shoulders shaking with fatigue, she finally passed out through a small, jagged arch in the rock wall into full sunlight. The texture of surrounding rocks became recognizable, features calling her to memory as if to a face. To visit a place like this, you couldn't tame anything in it or see much of it. *Just keep it company.* Gretchen took what was offered. She'd never put it to words.

It was then that she pulled her camera in front of her eyes and started to save the shapes of lava against water.

EPILOGUE

Len's estranged brother inherited his art, savings, and furniture. Ben di Noti did not purchase his art, as Len's brother had held out for a higher price. The fate of Len's paintings is unknown. Gretchen had already taken Len's archives and some of his paintings from his apartment. A few of his works and films of his protest theater remain at San Jose State and in Berlin and Australia.

Satchel made Caffe Trieste his haunt, hounding customers to join North Beach Artists. Later on he moved his pitch to Specs bar. These days, Satchel plays drums and bongo throughout San Francisco, sometimes with club groups, but often at subway stops for cash. Lately he favors a regular corner on Market Street. He says he has three, maybe four girlfriends.

Raggedly, the North Beach Artists stayed together, rabblerousing and occasionally showing their work at LiveWire. Following release of the film "Landlords," Ruby was discovered by a dealer. He bought her portrait of Nick from Ben Di Noti. A few years later, Di Noti died of liver cancer. His son runs their firm. Eleven years after Ruby's paintings started to sell, a woman she met in AA, who owned a music store, got her wealthy lover to help North Beach Artists develop an abandoned factory in Bayview Hunters Point. North Beach Artists changed their name to SF Arts for Life. After several grants from the City of San Francisco, based on the center's community education programs for youth,

SF Arts for Life houses studios, performances, and neighborhood workshops. On paper, Ruby lives next door, but she sleeps, works and eats on the second floor of the center. She gets regular mammograms. Her boyfriend produces local public-interest TV shows; he has featured the center several times.

For a year, Gretchen reluctantly served as interim managing director of the arts center. She created a darkroom there, sharing it with local people of all skill levels. A moneyed, enthusiastic Marin matron who loved the center's passion for art established a Board of Directors and raised funds. She installed her niece as executive director. Satchel recruited jazz musicians from the surrounding Bayview Hunters Point area, which is predominantly black.

Recently an organization has formed, Citizens Against Artwipes, intending to seize the arts center from its largely white staff and board of directors. Members of the small group Citizens Against Artwipes are also largely white. After demonstrating publicly, they made headlines by demanding the keys to SF Arts for Life, as well as a signed statement from its founders admitting guilt for harmful gentrification.

It's rumored that the building's owner, who has appreciated the arts center and its work, is so elderly and fragile that the venue may change ownership. If so, a major rent increase will be likely.

Two years after Len died, Julian and Gretchen shocked their friends by spending a couple of months in Amsterdam together. Julian went back to school, fixed his teeth, became a physicist, and married a Korean architect. He either plays guitar on weekends or, since his divorce, meets his two sons for tennis. Julian's been a loyal donor to the SF Arts for Life center. He has also bought many of Gretchen's black-and-white photographs.

Artists in San Francisco continue to dwindle dramatically, unable to afford rent in the city. Gretchen is still the exception, living in her gritty apartment that's still too cold. After administering SF Arts for Life in its first year, she went back to her previous job with a promotion. Weekends, she often kayaks. A New York exhibition of her pictures has been a satisfying success for her. She looks forward to Social Security and retirement, so that she can give photography all of her time and energy.

There's a painting by Len on her bedroom wall, and on her dresser a picture of him remains, laughing toward her camera.

ACKNOWLEDGMENTS

The film work of South African artist William Kentridge helped confirm my direction for this book: that two similar images seen together bring more depth and realization than one. Fellow novelist Robin Bullard's feedback was invaluable. Thank you, Robin, for showing me what my strongest critics would say about this book and inspiring me to stand up for my vision. Thank you, writers Kitty Costello, Dale Jensen, Geoff Rips, Anna Sears, Teck Swaybien, Judy Viertel, Judy Wells, and Olga Zilberbourg. I had fine, perceptive first readers in artist Emelle Sonh and my daughter Cielo.

Shout-out to places I've visited for the special exhilaration of North Beach San Francisco culture: Vesuvio, Live Worms Gallery, The Beat Museum, Mario's Cigar Store, Caffe Trieste, City Lights Bookstore, Yuet Lee, The Empress of China, NB Bauhaus.

I also want to thank my son Stefan and my daughters Kezia and Karina, whose love and vibrant lives made me a happier, more grounded person while I worked through eight drafts of this novel.

I'm so glad you came here to read it!

Also by Mia Kirsi Stageberg

Novel
CANDLES (Beatlick Press)

Novellas
EVERYTHING FOR THE BELOVED (Beatitude Press)
MENSTRUATION DIARY (The Sphinx Winks Press)

Creative Non-Fiction
RADIANCE AND COLD WIND (Silver Bay Books)

Stories
ICE BECOMES WATER (Smashwords)
SLOW-GROWING HAIR (The Sphinx Winks Press)
NISIO AND SHULA (Smashwords)
IN CRYING'S BODY (The Sphinx Winks Press)

Prose Poems
SNOWBANK (Silver Bay Books)
BROKENNOSEJOB (The Sphinx Winks Press)
HITSIDE LIGHTING (with Zim Emig,
The There's a Strange Car Following Us Press)
BIG YELLOW POEM (Mystic Pig Press)
LOUIE'S ICE HOUSE (Wounded Eagle Press)

Film Script
SACRIFICE (M&A Editions)

Mia Kirsi Stageberg started out as a published fiction writer in the New Directions annuals. Her work has appeared in *Exposition Review, North Coast Literary Review, sPARKLE & bLINK, Poetry at the 33 Review, Literary Orphans, Furious Fictions, Dream Machinery, Oxygen, Sloow Tapes, Kameleon, Revista Rio Bravo, San Francisco Peace and Love, Unmuzzled Ox, The Scribbler, Awaa-te* and *Maize,* as well as in numerous chapbooks and anthologies. Essays appeared in *Talking Cure; Art Practical; Entre Guadalupe y Malinche: Tejanas in Art;* and *Value: Essays, Stories and Poems by Women of a Certain Age.* Stageberg has been a single parent, editor, cloth sculptor, nonprofit fundraiser, and vocalist in 1980s bands Walking Rain and The Glands. She taught creative writing in a Santa Fe oral history project funded by the National Endowment for the Arts. She was also co-editor of *Caracol* monthly literary journal in San Antonio, co-founder of the theater group Corazoncitos del Pueblo and a regular cast member of Radio Free Children at KUNM in Albuquerque. Previously, in Toronto she was art writer for *artscanada* and, briefly, a radio documentarist for the Canadian Broadcasting Company. A native of Minneapolis, Stageberg has also lived in Indiana and New York, as well as Cambridge, Massachusetts; Austin, Texas; Washington, D.C.; and Haifa, Israel. She lives in Japantown, San Francisco and loves it.

www.ingramcontent.com/pod-product-compliance
Lightning Source LLC
Chambersburg PA
CBHW032236010726
47494CB00002B/515